Their skins are dark... and light. They inhabit islands ringed by gentle, sapphire-blue water... and dominated by awesome, fiery volcanoes. Their lives are marked by selfless acts of generosity... and bloody rites of human sacrifice. They radiate an ancient innocence... and betray an all-too-modern corruption. They are natives of the land and adventurers from abroad, proud kings and ambitious plantation owners. They are the Hawaiians, the people of...

Dark Paradise

ATTENTION: SCHOOLS AND CORPORATIONS

WARNER books are available at quantity discounts with bulk purchase for educational, business, or sales promotional use For information, please write to SPECIAL SALES DEPARTMENT, WARNER BOOKS, 666 FIFTH AVENUE. NEW YORK. N Y 10103

**ARE THERE WARNER BOOKS
YOU WANT BUT CANNOT FIND IN YOUR LOCAL STORES?**

You can get any WARNER BOOKS title in print Simply send title and retail price, plus 50¢ per order and 50¢ per copy to cover mailing and handling costs for each book desired New York State and California residents add applicable sales tax Enclose check or money order only, no cash please. to WARNER BOOKS. P O BOX 690, NEW YORK. N Y 10019

Dark Paradise

MARY S. CRAIG

WARNER BOOKS

A Warner Communications Company

WARNER BOOKS EDITION

Copyright © 1986 by Mary S. Craig
All rights reserved.

Cover art by Franco Accenero
Cover design by Anthony Russo

Warner Books, Inc.
666 Fifth Avenue
New York, N.Y. 10103

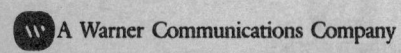

W A Warner Communications Company

Printed in the United States of America

First Printing: December, 1986

10 9 8 7 6 5 4 3 2 1

PART ONE

The Land and The Sea

CHAPTER ONE

THE GRAY OF BOSTON

There was one moment, as he ran toward the white church with its soaring steeple, when he thought perhaps he was doing the wrong thing. But the moment of doubt passed as he remembered all those years spent perched on his clerk's stool. That Robert Jameson had acted as if life were composed entirely of dutiful weeks: six days of recording barrels of sperm oil and jute sacks of cayenne; one day of divine services and family solemnity. It was certainly the course Jameson's prospective father-in-law had in mind for his future. But this Robert Jameson had different plans—and he was late for church for the first time in his life.

His intended, Martha Coopersmith, would be waiting for him in the church across the green. She was no longer the pale, shy child he had known as a boy, but a woman of eighteen with long golden hair (unfortunately pulled back rather severely) and a faint blush across her cheekbones (when he caught her staring at him). This woman he had chosen was as delicately appealing as a flower. And that choice was in no way altered by his more recent plans.

Even as he ran, Jameson realized how late he was. The parishoners began to pour through the vast doors of the church and gather in groups on the lawn. Martha, her arm held tightly by her great-aunt, was one of the few who didn't join a group to socialize, but hurried to the waiting family carriage. Her face was pale and she kept her eyes cast down, avoiding the curious glances of the people she passed.

Jameson slowed his pace as the curious stares turned toward him. He jammed his hat on his disordered dark hair, but had to remove it a moment later as he approached the Coopersmith carriage. "Miss Coopersmith, ma'am. Martha. Forgive my tardiness. I had no idea it was this late."

The old woman fixed him with beady eyes and said nothing.

Martha's eyes suddenly filled with tears. Her body shuddered slightly as she leaned back against the seat, turning her head away from him to hide her distress.

It wasn't like her to burst into tears for no reason. She was reserved and, though ardent in her attachment to him, not generally given to wild emotions. Her unhappiness wrenched at his heart. "Whatever has happened?" he demanded, reaching into the carriage to place his hand protectively on her shoulder.

A tear had started to roll down her cheek and she shook her head mutely. If she was incapable of speaking, her great-aunt Coopersmith was not. The first thing the tartar did was smack his hand off Martha's shoulder.

"How dare you behave in this fashion and pretend there's not a thing amiss? This poor child has been mortified—mortified, I say!—by your treatment of her this morning. I have never in my life witnessed a more distressing situation. There she sat with her prayer book in her hands and an empty seat beside her."

Jameson knew this was probably an exaggeration. Her mother, father, and brother would have sat beside her when he didn't appear. But he hid the smile that threatened to emerge, because there was obviously something wrong and the old lady was bound to come to the point sooner or later.

"Your bans, you young fool! Your bans were to have been read for the first time this morning. And you have humiliated the sweetest child on earth by not showing up." She sat forward to see what effect this had on the young reprobate.

He struck his hat hard against his leg in distress. "Oh, God," he moaned, "it completely slipped my mind."

"Slipped your mind?" the old woman hissed. "You are so lost to decency that a little matter of getting married slipped your mind? I wonder that you have the effrontery to admit it."

Martha's father, mother, and brother had reached the carriage. Edgar Coopersmith regarded Jameson with solemn disappointment. He waited in silence to hear the younger man's excuse, but it was his sister who hastened to explain in her piercing voice. "He forgot. That's it. He has nothing else to say for himself, except that he forgot."

Mrs. Coopersmith, a timid, colorless woman, looked as though she too was ready to burst into tears. Instead, she allowed her husband to hand her into the carriage, where she put her arms around her silent daughter.

The boy, Thomas, smelling faintly of lye soap and salted breakfast meat, had placed himself directly beside Jameson.

Like a small animal, he was quick and curious. His searching eyes rested on Jameson's face as he said, "Well, of course he has an excuse. He's all full of excitement, can't you see?"

In addition to being his betrothed's father, Mr. Coopersmith was Jameson's employer. This was not exactly the way Jameson had wished to break the news of his plans, to father or daughter, but there wasn't time for niceties now. He turned to the carriage and said urgently, "Martha, I want to tell you what has happened. Please listen to me. I'm sure you'll understand."

The girl's cornflower-blue eyes looked enormous in her pale face. She blinked helplessly, trying to clear the tears from her eyes. It didn't occur to Jameson that what he was about to tell her would make matters worse. He had known her most of his life, as he had known Aaron. He felt sure she would realize how important this was when he told her about Aaron.

"Who do you think I ran into two days ago?" he asked, his eyes blazing with excitement.

"She's in no mood to play guessing games, Robert," Mr. Coopersmith warned. "Just tell the poor child what has happened."

"Aaron Stoval. From Oliver Street."

Martha gave no sign of recognition. Jameson felt a trifle irritated. "You must remember Aaron. He and I grew up next door to each other. And you lived only half a block away in those days."

Martha continued to stare at him blankly. Her father, his mouth hardening, said, "I remember Stoval. A wild boy."

"Adventurous," Jameson corrected. "He went to sea. There's nothing wrong in that. My father was a sailor."

"The captain of a ship," Mr. Coopersmith retorted. "Hardly the same thing."

Jameson had begun to feel impatient with both of them. Here he had the biggest news of his twenty years, and all they could do was find distracting matters to plague him. He blurted, "I've signed on the *Felicity Ann*, Aaron's ship. She's the most beautiful schooner you've ever laid eyes on. We're going around the Horn to China."

Martha shrank back in horror, as though he'd told her he'd signed on with the devil rather than on a schooner. Her father grasped Jameson by the shoulders and shook him. "You're raving! You're betrothed to my daughter, and you know nothing about sailing."

"I can learn. Besides, they need someone who knows about storing supplies and shipping merchandise, which is something I've handled at the warehouse. Aaron will teach me the other things I need to know." He turned to Martha, his voice pleading for understanding. "This is the only chance I'll ever have to find out what it's like at sea. It's only for a year. We can be married when I come back."

Martha tried to speak. Her trembling lips opened and closed without a sound emerging. Another tear slipped down her cheek.

"You can't expect her to wait a year for you." Mr. Coopersmith raised an authoritative hand when it appeared that Martha would try to speak again. "You aren't to make him any promises, Martha. For all we know, he will change his mind in a year's time. Or he will be dead."

Martha moaned at the suggestion, and even Jameson stared at him. "Sailors die," Mr. Coopersmith said. "They die all the time from exotic diseases, the way your father did. It's a hard life. You have no idea what you're letting yourself in for. I daresay it's Stoval's doing. He could always talk you into the wildest schemes. But I thought you'd outgrown that failing."

Jameson regarded the older man coldly. "I'm a grown man. This is my own decision."

"And a very poor one. There won't be a job waiting for you when you return."

"Oh, Father!" Martha protested.

It was her first sign of understanding, and Jameson grasped at it. Turning to her, he plunged into a further explanation. "I used to go with my father to the docks when he was sailing. Sometimes I thought I would die of longing to go with him. I dreamed of places beyond the horizon, of places so different from Boston that you couldn't conceive of them. Rich with sunlight and lush with plants. Look!"

He drew a wrapped parcel from his pocket and began to open it. "This is for you, a going-away present. I bought it from Aaron. It's from China." He unfolded a swath of exotically colored Chinese silk and let it ripple to its full length. The lustrous colors glowed in the morning light, richer than any cloth he had ever touched. A million greens, like broad glossy leaves, pale fronds of fern, mosses and trailing vines. Hints of the endless sea, laced with foam, mirroring the sky. Even traces of gold and scarlet and orange.

Martha stroked the smooth fabric with a delicate hand. "It's beautiful."

"But what will she do with it?" demanded Aunt Coopersmith, who had until then remained mercifully silent. "It's totally unsuitable for an article of clothing, or covering furniture. Too gaudy by far. Whatever possessed you to buy it for her?"

Thomas piped up, "It's to remind her that he's gone to China, of course. She can put it in her hope chest and just look at it. And touch it."

Jameson saw no reason why she couldn't make a shawl of it, but he decided not to aggravate her family any further by saying so. Martha had begun to fold the silk into a manageable size. "Thank you, Robert. I'll treasure it."

As though they were alone together, he spoke directly to her. "I've been struggling over this decision for the last two days, ever since I came across Aaron again. I only signed on the *Felicity Ann* this morning. That's why I'm late. But, Martha, the ship leaves at daybreak tomorrow. This is my last chance to see you before I go."

Martha pressed the square of silk against her chest and tried vainly to hold back her tears. "This has come as a terrible shock. I don't know you as well as I thought I did, Robert. It will take me time to reconcile your wish to go to sea with your wish to marry me. Perhaps they can't be reconciled. I'll pray for you."

Her prayers were certainly to be valued, but he had hoped for more. He had hoped for a declaration of undying love, an assurance that she would be waiting for him when he returned. He had been so sure she would understand. Or, at the very least, that she would be pleased that he was doing what he had wanted to do all his life. Although he had never told her about this dream, he had assumed she would know it simply because she loved him.

It was her family's influence, of course. How could any girl coming from that virtuous setting, with a puritanical father, a forbearing mother, and a shrewish aunt, have any idea of his need to see more of the world than this cramped corner that was Boston? If only he had time to talk to her, to convince her... But there was no time. He had his few worldly possessions to pack before he met Aaron and went aboard the *Felicity Ann*.

"You'll be in my heart," he whispered to Martha as he pressed a chaste kiss on her white cheek. Then he bowed to her mother and aunt, ruffled Thomas's hair, and shook hands with the reluctant Mr. Coopersmith.

As he turned away, Jameson jammed his hat on his head

at an angle Mr. Coopersmith would surely consider unacceptable. But Mr. Coopersmith was gone from his mind before he was even out of sight. And so, to be truthful, was Martha. Not because he didn't love her, but because the excitement of sailing on the *Felicity Ann* eclipsed everything.

The heat and stench of the grog shop struck Jameson like a blast from a bellows. There was so little air in the low-ceilinged room that even the candles spiked along the wall sputtered for breath through clouds of tobacco smoke. Fat hens and a joint of beef vied with a string of skewered sausages in spilling their juices onto the glowing coals of the hearth.

Jameson paused inside the door, startled that so much noise could be confined in so small a space. Through the bawdy laughter and men's voices raised in song, Aaron's call barely reached him: "Over here, Jameson."

The men made room for him at the crowded table. Aaron thumped him on the back with boisterous enthusiasm. "You're one of us now," he declared. "A round of stout on me."

The man at Jameson's left, a ruddy fellow whose head gleamed hairless except for a red fringe above his ears, leaned back to stare at Jameson. "Think you can make the grade, eh?"

Before Jameson could answer, a barmaid leaned her square hip against the table, swept it clean of mugs, and accepted the order for stout with a gap-toothed grin. By the time she left amid a chorus of genial insults, the talk had moved to other things. The stories were never-ending—of strange ports and stranger natives, of exotic beasts and reckless crews.

Aaron speared a blazing sausage with his knife and waggled it in Jameson's direction. "Don't believe half of what they tell you. It's all to impress you with how brave and strong they are. That tale of Higgins's I heard three years ago from a Dutchman in China; Higgins has never been near the Barbary Coast. And maybe the Dutchman hadn't either," he added as an afterthought.

Jameson had almost forgotten how good it felt to laugh. How good it felt to say what he wanted, and to plan his life with an eye to what pleased him most. It was hard to believe, sitting there with the robust, rowdy crew, that he had spent years scratching in a ledger, never giving in to his desire to join the throngs on the wharf who lived a more exciting life than his.

On his way to the grog shop he'd passed the busy docks with a new feeling of belonging. The dense mist that curled around the masts in the harbor and the keening of fog horns had not seemed somber signs. The jangle of buoy bells, the stevedores' shouts, the shrieking of gulls, all of it took on a new significance. This was the Boston from which a man sailed out into the world. The pewter clouds that imprisoned the city were not going to imprison him any longer. One of those masts in the harbor would take him away from the wheels rumbling on cobblestones and the warehouses full of goods from distant lands.

Aaron's broad face beamed at Jameson in the flickering light of the grog shop. His friend's skin was a deeply sun-stained brown. His hair was tied back with a length of leather, and he wore a Moorish chain glistening at his throat and a brilliant sash wound around his waist. The contrast between the two was great. Jameson was tall and spare, while Aaron was stocky; Jameson was conservatively dressed and groomed, while Aaron was as colorful as a peacock.

But as boys they had shared the dream of discovering a more exciting world than stuffy New England. Jameson, a little late in following his inclination, was exhilarated to be here at last.

Aaron was speaking of elephants in Ceylon, and women with diamonds growing out of their foreheads, and a man who walked on burning coals. "Have you ever seen a parrot?" he asked Jameson, who shook his head. "They screech and curse like buccaneers. Of course, it's because they've heard the words, probably in some place like this. The blasphemy coming from those beaks is enough to set a pulpit to smoking."

It was not the first time Jameson had heard such tales. When he was a boy his father had told him similar stories, made somewhat more acceptable, perhaps, by the presence of the aunt who had cared for him. His father had eventually lost his ship, through an error in judgment. He had been too ill with a lingering, and eventually fatal, tropical disease to handle such matters, but no one had realized it at the time.

Jameson's only inheritance had been the volumes on navigation and geography and the journals his father had kept from his sailing days. His landlady, in exchange for the ship models he'd built as a boy, had agreed to store his goods against his return. They were few enough, and all, he had finally realized, from his father's life. How could he himself have lived for twenty years with no more to show for it than a few possessions.

"Well, this is it, lads," Aaron announced to the group at the table. "The last round before we take to the sea again. Here's to Jameson joining us on the *Felicity Ann*. God knows it's high time! No man should sit like a crow on a fence post scratching and scraping in a ruddy ledger in a cold waterfront warehouse when he can be busting his ass on board ship in a storm, eh, laddies?"

The evening wind had set the *Felicity Ann* dancing in the harbor. Strips of clouds against the darkening sky made ladders for the lean quarter-moon to climb. Jameson, following the example of his companions, slung his seabag over his shoulder and strode eagerly toward the gangplank.

A small figure detached itself from the crowd on the dock. Darting past hawkers with their carts and a fiddler singing chanties, the boy arrived at Jameson's side, breathless and grinning.

"Good lord!" Jameson stooped to make certain that it was indeed Thomas Coopersmith. "Surely your father doesn't know you're here."

"Nope." The boy's eyes danced with mischief. "He thinks I'm sick in bed. But Martha wanted so much for you to have this, and I told her I knew of a way to get it to you. Don't worry about me. It's not the first time I've come out on my own."

Jameson shook his head but didn't have the heart to scold the boy. It was exactly the sort of thing he and Aaron had loved to do when they were young. "What was it Martha wanted me to have?"

The boy dug into his pocket and dropped something into Jameson's hand. It was a silver locket on a fob chain. Jameson opened it to discover two picture frames hinged together. One side held a miniature portrait of Martha. For a moment Jameson thought the second frame was empty. Then, drawing it closer, he saw his own face reflected in a mirror. Held this way, Martha stared at his reflected face. Her fragile blond beauty contrasted sharply with his dark ruggedness. Jameson closed the locket and fastened it into his waist pocket. "Tell Martha I'll treasure it."

"It was to have been your wedding present," Thomas explained. "She thought this would be a better time for you to have it."

"Much better." He grasped the boy's hand and shook it firmly, as a man's. "Thanks for bringing it, Thomas. I hope you won't get in trouble."

"It will be worth it if I do," the lad assured him. His eyes drifted off to the *Felicity Ann*. "I only wish I could come with you. She's a proper beauty, that schooner."

"She is." Jameson watched as the boy disappeared into the crowd again, then swung the seabag up onto his shoulder. The others were already halfway up the gangplank and he had to hurry to catch up.

The captain of the ship, Hector Thomas, was standing on the quarterdeck beside the cannon. He was a bearded man with a weatherbeaten face and eyes that seemed to see right through a man. Aaron had assured Jameson that there wasn't a "solider man" one could sail with. "He's fair to his crew," Aaron had said proudly. And then, with a laugh, "He just expects everyone to work as hard as a slave."

Jameson was to find out what he meant before daybreak the next morning. Routed from sleep when it was still cold and dark, he managed to find his way onto the deck in the midst of experienced sailors readying the ship to sail. The anchor was being winched up and the hawser ropes hauled in. The last sails, straining against the wind, fluttered like trapped birds before bursting into place.

The bos'n frowned at him, taking a moment to place who he was. Then he pointed with a stubby finger toward another seaman. "Give Schuyler a hand there with those mizzen halyards."

Schuyler was a heavily muscled man in his late twenties. Short in stature, but with a great barrel chest, he chanted to himself as he winched up the sail lines. He glanced at Jameson with amusement when the younger man offered his help.

"First time out, is it?" Schuyler straightened. His limbs were as solid and heavy as his thick torso. "Let's see them hands."

Jameson extended his hands for Schuyler's inspection. Though strong and supple enough, they were pale and free of calluses. They looked exactly like what they were—the hands of a clerk.

"A strong one, are you?" Schuyler jeered. "All right, play out that halyard line."

As Jameson grasped the line to raise the rigging, Schuyler turned away. The small bow sail suddenly ballooned, throwing Jameson off balance. There was a burst of laughter from the watching sailors. Determined not to be the butt of their joke, Jameson braced himself before the whipping line upended him.

Schuyler stood with hands on hips. "You need to tie a quarter hitch in it first. Like this." He reached for the rope, but Jameson held it just out of his reach.

"Like this?" Jameson asked, expertly tying the quarter hitch himself.

Schuyler didn't answer. He watched the sail rise smoothly under Jameson's hands, then turned away.

Before Jameson realized what was happening, the lines had been cast off and the *Felicity Ann* surged forward. She seemed to tremble with anticipation, her great sails billowing in the wind, her prow cutting through the restless water. There were shouts of farewell all around him, but Jameson was more interested in the moving face of the endless sea than in the receding shore. He turned briefly to catch a glimpse of Boston and the crowd of well-wishers huddled in the gray morning light, waving their hats as the *Felicity Ann* drew farther and farther from land.

For a whole year he would be free of the dark buildings and the press of people, the strictures and duties of New England. For a whole year he'd explore a different world, a world of physical labor and foreign countries. There was a special kind of freedom in a sailor's life, as hard as it was.

And it was a hard life. For days the muscles in every part of his body protested against the unaccustomed labor. His flesh blazed, cracked, peeled under the sun shimmering off the sea. Blisters erupted on his hands, leaving raw painful scabs that hardened into horny calluses.

Aaron taught Jameson the skills necessary to lift him above the level of rank beginner and, consequently, the butt of the others' rough jokes. He learned to clamber in the ropes and work the winches, as well as the responsibilities of being in charge of the stores. And Aaron brought him into the inner circle of sailors.

These men seemed to Jameson as exotic as the strange birds that cried overhead. There were men of quick laughter and astonishing amorality, and ones of hasty temper and sullen hostility. All the sailors lived for the moment, for a tot of rum and a brisk chantey with a jig, telling tales of strumpets and drunken revels. They were entirely unmindful of the God who had hovered over Jameson's youth. Exposed to the endless horizons and the godless men, he continued to pray, but his words seemed strangely irrelevant.

Even the night sky bloomed with unfamiliar stars.

After leaving their first port of call, Aaron fell ill with a fever. The ship's doctor, an amiable man who depended mainly on nature and prayer to do his work, dispensed packets of powder and returned to his card game. Jameson was lulled by this casual attitude and assumed that his ignorance of the diseases sailors picked up in foreign climes made Aaron's illness seem worse than it was.

Aaron lay covered with sweat, his damp hair clinging to his forehead. "You look like old Coopersmith when you pull a face like that," he mocked Jameson. "I'll be right as rain in no time. Go finish your work."

Jameson's brows drew together. "Someone ought to stay with you. There's a storm brewing."

"All the more reason you shouldn't be shorthanded. I'm

not going anywhere." He closed his eyes and waved his friend out of the room.

Within minutes a violent storm had overtaken the *Felicity Ann*. Jameson was assured that this was not unusual as ships neared the Horn, but the towering gray swells were terrifying. Rain lashed the men and the ship, lightning speared the skies, and thunder rolled ominously across the waves. The sea was so wild that Jameson had to lash Aaron to his bunk to protect him from the pitching of the beleaguered ship.

There was no let-up in the fierce tempest and Jameson waged a continuous battle for his dry stores. There were no hands free to help him shift stores in the hold or to tie down the pens on deck. Hour after hour he struggled to keep the rain and waves from deluging the precious rations, but it was a losing battle.

On each of three attempts to approach the Horn, the ship was driven back by the storm. Jameson watched helplessly as the animal pens were swept from the deck and most of the remaining provisions were soaked. By the time they made the passage on their fourth attempt, the damage was done.

Without attendance, Aaron had grown much worse. Jameson was stunned to see the wasted face with its hollow eyes and cracked lips. "Hasn't anyone been here to give you water and food?" he demanded.

Aaron tried to moisten his lips but failed. Instead, he rolled his head slightly back and forth.

Jameson stomped out of the room, furious with himself and everyone else on board. Despite the fight for the ship's survival, there was no excuse for not taking a few minutes to see to Aaron's needs. He made his way to the galley and demanded food and water for the sick man, but the cook shook his head.

"You know what condition the stores are in," the man said. "Can't waste food and water on a dying man."

"He's not dying!" Jameson was infuriated by the suggestion and nearly grabbed the man by his collar. "But he *will* die if he doesn't have water. And he has to have it right now."

"Well, he ain't gettin' it, mate. Captain's orders."

Jameson was shocked. Surely Captain Thomas couldn't be so cruel as to let a man with a little fever die for want of sustenance. He went in search of the captain but found only Ben Horgan, the first mate. Aaron had always said Horgan was hardworking and capable but a bit of a coward. Jameson found that the man wouldn't look him in the eye.

"The cook won't give me food and water for Aaron Stoval. He's been neglected during the storm and desperately needs something to keep up his strength."

"You know better than anyone that we can't waste any of our provisions now," Horgan muttered.

"It's not a waste! He just has a little fever. He'll be perfectly all right if he's properly cared for."

Captain Thomas appeared in the doorway, his huge frame nearly blocking it. His voice was gruff but firm. "That's not what the doctor says, Jameson. Stoval's not going to make it. I'm sorry."

Until that moment Jameson had refused to believe it. Even now he wanted to insist that the doctor was wrong. But the realization that this was the truth hit his stomach like a blow, and his breath stopped for the space of several dull heartbeats. Horgan shifted uneasily beside him.

The captain continued after a long pause, "I know you did everything humanly possible to protect the stores, Jameson, but we're going to be in real trouble until we replenish them. We're nowhere near a source, and won't be for some time."

"He can have my share," Jameson said through rigid lips. "He's the best friend I've ever had, and I won't let him die without a drink of water."

"It will merely prolong his agony," the captain warned.

Torn, Jameson clenched his fists at his side. Better to let Aaron die quickly in pain, or more slowly in relative comfort? "I can't let him suffer this way. I'll share my rations with him."

"As you wish. Don't destroy your own health; we're all going to need as much strength as possible."

"Yes, sir." Jameson nodded to Horgan and left the cabin, still reeling with the enormity of the situation. Surely Aaron couldn't die—Aaron, with his beaming face, his stocky, healthy body. They had grown up together. They were both just twenty years old! You didn't die at twenty. Jameson hurried to the galley for his ration of water and food.

A sure, steady wind filled the *Felicity Ann*'s sails, speeding the ship westward. The crew grumbled over short rations but whistled in the rigging as one day of good wind followed another. Over their rum, they talked of China. They never spoke of Aaron.

The calm came in the night. On a sea as still as a country pond, the *Felicity Ann* shuddered to a stop. Her sails drooped limply from mast and rigging. Every man watched for the breeze. Through endless days of searing sun and hot heavy nights, the men waited for wind. With their bellies half-empty and their throats parched, they watched with resentment when Jameson took his rations to Aaron's bunk. Only Aaron, his eyes heavily closed, was unaware of the gravity of the situation.

Then, one blazing dawn, Aaron opened his eyes, whispered Jameson's name, and died.

Captain Thomas recited the funeral service from the *Book of Common Prayer*. The words sounded less comforting than Jameson had remembered.

"And therefore we do now commit his soul to heaven and his body to the sea."

Jameson ached with grief as the weighted, canvas-shrouded body of his friend was dropped over the rail of the ship. Widening ripples broke the still face of the sea, and Aaron was no more. The silent crew drifted away, leaving Jameson alone at the rail. Alone with his painful memories of Aaron, and his anger at the treacherous sea.

CHAPTER TWO

SOUNDINGS

The next day Jameson was called to the captain's cabin. He paused in the doorway, letting his eyes adjust to the dimness of the oak-paneled room with its velvet-draped bank. Leaning over a large wooden table, Captain Thomas and Ben Horgan studied the chart, the captain trailing his finger along a curve of markings. A compass and a quadrant held down the stiff paper.

"The Sandwich Islands," he said. "Our only hope of taking on provisions and water in time."

This comment was directed at Horgan, but the captain motioned Jameson into the room as he continued. "I'm sure I felt a touch of wind just now. We'd only need enough to catch the trade winds to the northeast."

Horgan measured distances on the map. "It's more than four hundred miles to the closest island, Hawaii." He looked up from the map to add a word of caution. "It's also where Captain Cook and a lot of his men were killed."

"Other ships have traded there for sandalwood since then. They've dealt with friendly natives."

"Not all of them."

The captain shrugged dismissively. "We have no choice. Either we get fresh provisions or we die. We'll head northeast to catch the trade winds. Give the orders."

"Yes, sir." Horgan's expression was grim as he passed Jameson.

Captain Thomas motioned Jameson closer. "I want you to learn how to use the quarterdeck cannon, Jameson. Schuyler can teach you, but he's not as good as he might be. I want you to be able to load and fire it in your sleep, no matter how difficult the conditions. Do you understand?"

"Yes, sir."

"Good. Get on with it immediately." As Jameson turned away, the captain said, "And, Jameson, I'm sorry about Stoval. He was a good man. I hate to lose good men."

They weren't all good men. Jameson had taken a dislike to Schuyler from the first day, and the forced proximity hadn't improved his opinion. Schuyler mocked him for knowing nothing about cannons and ridiculed him for expressing an opinion about how best to store the gunpowder.

Jameson ignored the jibes and taunts. His only goal was to become expert at using the quarterdeck cannon. When he proved uncommonly adept at managing the operation, Schuyler insisted on taking the credit.

It didn't matter. The wind that had been no more than a breath had continued to rise. Like a woman waking from a stupor, the *Felicity Ann* roused slowly. Then, with the assurance of a steady breeze, she sped forward, her graceful prow curling back the sea in wings of foam.

Jameson's excitement grew as the wind held. The sailors gladly resumed their posts, their hunger and thirst forgotten.

Once the fearful lull was past, it took a surprisingly short time for the *Felicity Ann* to reach the trade winds that would carry her to the inhabited islands. Jameson, along with every other crew member, scanned the horizon for the first shadow of land. When the first sighting was made from the cross-rigging, there was still nothing to be seen from the deck.

Gradually a dark line appeared along the surface of the sea. Jameson narrowed his eyes, straining to see the slowly rising mass. When it finally took shape, he saw a long, low contour crowned by dense clouds. And then the silhouette changed as the purple haze of several mountain peaks appeared behind the coast. Only as they neared the shore did the dark bulk turn into brilliant color.

A deep green came first, startling against the blue sky. Stark white clouds massed above the closest mountain. Then the lush jungle separated into a legion of green shades and shapes: the grace of palms, the delicacy of ferns, the glossy brilliance of giant vines, voluptuous with blossoms. Like the silk scarf he had chosen for Martha, the rich and varied greens of the jungle were irresistibly beautiful. Even the surf rolling lazily onto the black sand beach was as pure and transparent as crystal.

"Would you look at that?" Schuyler demanded. "A beach with sand as black as tar pitch."

The bos'n, standing behind him, said, "It's from the volcanoes. The lava flows all the way down to the water." He pointed to the banks of clouds. "That's a volcano there."

The glistening black beach with its fringe of palms and deep ferned paths had captured everyone's attention. The first mate withdrew his fascinated gaze and turned to the captain. "Should we head for the lagoon, sir? It looks sheltered."

"No, the beach cove. There's more room to maneuver if we're attacked."

Horgan nodded. "I'll have the guns made ready."

"Discreetly," the captain warned. He raised his voice to address the crew. "If they learn how desperate we are for food and water, they'll try to exchange them for weapons. It's my policy never to trade firearms to uncivilized natives. Remember that. Jameson, stand to your cannon. Wilkins, you and your men to the guns."

Jameson strapped on the leather cannoneer's sash and pried open the keg of gunpowder. Scooping the black powder from its oilskin container, he funneled it into the charge hole of the cannon. Then he lit a punk and held it, smoldering, where he could easily touch off the weapon. But his gaze was on the shore as the *Felicity Ann* made her way into the cove.

The island lay in an eerie silence. No birds flashed among the trees, no leaves stirred. Even the clear surf, thundering in from the sea, receded quietly, leaving circles of foam on the glistening sand. The sudden, distant cawing of an unseen bird raised sweat on Jameson's palms.

Captain Thomas swept the shoreline with his spyglass for long minutes, then signaled to have the anchor dropped. Immediately a soft sound, like a pulse, began to throb behind the curtain of green. The pounding of drums gradually swelled, filling the cove with primitive sound, and still there was nothing to be seen. Abruptly the drums fell silent and into the tense stillness rose the chanting of men's voices.

War canoes came rushing from the matted vegetation near one end of the cove. Warriors' faces were hidden behind grotesque gourd helmets with plumes that swayed like exotic birds. The canoes sped toward the *Felicity Ann*, propelled by incredibly powerful paddlers. Jameson sighted over his cannon while other crew members stripped and cocked their muskets. Captain Thomas's voice rang out above the sounds of preparation: "There will be no firing except on my command!"

The captain joined Jameson on the quarterdeck. As the canoes drew close, they saw the warriors more clearly, men of impressive size and strength whose faceless helmets were chillingly menacing. The natives wore only loincloth flaps and necklaces of brilliant feathers and beads. Their bodies gleamed from the water spray. One among them, larger than the rest, wore an ornate feathered cloak of vivid color.

Captain Thomas extended both hands in a gesture of peace. "We come only to trade. We mean no harm," he called out as the canoes came within range of his voice.

Horgan, beside the captain, pantomimed eating and drinking. "Food," Horgan croaked. "Water."

The canoes slowed. There was no way to know if the warriors understood either the captain's words or Horgan's gestures. The tallest warrior stepped onto the platform of his canoe. He looked like a giant towering above his companions. His flesh was the color of fine cognac, and his face, when he removed his helmet, was strikingly handsome. "I speak your English," he said to the captain. "I am Kekua, son of King Kamehameha." His English was clear but had a distinctive rhythm that made his words sound almost prophetic. "Tonight you will come ashore."

"Thank you," Captain Thomas replied. "We wish only to trade for provisions, food, water. I can send a boat..."

The young giant shook his head. "No. You and your men will come ashore tonight. Not before. Which of your men is in charge of what you want?" When the captain indicated Jameson, Kekua nodded. "Then he will come now. Alone."

Horgan whispered, "It could be a trick."

The captain nodded, his expression thoughtful. Horgan, his body stiff with suspicion or fear, jerked a thumb toward Jameson, who was at ready position by the cannon. "Give them a taste of that and we won't have any trouble."

"Or provisions either," Captain Thomas reminded him in a lowered voice. "Jameson, I think you'll have to go with them. I don't see any other choice."

Jameson realized then that any previous experience he'd had of fear was like a penny candle compared to the blaze he felt now. For a moment the terror seized him, softening the muscles along his thighs and pressing the air from his lungs. Only by a total effort of will was he able to force his body to move.

"Yes, sir," he said as he walked to the rail. He could hear Horgan whispering frantically to the captain.

"What if this is a trick? What if they kill Jameson before we go ashore? At the very least they can hold him hostage."

The last words Jameson heard as he climbed down the Jacob's ladder to Kekua's war canoe were the captain's: "We can handle any situation that arises. Jameson will be perfectly all right." He prayed it was true and took courage from the captain's words, enough courage to force himself to step onto the platform of Kekua's outrigger.

Instantly the craft surged to life. Jameson knew all his shipmates' eyes were on him as the span widened between the canoe and the ship. Ahead, nearer every second, was the green wall of jungle spilling a brilliant profusion of flowers onto the black beach.

No one spoke to him, although he knew the natives were covertly studying him behind their helmets. Kekua had nodded to him when he first stepped into the canoe, but now ignored him as he carried on a low-voiced conversation with one of his companions. Their words were incomprehensible to Jameson. He wondered if they were planning to kill him and what methods they would use. Hadn't the crew spoken of how Captain Cook was stabbed and clubbed to death, then dismembered and burned? And Cook had had a weapon with him. Jameson had nothing but his cannoneer's sash and his fists.

The canoes approached the dense growth at a reduced speed, and Kekua indicated that Jameson should lower his head as they passed through. After the first tangle of growth there was a cleared passage through which the canoes glided. Jameson could see the canoes ahead being pulled ashore. Bright birds flapped and screamed through masses of ferns taller than a man. There were blossoms all around him, but none he could identify; and the birdsong was such as he'd never heard.

"Come," Kekua said.

Jameson climbed ashore and followed the young giant on a well-worn path through the jungle. There were natives ahead and behind who talked among themselves, laughing and strutting as they walked. He could tell they were reliving the encounter with the *Felicity Ann* by their ferocious grimaces and growls, followed by mewling sounds that were a mockery of Mr. Horgan's high-pitched, frightened voice. Kekua held himself apart from this banter but made no effort to stop it.

The trail passed a waterfall that trapped rainbows between columns of flowering vines. Jameson paused to take in the incredible beauty of the scene, but the natives behind him muttered in what seemed a menacing way, so he quickly moved on. Kekua, who walked directly ahead of him, paid no attention to him until they reached a clearing where several huts formed a small village.

Dozens of natives were assembled, waiting for news of the morning's adventure. All of them stared at Jameson. Old men plucked at his clothes, and young girls giggled and touched his face. The women were half-naked, and Jameson couldn't keep his gaze from wandering to their breasts. His New England upbringing had been so circumscribed that he had never seen a naked woman. The sailors talked incessantly of the South Pacific women who offered themselves without the least hesitation, who walked bare-chested and unashamed. Jameson hadn't believed them, until now.

They were beautiful women, with smooth, dark skin and long, glossy black hair. Their eyes were bright with curiosity. The young women smiled at him and walked so close that their breasts occasionally brushed his arms. Mesmerized, Jameson felt the stirrings of arousal despite his concern for his safety. He looked around for Kekua and found him watching him from the doorway of one of the huts on the periphery of the clearing.

Kekua motioned for Jameson to join him. There seemed to be an air of expectation among the gathered natives as Jameson walked stiffly toward Kekua. If he was going to die, he must do it bravely. He prayed that his captor would be merciful, that it would be a swift blow that felled him. But too many tales of uncivilized natives and their barbarous customs assailed him. Tales of torture and sacrifice. Jameson feared for the limits of his endurance.

A fire burned beside the hut. Kekua stood over it, inspecting the glowing coals and the pot of simmering food. With a pair of sticks he lifted a coal and held it for a moment before returning it to a new position on the fire. Then he studied Jameson for a long minute, a slight frown between his brows. "Are you hungry?" he asked.

Food was the last thing on Jameson's mind and he shook his head. "Not particularly." But he had seen bananas growing along the path, and the thought of them stirred a rumbling in his stomach. How easily one's body gave one away! It had been weeks since he'd eaten a proper meal. "Well, perhaps a banana, if there's one here." Why die starving?

Kekua gestured behind Jameson to a bunch of bananas that a native girl was holding. Jameson snapped one off, then decided to take two. "Thank you," he said, addressing both the girl and Kekua. The fresh fruit tasted incredibly good after the weeks of foul rations. Emboldened, he asked for a cup of water.

Kekua spoke to the girl, who darted off, her bare feet soundless on the earth. She returned almost instantly, a bucket of water and a cup swinging easily in her hands. Her long, bare legs gleamed where spots of water had spilled, and she crouched down beside Jameson to dip the cup into the bucket. She had almost a boy's body, with its thin, lithe grace, and yet she was beginning to develop firm breasts. A girl, just becoming a woman. Jameson accepted the cup of water and forced his gaze back to Kekua.

The guarded expression of the young native had sharpened into a narrow-eyed shrewdness. "You have been at sea a long time. You want her?"

Jameson was startled and appalled by the suggestion. "Want her? Of course not!" As an afterthought, he added, "She's only a child."

Kekua considered this, running his eyes over the girl and pursing his lips. Finally he shook his head. "No, she is a woman. Or ready to be a woman. But you would rather have someone... older. A woman with more times."

At first Jameson didn't understand him. Before he realized what the native meant, Kekua was beckoning another young woman. This one was a few years older, and much more voluptuous, with softly rounded arms and hips, and full breasts. "Like this," Kekua suggested.

"No, no! You misunderstand." Jameson judged, by the expression on Kekua's handsome face, that this rejection was considered rude. "She's lovely. Beautiful. But I do not want a woman. I want supplies for the ship."

"There is plenty of time to get supplies. First you must refresh yourself."

"I'm perfectly refreshed, thank you," Jameson said rigidly. "If we are to have everything ready to take back to the ship this evening, we should gather it now. If you would assign some men to help me, they would be well rewarded."

Kekua shrugged. "As you wish." He waved away the young woman and gestured to several young men standing nearby. "These will help us. Come."

At least Jameson's life no longer seemed to be in danger. Once again he followed a short procession, out of the village and along a path leading upward. The men carried baskets and paused along the way to fill them with exotic fruits. In another clearing there were more huts, and a storage area of sorts, where dried and salted fish were added to their collection. The natives collected other plants that Jameson was not familiar with, something Kekua called taro, for making poi. It didn't matter what it was; Jameson was willing to add it to the *Felicity Ann*'s provisions.

He was shown the taro patches and the fish ponds. A different landscape was pointed out to him where there were giant rocks, gray and forbidding, that stretched away to one side. Among them, naked white-limbed trees twisted painfully toward the sky. Kekua explained that the goddess Pele had rained destruction on this area. Jameson assumed he was speaking of the volcano and merely nodded his understanding. There was no sense trying to talk a native out of his gods and goddesses.

But the lushness and the devastation were alien to him. When he heard the honk of a goose he looked around in delight, expecting to see a familiar sight. Instead of golden paddle feet, however, he saw a creature that clung to a rock with rough, curved claws. Only the cloud-capped mountain looked somewhat ordinary, and Jameson knew it was actually a volcano.

Kekua questioned him about his home and explained his knowledge of English. "There was a *haole*—a white foreigner—named Roberts who stayed with the *alii* chief Kawaiha. He taught me how to speak your language."

Delighted to hear that there was another foreigner in the area, Jameson asked eagerly, "Does he live near here? Will I meet him?"

"He's dead." Kekua uttered this in a perfectly matter-of-fact way, adding, "He learned of a plot to poison Kawaiha and warned him. When Kawaiha's enemies learned of this, they poisoned Roberts instead."

Poison. The very word made the hair at the nape of Jameson's neck rise. So foreigners were fair game in the natives' entanglements. And the natives used poisons as well as the more direct methods of knives and clubs to destroy their enemies. Jameson considered the foodstuffs they were gathering and decided none of them were good candidates for poisoning. Or were they?

When they returned to the first village, various breadlike goods were added to their collection. Then all the supplies were carried down to the place where the canoes were beached. "We will send them back to the ship after the men have come to the village," Kekua explained. "My men will guide the little boats to this place. Now you will wait in the village."

Jameson knew better than to argue with him. For all his melodious voice and the afternoon's helpfulness, Kekua still spoke with an authority that brooked no argument. It came from being a king's son, Jameson imagined. And if the son spoke with such power, surely his father must be absolutely imperious. Jameson hoped there would be no meeting with the absent Kamehameha while he was alone on the island.

Kekua led his companion back along a different path that came to a larger village than any of the ones they'd visited that afternoon. Here torches blazed and pungent smoke rose from numerous fire pits. The air was fragrant with too many scents to identify; decorations of flowers and feathers swayed in the breeze. Here and there, in startling profusion, stood pots and woven baskets filled with the strange and colorful tropical fruits that Jameson had come to recognize during the day.

"For a luau," Kekua explained. "A feast. This is our celebration of our gods, and you and your shipmates will join us."

There were no women in the clearing. The men had decorated themselves for a party rather than in their fearsome warrior garb. Jameson removed his colorful cannoneer's sash and presented it to Kekua. "This is for you. With thanks for your help."

Kekua, who, along with every other native, had obviously coveted the sash all day, accepted it with grave thanks. He slid it across his broad chest just as the party from the *Felicity Ann* arrived in the clearing. His chest seemed to swell under this novel decoration and he spread his arms wide to the new arrivals. "You are welcome,' he called. Then, raising his voice toward the jungle, he cried, *"Uhaele mai wahine!"*

Jameson heard the laughter and soft voices of the women before they emerged from the lush growth. The light was fading from the sky, but the wavering torchlight glowed on their richly colored skin and set lights dancing in their long, glistening black hair, which they wore loose. Braided flowers only half-hid their exposed breasts. Short slit skirts of tapa cloth covered little more. There were dozens of women, young and old, supple and portly, beautiful and plain. They were alike in only one respect—the glow of sensuality shone in their dark eyes and swayed in their womanly hips.

The startled crewmen stared in wonder as the women surrounded them, draped them with flowers and feathers, and pressed their naked breasts against them in unmistakable invitation. Jameson would have heard the crackle of hellfire behind their provocative laughter, no doubt, if it hadn't been for the roaring of his own pulse. He'd had no idea the temptation to carnal sin would be quite so overwhelming. Lust caught hold of him, as it obviously had the men around him.

He watched as a plump young girl, not so much beautiful as incredibly voluptuous, seized Schuyler. The sailor captured her in his arms and bent his mouth to her high, generous breasts. As Jameson turned away, his gaze fell on a slender young woman who stood across the clearing, watching him. Not only was she the most beautiful woman he'd ever seen, but some different quality set her apart. She seemed coolly removed from the scene of carnal revelry, poised and untouchable. Almost regal. But still remarkably sensuous.

Her steady gaze inflamed him. She was unapproachable, yet he felt himself take a step in her direction. Only the captain's voice speaking his name restrained him. As he turned to answer the captain, Jameson felt almost sure he saw her eyelashes flicker in a tantalizing wink. Almost sure.

Naturally, Captain Thomas was interested in the provisions. "Did you get them? Did the natives treat you all right?"

"Yes. We've stored the food by the canoes. The natives will come back with us to trade. There's water, fruit, breads, grains, dried fish, and some vegetables I don't know. Enough to keep us for a long time."

"You don't think there's any trickery at work?"

"They seem genuinely friendly. We aren't the only foreigners they've seen. I think they're more used to trading than we suspected. Kekua mentioned their desire for nails and other metals."

Captain Thomas nodded. His eyes became alert as Kekua, nearby, called out again to the women.

"Ia kanaka alakai!"

The women responded to this order by teasingly tugging the sailors toward the trees beyond the clearing. The men were quick to follow. Schuyler, made awkward by lust, lunged after his plump girl and fell. When he caught up with her, he swept her into his arms and headed into the darkness.

"We'd better pray they don't mean any harm," Captain Thomas said. "Even though our men are armed, theirs are in a position to kill off every damn one of us right now, if they've a mind!"

Distracted by the gasps and moans of sexual congress, Jameson barely heard the captain. His eyes searched the edge of the clearing for the slender young woman. She still stood there, serenely poised, smiling a challenge. Was it a challenge? If he went to her...

"Mr. Jameson." The captain's voice sounded impatient. "I want a list of the provisions. Mr. Horgan will need it for negotiating a trade."

"Yes, sir." As he turned to find Horgan, Jameson glanced once more toward where the woman had stood. There was only the lushness of the jungle, wavering in the light of the torches.

CHAPTER THREE

KAPU

The moon was high by the time the meat roasting in the pits was finished, the air filled with mouth-watering fragrance. Native men uncovered the pits to expose the succulent roasted pigs, then spread out the abundance of other food—fruits, breads, poi, bowls of colorful juices. To a crew close to starving, the feast seemed magnificent indeed.

As the sailors began wandering back into the clearing with the women still clinging to them, they stared at the native men peeling and mashing taro root, kneading poi, and tending the fire pits. The bos'n shook his head. "I don't understand it. The men are doing the cooking and they don't seem to care what their women do."

Schuyler laughed. "No accounting for heathen ways." He nuzzled the plump girl's neck. "Thank heaven!"

Jameson looked up to find the slender woman walking toward him. Her body swayed as gracefully as a flower. Her smile widened her delicate lips into an alluring bow. With each step her breasts peeked out from under the flower necklace she wore. When she stood before him, she touched a single finger to his cheek. His body stiffened.

Her lips parted in distress. "You do not... *i ono*... like me?"

"Oh, no," Jameson protested. "I do. It's just... You speak English!"

When she nodded, her long dark hair breathed fragrance. "Yes. There have been other *haoles*, other white strangers." She swayed toward him, her wide eyes filled with tempting mysteries. "What is your *inoa*?" She pointed to herself. "Nahana. *Inoa kou* Nahana."

"Robert Jameson."

"Jameson." She repeated his name thoughtfully. "Why are you not like the others, Jameson?"

"But I am."

"No. I don't think so."

Beyond the clearing several young Hawaiian men wearing only loincloth flaps and chains of polished animal teeth around their wrists and ankles were beginning to dance to the beat of a drum. At the sound of the instrument, Nahana began to back away.

"Are you going to dance?" he asked.

Her eyes widened. "It is *kapu*, forbidden, for women to dance with men, or to speak when men dance."

The rhythm of the drum changed abruptly and she backed farther away. He caught her arm lightly. "Will I see you again?"

Nahana touched one fingertip lightly to his lips before slipping away. Jameson watched her supple young back sway in the flickering light until she disappeared from sight. He fought against the need to follow her, a need so strong it took his breath away. Against the need his principles seemed untenably weak. What was happening to him?

Jameson joined Captain Thomas and Horgan where they stood with Kekua to one side of the clearing. Opposite them was a hawk-faced man of about forty whose dark eyes burned with intensity. He wore an elaborate headdress and a cloak that half-covered his chest, which was patterned with intricate scars. The men around him, huge, fierce-looking natives with heavily scarred faces, could only be guards. They were armed with knotted garroting ropes, thongs, and clubs. As Jameson watched, the central figure raised his hand, and the drums stopped.

"Who's he?" Horgan asked nervously.

"Maakoa," Kekua told him. "He is Kahuni Nui, the great high priest."

As Kekua spoke, Maakoa lowered his hand. The drums resumed their rhythm, the gourds rattled, and the singers chanted. The male dancers began to perform, their bodies glistening with oil in the flickering torchlight. The sailors were confused by the sudden disappearance of the women and puzzled that only men were dancing.

Schuyler stirred restlessly and slid a flask from his pocket. "Men!" he scoffed. "What kind of dance is that?" When no one responded, he raised his voice. "Where are the women?" Seeing his partner in the shadows of the trees, he called to her, "Come on. *You* dance. Understand?"

When he reached for her, she tried to flee. Catching her roughly, he tried to pull her toward the dancers. She resisted frantically, silently struggling. When she turned her terrified eyes toward the high priest, Maakoa, Jameson saw the priest's eyes meet hers in cold fury.

"What's wrong? Don't you know how to dance?" Schuyler demanded, holding the struggling girl firmly by the arm.

"Like this, see?" He staggered a few awkward, drunken steps before trying again to force her into dancing.

"Aohe!" the girl cried in terror. *"Kapu! Kapu!"* Finally managing to pull away from him, she fled into the darkness.

As the dancers finished and a hush settled over the clearing, a guard leaped into the clearing waving a feathered stick. His high-pitched cry sent a shiver down Jameson's back.

"Moi hele! Moi hele! Moi hele!"

As those in front of him drew back bowing, Jameson heard Kekua explain to the captain, "He warns that the king is coming."

"Warns? Why?" the captain asked.

"No one's shadow must fall on the king. It is *kapu*."

"What would the punishment be?"

"Death." Kekua quickly added, "Not for *haoles* like you, or for the *alii*, the nobles and chiefs."

King Kamehameha was of even more overwhelming proportions than his enormous son. He strode into the clearing wearing a feathered cloak and a giant headdress. Power shone from him like a beacon. He walked between two women of breathtaking beauty, one lithe, the other ample. The first, a woman of Jameson's age, radiated sensuality as strongly as Kamehameha did power. The other, older, was cloaked in an ornate long robe, but it was her regal serenity that struck Jameson. She seemed to absorb the chaos of color and sound around her into the still pool of her being. A boy of perhaps seven years walked at her side.

As the king and his companions passed, the people fell prostrate and the nobles bowed. When he reached Captain Thomas, the king stood waiting. Kekua whispered urgently, "You must bow."

For a moment Jameson feared that his independent Yankee captain would not be willing to bow to an "ignorant savage." But Captain Thomas was a shrewd man who adapted with grace to any situation. When the captain straightened from a truly magnificent gesture that might have been considered a bow by the courts of Europe, King Kamehameha smiled and clapped him on the shoulder like an old friend.

The king, in sonorous tones, spoke warmly to Captain Thomas. Kekua rapidly translated. "He says you are welcome. He is Kamehameha, king of Hawaii and most of the other islands. This is Keopuolani, his sacred wife. This is Liholiho, the son of his sacred wife who will be king. This is his wife Kaahumanu. These are his other wives behind. Pick whichever one you wish."

"He wants me to choose one of his wives? Is that what he means?" the captain asked, nonplussed.

Kekua nodded. "Yes, but you must not choose Kaahumanu or Keopuolani."

The captain's voice sounded choked. "Tell him many thanks. I will need time to choose. His wives are all so beautiful; he is a fortunate man. Perhaps later I can decide."

When this was translated for the king, he raised his shoulders in a puzzled shrug, but clapped Thomas on the shoulder again. *"Komo mai apau. Hoomaka!"*

This was the signal for the serving of the food. The roasted animals were carved, and generous pieces were offered to the Hawaiian men and the sailors. The women had withdrawn. On the other side of the clearing they sat with bowls of poi and portions of fruit. Even the king's wives went away to take their meal in a separate place.

Horgan ate the roasted pig with alacrity. "I'd almost forgotten what fresh meat tastes like," he said. "Might be a good idea to have some on board, Captain."

Captain Thomas glanced at Jameson for his reaction.

"There can't be enough on the island," Jameson suggested. "The women seem to have given up theirs for us."

Kekua stared to him. "No, no! It is *kapu* for women to eat with men or to eat meat."

Schuyler, sitting close enough to hear this, scooped up a mouthful of the poi and instantly spat it out. "I wouldn't feed this stuff to a dog, let alone my woman."

One of the sailors laughed at him. "Your woman! No woman would have you!"

Schuyler was too drunk to ignore this slur. "Not only would a woman have me, she'd go against a lot of silly superstitions for me," he insisted, swaying to his feet. "Just watch."

The disaster struck so swiftly that Jameson didn't absorb the enormity of what was happening until it was too late. Schuyler, smarting from his mate's goading, had crossed the clearing with a piece of meat in his hand, winking and holding it out to his earlier companion. When she and the other women drew back in terror, the sailors roared with laughter. Infuriated, Schuyler seized the girl and tried to force the meat on her. She knocked it out of his hand and it fell into the dirt. He bellowed with fury.

"All right, you savage doxy. If you're going to act like that, you can eat it dirt and all." Holding the struggling woman tightly, he grabbed the meat from the ground and forced it into her mouth.

The scarred *kapu* guards instantly descended on them with clubs and garroting thongs, and the battle lines were drawn. The sailors rushed to Schuyler's aid; the natives formed a ring around them. Jameson found himself with Horgan and the captain, both of whom were armed.

Silence fell as Maakoa strode into the ring, stopped, and pointed a finger at the weeping girl. *"Ia maake,"* he said sternly.

Kekua stood slightly apart from the two opposing sides. "Maakoa says she must die," he explained.

Jameson stared at him. "For touching meat?"

"She has broken a sacred *kapu*, the law of the gods. The punishment for breaking this *kapu* is death."

Schuyler still held the hysterical girl. The sailors stood their ground, knives and pistols poised to fend off an attack. Maakoa turned to the captain.

"Aohe wahine haole maake."

Kekua interpreted again. "He says you must give up the woman or you will all die."

For the second time that day, Jameson saw Captain Thomas driven to make a decision that conflicted with his principles. But he had no more choice now than he had had when Jameson stepped into the outrigger with the natives. The captain didn't even glance at the ring of warriors. "Schuyler, give them the woman."

Schuyler truculently released her. As two fearsome *kapu* guards bore the weeping woman away, the priest pointed to Schuyler. *"Haole maake o."*

"No!" the captain's word was unmistakable. "I will not turn over one of my men."

Maakoa gestured for the *kapu* guards to close in on Schuyler. The natives, many armed with spears and clubs now, pushed forward. Captain Thomas raised his pistol and fired into the air. The natives had obviously learned that pistols were deadly. They drew back slightly and the crewmen began backing from the clearing. But after a brief pause, the armed warriors and the *kapu* guards closed in again, walling them around. The crew of the *Felicity Ann* was hopelessly outnumbered.

"Hold steady," the captain ordered. "Don't fire until I give the order."

"They're going to rush us, Captain," the bos'n protested.

The captain and his men had leveled their pistols and the

warriors were holding their spears ready when King Kamehameha stepped between them. Moving without haste or fear, the king faced the captain, expressing by his carriage his disdain for these *haole* and their weapons.

"Hoi maku o maake haole."

"He says you must go," Kekua translated. "You are forbidden here now. If you *haole* come again, you will be killed."

The crew members slipped from the clearing onto the path down to the beached boats. Jameson brought up the rear with Captain Thomas. Maakoa, the priest, stood by the king's side, watching until the last of them disappeared, his hard eyes narrowed. To ensure that the crew understood they weren't to take the chosen supplies, the *kapu* guards and the warriors followed them at a distance, shaking their spears and clubs with taunting menace.

Captain Thomas had to make another decision soon after the men returned to the ship. China was still many weeks away. Word of the evening's problem might spread quickly to the other islands and prevent the crew from obtaining supplies elsewhere. Their best chance was to take the supplies already assembled on the island, and the only possible time to do it was now.

"I don't think they'll be guarding them," he said to Jameson. "They won't expect us to return."

"Probably not. But I don't like the idea of simply stealing the supplies. The natives have been generous; it was our fault this mess happened."

"Schuyler's, you mean," the captain said dryly. "Did they say what they wanted in exchange?"

"Nails, metal objects, cloth."

"Very well. You're in as good a position as anyone to determine the value of their supplies. Take some goods in exchange. But, Jameson, don't overdo it."

"Yes, sir."

"And take Schuyler. If there's trouble, I want him in the middle of it."

Two side boats were let down carefully in the middle of the night. The sailors who manned the boat with Jameson and Schuyler were armed with muskets. The cannon, along with a keg of powder, shot, and flints, was lowered in with them. It would hold off the natives, if necessary, long enough for the sailors to load some supplies. Mr. Horgan, the bos'n, and two more sailors took the second boat with the goods Jameson had chosen for payment.

Captain Thomas watched them over the ship's rail. "You're sure you'll be able to find the provisions, Mr. Jameson?"

"Yes, Captain." Jameson hoped it was true. What if the natives had moved them, either after he had left the landing area with Kekua, or when the *Felicity Ann*'s crew was driven off the island?

"The currents may be different at this hour, and without any torches they could be dangerous to negotiate. Mr. Horgan will know how to handle them."

Jameson thought the first mate looked too tense now to deal with anything more than a simple slipknot. But he nodded his understanding to the captain.

"Once you've loaded the provisions, stand to your cannon until Mr. Horgan's boat is away. Use the cannon if you have to. We need those provisions so we can set sail."

The moon, which had shone strongly not many hours ago, was now obscured by clouds. It made the night darker, which was both a help and a hindrance to the two small boats. Finding the narrow inlet through the thick growth of plants was almost impossible in the shadows.

Jameson had tried to pick out landmarks for himself, but it was too dark to see the misshapen tree he had noticed or the black boulder. Waves caught the boats as they neared shore and threatened to dash them into trees that seemed to grow straight from the water. More by luck than skill

Jameson discovered the narrow inlet through which the canoes had earlier slipped into the quiet waters beyond. His heart hammered as the two boats glided through the leaves and into sight of the landing area.

There was no one standing guard. The area was deserted except for the warriors' beached canoes and the stacked provisions. The canoes were upside down, some distance from the supplies. This left Jameson uneasy because the canoes had been directly opposite the supplies when he and Kekua had left the area. Then it occurred to him that the natives had shifted them to make room for the boats from the ship. Was that the way it had been when they had later departed under the threatening eyes of the *kapu* guards and warriors? There had been so much activity that Jameson couldn't remember.

Two sailors stood guard with their muskets while the others unloaded the trade goods from the ship and set them just beyond the supplies. Jameson stayed with his cannon, scanning the swaying plants for any sign of the natives. Mr. Horgan's boat was loaded first with the baskets of fruit, taro root, and breads, and the barrels of water. Everyone moved quickly; danger was almost palpable in the tropical night.

"It's getting on to dawn, Mr. Horgan," the bos'n warned.

Horgan nodded. "There's just one more load."

A brightly colored bird erupted from the brush, shrieking and cawing. Startled, the sailors raised their muskets. The extra moment of preparation was helpful. War cries exploded shrilly from the thickets around them. The warriors attacked with spears and clubs. Jameson's worst fears were realized.

Frantically Mr. Horgan cried out that they had left goods in exchange. He cowered behind the bos'n and tried to grab a musket from one of the sailors. In the moment of crisis Jameson suddenly felt a calm determination descend on him. He couldn't lose his nerve now. They might all die. With a steady hand he lit the fuse and sent a load of shot screaming toward the natives.

In the short respite that followed, he yelled to his companions while reloading the cannon, "Push off with the other boat. We'll stay here until you're clear."

Mr. Horgan was the first one into his boat. The others joined him, still firing their muskets at the scattered natives. Instantly the boat moved away from shore, the sailor pulling violently on the oars.

Jameson noted from the corner of his eye that some of the natives were heading for their canoes. He didn't doubt for a minute that the skilled native crews could overtake the side boat from the ship. He aimed his second cannon shot at them, spewing destruction on several of the vessels as well as the natives.

Horgan's boat was far from the landing now, out of reach of the natives' spears and quickly heading for the overgrowth that would veil it from view. Now Jameson's crew became the major object of the attacking natives.

But not their only object.

As Jameson loaded the cannon once more he noticed the natives approaching his boat more closely than seemed necessary simply to kill the sailors. Since it made little sense for them to try to recover the supplies, it took him a minute to realize what their real goal was—the cannon!

One of his sailors already lay dead in the shallow water, a spear sunk deep in his chest. Schuyler and the other sailor tried to hold off the natives with muskets and push off the boat at the same time. They were still outnumbered, and Jameson reached for the dead man's musket, which fortunately had landed in the boat as he fell.

Jameson saw the spear coming, but was unable to avoid it. He rolled to one side as the metal tip slashed his leg. Blood sprang from the wound, but Jameson was too intent on getting his boat away from shore to notice the pain. He raised his musket as another native leaped forward, and found himself looking up the barrel into Kekua's face.

The native's expression didn't change. He faced death as matter-of-factly as he had spoken of it during the day. A king's son would die as easily as anyone else, no matter that he had the voice of a prophet and the stride of a powerful animal. But Kekua had served Jameson and the *Felicity Ann* that day. Jameson couldn't bring himself to kill him.

Instead of squeezing the trigger, Jameson abruptly swung the musket, slamming the barrel against Kekua's head, knocking him senseless to the ground. By this time another native had sprung forward, but Jameson stopped the man by discharging his weapon.

Too late he realized that all of this had been a distraction to allow the natives to dislodge the powder keg and carry it away. The small cannon required two men to lift it, and Schuyler managed to kick one of them back over the side of the boat as the other sailor shoved the craft out into the water.

Horgan's boat was long gone by now. Schuyler and the sailor pulled fiercely at the oars while Jameson discharged each of their muskets in turn. Several warriors fell under the musket fire, but the natives refused to retreat. As Jameson's boat was moving out of range, he loaded his musket one more time. A warrior stood with raised spear, his perfect body arched in silhouette against the tangled richness of dawn light and jungle. Jameson's musket ball hit him just as the weapon flew from his powerful arm. Schuyler slumped forward, impaled by the spear.

The sailor attempted to shove Schuyler's lifeless body out of the boat, but Schuyler was a large man. "Help me with this," he called to Jameson.

"Couldn't we take him back to the ship with us?"

"Look!" The sailor pointed toward shore, where two natives were ready to launch one of the canoes that were still seaworthy. "They'll be a lot faster than we are. We'll have to dump the cannon, too."

It seemed wiser than letting the natives get hold of it, especially since the keg of powder had already fallen into the natives' hands. The current was pushing the small boat in toward shore again and every minute counted. Jameson said a silent prayer as they unceremoniously pushed Schuyler's body into the water.

The cannon followed him, though Jameson blocked its disposal from the view of those on shore with his body. No sense letting them know where the weapon could be found. The boat, much more responsive now, surged forward when the two remaining men set their shoulders to the task. They were rowing for their lives.

They burst through the vegetation that shielded the entrance to the inlet, losing sight of the warriors in their canoe. Out to sea, they could just make out Mr. Horgan's boat as it approached the graceful *Felicity Ann*. At least most of the supplies would get there safely. And Captain Thomas would have the swivels and the brass guns ready on deck to cover the second boat. Jameson breathed a sigh of relief. They were going to be all right.

A breaker wave suddenly roared over Jameson's head, swamping the boat. Choking and gasping, he fought his way to the surface, only to be driven down again, and again, by the relentless sea.

Dawn's muted colors were giving way to the full light of day when the surf nudged floating debris to the shore of the inlet. From a copse of thick palms at the edge of the beach, Kekua watched the remains of Jameson's boat drift ashore. The bodies of the dead warriors had been taken away, the exchange goods thrown angrily into the water. Kekua knew they would be recovered later, under cover of darkness.

Kekua was about to turn away when Jameson's body,

clinging tightly to an oar, was nudged forward by the current. The *haole* appeared lifeless, but as Kekua watched, he stirred, groaned, and elbowed himself a few feet above the lapping water. The long gash in his leg slowly spilled his lifeblood onto the black sand.

PART TWO

*Old Gods
and New*

CHAPTER FOUR

PELE

Jameson gradually became conscious of a pulsing sound. He lay motionless, half-convinced that the insistent rhythm was his own blood pounding through his body. But as he became more alert, he realized what it was: a drumbeat.

Confused, he opened his eyes and dragged himself painfully to his feet. The vines that grew everywhere in the jungle twined toward the sun through rustling bamboo and masses of flamboyant flowers. This could be any one of the verdant clearings he had crossed with Kekua. When the steady, cheerful twittering of birds was drowned out by a crashing breaker, he realized he was near the water.

His heart pounded from the exertion of rising to his feet. Leaning against a palm tree, he closed his eyes to steady his reeling head. At least the drums, accompanied by war chants, seemed to be receding. Braced against the tree, he stared into the green tangle beyond the clearing. Nothing.

But then his breath caught in his throat as he noticed a moving spot of color. Jameson pressed himself back against the tree, blinking at the two helmeted warriors, spears in hand, who moved silently through the jungle only a few yards away. One glance his way and they would see him. He had no weapon, and he doubted that he had the strength to use one even if he had. Still, he knelt and selected a lava rock. It was becoming automatic for him to fight for his life.

The two warriors had disappeared from his range and yet he remained perfectly still. He was no David to bring down even one giant warrior with a stone. He was *haole*, the white stranger in an alien paradise. His very presence on the island meant death if he was discovered.

After a while his ears attuned themselves to the whisperings around him and he determined where the water lay. It was easy enough to muster the courage to cross the clearing; the problem was strength. His every move was painful, his head ached, and his breath came in short gasps with the least effort. But mostly his legs felt like columns of shifting sand, unsteady, unreliable.

As he moved toward the sound of the water, he realized that one of his legs was wrapped in a primitive bandage. He couldn't remember having tied it there. He couldn't remember having dragged himself so far from the water, either. Perhaps he had drifted in and out of consciousness and that was why he couldn't remember now. At the water's edge lay an oar. Jameson remembered the oar and how he had clung to it.

There was other debris along the shore of the inlet, pieces of wood, bits of canvas. Jameson feared he would see the dead sailor floating in the water, but it was something else entirely that glistened up through the rippling surface. Puzzled, he tried to get closer, but the object was beyond his reach. What could possibly shine so brightly beneath the surface? Intrigued, he stripped off his torn pants and shirt and stepped gingerly into the warm water.

Fish of amazing colors and shapes darted indifferently around his legs. The sunlit water glowed a rich yellow green. A lazy octopuslike creature waggled past, fluttering its tentacles. Jameson filled his lungs with air and dived under the water. A moment later he surfaced, holding a marlin spike—it was part of the exchange goods; Jameson had seen that the keg of nails was under water, too. How incredible that the natives would throw away these metal goods that they had wanted so much!

Jameson would have kept on diving if he had had the strength. Instead, he decided to keep the spike as a weapon and return to see what else he could find when he felt stronger. As he turned toward the shore he saw Nahana watching him. Her eyes moved with interest over his streaming wet body. Her smile held the kind of tempting sensuality he remembered from the luau.

No woman had ever seen him undressed. He felt self-conscious in his pale-skinned nakedness. Trying to appear calm, he jerked on his pants and buttoned his shirt with awkward fingers.

Nahana stood looking at him, her head cocked a little to one side. "Why do you put those on your body?" she asked. "It's not cold."

"Where I come from, everyone wears clothes." Jameson knew he sounded cross, and tried again. "It's a symbol of modesty."

"What's that—modesty?"

"It's when you cover your nakedness because... Oh, never mind. You wouldn't understand."

Nahana grinned. "No, I wouldn't understand covering your nakedness."

"What are you doing here?"

She reached for his leg where his pants were torn and the bandage remained tied. His flesh tingled at her touch as she lifted the bandage to look at his wound. "I've come to see how your leg is."

"You bandaged my leg?"

She nodded. "It was still bleeding. Not anymore. In a few days it will heal."

"Yes. Thank you, Nahana." Her name sounded like music on his tongue. "But I can't stay here. I'll have to take a canoe and go to one of the other islands."

She shook her head. "That would do you no good. Kamehameha is king of all the islands except Kauai, and it is far, far away. Maui is closest. He conquered it many years ago, but there is a new chief who now challenges him. The warriors maybe come to fight even now. You wouldn't be safe."

"I'll have to take my chances."

When she shook her head, her soft hair swayed across her shoulders, casting delicious shadows in the hollow of her throat and along the smooth curve of her breast. "Some of our warriors have been killed. If you are found... *Maake! Maake!* You will be killed. You must stay here and hide. When it is dark I will come back to you."

This was the hard way to learn a new language. *Maake, maake*: kill, kill. He was totally dependent on her discretion. "Where are you going?"

"I must go to my brother. To be with him."

He caught her arm. The feel of her smooth, warm skin sparked a strong response in him. "Can I trust you? Will you think it your duty to tell others that you've seen me?"

"Duty?" Nahana frowned. "I would be killed for helping you."

"Then why did you do it?"

"I can't say. I must go."

She stood silently until he released her arm. Then she studied his face a moment before turning abruptly and walking away on swift, silent feet. As soon as she disappeared behind the screen of foliage, he thrust the marlin spike into his waistband and started after her.

Several times he thought he had lost her, as well as himself. Always he was saved by a swift glimpse of the scarlet flower wound in her hair. When she left the jungle to enter an area of huts, he sought cover in the thicket, watching.

The huts were more ornate than those of the villages he had seen with Kekua. The open common stirred with activity. Several young children, dark hair flying, laughed delightedly as they played a running game between two trees. Two young men, probably in their teens, had drawn a crowd for their boxing-wrestling match. Young girls wandered here and there while a circle of men talked volubly among themselves as they peeled taro.

The sun, his injuries, and the long walk conspired against Jameson. He slid to the base of a palm tree and fought sleep. He didn't dare close his eyes for fear of missing Nahana. When she finally appeared in an open doorway across the clearing he stumbled to his feet. A man followed her into the sunlight. Jameson stared in disbelief. The man was Kekua.

Nahana turned and stood very close to Kekua, looking up into his face. She rested in the loose circle of his arms as he caressed the bare flesh of her back. His whispered words must have delighted her. She stood on tiptoe to press her face into the curve of his neck.

Jameson's astonishment turned into suspicion. Her brother indeed! No brother and sister under the sight of God behaved like that. She had lied to him. She had lied to him not only with her words but with her eyes and her hands and her smile. Angry, he watched her graceful body slip out of Kekua's embrace with a farewell caress.

He caught her a few yards beyond the edge of the clearing. Clamping his hand over her mouth, he pulled her into the thicket with the marlin spike pressed against her throat. "You told him where to find me, didn't you?"

Nahana shook her head, wincing at his roughness.

Easing his hand from her mouth, but with the weapon still at her throat, he hissed, "I know who that was. The king's son."

"Yes, Kekua. You spared his life, so he sent me to help you."

"You lied to me. You said you were going to see your brother."

"Kekua is my brother."

"I *saw* you there at the hut with him! I would be more likely to believe that you are his wife."

"No. Kekua has many wives. But I am the sister he chose to one day give him a son to become a great *alii* warrior."

He stared at her in horror. "Have a son with your brother! I don't believe you. I've been a fool to believe anything you've told me."

Nahana remained silent, her dark eyes unreadable.

"You're going to come with me while I get a boat and leave the island. Don't try to get away." He lowered the spike but held it ready.

With the same poised disdain that King Kamehameha had exhibited in the face of the armed officers, she pushed aside the marlin spike. "I will take you, Jameson." Her tone was cool and detached. She turned her back on him and his weapon and started off through the jungle.

They had traveled ten minutes through the sun-dappled vegetation when Nahana suddenly stopped and signaled him to be silent. Muted voices sounded off to the side. Jameson peered through the vines to see where they were coming from.

The clearing was ringed with carved totem figures that glared hideously at the plump girl who was lashed to one of the trees. A rope looped around her neck had been drawn around a second tree. *Kapu* guards pulled on the rope, slowly garroting her to death while Maakoa looked on. Guttural sounds came from her swollen mouth as she tried to cry out. Her eyes were wide with terror.

Jameson drew back in horror. "It's the girl Schuyler was with," he whispered. "They're strangling her."

"Her name is Lahoa. She broke the law of the gods and she must die."

"Schuyler forced her to eat the meat. It wasn't her choice."

"It doesn't matter. The *kapu* was broken. Your sailor caused her death."

What Jameson had seen violated every tenet of his life. "My God holds human life sacred," he told Nahana fiercely. Lahoa's strangled cry filled the clearing. Her cry might have come from Jameson's own throat for the anguish he felt. Driven by the need to right this terrible wrong, he started forward toward the clearing.

Nahana raced in front of him and turned, fierce as an animal at bay. "Do you want me to die that way?" she demanded in a low, urgent whisper. "Because I will. And you will. Your recklessness will only cause more pain and death. Maakoa is not a stupid man. He would know someone was helping you. Try to save her and we will both die."

They stood staring at each other for long, agonizing minutes until there was silence in the clearing. Jameson shuddered and turned away. Nahana slipped in front of him and led him away from the clearing, up an overgrown path.

When they had gone some distance, he said, "Where are you taking me?"

"Somewhere that you can hide until it is safe." She glanced at the jagged volcanic mountain. "In Kilauea with the goddess Pele."

"In the volcano?"

"There are many *pohaku*, tubes, made by the lava. Come!"

The entrance to the lava tube wasn't much farther up the trail, though Nahana explained that some of the tubes started near the top of the volcano and ran all the way down to the sea. "Part of this one does, too, but you are safer to hide in the side section that is too small for any but a child to explore."

The main section of the lava tube was cavernous, taller than a man, and wider. But Nahana pointed out a small side shaft that went only a few feet. "You cannot be seen there from the main tube. And you should stay there until I can come. You are likely to fall asleep, and someone might stumble on you in the main tube."

"Is the tube used often?"

Nahana's studied shrug made him think she was avoiding an answer.

"When will you return?" he asked.

"When it is safe. When I have found a canoe for you. When I have gathered food. I can't tell when that will be. Rest. You will need your strength."

She touched his face with the tips of her fingers, gazing solemnly into his eyes. "I will return, Jameson." Then she turned abruptly and left.

Almost no light penetrated to the spot where he stood, his back pressed against the hard wall of the lava tube. It wasn't possible to get comfortable in the shadowy recess, but he was so exhausted that it hardly mattered. His body, already bruised, simply developed new aches as he settled in for the long wait. Between periods of heavy sleep he awoke to the black silence of the lava tube.

He became disoriented without the guidance of night and day. Once he awoke to find generous quantities of food and water placed beside him. He had almost forgotten how hungry he was until he bit into the ripe breadfruit and felt the juice trickle down his jaw. When he had satisfied his hunger, he immediately fell asleep... and dreamed of Nahana. In his dream she awakened him by curling her body against his and running her hands along his skin. Her touch was like fire, heating each part of him. Her mouth clung to his, her hips swayed against him. He could feel the rhythm of her body, pressing closer and closer.

He awoke in a sweat to the sound of marching feet. The cadence grew steadily louder as they approached the tube. Jameson shrank back against the wall. They were coming to get him! Nahana had betrayed where he was hiding. No, he couldn't quite believe that. She must have been seen, questioned, tortured.... He felt sick just thinking of it.

There was nothing he could do. Nowhere he could go. He remained in the alcove as the men, many men, drew nearer to his hiding place. Surely not so many men were needed to capture him! Inside the lava tube tunnel, their tread echoed and reverberated like thunder. But not one of them came into the alcove. They marched forward, a seemingly neverending column.

When the last one had passed, Jameson nerved himself to crawl to a spot that looked into the long tube. The last warrior wore a gourd helmet and carried a small canoe above his head; war clubs and spears swung down his back. A shimmering luminescence glowed from the path the warriors had taken. The last one seemed to sink into an unearthly bath of light, and the rumble of their passing echoed in the cave for long minutes.

Jameson breathed a sigh of relief. Obviously, these men were about to fight an enemy. They had no idea that he was hidden in the cave, nor did they care. But they would probably have killed him if they had found him.

A whisper of sound alerted him. He swung around, the marlin spike ready in his hand. Nahana stood at the entrance of the tunnel, motioning to him. He followed her out into daylight.

"Where are the warriors going?" he asked.

Nahana shook her head. "I can't say. Don't ask me."

"Yes, all right. I understand. But I have to get away. Were you able to find a boat for me?"

"I have found one and hidden it; but, Jameson, I don't think it's safe for you to leave now. There are whisperings of battle...."

"Then it's probably the best time for me to go. No one will be looking for me. Show me the boat, Nahana."

He followed her down the hillside to the inlet. She had concealed a small boat in a dense bed of ferns so well that he didn't even know it was there until she pulled aside the growth and cleared away the tangled vines she had wound around the mast. While he struggled to hoist the narrow sail, Nahana retrieved fruit and bread and water hidden close by.

Jameson packed the provisions carefully into the boat. It would be hazardous sailing to the next island, and he couldn't be sure of his welcome there. Surely there would be no one like Nahana to come to his rescue. He longed to hold her in his arms but instead he turned and clasped her hands. "Thank you. Thank you for everything. I'm in your debt."

"No. You saved the life of my brother Kekua." Then she fixed him with her steady, searching eyes and added, "And I would have chosen you."

A curious, sinking feeling struck him. It pained him to realize that he would never see her again, never touch her warm, satiny flesh or kiss her full, intriguing lips. Jameson forced himself to look away as he released her hands.

"Take care of yourself." There was so much more he wanted to say, but he couldn't find the words. "Good-bye, Nahana."

"Good-bye, Jameson."

The boat swayed gently as he pushed off. Nahana released the red lehua blossom from her hair and tossed it into the water in his wake. "A safe journey," she whispered.

Until the thick wall of vegetation along the bank of the inlet blocked her from his view, Jameson watched her standing there silent and watchful, beautiful in the dappled light. Jameson was not superstitious, but he drew comfort from her gesture with the flower. The water was calm under a smiling sky and the wind was favorable. Looking back, Jameson let his eyes absorb the remarkable beauty of the island with its towering green cliffs and its wild, colorful profusion of flowers and trees.

Then he tacked around the rock formation and headed toward the open sea.

A flotilla of war canoes was bearing down on him. The warriors were awesome in both ferocity and number, armed with slings, spears, and clubs. But the helmets of these warriors were vastly different from those worn by King Kamehameha's men. Without trying to figure out what this meant, Jameson scrambled desperately to bring his boat about and return to the inlet.

But it was too late.

On the beach Kamehameha stood calmly, watching the Maui war fleet approach. His son Kekua stood at his side and his warriors were ranked behind him. At his signal, an aide raised a conch shell to his lips and blew.

The moaning cry of the conch shell startled the birds from their trees. It reverberated through the lava tubes where the warriors waited, their canoes loaded with stones, their hands clutching long hollowed bamboo poles. One by one the warriors carried their weighted canoes to the end of the tube where the ocean flowed in. In their rock-laden canoes, they dropped into the water to disappear beneath the face of the sea.

To the two Mauian princes, the great Kamehameha and his warriors on the beach looked like a pitiful collection against their own overwhelming numbers. They didn't notice Jameson's small craft pushing back toward the rocks. With feathered pennants fluttering, they swept toward shore, already shouting victory cries.

Suddenly the ocean behind them roiled with Hawaiian warriors in their canoes. After emptying their ballast, the armed warriors who had entered the sea through the lava tube shot their crafts to the surface like so many dolphins flying for the sun, and launched a surprise attack from the rear.

Jameson's boat, pitching in the wake of the canoes, was trapped between the warring armies.

CHAPTER FIVE

THE BLOOD OF KAMEHAMEHA

The fierce clash lasted two hours. Jameson had no weapons to protect himself; the marlin spike was useless in a boat. He tried to brazen his way out of the area as someone not involved in the battle, but a Hawaiian warrior drove Jameson's small craft toward the shore with the threat of his spear. Jameson found himself a prisoner with the remnant of the Mauian army.

The prisoners were driven straight through the jungle to the king's compound. With his hands bound tightly behind his back, and other bodies pressed around him, Jameson couldn't dodge the lashing of low-hanging branches or sidestep the blades of stiff grass that sliced his arms and legs. Tangled roots and vines on the forest floor caught at his feet, forcing him to fight for balance with every step.

The two captured Mauian princes, Hanakea and Mokilho,

were driven ahead of the other prisoners. Even with their feathered garments torn and bloodied, they walked proudly, as befitted the sons of a king. Most of the prisoners were not imbued with such *alii* pride; they uttered strange cries and moans in the agony of defeat.

Before they reached the royal clearing, Jameson heard the high priest Maakoa chanting. The prisoners fell silent at the sound of his voice. At the edge of the compound, Kamehameha's warriors separated the two Mauian princes and Jameson from the rest of the defeated warriors. The three men were brought into the clearing, but no one acknowledged their arrival.

All eyes were on Maakoa as he chanted over a tapa-covered body on a pallet in front of the king's elaborate dwelling. Jameson saw Nahana at once, standing in a group of women. King Kamehameha stood between his wives, his sacred wife Keopuolani, on his left with her son Liholiho beside her, and Kaahumanu, his favored wife, on the right. Nahana's face was filled with grief as she watched the high priest.

Maakoa fell silent and backed away. Only then could Jameson see that the dead man lying in state was the king's son Kekua. A great sadness filled his chest. He watched as the women walked forward in single file. Each laid a white flower on Kekua's body before moving on. As clearly as if it were a waking dream, Jameson saw Kekua at the door of his dwelling, smiling as Nahana lifted her lips to him in that nuzzling embrace. His chest tightened, but whether in grief for the dead warrior or for some other reason he could not be sure.

Nahana approached him silently, her dark eyes troubled. "They told me you had been captured."

"You were right that it wasn't safe to leave. I'm sorry about your brother."

"Kekua isn't dead. Only his breath is gone. Now it will be everywhere until a new life calls it back."

He glanced at the handsome young man under his coverlet of fresh flowers. "May his soul rest in peace."

Nahana looked puzzled but she said only, "I will tell my father that you once spared Kekua's life."

"That might have helped, if Kekua were alive. Now . . ."

King Kamehameha walked to the center of the clearing, absorbed in his own thoughts. He studied the captured Mauian princes, who bowed before him. Jameson felt Nahana tug insistently at his shirt, and he, too, lowered his head to the king. Mokilho wavered under Kamehameha's fierce scrutiny, but Hanakea stiffened and defiantly bared his chest. The young prince spoke swiftly, a long speech that ended in the words, *"Keiki no keiki."*

Kamehameha repeated the words thoughtfully before glancing at Kaahumanu, as though to read her reaction. Then, in the solemn manner of a pronouncement, the king spoke, using the phrase again: *"Keiki no keiki."*

"What is he saying?" Jameson whispered to Nahana.

"Those are the sons of Kamauli, the chief on Maui who challenges Kamehameha's conquest of the island," she told him. "Kamehameha says he will keep one of the princes as his own son." She glanced toward the body of Kekua. *"Keiki no keiki,* a son for a son. Kamehameha will send the other son back to his father. If the chief of Maui will surrender and become one with the rest of the islands again, we will have peace."

At the king's gesture, the two young men were separated. Hanakea remained in the clearing but Mokilho was led away. Kamehameha strode to the group of captured warriors. They fell to earth at his glance.

When the king spoke again, Nahana breathed with relief. "He is going to let them live as slaves."

"Slaves?" Jameson shuddered. "It would be an awful

fate." As he spoke, Kamehameha turned toward him. Before the king could pronounce Jameson's sentence, Nahana moved to her father's side. Jameson watched her plead with him in that liquid language they shared. The king looked toward the body of Kekua and then at Jameson before speaking tersely to Nahana. He knew from her stricken expression that her plea had failed.

Nahana approached him slowly.

"He didn't believe you?" Jameson asked.

"He said you were forbidden to be on the island. He said Kekua is dead anyhow."

"What will he do with me?"

Her voice was barely audible. "I don't know."

Maakoa, trailed by lesser priests, crossed the clearing to the king. As he spoke, he gestured toward Jameson. Nahana translated his words quietly. "Maakoa says you *haoles* have brought death. This is a warning from the gods. If you are allowed to live, many more of our people will be killed."

She fell silent as her father approached to confront Jameson.

"Ana o ka la opopo maake, haole maake."

Jameson recognized the worst of the words even before Nahana translated them for him. "When the sun dies tomorrow, you will die."

"But our coming had nothing to do with this attack by the Mauians! And I wasn't even on the island when I was captured! I came to this island in peace. I spared Kekua's life when..."

"Enough!" the king thundered. "I have spoken and it is done!"

Jameson stared at him. "You speak English!"

"Sometimes." The king shrugged, sending ripples down his feather cloak. "When you came back to the island you broke the *kapu* of Kamehameha. If one *haole* can break the *kapu* of the king and live, will not others?" He turned his back on Jameson and said as he walked away, "You must die."

Jameson stood stunned by this final sentence. Two warriors stepped forward and seized him. Nahana reached out to him, but he was already beyond her grasp.

The totem figures were horrifying by torchlight. Jameson was bound with his back tight against one of the stark, stripped trees as Lahoa had been. When his executioners had finished tying him, they took positions on either side of him, staring straight ahead.

Jameson worked feverishly to loosen the painfully tight ropes around his wrists, but they had little give and were cleverly knotted. He finally managed to loosen them enough to feel a faint stirring of hope.

Almost as if his optimism had alerted the guards, one of them grabbed the garroting rope and tugged it. With his head forced back and the rope pressing on his throat, Jameson ceased struggling for anything except his next breath.

Nahana stood uncertain outside her father's sleeping hut. Taking a deep breath to summon courage, she stepped inside. Her father was sleeping on his mat, his beautiful young wife Kaahumanu pressed against him. The passion of their joining was still tangible in the air. Kamehameha's sacred wives and those who were currently favored also slept on mats around the hut. Nahana forced herself to kneel by his side and whisper his name.

Kaahumanu stirred and opened his eyes. "What is it?" she asked softly. "What's wrong?"

The king opened his eyes and frowned at Nahana.

"I tried to see Jameson and the guards wouldn't let me," Nahana explained.

Her father sighed. "Why do you want to see him? He is just another *haole*."

"No, he's different. He's not like the others."

"Be careful, Nahana," her father warned. "Even a king's daughter is not free to break the *kapus*. Have you forgotten that?"

"Please. Before he dies. I only want to..."

"No." Her father's tone was more frustrated than angry. "Leave! Before my anger rises." He saw the sadness in her face and sighed. "Maybe tomorrow. Maybe."

Nahana rose and turned to leave. She knew from her father's voice that he was fully awake. Now he would lose himself in lovemaking, forgetting his daughter's sorrow in his passion. She heard his low murmurs of arousal as Kaahumanu pleased him with her hands and body. The heaviness in Nahana's heart slowed her steps, and she heard the words that passed between them.

"I'll be right back," Kaahumanu said.

"Maybe I won't wait for you."

Nahana paused outside the door, holding her breath. In the silence that followed, Nahana knew that Kaahumanu, who was adroit above all other women in giving joy to men's bodies, was stroking the king to a passion that no other woman could satisfy.

With chiding laughter, Kaahumanu whispered, "You'll wait for me."

Kaahumanu appeared at the entrance to the hut and linked her arm with Nahana's. "You think the *haole* is handsome?" she asked.

"Yes."

"So do I. Come, you will see him."

At the execution clearing the guards moved to bar her way. But Kaahumanu strode regally into the torchlight. "Move away," she ordered. They backed away with lowered heads. Kaahumanu led Nahana past them but drew back into the shadows as Nahana hurried to Jameson's side.

"Nahana!" he cried. "I didn't know if I'd see you before... Did you talk with your father again?"

Kaahumanu spoke from the darkness. "You should not have come back and broken the *kapu* of Kamehameha."

"I had no choice but to come back for the supplies." He stopped and peered through the night at Kaahumanu. "Who is that?"

"I am Kaahumanu. I am a queen."

"Would you talk to the king for me? Would you try to persuade him not to have me killed?"

"Kamehameha has larger concerns than you just now. He must win this challenge from the Mauians so that he can be king of all the islands and we can be one people."

Suddenly Jameson felt a shock of hope. There was something he could offer in exchange for his life. He spoke carefully, never taking his eyes from Kaahumanu's face. "The night of the raid Kekua and the warriors got our keg of gunpowder, but they didn't get the cannon. They obviously wanted it, so they must know how powerful a cannon is."

"The warriors have faced cannons," Kaahumanu admitted.

"I can get a cannon for you."

"Where? Your ship has left."

"The cannon is where I can get it. And I know how to use it. Your warriors would only ruin it without my help. Let me tell Kamehameha."

"I will tell him."

"What if he won't listen to you?"

Her tone turned imperious. "I am Kaahumanu. He will listen to me when I wish him to listen."

She smiled and turned away, taking Nahana with her. But not before the younger woman pressed Jameson's arm in a sign of hope.

* * *

The sun was not all the way up when the *kapu* guards released Jameson from the tree and led him down to the inlet where the raid had taken place. Jameson flexed his stiff hands as he watched Kamehameha approach with Nahana and Kaahumanu. The king motioned the guards away.

"Where is this cannon?" he asked.

"I will give it to you and show you how to work it, if you will let me leave the island," Jameson bargained.

"Where is it?" the king asked more sharply.

Jameson pointed toward the water. "Out there."

"Lost in the water!" He turned on Kaahumanu and spoke swiftly in Hawaiian. Nahana reached for her father's hand before the queen could respond. Kamehameha frowned as he listened to his daughter's urgent words. Finally he nodded.

Jameson waited anxiously for an explanation.

Kaahumanu said, "Nahana said you do not lie and you will prove it by giving the cannon to Kamehameha now, this minute, or he can have her killed, too."

Jameson's stomach lurched. "But I can't do that!"

Nahana stared at him, aghast. "You lied? The cannon is not there?"

"It's there," he assured her. "But it's heavy and it's under water." He turned to Kamehameha. "It's just that it will take me a little while to get it."

The king looked thoughtful. "The sun is only now here. You will not die until it sinks into the sea over there."

"It might take longer than that," Jameson protested.

"The sun will not take longer."

Jameson stared at him. No wonder this man was king. "All right. I'll need half a dozen men."

"No. Two men."

"I don't know if I can get it done with two men."

"You have until the sun is no more," King Kamehameha

reminded him. He traced an imaginary arc with his hand, pantomiming the sun's death at the end of the arc by turning over his hand.

Nahana's anxiety showed in her face. Jameson would have given anything to be able to reassure her. But she herself had said that he did not lie, and he would simply have to prove it. As the morning sun crested the line of the hills, he stripped off his shirt and shoes and motioned to the two natives Kamehameha summoned to be his helpers. There was no time to lose.

In order to locate the exact position of the cannon, Jameson re-created the sequence of events on the raiding night. Using a four-man canoe that was approximately the size of the side boat he and the other sailors had been in, he started from the same point on the beach. The canoe moved more quickly than the cannon-laden boat, but Jameson was able to judge distances by how far the skilled warriors could throw a spear.

When they reached the spot where they had thrown Schuyler's body overboard, and then the cannon, Jameson prepared to dive. The water was clear, but too deep to determine what lay on the bottom. Again and again he dived, spending so long beneath the surface that he raced in anguish for air each time.

The two natives who accompanied him watched his progress with curiosity. Since they couldn't speak to him, nor he to them, there were no explanations and no suggestions made. The royal family watched from the shady beach. Only the king's son Liholiho appeared indifferent. Kamehameha's face showed interest and Kaahumanu's a distant calculation, while Nahana's was openly hopeful. The priest Maakoa stood apart, his expression unreadable.

The canoe drifted from the spot where Jameson had originally started diving, and he tried to calculate whether even the strongest current would shift the weight of a cannon. In his exhaustion he harbored suspicions that the natives had already rescued the canoe and were merely allowing him to make a fool of himself. No, it had been dark. They couldn't really have known when the cannon went overboard. They would have assumed that it went down with the side boat itself, farther out.

Time was passing quickly. Jameson was offered food at midday and ate ravenously. But his hope was fading. The distances at night were probably deceptive. Possibly his guess about how far a spear could be thrown was inaccurate. When he had finished his meal, he motioned to Nahana.

She hurried to his side. "Can't you find it?"

"No. Will you tell this fellow something for me?" he asked, indicating one of the natives. "I want him to throw a spear, from the shore, while I'm out in the canoe with the other man. I want to see how far it goes."

"His name is Hopu, but it is Honolii who would be able to throw his spear the farthest. Let me have him be the one."

Jameson agreed. He and Hopu paddled out to the spot where he had started his search and called for Honolii to throw a spear. It occurred to Jameson that the native might be tempted to aim for him, but that was a chance he would have to take.

Honolii had massive shoulders and stood well over six feet tall. He drew back his arm and then swung it forward with astonishing power, releasing the spear at the height of the arc his arm made. The whole process looked amazingly effortless.

Jameson remembered thinking the night of the raid that they were almost out of range of the spears. Now he saw demonstrated again how incredibly far the natives could throw. The spear easily sailed past his canoe and landed in the water a good fifteen feet farther out.

Jameson would have to start his search all over again, much farther out, much later in the day.

On his third attempt he spotted a gray bulk that he prayed would not turn out to be a rock. Without enough air left to sustain him, he was forced to surface before he could investigate. This time he would dive with a rope curled in his hand. He was physically exhausted from his efforts, and the still-raw wound on his leg grew more painful.

Taking a huge gulp of air, he descended to the area where he had seen the gray bulk. This time he was able to touch the hard metal surface, but he found that the cannon's brass muzzle was deeply embedded in the bottom of the inlet. Though his efforts to shift it were unsuccessful, he did manage to slide the rope around the mounted firing tube before racing to the surface for air.

Hopu was watching intently when Jameson surfaced. There was a question in his eyes as he took the rope from Jameson, but when Jameson nodded, the native grinned broadly. Hopu pulled on the rope and felt the great resistance. He pulled again, harder, but still the cannon did not budge.

Jameson indicated that he needed another rope. Then once again he dived to the cannon, slinging the second rope around it in a different direction. With little remaining air in his lungs, Jameson dug furiously at the mud surrounding the sunken carriage. When he surfaced, Hopu helped him into the canoe and drew the rope up over the other side. Each man pulled on his rope, using the leverage of the canoe sides to give him more strength.

The solid resistance of the submerged cannon discouraged them again and again. Jameson dived once more, spending his energy and his air, scraping away as much mud as possible before returning to the canoe. This time the dead weight yielded, a small bit. Encouraged, the two men pulled again, and felt the cannon shift. They had freed it!

But there was no possibility of lifting the cannon. Its weight in comparison to the size of the canoe made that impossible. The only thing they could do was begin the laborious task of dragging it back to shore, even though it was already late in the afternoon, the two men were tired, and Jameson's leg ached almost beyond endurance.

Slowly they made their way toward shore, the cannon dragging heavily along the bottom of the inlet behind them. When they were close enough to the landing area, Kamehameha sent other natives to help drag the cannon onto dry land. Jameson drained the water from it and wiped it down with a rag. Kaahumanu studied it proudly, but the high priest Maakoa wore a dark frown.

"Well, there it is," Jameson told the king. "Just as I promised."

"Make it shoot," the king ordered.

"Your men will have to return the gunpowder they took from the boat. Then I can shoot it." Maybe. Provided the gunpowder had been kept dry, and the cannon hadn't gotten clogged with debris, and...

Kamehameha pointed toward his young son. "There is the keg. The sun is dying."

Liholiho was sitting on the familiar keg, kicking his heels against its sides and bouncing up and down. He was not pleased when Hopu took it away, but he came forward to watch what was going to happen.

Jameson pried open the keg and unwrapped the oilskin that contained the powder. He held his breath while he tested it between his fingers. To his relief, the powder was dry. He poured a good quantity into the flash pan, then gathered stones and broken shells and forced them into the muzzle of the cannon.

There was no fire on the beach and Jameson had no flints. He could have sent for a burning branch from the closest village, but the sun was quickly sinking. He decided that it would do no harm to surprise the natives with one of civilization's tricks. As always, he had the mirrored locket Martha had given him in his pants pocket. He turned the cannon toward a line of trees and knelt to focus the last rays of sun on the fuse.

There was a curious silence for a few minutes, and then whispers and a few impatient murmurs, even a little derisive laughter. Just as the last rays of sun left the beach, a slender plume of smoke began to rise from the fuse. Jameson turned away and covered his ears.

Rocks and shells exploded thunderously from the muzzle, shattering the line of trees. The land trembled from the blast. The natives stood in open-mouthed amazement. Liholiho cried out and ran to his mother's side.

Kamehameha nodded with satisfaction. Maakoa came to stand before him. Gesturing toward Jameson and the cannon, he spoke swiftly. From Nahana's sudden look of terror, Jameson guessed what she was hearing.

"He still wants to have me killed, doesn't he?"

"He says the cannon is proof that *haole* ways are evil. The gods will send punishment if they are not made *kapu*."

Kaahumanu boldly strode over to confront both the high priest and the king. Nahana translated her words. "Kaahumanu says you are powerful. You know how to shoot the cannon. And Kamehameha can use the cannon to conquer Maui again and unite our people."

The priest raised his voice to drown out Kaahumanu's words.

"Maakoa says that if a stranger defies the gods, he must die."

The sun was a blazing memory behind the hills and the wind had turned chill. Jameson shivered in his wet clothing.

His leg ached. He was tired to the core. As he watched the high priest defiantly demanding the king's reply, he wouldn't have wagered a pint of stout on seeing another dawn.

The king glanced at his son Liholiho and then back at Maakoa. When he spoke, his tone seemed amused.

"He says he who shares the king's blood cannot be a stranger."

Excited whispers stirred among the natives as the king's sonorous voice continued. Jameson couldn't follow this new direction. "I don't understand. Is he going to let me live?"

"Yes. You will not be a stranger if you are part of the king's family."

"But I'm not part of the king's family."

"You can become a part of it by marrying the king's daughter." Her smile was slightly tremulous. "Kamehameha says you are to marry me."

CHAPTER SIX

HONI

Jameson had little choice but to accept this decree, as it was a matter of life or death. But he spent the next hour considering just what it meant to "marry" Nahana. A heathen ceremony could mean nothing to him as a Christian, surely. And yet, he would be expected to join himself with her as though they were truly wedded.

The thought both excited and alarmed him. Nahana's body was incredibly desirable and he could imagine possessing it. But he had promised himself to Martha. Martha. How long had it been since he'd even thought of her?

Still, these circumstances were extraordinary. If it had been a quiet, uneventful passage on the *Felicity Ann*, he would have lain on his bunk thinking of her occasionally, eventually returning to her, full with his new knowledge of the world. Who would have thought his life would depend on "marrying" a native Hawaiian girl whose eyes shone with delight and whose body blossomed with temptation?

But no, he was actually anticipating the physical union with Nahana. That was not the way it should be if he truly held to his religious scruples.

Jameson decided that the principled thing to do was to go through with the ceremony but to explain to Nahana that he was betrothed to Martha. In the presence of the other natives they would pretend to be man and wife, until Jameson had an opportunity to escape from the island. From what Jameson had seen of Hawaiian society, Nahana would not suffer from his leaving. Her father would simply give her to another man.

The thought distressed him, and he put it aside.

Kamehameha had decided that they would be married immediately. Jameson was brought to the royal compound wearing a colorful feathered cloak over his bare torso. Nothing could have been a greater contrast to the somber clothing he would be expected to wear when he married Martha.

Jameson had never seen any creature as beautiful as Nahana that night. Her dark hair bloomed with flowers, her glowing breasts were enticing beneath flamboyant leis, and her eyes as she watched him were warm with enchanting promise.

The ceremony started with dancers surrounding him, filling the royal compound. The music and the hypnotizing movement of the women caught his full attention. And then Nahana danced alone. He watched her breathlessly. Passion, tenderness, and regal grace combined in her lithe body. Her hands moved with fascinating agility as her body swayed and twisted before him.

It was like a forbidden dream, the sinuously winding bronzed body, the music-filled erotic excitement. The scent of flowers, the wavering torches, the black sky wild with stars. And then the other dancers circled the two of them, caressing Jameson, stroking Nahana. Drawing back, they undulated in the ritual love hula.

The hula ended abruptly when the drums stopped. The dancers stepped back as Nahana took his hand and led him to the palace hut. Two mats lay on the earth, one decorated with a white flower, the other with a red.

Nahana knelt on the mat with the white flower and motioned Jameson to the other. On their left sat twenty-five girls, ranging from children to ample women, watching them, giggling softly and whispering.

"Who are they?" Jameson asked.

"My sisters."

"All of them?"

She laughed. "No, only some of them. There are many more." As she spoke, the sisters descended on them, patting, embracing, and fondling both him and Nahana. To his embarrassed relief, they scattered as Kaahumanu approached. She embraced them in turn, lightly pressing her cheek to theirs. Her arms lingered around Jameson seductively. As she released him, Jameson saw the high priest outside the hut turn and walk into the darkness, followed by his lesser priests.

Nahana lifted the white flower and placed it between them, motioning Jameson to do the same with the red one. The king, his eyes still on the departing priests, shrugged and approached them. Kamehameha held a gleaming, honed dagger. Lifting Nahana's arm, he cut her wrist just enough to bring blood welling forth. He did the same to Jameson, then pressed their wrists together, symbolically joining their blood. When this was finished he smiled and gestured to a small hut on the other side of the clearing.

They had to make their way past a congratulating, enthusiastic crowd. Nahana guided her new husband through the low door of the hut. The quiet inside was a relief after the noisy, close-pressing crowd. Nahana turned to him, sliding her hands across his bare chest under the feathered cloak. Her breasts pressed against him as she fitted herself to the curves of his body. Only his consciousness of the crowd outside the hut gave Jameson the strength to fight off his arousal. Pulling away from her, he peered out at the revelers, who had begun to divide off into embracing couples. "Why are they all out there?" he asked.

"They wait for us."

"To come out again?"

"No. They cannot be together until we are, until we become one."

"Until we . . . ?" Jameson stared at her. "While they all stand out there waiting, you mean? I can't do that."

Nahana considered him with wide, pleading eyes. "You must. It is our way. When you wish to take other wives, they will know it is all right."

"Other wives! I won't be taking other wives."

"Why not?" she asked with a puzzled frown.

"Because, where I come from, a man marries only one woman. It's what my religion says is right." His voice trailed off as she pressed against him, but he knew he had to continue. "Of course this isn't like our kind of marriage. I don't consider myself really married to you."

A lone tear trickled down Nahana's cheek and she brushed it quickly away with the back of her hand.

"It's not that I don't think you're beautiful!" he insisted. "If I were going to stay here, there is nothing I would rather have than for you to be my wife. But I'm not going to stay. You know that. Kamehameha can't keep me here forever."

Nahana stroked his arm and laid her cheek against his. "But you are here now."

"In Boston there's someone else, a woman I plan to marry."

"And you don't want me?"

"Oh, Nahana, I do, but..."

She moved her lips along his bare chest, past the hollow of his throat, and up toward his mouth. Overwhelmed, Jameson leaned toward her lips.

"No," she said, holding him back. "Hawaiian way is called *honi*. We breathe into each other's soul."

She tilted his head and gently parted his lips with her fingertips. Without touching him, she brought her open mouth so close that he could feel the heat of her lips. And then she seemed to fill all of his senses. Her musky fragrance, her satiny skin, the melody of her voice, the radiant beauty of her enchanting face, the rich taste of her mouth... As her breath mingled with his, he felt an uncontrollable passion. A word whispered through his mind—*forever*. This must go on forever.

Nahana's fingers moved caressingly across his face and throat. Her insistent lips tasted him with exciting boldness. She tasted his mouth, and his throat, and his chest, even as her hands explored farther down his body. She placed his hands on her firm breasts, sighing as he touched her there for the first time.

Jameson had not intended to take part in this game of passion, but he was too intoxicated even to remember his own strictures. The soft skin of her breasts, the hard tips that somehow begged him to taste them, the feel of her hands on his manhood—all of this drove him to an ecstasy of arousal that he wouldn't have believed possible. The exquisite urgency that raced through his body and coursed through his veins was so enthralling that he could think of nothing else. His manhood throbbed with the need to enter Nahana's body, to join with her in an agony of spectacular release.

Nahana pulled him closer. Her thighs opened willingly and her hands guided him to her. How incredible to become a part of her, to fill this empty space with his swollen member, to feel the velvet grip of her womanhood! Jameson became more inflamed with each stroke. Nahana's moans rang in his ears like the most exotic music. The final release made them soar together somewhere outside of time and place.

Jameson clung to her, stunned by the experience.

The world seemed to explode into sound around them. At first Jameson thought it was all part of the native ritual, this piercing wail of the conch shell. Embarrassing, certainly, but nothing to alarm him. It was only when Nahana started up in surprise that he realized this was something out of the ordinary.

They dressed hurriedly and followed the rest of the celebrants, who were running down the path toward the ocean. The warriors had grabbed spears, and the others followed immediately behind with rocks and stones they picked up along the way. The sight that greeted them was startling.

The body of the young Mauian prince Mokilho, lit by pale moonlight, shone against the blackness of the sand. Fresh, warm blood bubbled silently from around the base of a feather-tipped Maui spear buried in his chest.

It made no sense to Jameson. Why would his body be here? This was the prince Kamehameha had sent back to his father as a bid for peace. Nahana grasped Jameson's arm tightly, her eyes staring past the dead man toward the water.

Jameson followed her gaze. Surely only a king could bedeck himself like this, with exquisite feathered cloak and plumed headdress. But what king could stand so defiantly erect on his decorated outrigger platform with so few warriors around him? He was shouting in the native language.

"Kamehameha! Kamauli Maui *moi kauoha he alo he alo!*"

"What's he saying?"

"He is Kamauli, the king of Maui. He calls to my father and demands to speak face to face."

"Kamehameha!" the king shouted again.

In addition to the warriors and wedding guests, Kaahumanu and the royal household had reached the beach. King Kamehameha strode forward regally. Waving his warriors aside, he crossed the beach alone to face Kamauli.

The Mauian king raised his hand to point at Kamehameha standing above the body of Kamauli's son. His words held such anger that his fury survived even Nahana's soft translation: "Kamauli, king of Maui, returns a dead son for a dead son. He will not surrender to Kamehameha and join the Hawaiian kingdom. He vows to destroy Kamehameha."

In the silence that followed, the outrigger turned, carrying the king and his challenge off into the darkness.

Kamehameha stared at the dead prince. Slowly and with great deliberation, he pulled the Mauian spear from the young man's chest and snapped it between his immense hands. *"Kaua kuloko,"* he said, sighing.

From the shelter of Jameson's arms, Nahana watched her father. "He says, 'Now there must be war.'" Her eyes rose to Jameson's face with dark foreboding.

Jameson had paid scant attention to Kamehameha's son Liholiho. Although, like all the king's heirs, he was physically beautiful, he was not otherwise an appealing child. Every time Jameson had seen him he had either been clinging to his massive mother or yawning with indifference at whatever was going on.

But Liholiho had apparently expressed an interest in the

cannon. As the king prepared his forces to go to war against the Mauians, he ordered Jameson to teach Liholiho to fire the cannon. Kamehameha believed one could never start too young with a child in preparing him for leadership.

The beach hummed with activity. War canoes lined the sand in ranks. The sounds of warriors honing weapons and polishing spears nearly drowned out the exotic bird cries from the nearby palm trees. Burdened like ants, workers steadily toiled across the beach carrying provisions for the supply boats. The king, his golden feathered robe rippling behind him, strode back and forth, checking details and testing equipment.

Jameson wished he had established some rapport with Liholiho before now. Unaccustomed to the role of teacher, he fought impatience as he repeated his instructions to the young prince. The cannon had been lashed to the platform of a large canoe. With Jameson leaning over to watch, Liholiho tried again to turn the lever to elevate the muzzle. Instead of raising it, he jammed the lever into a locking slot so the muzzle would not move. Before Jameson could stop him, Liholiho scowled and tried to force the lever.

"No, no," Jameson said. "Watch *haole*. Watch me." He pointed to himself, gesturing that the boy must observe carefully. He went through the process again very slowly, unlocking the lever from the slot and turning the elevation wheel until the muzzle was aimed correctly. When he had locked the lever into its slot again, he pointed to Liholiho. "Now, you do it."

Liholiho jammed the lever yet another time. Jameson saw the king watching them and leaped from the canoe onto the beach. Fighting frustration, he crossed to the king and lowered his voice to keep from being overheard by Liholiho or the warriors. "It's no use. He's too young to learn something this complicated. Perhaps I could continue to teach him and a young warrior at the same time. You don't want it to blow up and kill your own men."

"It won't blow up. You will be there to see that it works properly."

"On Maui?" Jameson asked incredulously. "You can't make me fight in your battles."

Amazingly, the king didn't bridle at this challenge. Instead he spoke quietly, thoughtfully. "Jameson, I have fought wars for more years than you have lived. Now I will do anything to end it."

"But you have promised that I can leave the island."

"When another *haole* ship comes."

Their voices had risen. Jameson felt the watchful eyes of Liholiho and the warriors on them. "Fine," he said, lowering his voice. "Then I'll stay right here until one comes."

"No, you will go with your cannon. I have decided."

He had decided. It was really too much, after a fruitless morning fighting Liholiho's apathy. Being confronted with the king's intransigence flooded Jameson with anger.

"Well, I've decided that I won't," he said, not bothering to lower his voice. He whirled to walk away, but before he could take a step he was roughly stopped. The king, with catlike speed, had snapped his huge hands around Jameson's arm, holding him fast.

Instead of a blow, however, the king looped his arm around Jameson's shoulder and began to walk. Although Jameson's impulse was to balk, the king's massive strength propelled him along.

"Come," the king said cordially. "There is something I want to show you."

The king's path led up the hill above the beach to a clearing. A column of lava rock thrust upward, casting a shadow toward the ocean. The flat-based monument was adorned with carved totem figures. In its center rested a single, huge lava rock. Kamehameha stared at the immense stone for a long moment. He seemed to absorb some inspiration from it. His face shone with pride and inner strength and reverence. Jameson was fascinated.

Almost as if he were returning from a trance, Kamehameha turned to Jameson. "This was built by warriors who would not surrender. Many died, but they would not surrender."

The lace of undisturbed lichen gave the monument a sense of great age. "When?" Jameson asked.

"Only the chants remember. It was long, long ago. But their spirits are still here. They speak to us. They call for peace. One land, one king. That was their dream. It is my dream. And it must happen. That is why you will come. Do you understand now, Jameson?"

Jameson sighed inwardly. Even though this man worshipped heathen gods and yielded to the bloody dictates of a high priest, Jameson was impressed by his worth. "I understand. But this isn't my war. And I don't know anything about fighting wars."

"In the land from which you come, is there no war? No battles with other lands?"

"Well, there were thirteen colonies. Something like the islands here. And they had to become united to fight against another land."

Kamehameha nodded. "You see? One land. One king!"

"No, there is no king. Once there was a king far across the sea, but he was defeated, thrown out."

"Just as we will defeat this chief of Maui so that we can be united." He led Jameson onto the stone platform where the immense rock stood. "Here, Jameson, I will show you. Long, long ago it was spoken in the chants of Kahuna. It was foretold that when a great king raised a rock until its shadow touched the sea, then all the islands would swim to him and be one land and there would be peace. That rock," he added, pointing to it.

Intrigued, Jameson leaned against and attempted to move the rock, without success.

"*I* will raise it," Kamehameha said quietly. "I will make one land, one king. This will be the last war. When I have overcome this challenge from Maui, our people will be united in peace and we will be a great land. You understand, Jameson?"

"Yes. I do understand what this means to you and your people, but..."

"I need you and your cannon, Jameson. The Mauians do not have guns because the *haoles* refuse to trade us weapons. With your cannon, the battle will be short and few will be killed. I ask you to come with me."

"No."

"Then I will make you come."

"You can't do that."

"Perhaps not, but I can still have you killed. Believe me, Jameson, if you do not come, you will die." Then he smiled. "Or I can make you a chief, a great leader of warriors. Which fate will you choose?"

The old bandit. He must think he was dealing with a child of Liholiho's age, to make such a hollow promise. "If I do it, you must promise to let me go, and no more tricks."

"You have the word of Kamehameha."

Jameson met the king's eyes, as black and shining as the polished sand of his island. "I'd like you to swear it on that rock."

The king's face registered incredulity at this impudence. "You do not trust the great Kamehameha?" he thundered.

Jameson met his eyes steadily. "I trust you, Kamehameha. I trust you to sacrifice everything that lies between you and this goal of unifying the islands. Because my cannon and I happen to stand squarely between you and that rock, I want you to swear to let me go without any more tricks."

A shadow of a smile tugged at Kamehameha's mouth.

The king laid one huge bronze-colored hand on the rock. "I swear it."

Jameson remembered the euphoria he had felt back in Boston when he decided to sign on the *Felicity Ann*. The same glorious exhilaration came over him now and he grinned at the king. "All right. I'll fight with you and become a great chief. It's better than being a clerk or a sailor!"

Kamehameha clapped him on the shoulder. "You will be here when I raise that rock. You will tell your children, and they will chant it for all time. Forever."

In the nights Jameson held Nahana to him, made love with her, and drank in her beauty as though it were the sustenance of life itself. At night it was easy to forget that he came from another world, that these people were not his people, that their gods were not his God. Only Nahana mattered then, her warm, yielding body, her soft, caressing voice.

But during the days he remembered, and drove himself to work hard toward the launching of the war fleet. The sooner their expedition got under way, the sooner they would return and he would be free to find passage home. To return to Boston, to a clerk's job, no doubt, and to Martha. He shivered in the hot sun when he realized that when he returned to Boston this whole episode of his life would be over, gone, lost. He couldn't even hold on to the memory of it and feel true to his New England convictions.

And yet, what kind of life could he have here, among these natives who killed others for disobeying the most minute command? The *kapus* appalled him and terrified him by their arbitrariness. If these people were frequently kind and generous, they were also tightly bound by superstition and ignorance. If their island was a paradise, it was also a fearful place wrapped with dangerous *kapus*. Jameson was constantly torn by his conflicting feelings about the place and the people. It was almost a relief when the day came that they were to sail for Maui.

Jameson, his cannon lashed to the platform of the largest of the double-hulled boats, watched the king bid farewell to his family and his people who crowded the beach. The fleet was impressive: war canoes, outriggers, sailboats, a forest of craft swaying on the water. Although he and Nahana had already said their farewells, he tried to pick her out from the masses of people. When he found her he would have gone to her one more time but the king appeared beside him, his hand on the shiny brass muzzle of the cannon.

"Is it ready?" he asked.

At Jameson's nod, Kamehameha raised his arm in a gesture for silence. Maakoa's benediction was for the war canoes. For Jameson and the cannon he showed only scorn. Liholiho scowled, hurt at not being allowed to accompany the warriors. Kaahumanu stood proudly erect, confident that her husband would bring victory back with him. Kamehameha raised his hand once again and the flotilla began to move away from shore. The cannon boat led the ranks of war canoes, like the poisoned tip of a waterborne arrow.

By night a storm had risen. The waves crashed over Jameson's boat, plunging it wildly in the channel swells. After strengthening the lashings that held the cannon to the craft, Jameson cautiously worked his way forward to where the king stood on his platform. The king, staring toward the dark horizon, appeared indifferent to the mountainous waves and the howling blackness. Jameson had to call twice before he got Kamehameha's attention.

"It's getting rougher. Perhaps we ought to turn back."

"No."

"But we've already lost a dozen war canoes. If we don't turn back now..."

The king refused to let him finish. "No. Even if we are

fewer, with your cannon we are more." The king turned away, fixing his gaze again on the horizon. Jameson shrugged and returned to his cannon. He had learned that the king's will was everything, a state of mind closed off to reason or common sense or acceptance of defeat. Kamehameha was determined to fight and win this battle, if it cost him every last man.

CHAPTER SEVEN

SHADOWS ON THE SEA

Bright sunlight gleamed on the island of Maui as the war fleet arrived. Behind a wide sweep of white sand dotted with outcroppings of rock rose dense junglelike vegetation set between two stony, overgrown hills. Standing there, Jameson was reminded of the *Felicity Ann*'s first approach to Hawaii, of how the island seemed devoid of life, wrapped in eerie silence. The same feeling came over him now. By the exchanged glances and quiet words between the warriors, Jameson knew they were apprehensive about this abnormal stillness.

"Kamauli was the one who challenged you," Jameson said to the king. "Why isn't he here? Maybe they've learned that we have a cannon and have changed their minds."

"If we cannot make them come to us, we will go to them. We will land."

"Couldn't you send some men on ahead?"

"No. I am first. I will go first." He raised his arm to signal the fleet forward.

When his war canoe reached the beach King Kamehameha stepped alone onto the sand, his stance one of challenge. There was still no motion, no sign of waiting opposition. With the help of a half-dozen warriors, Jameson moved the cannon to the shore. Not a bird called in the dense green screen beyond the sand.

Jameson lit a torch and thrust it into the sand. "They must have seen us coming. Maybe they're afraid and have run off."

Kamehameha pointed to the jungle. "No, they are not afraid. They are there, waiting."

"Where do you see them?" Jameson asked, peering again at the vegetation.

"I feel them," the king replied. He raised his sword and called for his warriors to follow. The massive army pressed deliberately toward the plateau ahead. When they were within a dozen yards of the plateau, the air exploded with sound. Sharp reports and bursts of gunfire threw the warriors into disarray. Musket balls ripped through the ranks, felling men on all sides. The attack, overwhelming in its surprise and ferocity, forced Kamehameha's army to fall back under the onslaught.

Jameson had not expected them to have guns. No wonder Kamauli was so confident of his victory that he sacrificed his own son! As Kamehameha's warriors sought cover, the Mauian chief rose to the top of the plateau. His army poured around him, a few warriors still firing muskets. Most brandished the traditional weapons, clubs and spears.

Kamehameha refused to take cover. Fending off the host of Mauian warriors who descended on them, he shouted rallying cries to his men. Jameson, torch in hand, moved toward the cannon. Spears sang past him. But before he could light the fuse, a musket ball crashed into the torch, knocking it from his hand. He scrambled to retrieve the torch, sheltering the flame to keep it burning.

The Mauian warriors bore down on him as he sighted the muzzle and raised the torch. With upraised clubs, they were almost upon him as he touched the torch to the fuse, then rolled away from the cannon blast, while his assailants felt the earth vibrate from the explosion. Screaming with astonishment and terror, the Mauians retreated in disorder to the plateau rise.

Each side regrouped and removed its wounded from the battlefield. Kamehameha's forces took shelter behind the rock outcroppings. Kamauli's warriors waited for the opposition to make the first move. Except for an occasional muted moan, the same eerie silence fell on the island.

Jameson experienced a rising frustration. A stand-off was really a defeat for an invading force, surely Kamehameha realized that. Yet the king stood apart, calmly studying the situation. Jameson approached and waited to be acknowledged.

"Somehow they have gotten guns from the traders," the king said.

"I can hold them back with the cannon until you get your men into the boats."

"I will not run."

"But it would be dangerous to stay until nightfall. They could rush us in the dark before there was time to get off more than one or two cannon shots."

"It is not night yet."

Jameson failed to keep the edge of irritation from his voice. "There's a time to be brave and a time to be wise."

Kamehameha seemed amused. "Isn't it possible for a man to be both?"

"Only when he's dead. Look, there's still time to get

away. Now that they know about the cannon, they won't attack."

"Then we will attack them."

The man was unbelievable, Jameson thought. But let him plan the impossible, since he was the only one mad enough to attempt it. "How?"

"They have many little guns, but we have a big gun."

"You don't understand," Jameson said, trying desperately to break through the king's wall of stubbornness. "I can't hit them with the cannon from here. The muzzle won't go up that far. In order to attack them up there with this cannon, I'd have to be higher than they were. So I could fire down on them."

"Then you will go higher." The king pointed toward the hill beside the plateau held by the Mauians.

"You mean take the cannon on top of the hill? But there's no path. It's almost like a jungle." Jameson considered the distant hill thoughtfully. "Of course, in a way that helps. They wouldn't be able to see me."

The king's idea should have filled him with horror. Instead, it inspired him with excitement. "It would be possible if I had enough men to drag the cannon. Maybe there's some way we could take it up from the other side of the hill. Like Hannibal."

"Who's Hannibal?"

"He was a general a long, long time ago. He took his whole army over a mountain where no one thought he could go. Then he attacked his enemy from behind."

"Did this general of yours win that battle?"

"Yes. He won that one. But then he lost all his other battles after that."

"I am different. I will win this battle and there will be no more."

"We could drag it behind those sand bluffs. They wouldn't know it was gone. Then we could take it around... No. It won't work. Even if I got it to the top of the hill, as soon as I fired once they'd know it was gone and they'd attack you here."

"Take the cannon." The king turned to summon several of his largest, fiercest warriors. After he spoke to them they bowed their understanding and joined Jameson.

With pantomime gestures, Jameson showed each man his task. Keeping below the level of the sand bank, they dragged the cannon into the dense vegetation at the base of the hill. Jameson chose a route that was difficult but kept them out of sight. Halfway up the hill, he looked back at the beach.

Kamehameha had obviously directed his men to a sensible holding position. The plumed helmets of his warriors were clearly visible where they had taken defensive places behind rock outcroppings. Nothing else moved or indicated the size and strength of that great army waiting on the beach.

The warriors helping Jameson were sweating heavily by the time the cannon was set in place. He leveled it firmly, adjusted the position, and filled and tamped the flash plan. As he began to traverse the muzzle to point down at the Mauian forces, a glint of sunshine on the polished brass almost blinded him. Only after he finished priming the cannon did he realize that those same flashes of light had alerted the enemy.

The Mauian warriors below had swung around and turned their fire in his direction. He shouted at the men behind him, motioning them down. Musket balls howled past him as he lit the cannon fuse. With the fuse sputtering, he dived for the dry earth.

His aim was perfect. The cannon's shrapnel exploded into the tightly grouped Mauian warriors on the plateau below. Jameson had not envisioned how frighteningly destructive the cannon would be. Natives fell dead and wounded, sand

and dirt filled the air, and brush and foliage spewed in all directions. Even the uninjured Mauians scattered in confusion.

The chief Kamauli was no part of the disarray. He realized that if the cannon was above him, it was gone from the beach. Gathering his remaining warriors, he ordered an attack. Kamauli was in the forefront of the charge toward the beach where Kamehameha and his warriors had their backs to the sea.

Jameson watched with trepidation as the tide of howling Mauian warriors raced down the hill. Maybe Hannibal's strategy was destined to work only once. But Kamehameha's will had been done: the stalemate had been broken. Now Kamauli's force, still greatly superior in number, was bound to spell doom for the forces trapped on the beach, and eventually for Jameson as well.

The smoke and dust cleared from the plateau. The warriors with Jameson started to laugh and crow as if victory was theirs. Jameson stared at them. Didn't they understand what had happened? Then he saw that the Mauian charge, launched with such surety, had faltered. Not realizing that the plumed helmets behind the rock outcroppings were only decoys, the Mauian king had led his men into Kamehameha's trap.

While Jameson and his companions had been pushing the cannon up the hill, Kamehameha, bareheaded and in silence, had led his army to the top of the second hill flanking the plateau. They streamed to the attack now, forcing the Mauian army back toward the thundering sea.

The battle that followed was fierce and bloody. Kamehameha killed Kamauli in hand-to-hand combat. The cries of battle, the wailing gasps of the dying and wounded, reached Jameson on his hill. Sickened, he turned to the removal of his cannon with an aching heart.

As they began their descent from the hilltop, a band of Mauians appeared to block their way. The fierce warriors rushed at them with raised clubs and glittering spears.

Jameson was unarmed, save for a knife tucked through the cord at his waist, and what good was a knife against a spear?

But he found a reserve of courage in himself and stood his ground as the attackers came closer. If he was to die, he would die defending himself. His heart pounded but his hand was steady, holding the knife threateningly poised to strike. Immediately Jameson found himself facing a native with a spear aimed at his chest.

Instinctively he ducked to one side and leaped forward under the man's guard. But he lost his footing on the rocky hillside, and his knife merely grazed the Mauian's chest. The Mauian instantly raised his spear above Jameson's heart. The blade flashed in the sun as the man grasped the shaft firmly for the final thrust.

Jameson tried to roll aside but his way was blocked by a boulder. And then, as death stared Jameson in the face, the Mauian fell forward, dead from a blow by one of Jameson's companions. Jameson rose shakily and retrieved the deadly spear that had almost ended his life. He would be prepared if another attack came.

His Hawaiian savior shrugged off his thanks as if nothing had happened and indicated that they were ready to continue down the hill, leaving the dead and dying without a backward glance.

By the time they had worked the cannon down the rocky slope to the beach, the white sand was red with human blood. The surf pounding against the shore left a bright, deadly pink foam as it receded. The surviving Mauians waited stoically to be beaten to death. Jameson was sickened at the thought of the slaughter.

Always the king, Kamehameha walked solemnly and without haste from where his wounded warriors lay. Sometimes Jameson forgot that this man was literally a giant, a man who towered physically over those around him. His very presence now proclaimed absolute power as he stood silently looking at his prisoners. Kamehameha's warriors, their clubs raised, watched for the king's signal to kill the captured men.

Jameson could not remain silent. "Surely you don't have to kill all the Mauians!"

"They are no longer Mauians," Kamehameha told him calmly. "We are all Hawaiians now." As he spoke, he clapped his arm around Jameson's shoulder. "All Hawaiians now, Jameson. All."

Turning to the Mauian captives, he repeated the words in his language. The king's warriors lowered their clubs. The Mauians regarded him with disbelief, then rose to cheer him as their new leader.

With the warriors' spears turned skyward to signal success, King Kamehameha's fleet rounded the promontory at the mouth of the bay. The island drums pulsed an ecstatic welcome and the crowded beach fluttered with feather pennants and tapa banners held high among flower-bedecked poles.

The triumphant tattoos blown on the conch shells drowned out the shouts of the people. They watched their proud warriors arrive, their canoes in precise ranks slicing through the clear water, pressed forward by the perfect rhythm of the warrior paddlers. The king towered above all on his decorated outrigger platform.

Kaahumanu was the first to welcome her king. Almost in jest he asked if she had sacrificed to Kukailimoku, his fearsome war god, for them. She smiled, admitting she had not. "I knew you would return. Now you will rule all, and I will be with you."

After he had greeted his people, Kamehameha picked up a Mauian spear, showed it to the crowd, then held it out to the high priest Maakoa. Maakoa offered his thanks to the gods for this victory.

Then the king took the spear and crossed to Hanakea, the surviving son of Kamauli. The crowd watched in silence as the king joined his own spear with that of the Mauian. Then he snapped both spears in half between his huge hand. The young man bowed when Kamehameha ceremoniously held the broken spears out to him.

"We are one people, one land," Kamehameha told him. "You will marry one of my daughters and return to Maui to rule for me."

Jameson had been searching the crowd for Nahana since the boat neared shore. Just as he finally saw her, Kamehameha caught him and drew him forward. *"Puali alii mahalo, hanohano,"* he shouted.

As a great cheer rose from the crowd, young girls pushed past Nahana to drape Jameson with leis and bright feathers. The men draped the muzzle of his cannon with flowers.

Kaahumanu, smiling in a teasing way, stood very close to Jameson's side. "Kamehameha says you are a great warrior. You are to be honored."

As she spoke, a leggy girl darted out of the crowd to thrust an orchid lei around Jameson's shoulders. *"Nonohea oi,"* she whispered with a giggle.

"She says you are beautiful," Kaahumanu translated.

"No," Jameson protested, feeling his color rise.

Kaahumanu seemed to trace the lines of his face with her eyes. "Yes," she corrected him.

Again Jameson tried to work his way toward Nahana, only to have the king catch him in those viselike arms.

"What do you wish, Jameson? Speak it."

"Nothing."

"You are a warrior now. And a noble, an *alii*." The king raised his hand, his voice overwhelming the laughter and talk. *"Ku alii koa e wahine."*

At his words, the commoners bowed, backing away, and

a half-dozen young women were ushered before him. "You may choose any one of them, Jameson," the king said.

Startled, Jameson fell back a step. "Choose one of them?"

"You wish more than one?" the king asked. "All of them?"

"No. Only one." Looking past the giggling girls, his eyes met Nahana's and she smiled, waiting.

King Kamehameha strode from the beach up the path to the sacred monument. His people followed him, falling silent as he stepped onto the stone platform. For a long moment he appeared to be in prayer or meditation. He bent and grasped the huge rock that stood in the center of the platform.

For a moment it looked as though not even he could lift it. Then, kneeling deeper, he slowly raised the stone and carried it to the ancient monument. It was terrifying to watch him balance the enormous weight above his head. If his strength should give out... But he continued to move forward until he had set it on the topmost ledge. With the rock in place, the monument's shadow lengthened, crossed the beach, and fell darkly on the face of the water.

The chanted prophecy had been fulfilled.

The king stood alone in godlike isolation beside the monument. The sun glistened on the golden feathers of his cloak and on his handsome face. "Now there will be peace," he said. "We are one people, one land."

Jameson tightened his arm around Nahana. This was a moment he would always remember, the kind of moment one passed along to one's children. The thought brought a memory of Martha Coopersmith sitting in her family's carriage with the piece of green silk pressed against her chest. She was supposed to be his wife; she was the one who was supposed to bear his children. And he somehow knew that those Boston children wouldn't be interested in a Hawaiian legend. He pushed aside these thoughts, but the happiness of his return was shadowed by guilt.

Nahana took him to their new quarters, a small thatched hut on the beach. It was furnished with a single tapa mat, surely plain enough to satisfy any puritan's asceticism. But the setting was a complete contrast. Surrounded by wildly flowering bushes and exotically blossoming vines, the hut opened onto a dazzling white coral beach and the cool azure of the sea.

At the door of the hut Jameson hesitated. He had come to the island too well schooled in guilt. For some time the necessity of saving his life had kept his mind from the past and his promises in another world. Now he had to face them again.

The marriage ceremony was at the heart of his dilemma. No matter how often he rationalized his marriage to Nahana as a heathen ritual, a temporary measure to save his life, he knew he was only adding one more lie to his growing list. Because he loved her.

God help him, he loved her, even if that love opened to him the dark portals of hell.

Nahana slid her hand across his chest and laid it on his heart. The liquid brilliance of her eyes and her gentle, puzzled smile struck him with amazing force. He drew her close, feeling the warmth of her body, the soft firmness of her breasts, the excitement of her touch. The passion that had been interrupted by the alarms of war flowed back into him now as inexorably as the curling sea swept the beach.

Her eagerness for him served only to fan the flames. Before he could do more than taste her lips, she was unfastening the buttons on his pants. She pushed the material down his legs with feathery strokes, her mouth sliding down his body as she knelt. When he was naked she remained kneeling in front of him, her tongue flickering madly on the most sensitive of places. He moaned with pleasure.

He reached down to her breasts and cupped them in his hands. The hard knots of her nipples made his fingers tingle. She was driving him crazy with the pressure, the moistness, the urgency of her mouth on him. Surely his arousal was more than a man could bear!

But the native women were schooled in the arts of lovemaking. Nahana had been taught secrets by Kaahumanu that many of the other women did not know. She had been taught to heighten the arousal, then to allow it to slowly relax for a few minutes.

Then her fingers would stroke, her mouth massage, her body sway, until a slightly higher peak was reached, only to have the stimulation withdrawn again. Like waves at high tide, cresting higher and higher, Jameson felt the desire in his body grow and grow to unbearable, unbelievable new heights.

Her fingers touched him everywhere. In sensitive, forbidden places that made his heart hammer with shame and delight. Her mouth was the moist, velvet trap that captured his lust, that toyed with him, that teased and tempted, lapped and lashed. He felt almost bewitched, unable to maintain rational thought. His body burned with desire, while his mind sailed free of earthly strictures.

Intoxicated with physical euphoria, he gently pushed her down onto the tapa mat. She was completely open to him, her breasts pressing upward, her thighs wide apart. He took one breast in his mouth, urgently drawing on it until she moaned and wriggled against him, her hips spasmodically thrusting upward with need.

Nothing in the world was like their joining, the slow yet urgent satisfying of their desires. He was a part of her and she a part of him, too close, too linked, to be anything but one crowning explosion of joy. The shuddering of their bodies, naked, moist against each other, was a physical and spiritual mating beyond anything Jameson could have imagined.

Stirring against him, her lips buried in his neck, Nahana whispered, *"He moeuhane aku."*

"What does that mean?"

"It is what the gods dream," she explained, stroking his bare chest lightly with her fingers. "It is a saying among our people. The gods do not have bodies, so they cannot have this that we have. They made death because they were so angry and jealous of our lovemaking."

"Do you believe that?"

"I believe the gods would be jealous of us, of this."

She turned her wrist to expose her marriage scar, and traced the same mark on his. She pressed her scar to his and nuzzled her face in the nape of his neck. Her silky dark hair shone against his pale flesh. Jameson realized that he was losing all sense of who he really was and where all this fitted into his life.

Nahana, sensing a change in him, propped herself on an elbow to look down at him. "What is it, Jameson?"

How could he answer in words she could understand? She could not imagine the gray imprisoning sky of Boston, the narrow austerity of his old loft room, the tense strictures on his old life.

"It was not good? It was not like *haole wahine?* You did not like having me?"

He caught her to him, holding her close. "It was like . . . I never imagined a woman could be like you."

Her dark eyes clouded with confusion. "Then what is wrong? Please tell me. I will learn."

"For one thing, you believe we're really married."

She held out her wrist with the faint wedding scar on it. "We *are* one, married."

He had known he wouldn't be able to make her understand. "I mean a real marriage, in a church, with someone you're going to be with forever. There *is* someone else, I told you that." Reaching for his shirt, he took out the locket and opened it.

Nahana studied Martha's face with mild curiosity, then handed back the locket.

"Her name is Martha," he explained. "We're supposed to get married. Do you understand that?"

"Yes. You wish her to come here and be your wife, too."

"No. I can't have two wives."

"But you are an *alii* now, a noble. The gods say you can have many wives."

"I don't believe in your pagan gods. I can have only one wife."

Nahana took back the locket and looked at Martha more closely. "Do you like having love with her better than with me?"

"No." Her sudden look of delight forced him to try to explain further. "I don't mean that. I haven't done this with her. We're not allowed to do it until we're married. That would be a sin."

"Like a *kapu*."

"Sort of."

Her eyes widened with amazement. "You would be killed in this Boston for making love?"

"No, no. But if you sin, then you go to hell when you die."

"And what is hell?"

Jameson knew that by heart! "It's a huge pit with terrible fires and burning oil, and if you've sinned, then after you die you're thrown into the pit and you burn forever and ever in the fires."

She suppressed a giggle. "Because you have loved with someone? But then, everybody would go there, to this hell."

"You don't understand!"

Nahana studied Martha's face more critically. "She is very... very..."

"Pretty."

"Do you think I am pretty, too?"

He took the locket from her and closed it before meeting her gaze. "No, I think you're beautiful. I think you're the most beautiful woman I've ever known."

Satisfied, she lay back down. "And you are the most beautiful man I have ever known." Drawing his face to hers, she kissed his eyes, his nose, and his lips. And then she fell instantly asleep.

Jameson watched the moon pass overhead to be replaced by the rich apricot light of dawn. With Nahana's smooth flesh pressed against him, he considered his situation, but came to no conclusions.

CHAPTER EIGHT

MYSTERIES

A vine trailing across the thatched roof of their hut produced massive flowers that unfolded one petal at a time, as the light came. Each petal disclosed that there was yet another one within it, waiting its turn to be revealed. During those days with Nahana, Jameson felt his own understanding of her and her people flowering in the same way. Every mystery had a new mystery hidden within it.

Nahana taught him the ways of the natives. The first day, as they crossed the receding froth of waves, she darted off to return with a string of reddish seaweed. Plucking two bulbs from it, she handed one to Jameson.

"What am I supposed to do with it?"

"It is for you to eat."

"Eat! But it looks like some kind of seaweed."

"It is *kailii*. Small children come to hunt for it."

When she ate the berry with obvious enjoyment, he tasted his. "It's sweet, like fruit, almost."

"*Kailii* means 'sweet berry that comes from the sea.'" She stripped off the rest of the berries and shared them with him.

"What does *Nahana* mean?" he asked.

"*Nahana manu*. It means 'small bird that has fallen from a nest.'"

"Why did they call you that?"

"My mother was *manu hei*, a catcher of birds for Kamehameha. Some say Kamehameha wanted her because she brought the most feathers, but I think it was because she was very beautiful."

"You think? Is she dead, then?"

He was always startled when some innocent reference filled his mind with stark scenes from his life back in Boston. At her words he saw the churchyard with the cold stone bearing his mother's name, and felt his father's hand gripping his. "To God," his father had said. "Your mother was called back to God."

But Nahana, her voice still cheerful, explained, "Not dead at all! But she was not an *alii*, so she could not be a wife of Kamehameha. She had to go away and never return."

"I'm sorry." He stroked her beautiful silken hair. "I know what it's like to be without a mother. Mine died when I was young, and my father was away at sea so much. . . . It was lonely growing up."

"But I had many mothers! And many brothers and sisters. And many . . ."

"That's different. It's not like having someone who belongs to you, who loves only you and makes you feel special."

"Like having only one wife makes her feel special?" she asked.

"Yes. That's what love means, belonging to someone you feel special about, different than you do about anyone else."

"The one in the locket, she loves you that way?"

"I think so."

"And you love her in that way, too?"

Since he could neither answer that question nor explain why he couldn't, he grasped her hands and tugged her into a race along the beach.

At sunset they watched a fisherman pulling up a catch in his net. His young son kept the tie line untangled and waited for the fish with his basket. Jameson and Nahana watched him unload his net, fill his basket with vividly colored fish, and then empty the remaining fish into a tide pool back up the beach.

"Why did he put the rest of what he caught in the pool?"

"His basket was full. It was all he had need of. This," she said, pointing to the pool, "is for others. Our gods say that one who shares will never want."

"Then the fish are for anyone who comes by?"

"Yes, for anyone."

Jameson chuckled. "Well, I guess that's our dinner, then." He glanced up and said, "Thank you, gods." He slipped out of his bark sandals and stepped into the shallow tide pool. The darting fish eluded his awkward fingers, slipping easily away from him. Nahana's soft laughter pricked him. "What's the good of leaving fish for someone if they can't be caught?"

"You must be like the fish."

She stepped into the pool without a ripple. Standing absolutely still, she fluttered her fingers under the surface of the water. The fish circled curiously. When one came near, she slid her hand under it, scooped it up, and flipped it onto the rocks beside the pool.

"Bravo!" Jameson exclaimed, clapping.

When she had collected enough fish for their meal,

Nahana knelt beside him while he cleaned them. Her slender hands rested on her knees and her eyes were watchful. After he rinsed the fish at the water's edge, she held out strong flat leaves for him to lay them on.

"Now what?" he asked.

She looked confused. "You cook it."

"Me? I've never cooked anything in my life. Women cook."

"Women cook?" Her tone was incredulous.

Jameson laughed. "We may have a problem. Can you make a fire?"

She shook her head, her eyes dancing with amusement.

"Well, do you know how to make a fire pit like they use in the village?"

"I've never really watched, but we can try."

By the time the smell of baking fish mingled with the scent of wood smoke, Jameson was ravenous. He felt positively triumphant when the fish's flesh flaked at the touch of his knife blade.

"I may not be much of a cook, but this is better than eating it raw," he told her as he cut it into portions. Glancing up, he saw her waiting at the other side of the hut. "It's ready. We can eat. Come on."

"I must wait until you have finished because I am a woman."

"What's that got to do with it? Come on. I won't tell anyone."

"*Haole* wives can do that?"

"Of course, and almost anything else they want to do. Come on, before it gets cold."

She shook her head. "It is *kapu*."

The very sound of the word grated on him. "You can't cook! You can't eat with me! Yet you can make love with me. Don't you realize how ridiculous that is?"

"No more than your *haole kapu*."

"What do you mean? We don't have any nonsense like that in our religion."

"Then why must you burn forever in a place called hell just for having pleasure?"

"That's... that's different."

"How is it different?"

Irritated and no longer hungry, he shoved the food aside, rose, and strode off down the beach.

Nahana followed him with her eyes and touched the wound on her wrist. He was her husband. It was her duty to please him, and to obey him in all things. Yet, the gods forbade this thing he asked of her.

His anger was visible in his every step. She shivered as she ran along the beach after him, calling his name. He turned and waited for her to catch up.

"Jameson, I will do what you order me to do."

His anger disintegrated at the sight of her solemn face. "I don't want you to do things because I order them. You'll come to understand my ways, as I will come to understand yours." He smiled ruefully, put his arm around her, and started back to the beach hut.

Jameson abandoned his civilized clothing a little at a time. First he replaced his *haole* shoes with bark sandals, then he stopped buttoning his shirt against the warm sun. Since he had only one shirt, he soon forfeited it altogether, except for those rare times when it was appropriate. He cut off his damaged trousers just below the knees; and he left the locket with Martha's picture in the hut, under his folded shirt.

His progression toward native dress was more swift than his skill in the language. His attempts to learn Hawaiian brought out the mischief in Nahana. On the warm beach, just beyond the curl of the waves, she sat facing him. She traced his forehead lightly with her fingertips. *"Lae,"* she said softly.

Touching her forehead with her fingers, he repeated, *"Lae."*

Her fingertips trailed across his eyes. *"Maka."*

Her lashes felt like silk curls under his hands. *"Maka."*

The nose was *ihu*, the lips *lehe lehe*. She moved her face close to his. "What do you call a kiss now?"

He smiled at her. "Your kind of kiss. *Honi.*"

With her lips so near, and her breath sweet in his mouth, he succumbed to their mutual passion.

One day he found Nahana standing behind the translucent veil of a waterfall, lathering and washing her hair with the milky oil from a split coconut. He was enchanted, as always, with her loveliness. She flung back her long hair, letting the full force of the tumbling stream rinse out the coconut oil. Then she dived through the waterfall and into the glistening pool below. When she surfaced, she beckoned him to join her.

Jameson removed his short trousers and dived in. The water felt exhilarating against his bare skin. He swam slowly to where Nahana waited and took her in his arms. Her gleaming black hair made a moving veil around their shoulders, and the split coconut slipped from her hand. Robert reached for it, but it floated away.

She shrugged. "It is no matter. They are everywhere. Don't you have coconut trees in Boston?"

"Not coconut trees. But there are other kinds, all along the sidewalks."

"What are sidewalks?"

He had none of her poetry and legend to explain his own language. "I don't know if I can explain. They're like paths, but a hard surface raised up so that you don't get your feet muddy."

"Do the girls in Boston wear flowers?"

Martha's severe, dark garb flashed in his mind. "No. They wear dresses and petticoats, and... well, other things."

"Would I wear them?"

"Yes, in Boston."

"I would go to Boston with you, Robert."

The intensity of her tone startled him. He kissed her wet lips and hugged her. "I know, but it wouldn't be the same. It wouldn't be like it is here for us."

"If you are not here, it cannot be the same for me."

"There will be someone else, like there was for you before."

"They were not like you."

"Even Kekua?"

"Kekua had many wives. You would have only me."

"Yes, only you, if this was where I was going to be forever." He sighed without meaning to. "But sooner or later another ship will come."

"Maybe it will not come," she said, winding her arms around him. "Then I will belong to you always."

Each day dawned in splendor and went down in glory, each the same and yet filled with wonder and joy. Life was sweet, as sweet as the scent of Nahana's breath. As the days and weeks passed, Jameson thought less and less about the world he had come from.

And then a different morning came. Nahana awakened him with a kiss. Then, like a mischievous child, she wriggled from his grip and ran out into the early morning sunshine.

Pulling on the short *paa* that the native men wore instead of trousers, he lazily followed her down to the beach. Though he called for her, there was no response. He finally located her on a low overhanging cliff, staring out to sea. Before he had scrambled all the way up to her side, he knew something was wrong.

"What's the matter, Nahana? What do you see?"

Instead of replying, she looked away from him again, toward the brilliant sunlit water. He followed her eyes and caught her close against the sudden pain in his chest.

Billowing white sails were cresting the distant horizon.

A clock had been ticking in Jameson's head since the day Kekua hauled him from the lagoon and put him in Nahana's care. No dawn had ever turned the endless face of the ocean to moving color, no sunset blazed into darkness behind the mountains, that he had not thought of that ship somewhere out there, the ship that would take him back to his own world.

Through threat and war and deepening emotional ties, time was measured only against the arrival of the ship. Yet, when he had asked himself how he would feel when it finally came, his answers had been defensive. *Of course I will be delighted,* he had told himself. *After all, I'm alien here among alien gods, and alien people. Martha is in Boston.*

And Nahana is not, his mind would insist. He could not force himself to consider the matter further.

The ship dropped anchor and longboats approached the shore. When Nahana turned and ran back to the hut, he followed her. He lifted her from the tapa mat and held her close until the distant drums began.

She pulled away without meeting his eyes. "They will be coming for you," she said. "You will have to go to the ship."

"You can't know that," he protested, reaching for her.

"We both know it."

She was right, of course. But it was too soon. The moment she pulled away he felt cold. Yet even in that bleak moment he knew he would have to go to the ship—with his trousers cut short, his shoes ruined, his shirt missing its buttons.

"They have come for you," Nahana insisted.

Now he, too, could hear the king's messenger hurrying toward their hut. "I'll be back," he promised.

She didn't even try to smile.

Not since coming to the island had Jameson felt as alien as he did going aboard Captain Homer Fairburn's ship. He might as well have been a collared ape on the wharf back in Boston. The officers clustered around him and the crewmen stared from their posts. They peppered him with questions while a bos'n was sent to assemble "decent raiment" for him from ship's stores. Their congratulations were as hearty as if he had been transported from death back to life.

An indeed, he had passed from Nahana's world to his own. The captain's mess, paneled in maple and boasting fixed sideboard pieces, offered all the comforts of a proper Boston house. Over his meal, Jameson tried not to fiddle with his borrowed clothing. His jacket bound his shoulders too tightly and the fabric of the trousers scratched his thighs.

Captain Fairburn's lean face and crisp accent branded him a true Yankee. Jameson was not surprised that a man of his age ate lightly, but the first mate, Jerome Higgins, didn't look like an ascetic in these matters. He was young and heavyset; Jameson was surprised to see him merely pick at his food.

The second mate, James Darden, deferred to the others so humbly that he reminded Jameson of a particularly servile clerk. The ship's doctor, Lemuel Benthurst, a man of fifty or so, was convivial and inquisitive. "Some more pickled rutabaga, Mr. Jameson?" he asked, offering the dish.

"No, thank you, Doctor. I've eaten my fill." In truth, his

fill had come quickly enough. Could he have lost his taste for that biting flavor so quickly?

"Understandable," the doctor said, filling his own plate again. "Been some goodly time, I expect, since you tasted real food—New England food."

They wouldn't understand about the abundance of fresh fruit, the plenitude of fish. Jameson merely nodded.

Captain Fairburn's eyes were on him, thoughtful. "Quite a story yours is, Mr. Jameson. Washed ashore after a raiding expedition, nearly killed by the natives for breaking their taboos, involved in a war... You'll have some tales to tell when you return home."

Young Darden leaned toward Jameson. "It must have been a fearful experience."

"Not all of it, Mr. Darden."

The captain winked at Darden, though his words were clearly spoken for Jameson's benefit. "You forget the beautiful princess. I'll warrant you made that up, Jameson."

"Oh, no, sir."

"Well, if you didn't, you could have, and no blame attached. But I'll tell you: wait till your first sight of a real white woman again, back in Boston. Of course, that will be a while, but worth it if we can take on a full load of sandalwood here."

"You're bound for China then, Captain Fairburn?" Jameson asked.

"Yes, that's where sandalwood is fetching top prices right now. Then back around the Horn and north to home. Best part of eight months, I imagine. Are you prepared to work your passage?"

"Yes, Captain." It struck him that eight months from now it would be gray in Boston again. "We'll be returning to snow and ice."

"And none too soon for me," Higgins remarked. "That's

when you really feel to home again, Jameson, when you see real ice and snow after this endless sun."

"A spot of rum to finish off?" The captain lifted the decanter and began filling glasses around the table.

Higgins covered his glass with his hand and shook his head. At this, the doctor leaned to have a closer look at him. "Feeling all right, Mr. Higgins? You look a touch pale. You know we've got a bit of tropical ague on board. I've already had to blood-let one of the mizzen crew."

Higgins drew back. "I'm all right. Save your leeches for someone else, Doctor."

The captain turned to Jameson. "This King Kamehameha. How long is he going to keep us waiting out here? Why doesn't he just let us come ashore and start trading?"

"I'm afraid he's learned not to trust *haoles*—white foreigners like you."

"Like me, Jameson?" the captain asked, amused.

"Like us, I mean," Jameson quickly corrected himself.

"Well, here or ashore, Christian or heathen, no matter so long as I can strike a bargain. Tell me about this king. What sort of man is he to deal with?"

"It's hard to say. Everything seems to depend on his mood."

The captain's long face grew thoughtful. "Hmmm. But you've got his ear, I gather. If you were to sweeten his mood a little, persuade him to pay premium price for our goods, I'd take it favorably. When we get back to Boston, perhaps I could find you something a little more ambitious than clerking to do with your future."

Jameson thought of himself perched on the high stool in the warehouse on the docks. And then on the sunny beach eating juicy fresh fruits and watching Nahana weave flowers in her hair. With mixed emotions, he caught the captain's final question.

"Do we understand each other, Mr. Jameson?"

CHAPTER NINE

ALOHA

The *heiau* shrine to Pele was set in a wide clearing back from the bay and the beach. The feathered headdresses and bright costumes of King Kamehameha and his counselors and family were a startling contrast to the simple pyramidlike tier of rocks.

"You must send the *haole* ship away," the high priest Maakoa said. He pointed to the mighty volcano, dark against the sky. "The goddess Pele warns there will be evil if the ways of the *haole* come among us." His voice turned persuasive. "The gods have given us the sea, they have given us the sun. They have given us food. We have no need of what the gods have not given us."

Kamehameha frowned. "But perhaps now the gods want to give us *haole* things."

"No. If we take what the *haole* brings, our gods will take back what has been given to us."

"There have been *haole* ships before," the king reminded him. "The sun is still ours. The sea is still ours."

Kaahumanu agreed. "The ship does not bring *haole* gods, only things of the *haole*, like the cannon of Jameson. Now we rule Maui in peace."

"What if other *haole* ships bring other cannons?" Maakoa challenged her. "Who will rule Maui then?"

"Only Kamehameha will rule Maui," the king announced imperiously. He turned to his sacred wife. "What does Keopuolani think? Shall I trade with the *haole* ship?"

"I think whatever Kamehameha thinks," she said.

The king nodded as if he had anticipated her answer. He turned to his son. "Liholiho?"

The prince hesitated. "I don't know."

A flicker of irritation crossed the king's face.

Jameson approached him. "Kamehameha, the captain is waiting. You have to go."

The king scowled. "No, I do not have to. I rule. I will decide whether to trade with the *haole*."

"There are things you don't have here. Like plows to help you produce more food, and hooks to help catch more fish."

"I have food. I have fish."

Jameson sighed. "But there are other things. Inventions, tools, clothing, many things you don't have, things I couldn't even explain, that will make life better. This captain tells me that he has traded on the other islands, with other chiefs. Not trading with this ship won't change anything. There will be more ships. You can't put up a wall in the sea."

Kamehameha turned to study the wide sweep of ocean that surrounded his island kingdom. Jameson knew the king would like to wall off the rest of the world if he could, to remain the only powerful figure in his paradise. After a while, though, he turned back and nodded. "You will tell them that I will trade."

One of the lesser priests translated Kamehameha's decision to Maakoa. He stared at the king with narrowed eyes for a long moment. "I warn you. There will be punishment because of the *haole*— Send them away or I am afraid for you."

When the king paid no heed to his words, the priest scowled. "The gods can teach fear even to Kamehameha," he warned.

The *haole* goods—bolts of cloth, shoes, farm implements, cooking utensils, miscellaneous tools—were displayed on the sunlit quarterdeck of the ship. The captain and his officers faced the Hawaiians for the trading session. The native warriors, still in their war canoes, surrounded the ship. Although the sailors kept a wary eye on the helmeted warriors, they found it hard not to stare at the king's entourage. The deck of that sober ship flamed with brilliant color and feminine beauty.

Unwinding a yard of cloth from a bolt, Higgins passed it to the king's party. "That cotton comes from one of the finest New England mills," the captain told Kamehameha. "Fifty sandalwood trees for the bolt."

Kaahumanu and Keopuolani fingered the cloth and smiled with delight. Liholiho tested a swath of the fabric around his neck and shoulders, preening. Jameson managed to run the cloth through his fingers before it was passed on to the king's lesser wives.

"Is that muslin or cotton, Captain?" he asked.

"What does it matter? They don't know the difference."

Jameson heard the sound of ripping cloth and turned to see Kamehameha with the bolt of fabric in his powerful hands, tearing off lengths of it. *"Maikai O!"* he said.

The captain turned nervously to Jameson. "What's he

saying? I don't want him to get angry. Talk to him, Jameson. Tell him he can have it for twenty trees.''

Jameson went to the king's side and relayed this message, in a mixture of quiet Hawaiian and English.

The king shrugged. "Twenty trees, fifty trees, one hundred trees, if I wish it."

"That's not the way to trade. Don't offer him any more than you have to. You see how weak that cloth is, how easily it tears."

Kamehameha motioned toward his wives. "That's good. That way all my wives can have some of it. I want that cloth."

"All right. But let me bargain for it. There's no point in your giving any more than you have to."

Jameson returned to the captain and shook his head. "The king says the price is too high." Kamehameha glared at him with sudden suspicion, but Jameson hurried on. "He will give only ten trees to the bolt."

The captain nodded. "All right, ten trees then. Higgins, mark it down."

As Kamehameha relaxed his scowl, the captain turned toward his first mate. "Did you get that, Mr. Higgins?" The first mate staggered against the rail and braced himself with one hand. The captain regarded him with concern. "Are you all right?"

Higgins forced himself to stand. "Yes, Captain, just too much sun, I think."

"You'd best get below. Mr. Darden can help me keep the count."

Higgins saluted and staggered uncertainly down the stairs.

Jameson picked up a pitchfork and examined it before asking the captain how many of them he had to trade. "Two gross," the captain told him. "The lot for a hundred trees."

"I'll ask the king." With his back to the captain, Jameson

showed the tool to Kamehameha, who tried to bend the tines of the pitchfork with his hands. When he could not force the metal to yield, he nodded with satisfaction. He passed the tool to Liholiho, who jabbed the air with it before turning his attention back to another bolt of cloth.

"It's strong enough but it won't catch fish," the king told Jameson.

"That's not what it's for," Jameson said. "It's used for digging in the earth and for planting. With tools like this you could dig up taro roots in half the time. Like this."

When Jameson pretended to dig into the deck as a demonstration, Kaahumanu, impressed, took the tool from him and turned to the king. "It is useful. Jameson can show us."

"The captain is asking a hundred trees for them," Jameson said, "but let me bargain with him."

Once again he approached the captain. "The king says yes but only twenty-five trees for all of them."

"Twenty-five!" the captain cried. "I can't do that. Seventy-five."

Jameson felt the captain's eyes on him as he spoke with the king. When he returned, he shook his head. "Fifty. That's as high as he'll go."

The captain sighed and considered the flamboyant giant across the deck in his gold-feathered cloak and massive headdress. "I must say he drives a hard Yankee bargain for a heathen. Well, all right, fifty. At least you got him up a little. Thank you, Mr. Jameson."

Jameson watched as the king rose and crossed from the trading area to the side of the quarterdeck. He stopped and pointed toward a gunnel bay. A tarpaulin covering had blown back to reveal the highly polished side of a marble slab.

"He aha kela?" the king asked.

The captain tried to answer with gestures before turning to Jameson for help. "That's marble. But it's for a Siamese king. For his statue on a tombstone."

Kamehameha pulled off the rest of the tarp and saw his entire figure reflected in the polished surface. *"Kela makemake,"* he said with satisfaction.

The captain chuckled with delight. "He says he wants it, right? Maybe we can do some real trading after all!"

Jameson turned away, frustrated.

The sun was setting when the trading session finally ended. Still wearing his *haole* clothes, Jameson walked along the beach toward the hut. Sun-shadowed waves rolled gently toward palm trees bathed in golden light. He scarcely noticed the beauty. He was trying to decide what to say to Nahana.

Not since the war on Maui had he spent this many hours away from her. Yet she felt as near as his breath since he had left her side. But time was running out, and he couldn't rest until the future was settled between them, difficult as that would be to do.

Even before he reached the beach hut he knew she wasn't in it. There was a sudden bleakness about it that chilled him. He stood by the fire pit they had clumsily built together and called to her. An impudent mynah bird teetering on a nearby limb aped his tones. There was no answer.

Jameson scouted her favorite places along the beach. When he didn't find her, he followed the path they had so often walked together, which led to the waterfall.

The same sunset light that had rippled on the waves glistened on her wet body. She was shaking her hair dry and the jeweled droplets danced like motes of light all around her. Unaware of him, she began to comb her long, lustrous fall of hair, drawing the comb through it slowly, sensuously, her body swaying with each stroke.

Jameson watched her for a long time, while storms of feeling raged within him. Nahana's beauty and grace seemed beyond human reach. Yet, she was his, his wife, his mate.

As he started toward her, spurred by desire, a sense of impending loss constricted his chest and burned hot behind his eyes.

She stepped from the pool and pulled on her skirt as she heard his step. "Jameson?"

"I'm back," he called.

She thrust a bright flower into her hair and leaned down to pick up a lei she had woven for him. As he entered the clearing she paused. The change in her face filled him with foreboding.

"What is it?" he asked.

"You are different."

"Different?" Jameson tried to make the word sound light. "No, it's just the clothes."

He bent to let her drape the lei over his head. Instead she looked from the harsh fabric of his stiff coat to the delicate flowers she had woven together and lowered the lei.

"No. You are different," she insisted.

When she began to walk away, he caught up with her and buried his face in her damp, fragrant hair. "I'm not gone yet, Nahana," he whispered. "And maybe..."

"What?" Her voice rose with hope.

"I don't know. I don't know."

He held her very close, conscious that the delicate flowers she wore were being crushed against his coat. It didn't matter. How could he bear to pull away, much less leave her forever?

The king chose his strongest workers to haul the black marble slab to the monument clearing. By the time they had set the marble where King Kamehameha indicated, their flesh gleamed with sweat. Jameson slid his finger around the inside of his stiff collar. It was one thing to sweat with the breeze fanning your flesh. Sweating inside a ship's uniform was an unpleasant business. But then, this whole affair of the marble slab had been sticky and unpleasant.

The workers backed away with their heads bowed, and Kamehameha studied his new acquisition with proud, excited eyes. He strode up to the polished face of the marble and studied his reflection intently, then nodded.

"Vanity, vanity, all is vanity," Jameson quoted to himself, watching. Then, unable to restrain himself, he asked, "What good is it? It's not like wood you can carve. Who's going to make it into a statue?"

"You will make it, Jameson," the king said, without turning around.

"I'm no sculptor. I don't know how to do that kind of thing. Anyway, it's none of my concern."

As he turned away, the king caught his arm lightly. "You are angry with me about the *kii* ... the statue. But you don't understand, Jameson. Yes, I have conquered the other islands, even Maui. I have forced them to be one. But that is not enough. Now I must make them *want* to be one."

"What has putting up a fancy statue for yourself got to do with that?"

"The *kii*, the statue, is for the time when I am gone. My breath made one land, one people. The sons of my son will not have that same breath. If they need me one day, the spirit of my breath will be in the *kii*. Besides, don't other kings have statues?"

"I suppose so." Jameson glanced at the marble. "But two hundred trees!"

"Then I will give only a hundred."

"You can't do that. You made a contract, a bargain. If you make a bad trade, you are still stuck. That's why I was trying to help, to act as your adviser." He shook his head, still irritated by the scene on the quarterdeck. "Two hundred trees. Do you realize how valuable the sandalwood is? It won't last forever."

"This is the way of the gods." The king's face hardened with stubbornness. "When the sandalwood is gone forever, the *haoles* will be gone forever, too."

"No. Then they'll want other things."

Kamehameha stared out to sea and sighed. "You are right. I cannot build a wall. More will come." Almost to himself, he repeated Jameson's word, "Adviser." He turned to clap Jameson on the shoulder, smiling broadly. "Yes, good. You will be my adviser! You will advise, I will decide."

"What are you saying?" Jameson asked in astonishment. The sails of the Yankee ship shone out on the sea, Jameson himself was back in the uniform of his people, yet the king was talking of making him an adviser.

"I ask you to stay. I need you." Then he became expansive. "What do you wish, Jameson? Slaves? Wives? My law says no *haole* can own the land for always, but I will give land to Nahana, then it will be yours. You will be a great *alii* if you stay here."

"But my life is back in Boston."

"This Boston. You are an *alii* there? People bow to you there?"

Jameson had to chuckle as he shook his head.

"No?" the king exclaimed with mock surprise. "But you must have land, and houses, and servants there. You must have a wife like Nahana."

"No," Jameson admitted. "Not like Nahana. But there is someone there, who's waiting to marry me."

"She will come here, then you will have two wives."

Jameson had failed miserably trying to explain Christian morals to Nahana; he didn't even try with Kamehameha. He simply said, "I couldn't do that."

"If you were adviser to Kamehameha, whatever you wished you could do. Whatever you wanted you could have."

It was a tempting offer, but he couldn't consider it. "I am a stranger here. I don't speak your language well. I don't even know if I would be a good adviser."

"I know you would," the king assured him jovially. "Then it is settled. Tonight I will announce it. Jameson will stay."

"Wait a minute," Jameson protested. "I didn't say yes."

"I said yes, and that is enough."

Jameson's frustration in dealing with the king erupted. There was no getting through to him that his word was not universal law. "You're not going to tell me what to do. If I want to leave on that ship, nothing is going to stop me. Not you, not anything!"

Angrily he swung away from the king, only to have his arm caught again. Jameson whirled to face the king. Kamehameha's expression had softened. His tone was almost humble.

"I wish it, Jameson. I *wish* you to stay."

Jameson stared at him, touched in spite of himself. "I'm sorry, really, but I can't. I want to go home and you promised that I could."

"Yes, I promised. And Kamehameha keeps his word."

Dealing with Nahana was even more difficult. From the day the ship arrived, she had become an obsessive housekeeper, washing food bowls, brushing out the hut, always busy when Jameson wanted to be with her.

Worse, she stared at him with eyes empty of luster. She might have been hurting just as badly as he was, but her actions simply made everything worse for both of them. When he offered to help her carry wood, she ignored him.

Then she strode past him, threw the tapa mat over a limb, and swept at it furiously with a broom.

"Why are you doing this?"

"I'm cleaning the tapa. I do this every day."

"I don't mean that. You know what I mean. Why are you acting like this? You always knew I was going to leave sooner or later. I never lied to you."

"I do not wish to talk of it."

"Well, I do," he said firmly. "Put that thing down. You don't have to clean now."

He took the broom from her hand. Nahana faced him, her expression defiant. "It is the duty of a wife to clean and bring wood and—"

"It's not your duties we're discussing. We're discussing us. From the beginning we've been different from the others. And from the beginning we've both known that someday I would go back to my own people. It won't be the end of the world for you, Nahana. There will be no disgrace to you in my leaving."

Her hands clenched into fists. "What do I care of disgrace? What you are doing is worse! You are going away from me when you are my only happiness."

"You will know happiness again. After I am gone there will be someone else. It's the way of your people to have many husbands and wives. You'll soon forget me."

She stared at him. "No. I will not forget. Will you?"

It might have been better for both of them if he could have lied, if he could have said yes, he would forget her. It would have encouraged her to get on with her life when he was gone. But he couldn't manage such dishonesty, even for her sake. He wanted to take her in his arms and hold her, but before he could make a move her expression changed.

The cadence of the distant drums was not the usual pulsing rhythm but awkward and arrhythmic. As Nahana listened, the light seemed to fade from her eyes. Her shoulders drooped and she turned her face away from him. Jameson was almost relieved that there no longer seemed a need to answer her question.

Jameson and Nahana followed the drums to the royal compound. By the time they arrived, the grounds were filled with chiefs, their wives, and other members of the nobility, all dressed in ceremonial attire. The Mauian prince, Hanakea, stood among his attendants. The drum in front of the thatched palace continued its odd, erratic beat.

"What's this about?" Jameson asked Nahana. "Some sort of official ceremony?"

She nodded. "The *makala*. The king calls all the *alii* to tell them something. He has made a great decision. It is *Kauoha moi*. It must be obeyed."

When the drums stopped, the crowd stood silent, all eyes on the king's palace. The king, resplendent in feathered cloak and headdress, stepped out with Kaahumanu, equally regally attired, just behind him. The *alii* lowered their eyes and bowed to him. Next he pointed to Jameson.

"*Kanak aa nui na pilikia, kanaka koa ua hele aku oia,* Jameson."

Jameson turned to Nahana, who translated quietly as the king continued. "He said you are a great hero, fearless in battle and with much wisdom in peace, but soon you will go away forever, and so he orders that there will be a chant of your deeds to be in the memory of the people forever."

A wave of surprise and pride washed over Jameson, but he felt Nahana stiffen at his side. Kamehameha, still speaking, pointed to her and mentioned her name as he continued his pronouncement. Jameson's eyes begged her to explain to him.

She seemed suddenly emptied of life. Her voice was flat, as if she were reciting something from memory, without meaning. "What is of one blood will now be of all blood.

Hanakea and Nahana will be one. Maui and Hawaii will be one." She glanced across the clearing to where Hanakea was watching her. "My father says I must marry Hanakea."

As Jameson struggled to believe what he had heard, Kamehameha held out his hands, one toward Nahana and the other toward Hanakea. As he brought his hands together again in a joining gesture, Nahana left Jameson and walked across the clearing to take her place beside Hanakea.

If his life had depended on it, Jameson couldn't have said how long the ceremony lasted. He stood like stone, unable to absorb the enormity and swiftness of his loss. It was inconceivable to him that Nahana could be promised to another man before he was even gone.

The tempo of the drums changed and the clearing began to empty. Jameson roused himself and looked around for her. She was gone. A tangle of conflicting emotions, not the least of which was guilt, stormed through him as he made his way back to the beach hut. He stood a long time staring at the moving face of the sea before forcing himself to enter.

With only the dappled moonlight for illumination, she was gathering her things into a net. The sight of her brought pain to Jameson's chest. Her lovely skin glowed in the pale light, glistening with perspiration. Her usual grace was gone, leaving her unsteady on her feet. She tried to put a comb in the net bag, only to have it fall from her trembling hands. Bending to retrieve it, she was forced to brace herself against the wall.

Jameson had never seen Nahana like this. She had always exhibited her father's strength. To see her so distraught was like a knife in his gut.

"Nahana," he whispered.

She straightened at his voice. Wiping her brow with a swift, surreptitious movement, she made a visible effort to be calm as she turned to him.

"I didn't know where you'd gone," he said. "I thought maybe you'd already . . ." He watched her store more of her things into the net bag. "Do you have to leave now? Surely you can't be expected to go to him so soon!"

"No. First I have to stay with the Mauian women."

"For how long?"

She shrugged her slight shoulders. "I will be guarded by the women until Hanakea chooses me. Kamehameha has promised me to him, but a marriage will take place later on Maui when all the chiefs come."

"How does Hanakea choose you?" Jameson asked, not wanting to know.

Nahana looked away from him. A sickness of mingled jealousy and pain caught at his breath.

Nahana spoke softly. "It is *maamea*, a way only for kings. When he wishes, we will trade leis. Then he will take me, and decide if I am to be his wife."

"Like trying a dray horse? You don't have to do that, Nahana."

"Kamehameha has spoken it. I must."

Jameson expelled a long, angry breath, striving for control. Nothing on this island, this dark paradise, was under his control. He had made his choice. But he wanted to say something that would bring a glow back to Nahana's pale face.

"When he chooses you, you'll live on Maui as his queen. That will be . . . wonderful, I guess."

She glanced at his old shirt on the floor, the one that covered the locket from Martha. "You'll go to her, the one in there?"

"Yes, I suppose so."

She lifted her bundle, steadied herself, and started toward the door. She was too pale. Even her walk was wrong. When he caught her arm, her flesh felt cool and damp.

"I must go now," she said.

God, if he could only beg her to stay, somehow keep her with him. He had relinquished all right to her. He released her arm and she stood looking up into his face.

"Good-bye, Jameson," she said softly.

The magic that had stirred between them from that first night at the luau was there, palpable in the air, a lasting magic, strong and vital. Caught in it, Jameson started with shock as she tore her eyes away and darted out the door. In a moment she was gone from sight.

The faint, sweet coconut smell of her hair lingered in the room along with the fragrance of her flowers. "Oh, God," he groaned.

Waves of pain coursed through him. His fists clenched and he gulped back tears. It would be stupid, senseless, to run after her. He would have to fight her father and that overgrown Hanakea, maybe the whole damned island chain, to get her back. And he alone was responsible for letting her go.

"Aloha, Nahana," he whispered in the silent room. "Aloha."

CHAPTER TEN

PELE SPEAKS

Jameson threw himself into his work with Captain Fairburn and the crew of the ship. It was one way to keep his mind from the constant pain of losing Nahana. He knew enough about the natives and their sandalwood to be of some help, but his advice was rarely heeded. This was not the first time Captain Fairburn had encountered natives, and he knew just how to deal with them.

The Hawaiian workers dragged freshly cut sandalwood trees down the hillside, where they were stacked in the field below. The workers, fitted with harnesslike ropes, moved slowly under the blazing sun, while the captain impatiently gestured them to speed up.

"Take some of the crew and start clearing a path down to the beach," he ordered Jameson. "Make it wide enough for three men abreast."

Jameson had started to gather men when he heard a piercing cry from one of the sandalwood haulers. The man staggered and fell, doubled over with pain. The other haulers stopped in confusion and Jameson moved to the fallen man. When Captain Fairburn motioned impatiently for the workers to continue, Jameson rushed to help the injured man wriggle free of his harness. Unhampered, the man started to stagger off. Jameson started after him.

"Let him go," Captain Fairburn said. "He's of no use now."

"But he may be hurt."

"Not likely! I know all about these native fellows. They'll do anything to get out of work. You worry about clearing the path."

"Yes, Captain."

As Jameson gathered his men, he saw the doctor puffing up the hill, swearing in the oppressive heat. Jameson then overheard the captain ask, "What is it, Benthurst? Why have you come up here?"

"It's Higgins, sir. He took a sudden bad turn.... Well, he's dead."

"Dead? But you said it was just ague, like Foster."

"And so I thought, at first."

The two men were moving away now and Jameson could not catch any more of their conversation. Higgins dead! Jameson was instantly reminded of Aaron's painful death at sea. Saddened, he hurried back to the men clearing the path.

Not more than a mile from the royal compound Kamehameha had a smaller compound set aside for Hanakea and the Mauians. In the Mauian women's hut Nahana sat apart from her chaperons, two older women dressed differently from the Hawaiian women. A third woman entered bearing a tray of fruits and poi for Nahana.

"Here's your dinner," she said, setting it in front of the younger woman.

The sight of food made Nahana feel ill. She was already flushed and shaky. "I'm sorry. I'm not hungry."

"But you didn't eat earlier, either," the woman protested, concerned. "Are you sick?"

Nahana lifted a listless hand. Was she sick? Or was she merely too sad to care?

The chaperon, who wore her black hair tied in a topknot, tried to encourage her. "You must eat for Hanakea. He will want you big and strong when he makes love to you."

With an effort Nahana rose unsteadily to her feet. "I want to go outside, alone."

"No, no, you mustn't," the chaperon said. "If we let the shadow of another man touch you, Hanakea will have us killed!"

"No man's shadow will touch me," Nahana promised. She pushed her way past them and walked to the edge of the clearing, where she stood looking out toward the stretch of beach she and Jameson had once shared. Only when the light had long since left the sky did she return, stumbling, to the hut.

Keopuolani was racked by chills and fever. She lay propped on a mat in the royal palace, with her young daughter Kalono beside her. The child was pale and listless. Liholiho hovered near his mother with nervous trepidation. Several of Kamehameha's other wives were gathered, too, watching Maakoa minister to Keopuolani.

The high priest massaged her with medicinal oils. His touch was gentle, his chant soothing. When Maakoa stepped aside to prepare an herb potion, he was accosted by Liholiho.

"What is the matter with my mother? You must make her well!"

Maakoa ignored him. He brought the potion to Keopuolani,

who then forced herself to raise her head and drink. But a paroxysm shook her body and the medicine poured back out of her mouth. When the spasm had passed, she sank back numbly on the mat.

Kamehameha shuddered at this distressing scene. Liholiho crept over to him, a pleading look on his face. Kamehameha put a comforting arm around the boy's shoulders, but his frustration at being unable to help Keopuolani soon drove him out of the palace. Outside, he found more afflicted victims, both the *alii* and her servants.

Maakoa followed the king from the palace. "This sickness cannot be cured," he told the king. "Therefore it is not of the body, but of the spirit."

"What can I do?"

"Nothing." Maakoa pointed to the sacred monument in the distance, where the *kii* god statues surrounded Kamehameha's marble slab. "A man can make his likeness as a god, but he cannot breathe the power of a god into it."

Kaahumanu had come out of the palace and stood listening silently to their exchange.

"Only the goddess Pele holds the answer," Maakoa insisted. "And only I can hear Pele. If you command me, I will go to her."

There was a moment's pause before Kamehameha agreed.

"And only that which Pele speaks to me shall be," Maakoa pressed.

Again the king hesitated before nodding.

Satisfied, Maakoa left without a glance toward Kaahumanu. She stepped forward and ran her hand soothingly along Kamehameha's arm. "You will find an answer," she said.

The king shook his head. "There's nothing I can do."

In the Mauian compound Hanakea watched as one of his priests examined several of the stricken. The victims writhed in fevered spasms while the other Mauians, his royal attendants and servants, drew back from them. Hanakea stood firmly beside the priest, disturbed by the afflicted and by the slow, solemn drumbeat in the distance.

"What's wrong with them?" he asked.

The kahuna shook his head. "This is not a sickness of Maui. I cannot cure them here."

"Then we will return to Maui." Hanakea turned to an attendant. "Prepare the canoes. Tell the old women to bring out Nahana."

While the preparations progressed, Hanakea strode quickly through the jungle to the king's compound. Kamehameha stood outside his palace, his gaze resting on the peak of the volcano. Hanakea bowed to him before stating his business.

"With your permission, we will return to Maui. My kahuna says he cannot cure my people here."

"Maakoa has gone to ask the goddess Pele for an answer. When he returns, all will be well," Kamehameha assured him.

Hanakea waved an impatient hand. "I wish to return my people to their land. They should not be away when such a dread affliction has stricken them. They will gain strength from the earth on which they were born."

Kamehameha nodded. "Yes, yes, you must return to your land. It will restore your people. Go with my blessings. But what of Nahana?"

"She will go with us. My women will care for her. When this sickness has left our people, we will return."

"But what if Nahana should become ill?" Kamehameha frowned. "My sacred wife Keopuolani and my daughter Kalono are ill. At least they are here on their land. Nahana would be a stranger on Maui."

"My women will care for her," Hanakea repeated.

A cry from inside the palace pulled Kamehameha back toward his wife. "Very well, then. Nahana will go with you."

By the time Hanakea returned to the Mauian compound his preparations had been carried out. He called to the chaperons to bring Nahana out of the women's hut. He could hear them urging her forward, but it was several minutes before she stood in the doorway.

Her face was flushed and she seemed dazed. Her knees were so weak that she clutched the arm of one of the chaperons for support. Hanakea smiled reassuringly, beckoning her with a white lei he held out to her.

One of the chaperons nudged her. "Hurry! Hanakea is waiting to take you to Maui."

She stared at him for a moment, trying to understand what she was being told. Then she started to shake her head, gently at first and then more wildly. "No! No! I can't!"

Suddenly, with a burst of feverish energy, she pulled free and darted across the clearing, running blindly toward the obscuring growth of the jungle. The servants and chaperons started to run after Nahana, but Hanakea restrained them. His great pride wouldn't allow him to reclaim a woman who had rejected him.

He stared after Nahana for a moment, then ripped the white-flowered lei apart, shredding the petals onto the dirt at his feet. When his hands were empty, he said, "We will go now."

Instinctively, Nahana ran toward the sound of the drum. The drummer, a young priest, sat in a trance near the pyramid-shaped *heiau* shrine to Pele. Here Nahana found herself caught up in a mob of the afflicted, many delirious and clawing at their skin or tearing at their hair. There was no longer any distinction of class; they were all pressed together—nobles, commoners, slaves. With dazed eyes she tried to take in the enormity of the scene, but it was too appalling. She backed away, stumbling in her fear and anxiety. This was not where she would find Jameson.

The ship. He was going on the ship. She must get to the bay. Her legs felt wobbly and her head was spinning, but she forced herself down the path to the water. Suffering people passed her but she scarcely noticed them. The only thing she could think of was that she must find Jameson.

When she reached the beach it was filled with sailors working frantically to prepare for departure. They were loading the sideboats with sandalwood and gathering all their equipment to be returned to the ship. There was a sense of urgency among them, an almost surreptitious haste.

Nahana pushed her way through the sailors, searching for one man. "Jameson! Jameson!" she cried, desperately raising her hoarse voice above the racket. "Where is Jameson?"

A sailor reached for her but dropped his hand when he saw her fevered eyes and unsteady stance. Dr. Benthurst moved quickly to her side. "Who is this girl?" he asked.

"I am the wife of Jameson," she told him. "I must find Jameson."

The doctor put his hand on her forehead but she brushed it away. He frowned. "I'm afraid you have a fever."

Nahana didn't hear him, she was so intent on her mission.

"I will go with Jameson to his island, to Boston," she said.

"On the ship, you mean?"

"I will go with Jameson. Please! Where is he?"

"I think he's gone to his hut to get his things. But, wait! You can't go there. You're sick!"

Nahana pulled away and pushed her way past the doctor and the sailors. She knew only that she must reach the beach hut where she and Jameson had lived.

* * *

The rhythm of the drum changed as Maakoa crossed the clearing to the shrine. When he reached the monument to Pele, the drum ceased entirely. Kamehameha stood to one side of the mass of afflicted, towering over Keopuolani, who was now very ill. Little Kalono lay beside her, too frail to move. The priest glanced at the king and his family before mounting the shrine, where he stood, every eye upon him.

"I have warned that if the *haole* were allowed upon the land, the gods would be angered. The goddess Pele has spoken to me. Pele punishes us with a curse because we have taken the strangers among us." He pointed down to the beach where the sailors stood. "They are the reason we have been cursed! Unless you turn from them to Pele, you will all be cursed!"

The mass of people turned to stare at the ship's crew, then slowly started toward them. The sailors began looking around nervously for weapons. But Maakoa's stern voice rang out over his people.

"No! Leave them! Pele is not angry with them, but with you!" He pointed to the looming volcano. "Those infested by the evil spirit must be given to Pele so the curse will be burned from the land."

Kamehameha's hands clenched at his sides. His eyes could barely meet those of his sacred wife and daughter. But Keopuolani remained calmly courageous. She held her young daughter against her, grateful that the child was too ill to understand what was being said. "We will obey the will of Pele," she said softly to the king.

Maakoa's voice continued now with the dirgelike beat of the drum. "Pele waits for you. Go now! Go! Go! You who are cursed must go to Pele and give yourselves to her fires!"

Already the *kapu* guards were herding the crowd toward the mountain. Most of the sufferers, resigned to their fate, struggled to their feet to start their last journey. Keopuolani lifted Kalono into her arms and smiled bravely at Kamehameha.

Liholiho cried out to his mother, "I want to go with you. Please!"

"No. You are a king's son," she reminded him gently. "You must be strong and live for your sister's sake and mine. And for your father's. I will always love you."

Kamehameha held the boy back. As Keopuolani walked away, Kaahumanu joined the king where he stood with his son. She clasped his hands, warming them with hers, offering him what comfort she could.

Jameson had few belongings to gather. There was his war necklace and his *alii* cloak, and the locket with Martha's picture. He had thought of bringing the tapa love mat, but dropped it on the floor of the hut, unable to bear the memories it stirred.

As he neared the area where the sideboats had been pulled onto the beach, he heard Captain Fairburn ordering the men to hurry with their loading of provisions. The urgency of the captain's voice startled him. Dr. Benthurst came hurrying over and grasped his arm.

"What is it?" Jameson demanded.

"Didn't your woman tell you? She was here looking for you. She said she wanted to go away on the ship with you."

"Nahana? Where?"

The doctor waved off along the beach. "Your hut, I suppose. I told her you'd gone there."

Jameson swung around to start back, but the doctor held on to his arm. "You don't understand," the doctor said. "She's sick. They're all coming down with it. You can't go to her now."

"She's sick? With what? What is this wretched sickness?"

"Cholera. It's all over the island. The captain's decided to leave now and he isn't going to wait for anyone."

Jameson pulled away from him. "But I have to see Nahana before I go."

"There's no time. They're loading the boats."
"I'll be back."

There was no one in the thatched hut. Even the tapa love mat was gone. Nahana must have taken it. She was probably delirious, and likely to stumble onto paths where *kapu* guards were forcing the afflicted toward the volcano. Jameson panicked.

Jameson ran along the path toward the volcano, his eyes watching for any movement in the undergrowth, for any sign of Nahana. But he heard only the incessant pounding of the drums, the wails of the sick, the muffled pounding of footsteps all around him.

When he reached the *heiau* shrine Jameson looked back at the bay. There were still three sideboats on the beach, but crew members were already climbing into one of them. Captain Fairburn was no longer on shore, but Dr. Benthurst stood looking anxiously toward the beach area where Jameson had disappeared earlier. Jameson pressed on. He still had a few minutes.

"Nahana! Nahana!"

The shrine was deserted now. He began a search of the area, peering behind the wooden figures, looking through the undergrowth. As he moved closer to the path he heard another group of the afflicted being prodded along by the *kapu* guards. His time was running out. On the beach below, the second sideboat was being loaded. Now only one remained, and he had to give himself time to reach it.

Suddenly he stumbled and, glancing down, saw the tapa mat. He recognized the design immediately and clutched it against his chest. "Nahana! Where are you? Nahana!"

The band of cholera victims moved past him, oblivious to his presence. But Nahana was not among them. His heart twisted with pain as he thought of her sick, being forced up to the volcano.

His gaze fell on the last of the sideboats on the beach. Dr. Benthurst was still standing on the sand, but the other crew members were beginning to climb in. Jameson's time had run out. As he turned to head down the path, a faint movement in the undergrowth caught his eye.

Nahana staggered out onto the path, perhaps in answer to his call, just as the cholera victims reached her. She saw Jameson at that instant and reached out to him, but was suddenly swept up in the mass of people marching to their death. Jameson could not move, paralyzed by the horrifying scene he had just witnessed.

He stood there clutching the tapa love mat. Below, on the beach, Dr. Benthurst was boarding the last sideboat. Time had run out.

CHAPTER ELEVEN

IN THE CRATER

The worship of Pele had begun in the mists of time. For centuries the people of Hawaii had climbed the steep face of the volcano Kilauea, which housed the goddess. So many feet had passed along the trails of the mountain that the rich earth no longer grew trees to block passage.

Now these paths were crowded with the afflicted. Having gathered his wits, Jameson hid away from the trail and watched the *kapu* guards ruthlessly prod the helpless victims along. Somewhere in that anonymous throng Nahana was stumbling toward her death. It would be foolhardy to challenge the guards; they were many and he was one. If he was going to save her, he must do it by stealth.

The sounds of human misery grew dimmer and finally faded to a faint moan on the wind as he made his way toward the opposite side of the volcano. No inch of his progress was easy. Massive trees were scattered above; tangled undergrowth covered the ground. Jameson plunged into hidden pits and scrambled through nearly impenetrable masses of knee-deep vines.

The sunset blazed across the sky as he forced his way upward. The ship's uniform, which he had cursed for its clumsiness only a short time earlier, now proved to be his salvation. The briars that slashed the sturdy fabric would have left his arms and legs bleeding. There was no way to protect his hands and face, but the pain of the scratches was temporary. The death he was trying to prevent was permanent.

When he began again to hear the sounds of suffering, he knew he was nearing the top. Breaking from the brutal, dense thicket, he saw before him a landscape that might, for its horror, have been painted in hell. A field of black lava, marked by giant stones, curved up to the mouth of the smoking crater. Doubled over, Jameson scrambled from one lava outdropping to another until he reached the top. He lay flat on a black stone and looked down.

The wide projection in front of the open crater was a beehive of human misery. Wailing, anguished cries rose along with the acrid smoke and the stench of human excrement. Victims too weak and ill to move huddled in helpless clusters. *Kapu* guards, their scarred faces forbidding in the flickering light, moved briskly among them, carrying the newly dead to the mass of corpses already lining the crater's edge.

Priests dominated the center of this scene of horror. Their dark silhouettes were distorted against the flickering flames as they made their ritualistic gestures. They were purifying the hapless victims who could still drag themselves to this spot. The priests chanted and spilled handfuls of gray volcanic ash into the hands of the sufferers, who rubbed it over their faces and chests.

Jameson felt sure that hell itself could be no worse than this.

The daylight was quickly dying. Jameson edged as close as he dared and squinted desperately at the moving mass of bodies scarcely lit by the occasional torches and the flickering light from the crater.

A movement on the horizon caught his attention. Far off, a billowing sail floated on the placid sea. That swelling canvas was to have meant freedom for him. Now it barely registered on his mind. His eyes were already back on the scene at the crater's edge.

He stripped off his uniform and scooped up the coarse volcanic ash to darken his body. But not even the dullness of the ash could entirely conceal the *haole* whiteness of his flesh. When the light was gone from the sky, he moved stealthily into the area of the afflicted. A tapa robe lay abandoned alongside the place of the dead. He draped it around his body and tied it on one shoulder, trying not to think of what had happened to its previous owner.

The sufferers were as indifferent to him as they were to their own fate. It was the guards whom he watched warily. When he caught a guard's eye on him, he lowered his head and groaned and twitched in agony as those around him did. When the guard's gaze moved on, Jameson continued to move from group to group, searching for Nahana.

When he saw the slender figure with glowing dark hair falling over her shoulders, his heart leaped with relief. Kneeling, he took the girl in his arms and turned her face toward him, softly speaking her name.

She stared at him blindly and his arms dropped away. This hapless girl must once have been as lovely as Nahana. Now he recoiled from the horror of her face. Her flesh was deeply wrinkled under the crust of lava ash. Her eyes had shrunk to blind pits above her hollowed cheeks. When she tried to speak she succeeded only in thrusting a thick white tongue between her split lips. Shaken, Jameson gently laid a comforting hand on her arm and then turned away.

Time after time he was mistaken in thinking he had found Nahana. Each time, a different, destroyed face stared back at him, unseeing. He found himself moving closer and closer to the priests in his search. Those sharp-eyed kahunas wouldn't be fooled for a moment by his disguise.

When he finally saw Nahana curled against a lava rock, her head bowed, he was afraid to believe it. Her glazed eyes, the death mask that the ash made of her face, filled him with horror. But she was alive.

"Nahana!" he whispered, kneeling and brushing at the ash. Her face felt feverish. She gave no sign of recognition. "Come on," he urged. "Come with me."

She pulled away with what strength she had. "No! I cannot go. I must die in Pele."

"You're not going to die here or anywhere else. I'm not going to let you die."

They were within a dozen yards of the kahunas. Jameson didn't dare make a commotion. Enfolding her within his tapa robe, he held her tightly until she stopped fighting him. He could feel how little strength she had. But she refused to cooperate, and opened her mouth to cry out. He clamped his hand over it, stifling the sound. There was so much sound around them, groans, screams, that it would have been impossible to sort out any one voice.

And yet the closest priest had turned to stare at them, his cold, deadly eyes fastened on Jameson's face. Jameson held tightly to Nahana but forced his body to twist with the anguish of those around him, slumping onto the lava rock. With his face averted, he still kept an eye on the priest, who had taken a step toward them.

There were so many victims for the priest to attend to. He paused, aware that he had no time to discover if something was wrong. Jameson breathed a sigh of relief as he saw the man turn back to his work. Once again he bundled Nahana against his body and drew her to her feet.

She had no strength to walk, so he carried her, but awkwardly, at his side. They had moved only a few steps toward the surrounding darkness when he saw the suspicious kahuna priest motion to a *kapu* guard. Jameson's heart seemed to freeze in his chest. He didn't know whether to keep walking or to sink down at the crater's edge.

Nahana murmured in her delirium and swayed dangerously. Jameson attempted to steady her and still keep an eye on the priest. The guard had almost reached the priest, who was pointing in their direction. His message delivered, the priest returned to his work.

The *kapu* guard started toward them. He was a huge man, with the hideously scarred face of his position. Jameson forced himself to walk slowly, even to stumble, as if he were merely wandering around in a daze. It seemed unlikely that he would be able to convince anyone of this, but he had to try. Nahana's life, and perhaps his own, depended on it.

Jameson tried desperately to think of something to distract the guard's attention. The man continued to follow them, but in an erratic fashion, almost as if he were toying with them. Jameson would move toward the darkness, pretending to stumble, and the *kapu* guard would lumber after them, only to stop and stare at them.

Nahana moaned softly against his chest. She was too sick for this kind of forced walking. He should simply raise her in his arms and walk off into the night with her. But they were already conspicuous as the only ones standing, except for the priests and the guards. Fearful that the longer he delayed, the more attention that might be called to them, Jameson scooped Nahana into his arms and headed for the blackness beyond the crater's rim.

When he heard the *kapu* guard call out, he walked faster. At any moment a club might rain a deadly blow on him from behind, but he kept going. All he cared about was getting Nahana away from this pit of disease and death. Otherwise she would die.

There was a sudden commotion behind him—a heavy thudding followed by new cries and moans. Jameson allowed himself one swift, backward glance, afraid the guard was gaining on him. Instead, he saw that the man had fallen, himself a victim of the dread disease. Without hesitating, Jameson ran the last few yards that took him out of sight of those at the crater.

Once again he was forced to fight his way through the dense vegetation, this time with Nahana in his arms. The trails were still crowded with new victims and the *kapu* guards who drove them. When Nahana stiffened in his arms and cried aloud in pain, Jameson rocked and comforted her as best he could.

They skirted mourning villages and stopped at streams and waterfalls. Jameson always cupped his hands and brought water to her lips. She moaned in protest, twisting away, but he forced her to drink. There was nothing else he could do for her until they reached a safe resting place.

For hours and hours he struggled downward, until finally the salt scent of the sea reached him. He knew they were nearing the area where Nahana had nursed his injured leg. She lost consciousness; her head rolled back against him and her slender arms dangled like living ribbons. But he didn't dare stop. He didn't dare think that she might be dying.

When he reached the secluded clearing that he had sought, he laid her down on the matted grass. Her head flopped to one side and she lay as if lifeless.

"Nahana," he whispered. There was no response, even when he called her name louder. Desperate, he shook her shoulder gently until her eyes fluttered open. She stared at him in a fevered daze, frowning a little as if she could not see. Her eyes closed again and her body was racked by a painful spasm. Jameson seized her and held her close, as if the pressure of his arms could stop her dreadful trembling.

But this wouldn't do. He was reacting, rather than thinking. He needed to treat her, to do everything he had ever heard to battle this sickness. Her spasm passed and she fell back senseless again. This time he couldn't rouse her, but her breast rose and fell with labored breathing.

He wiped the ashy sweat from her face and brushed back her damp, clinging hair. Then he took the tapa robe to the lagoon's edge and dipped it in the clear water. When he spread the soaking robe over her, she flinched, stirred, and opened her eyes. Then he fanned her with a wide leaf, but she frowned and tried to throw off the tapa robe.

"No, Nahana. Leave it where it is. It will help to bring your fever down."

He tore a strip from the robe and laid it on her forehead. She submitted to this treatment, but muttered in a distraught voice, "Jameson. Where is Jameson? I will go to his island. I will go to Boston. Where is Jameson?"

"I'm here, Nahana," he said, gently pressing her shoulder. "We're here together, where you first brought me when I was injured."

Her eyes wandered idly from his face, almost as if he hadn't spoken.

"Nahana, Nahana! Can't you hear me? Don't you remember?"

She looked up, forcing herself to focus on his face. Her eyes registered disbelief. "Jameson. But you sailed away on the ship. You cannot be here with me."

"I *am* here with you. I'm not going to leave you."

Suddenly she began to shiver violently. Jameson threw the tapa robe aside and held her trembling body next to his.

"I'm so cold," she whispered against his chest. "Jameson, Jameson. Are you still with me?"

"I'm still here," he promised.

In time her flesh began to warm and she drifted into a shallow, restless sleep. He cradled her in his arms, willing his strength to be absorbed by her slender frame. She sighed in her sleep and he gently stroked her forehead, her cheeks, and her lips. Then he breathed into her the spirit of his love, as she had taught him.

"I love you, Nahana," he whispered softly. "I love you and I won't let you die."

In the palace hut of the king, Kaahumanu sat with her dark eyes half-closed, covertly watching her husband. Her heart ached to see his greatness so visibly diminished. The past days had scarred him in a way that a lifetime of fighting wars had not.

He was still a giant among men, but much of his kingliness had seeped from him. The grand vitality that had powered his arms and his loins glowed dimly, like a raging fire fallen to ash. His voice—the voice of the Great Kamehameha—was hesitant. His head was bowed as he watched the high priest Maakoa chanting over Liholiho.

The young prince twisted in pain on his mat. His movements were awkward and his young flesh poured sweat. The king moved restlessly around the room waiting for Maakoa's pronouncement.

The high priest spoke abruptly. "Yes, it is a curse."

Anguish distorted Kamehameha's face. "Why?"

"You let the foreign traders come with their false ways and their false god," Maakoa reminded him. "You even let the foreigner Jameson live among us. The gods are angry."

"What can I do? Tell me what I can do."

Kaahumanu stirred, hoping the king would glance her way. He *must* not make hasty promises to Maakoa. Kaahumanu knew that she loved the gods as well as any woman did, but she didn't trust Maakoa. Though he was a kahuna, even a high priest, he was also a man. And the weaknesses of men had not been burned from his heart when his flesh was scarred for priesthood.

Only the priests could read omens and hear the gods speak. Kaahumanu had known priests who prayed men to death without ever touching them. The kahunas were powerful men, and they didn't always use their power in the best interests of the king or his people. They were to be feared, and Kaahumanu feared Maakoa more than any. She sensed he had no scruples about the use of his power.

"You must swear never to let the foreigners again come on the islands," Maakoa told the king.

Kamehameha hesitated. Kaahumanu knew that he felt her eyes on him, asking for a glance, only a glance, so that she might warn him. Instead, he looked down at the sagging body of his son. Fear for his own blood proved stronger.

"Yes. Kamehameha swears it! To save my son I will swear it. No more foreigners."

Kaahumanu knew she must speak or forever be silent. "But then we will not have..." she began. When the king turned on her with a furious glare, she fell silent. Her heart plunged at his next words.

"Anything Maakoa says the gods ask of Kamehameha, he will swear. Then the curse will be no more?"

Maakoa's expression was complacent. "Yes." With scarcely a pause, he reached for Liholiho's hand. "But Liholiho must go to the volcano of the goddess Pele."

The king surged with sudden life, thrusting himself forward. "No! Not my son. Not Liholiho! The gods have sent my sacred wife Keopuolani and my sacred daughter Kalono to die in Pele. But no, not Liholiho. Now that I have sworn all you asked, they will leave him to me."

"No," Maakoa told him sternly. "He must go, or what

you have sworn the gods will not believe. There will be even greater punishment."

Kaahumanu looked away. She could not bear to watch so great a man humbled so pitifully. Liholiho whimpered as his father embraced him. Then Maakoa dragged the boy stumbling from the hut. Kaahumanu crossed the room to stand silently by the king.

Even though he knew she was there, it was a long time before he spoke. "Now I will have no son to rule after my breath," he said, defeated.

"But *you* still live," she reminded him. "You will have another son to take your place."

He shook his head. "That cannot be. You know the prophecy of my birth."

"Everyone knows it. When a long flame filled the sky, a great king would be born and he would be chosen to make the islands one and to lift the last rock so that the people would look up to him as a god. And it has happened. Everything that the chants foretold."

"Yes. And so the rest of the prophecy of the old kahunas must happen, too."

"What is the rest of the prophecy?"

"The old kahunas foretold that a great cloud of death would strike the land, but I would be spared."

"And you have been spared."

His voice became bleak. "The people will believe even more that I am divine, and the gods will become angry and strike me down."

"How?" she asked, troubled by his words.

"It is foretold that when the gods grow jealous of Kamehameha, they will let the people tear a royal cape from his shoulders so they will see that he, too, is only a man. Then Kamehameha will die."

His words struck coldly at her heart. She gripped him by the shoulders. "That will not happen!"

The king was thoughtful. "The chants have already spoken. Why else have I been spared?"

"To rule!"

"If the prophecy of the chant has come true, I will have no strength left to rule."

Kaahumanu had thought of the time when Kamehameha would be dead. Of the time when Liholiho, a delicate, unwarriorlike lad, would come to the throne. If Liholiho was gone, if Kamehameha had no strength...

"You will have me," she said. "I will help rule with you, for you."

He stared at her in disbelief. "Rule for me? But you are a woman. The people would not accept that."

"They will accept what Kamehameha accepts."

The blaze of dawn awakened Nahana. She watched it idly, content to let her eyes follow the dark swaying of the palm trees against the flood of colored light. When her gaze fell lower, to a makeshift shelter standing in the shadow of the vines, her brow furrowed with concern. Where was she? The embers of a cooking fire still winked in the ashes of a cooking pit. Bowls and a tapa robe rested beside the pit. Nahana herself was lying on a tapa mat in a clearing. None of this made sense.

Then, almost to herself, she whispered, "Jameson?"

As she spoke, he appeared from the thicket. He was carrying a bowl, stirring something in it as he walked. She watched him kneel beside her, still unable to believe this was happening.

"I'm here," he said.

"Then I didn't dream it. You were here with me."

"And I'm going to stay here, on the island with you. You're my wife, Nahana."

"But you said..."

He shook his head and handed her the bowl. "Don't talk now. Drink this."

"What is it?"

"Water and salt, and some sweetening from berries. They say the Indians used it."

"Indians?" The new word confused her.

"I'll explain sometime, along with a lot of other things. We've got our whole lives for that. But right now, drink it all."

She took a cautious sip and made a face.

"It's not supposed to taste good," he assured her. "It's medicine. Hold your nose, like this, see? If you won't do it, *I'll* hold your nose."

She laughed at him, held her nose as he had shown her, and swallowed the bitter stuff. When he had set the bowl aside, he laid his hand on her forehead and smiled.

"Every day that fever gets better."

"Every day?" She frowned. "But it was night and now it is morning."

"I brought you here three days ago. You've been too sick to remember."

Nahana caught his hand and pressed it against her cheek. "I remember some things. I thought they were a dream."

"I love you, Nahana. I want you to know it wasn't a dream when I said that." He put his arms around her, but she pulled back, tense with fear.

"You mustn't love me, Jameson."

"Why not?" he asked, his tone almost amused.

"I defied the gods. They might take revenge on me by striking you down because you love me."

Looking up into the bright sky, she spoke fervently to her gods. "I will do what you ask. I will go back and give myself in death to Pele if you will only spare Jameson."

He seized her shoulders and forced her to look at him.

"Listen to me, Nahana. This illness is not a curse. That's all just superstition. Believe me, there is no such thing as a curse."

"But the great priest Maakoa said..."

"I don't care what Maakoa said. There's no curse. You were sick, just like all those other people up on the crater."

"No," Nahana said sadly. "It is not like a sickness. It was never here before."

"I know. Maakoa was right about that. It was a disease that came from the foreigners, the *haoles* on the trading ship. Cholera, most likely."

"How do you know?"

"Because this is how epidemics happen. There was a sailor on the ship who was ill. I didn't think much of it at the time, but he might very well have had some disease that has been passed along. Some people can live through it, the way you have. A lot of those people at the volcano would have survived with proper care."

"They would not be able to live. If I have been here three days, then tomorrow is the day they must give themselves to the goddess Pele."

Jameson was struck dumb for a moment. "You mean kill themselves? Jump into the volcano? My God, Nahana. There must be some way to stop that!"

Her shoulders slumped. "Only Maakoa can do that."

"You're probably right." But his eyes narrowed in thought. "And only Kamehameha can make him do it."

CHAPTER TWELVE

WARRING MAGIC

Nothing less than the horror planned at the crater would have persuaded Jameson to allow Nahana to move from her tapa mat. She was weak and they stopped frequently for her to rest against him, her breath shallow from exertion. When they arrived at the royal compound, Kamehameha was the first to see them step from the jungle path into the clearing. He stared at Jameson in astonishment and called his name.

The three men with the king—Maakoa and two of his priests—swung around. Kaahumanu, on the king's other side, seemed unable to believe her eyes.

"Why are you still here, Jameson?" the king asked. "Why didn't you go with the *haole* ship?"

"I decided to stay here on the island with Nahana." She clung to him, saying nothing.

"Aole!" Maakoa roared at the king. "Kamehameha *paa haole kapu. Jameson haole, Jameson kapu!"*

"What does he man, *kapu?"* Jameson asked.

"He means you cannot stay on the island."

"Then I will go with Jameson," Nahana told her father. "To his island. To Boston."

"Aole!" the priest said again. *"Kanake hele kapu!"*

"Now what's he saying?" Jameson asked.

Nahana translated dully, "None of our people shall be allowed to leave the islands."

"You mean you can't leave and I can't stay?" He turned to the king. "Just because Maakoa says so? You are supposed to be the one who makes the rules."

Kamehameha sounded old and defeated as he said, "You cannot stay on the island, Jameson. I have sworn that to Maakoa before the gods."

"But I don't understand," Jameson protested. "You wanted me to stay. You practically begged me to stay!"

"I was wrong to break the ancient way of the gods. And now a great curse has come upon the people. Until you and all the *haoles* are forever gone, the gods will not take away the curse."

Nahana stepped toward her father. "But Jameson says it is not a curse. It is a sickness."

"Is this true?" the king demanded. "Is it only a sickness, Jameson?"

"That's right. Cholera. People who get this sickness can be cured, like Nahana was."

Kamehameha caught eagerly at Jameson's arm. "Do you mean that? You could make all those on Pele well again?"

"Not all of them," Jameson admitted. "But many of them, yes. They do not all have to die."

"Aole! Akua amu mai!" Maakoa shouted.

Kaahumanu answered the priest, *"Nahana aole amu. Jameson hoola."*

The king was torn between the opposing views of his wife and the priest. He turned to Jameson. "You say you could make many well again, Jameson. Could you make my son Liholiho well again?"

Kaahumanu grasped this opportunity. "Yes! Jameson could save Liholiho. He will prove that Maakoa is wrong. The gods do not want the islands closed to the *haole*."

"But I'm not a doctor," Jameson protested.

Maakoa, scowling fiercely, pointed at Kaahumanu. *"Akua amu ka!"*

She turned away, deliberately replying to his threat in English, "Kaahumanu does not fear your curse. I believe in Jameson and what he can teach us." She stopped before Kamehameha, her hands outstretched. "Let Jameson go to Pele. I am not afraid. I will go with him."

The king looked doubtful. "But Kamehameha has spoken his word to Maakoa before the gods." His gaze moved from Kaahumanu to his recovered daughter to Jameson. "How long did it take your *haole* magic to cure Nahana?"

"Three days. But it wasn't . . ."

Without giving him a chance to explain fully, Kamehameha set the rules, just as he had always done. "You will go to Pele, Jameson. And you, Kaahumanu, will go with him. For three days, and you will save my son."

He moved off swiftly before Maakoa could intercede, but it was Jameson who stopped him. "Wait a minute! I said three days, but . . ."

"Three days and no more," Kamehameha replied, striding into his palace.

Nahana clung to Jameson's arm, unwilling to meet Maakoa's baleful glare. Jameson hugged her to him, and tried to smile encouragement at Kaahumanu, but he couldn't summon the conviction. Once again he was being forced to bring off the near impossible, and he feared total disaster.

* * *

Jameson and Kaahumanu reached the sacrificial area of the volcano at sunset. The scene had become an even worse hell in the days since Jameson had rescued Nahana. All order was gone. The living lay in stupors or thrashed about in agony, mixed indiscriminately with the newly and the long dead. Torches cast terrifying shadows. The air reeked with the stench of the dead and the acrid breath of the fiery pit below.

Some of the afflicted still staggered around, blindly brushing into one another. When Kaahumanu and Jameson were recognized, there was a pitiful attempt at bowing, which often led the sick to fall and not to rise again. The priests and *kapu* guards were merely confused by their coming.

"This is even worse than I expected," Kaahumanu admitted. "What do you command to be done?"

Jameson studied the scene, fighting discouragement. "First the dead bodies must be buried and all their clothing burned. The sick who are hot with fever must be put to one side and kept under wet tapa cloths. The ones who are cold and shivering must be moved near a fire and kept covered and warm."

"The dead must be given to Pele," Kaahumanu insisted. "It would take too long to bury them. The labor is better spent in helping the living."

It disturbed Jameson to think of the bodies being thrown into the volcano, but he knew she was right. Even then, the remaining tasks seemed impossible. There were so many victims. "And fresh water. We're going to need a lot of that. And salt. And anything sweet, juice from berries or some kind of fruit."

"I will command it," Kaahumanu agreed.

"But will the priests and *kapu* guards listen to you?"

Arrogance stiffened her body and brought her head high. "I am Kaahumanu, queen of Kamehameha. I will tell them the king has sent me and they will listen."

Jameson watched her gather the milling victims around her. If he had worried that no one would listen to her, he had underestimated her power. *"Lohe!"* she cried. *"Kaahumanu hele."*

She explained that they were here to help the sick, and that Jameson had already saved Nahana's life. When she was challenged by one of the priests, her reply was firm.

After a moment of confused consultation, the guards and priests began to carry out her instructions. By the time darkness fell, the fires fed by the clothing of the dead sent pillars of flame rising into the sky. Beyond the fire the guards labored to dispose of the dead bodies. Many of the fevered had already calmed under the chilling wet tapa mats and the sounds of suffering had abated somewhat.

Jameson and Kaahumanu had found the king's son Liholiho huddled on the ground, semiconscious and barely moving. Beside him his mother, Keopuolani, cradled her silent, motionless child Kalono. Keopuolani's face was a distillation of pain and despair.

Kaahumanu knelt swiftly at the queen's side and took her in her arms. When Jameson reached toward the child, Keopuolani tightened her hold, pressing the girl against her chest in fear. Only at Kaahumanu's urging was Jameson allowed to examine the child, to feel the temperature of her flesh and search in vain for a pulse in the tiny wrist. He closed the lids over the now-sightless eyes and tried to signal the truth to Kaahumanu. The mother, seeing Jameson shake his head, clutched her child even closer and tried to draw away from both of them.

"No," she insisted. "Her breath has not flown from her body. I will hold her, then her breath cannot flee." She sobbed weakly. "Say to me she is not dead."

Jameson leaned to her. "I'm sorry, Keopuolani. She was just too young, too frail."

"I would have given my breath to her," Keopuolani whispered.

"I know. I have to take her body. I'm sorry."

As he slid his hands under the child's frail body, her mother cried, "Wait!"

Keopuolani cupped her hands over her mouth, breathed into them, then carried the air to her child's still lips. She watched with eager hope to see the girl move or speak. Only when nothing happened did she turn away, heartbreak in her face, and let Jameson lift the child from her arms.

Helpless grief tightened Jameson's chest. He could do nothing to help this tiny victim. A priest carried off the corpse and Jameson saw Keopuolani rise to follow. When Jameson touched her arm to hold her back, he found that she was trembling.

"Ask the guard to take her by the fire and keep her covered," he told Kaahumanu.

But the guard was unable to obey her command. Keopuolani, weak and ill, refused to leave Liholiho's side.

"He could live," Jameson told her.

Keopuolani stared at him. "But how? Maakoa says..."

"Maakoa is wrong," Kaahumanu said. "Kamehameha sent us here because Jameson has *haole* magic. The breath of Liholiho may be saved."

The king's sacred wife regarded Jameson with mingled hope and fear, and allowed herself to be led to the warmth of the fire.

"You know I don't have any *haole* magic," Jameson insisted angrily to Kaahumanu when they were alone.

"Liholiho must live. Then Kamehameha will know that Maakoa's way is wrong, and that there should be new ways for our people. Jameson, together we can do this. But if Liholiho does not live, your ways will be lost to us, and Nahana will be lost to you forever."

Liholiho had already slipped into delirium. As Jameson

bent over him, the young boy grabbed his arm and spoke with desperate intensity. Though his dark eyes gazed up at Jameson, the focus was wrong, as if the boy were looking past him into a different time, a different place.

"*Kaua me makua moi puali pono,*" Liholiho begged.

Kaahumanu sighed softly as she explained, "He wants to fight beside his father, the great Kamehameha, to prove that he is worthy."

Jameson remembered the day the war fleet had sailed, leaving the boy watching wistfully after them. "He must think it's the day we sailed to conquer Maui. Poor child."

"Will he live?" Kaahumanu asked.

"I don't know. His fever;s very high, his pulse is erratic. We've got to keep the tapa wet."

The queen signaled for a guard to bring more water. She herself soaked the cloth and patted it over the boy. "He *must* live, Jameson."

"We'll do everything we can."

As the third dawn stained the sea and the sky scarlet, Kamehameha awakened to stare hopefully toward the mountain. Each day he had watched Maakoa supplicate his gods at the *heiau* shrine. Each day the king feared that a messenger would come bearing awful news. Today he waited no longer.

Preceded by his guards, and followed by his priests, Kamehameha strode up the mountain path. He was resplendent in a feathered cloak and headdress, and the rhythmic beat of the drums heralded his progress. Nahana followed silently, fearfully, her strength barely up to the hike, but her need to be there too compelling to be ignored.

At a jutting outcrop of rock near the top, the guards stopped and waited for the king's instruction. Kamehameha curtly motioned them forward. The drums fell silent as the king stalked to the rim of the crater. Instead of chaos, the sacrificial site was now orderly and clean.

Almost half of the afflicted had survived. They stood massed before the king, their faces ravaged but hopeful. Even the weakest attempted to bow. The king surveyed the scene, searching for a single face in the multitude. Just as he began losing hope, Jameson stepped forward with Liholiho at his side.

Kamehameha cried aloud and rushed to embrace the boy. Maakoa scowled, but Nahana moved joyfully to Jameson's side and slipped her hand into his.

"Liholiho ola, Kamehameha ole," the king cried. Clinging to his son with one arm, he embraced Keopuolani with the other. Then his gaze moved beyond the little group and back to his sacred wife. "Kalono?" he asked.

Her eyes dropped. *"Maake,"* she said softly. "Jameson came too late to save our daughter, but he has saved our son."

The king nodded, tightening his arm around Liholiho's shoulder. "Jameson shall be rewarded. What do you wish, Jameson? Name it."

"Only to stay here and live with Nahana as my wife."

Maakoa stepped forward. *"Jameson e haole. Ina haole kapu, nui ami."*

Jameson felt Nahana quiver at his side. Then she was out of the circle of his arms, confronting the two men.

First she turned to Maakoa, then to her father. "Jameson is not *haole*," she insisted. "He is my husband." Lifting her arm, she displayed her wedding scar before grasping Jameson's wrist to exhibit the matching scar.

The king smiled at his daughter's determination. "Jameson may stay here with Nahana, always," he proclaimed. Then he turned to let his eyes rest intimately on Kaahumanu as he reached for her hand. *"Mele Kaahumanu. Kaahumanu nui!"*

The people picked up the chant and made it ring from the mountainside: *"Mele Kaahumanu. Kaahumanu nui!"*

Jameson thought this queen was in many ways a match for the towering king in courage, strength, and physical beauty. At the moment the royal couple seemed joined, equals in every way. Then the king's massive hand seized Jameson's and held it high, adding a new phrase for the crowd.

The multitude shouted his name. *"Mele Jameson, e Kaahumanu nui!"*

Maakoa's scarred face stared back at them, darker and more ominous than the lava rocks on which they stood.

PART THREE

The Wall In The Sea

CHAPTER THIRTEEN

THE STINGRAY

The cholera epidemic ran its course. The dead were consigned to the volcano and the survivors returned to their villages. Though the priests darkly remembered that a *haole* ship had brought the sickness, the people remembered only that *haole* magic had saved many from a flaming death in Pele.

Kamehameha rejoiced. His son had recovered, and his islands were united. If he was still wary of strangers in his land, he listened to Jameson, his adviser, and welcomed the traders who bartered new and strange objects for his precious sandalwood.

The king's whimsical extravagance appalled Jameson, but he was unable to do much to temper it. And the Yankee traders had no such qualms. Sandalwood was highly treasured in China for carving, for incense, and for rich perfumed oil. They were delighted to haul off the great logs in exchange for whatever captured the king's fancy.

Kamehameha's palace in the royal compound became as much *haole* as Hawaiian. A huge, ornately carved four-poster bed was crowded in where his tapa sleeping mat had lain. Coat racks, umbrella stands, even handsome oriental rugs cluttered the royal quarters. Kamehameha sported satin knee pants while Kaahumanu topped her traditional short slit skirt with a lustrous silken shirt that half-concealed her perfect breasts.

Robert Jameson was wholly committed to Nahana and to serving as adviser and friend to the king. He even convinced himself that God would not have left him on the islands without a reason. Over the years since his arrival on Hawaii, he had worked hard to teach Kamehameha the principles of government that he had known in New England. The work was challenging and frustrating by turns. When the king finally listened to Jameson's warnings about the sandalwood, he did too little, too late.

Kamehameha placed a royal monopoly on the remaining trees. He protected the younger trees from cutting and ordered new seedlings to be planted. But sandalwood trees grew slowly, and every canny trader could convince Kamehameha that there was one more thing he had to have, in exchange for the dwindling trees.

Jameson gradually Americanized the hut on the beach that he shared with Nahana. He wielded a straight razor over a pewter bowl and replaced the fragrant fire pit with a wood-burning stove. When they were alone, Nahana ate with him, sitting on a chair at the maple table.

To her the breaking of the *kapu* against women eating with men was more significant than the acquisition of New England furniture, but she said little about it. Her love for Jameson was stronger than her fears. But in public she followed the rules of her native society, and Jameson in turn kept silent about his distaste for such unchristian practices.

The trading ships from Great Britain, the United States, and Russia stopped more frequently on the islands now that there was sandalwood to be traded. These ships loaded furs and other goods in California or farther north up the coast, wintered there, and then made brief stops on the islands on the way to and from Canton.

Jameson taught the king to be a sharper trader, taught him the worth of the hogs, fruits, vegetables, firewood, salt, and water that he could trade with the foreign ships. Barter was his usual method of trade, but he sought hard cash and stored it in well-guarded storehouses with many of his western goods.

When the chief on Kauai refused to acknowledge Kamehameha as ruler of all the islands, Kamehameha planned an invasion that required hundreds of ships. His expenditures on this fleet were not, perhaps, perfectly practical by Jameson's standards, but the results were impressive.

Kamehameha ordered the building of eight hundred peleleu canoes—twin-hulled, broad and deep, with covered platforms, and some even rigged with a main sail and jib. The fleet could carry an army of several thousand and took five years to complete. Kamehameha used Jameson's services in collecting muskets, cannon, and schooners as well.

In the end, the king was not forced to do battle with the chief of Kauai, who understood that Kamehameha's strength was far superior to his. Kamehameha allowed the Kauai chief to pay obeisance to him and to remain as the king's governor on Kauai.

Kamehameha developed an impressive government, with the advice of his high chiefs and Jameson. He appointed a governor to rule each island and set up a system of navigators to deliver his commands to these men. He gathered skilled workers and craftsmen around him—warriors, canoe makers, athletes, surfers, feather workers, wood carvers, dancers, chanters.

Jameson would join the king on his travels to other islands. Nahana generally went along, too, as they did not like to be separated if possible. Over the years, their love had only grown stronger, their only frustration being that Nahana still had not become pregnant. Nahana had come to accept this as some sort of punishment from the gods, and was grateful that her penalty was no greater. So eventually Jameson had stopped talking of the day when they would have children.

Then one day as they walked along the beach, she said, "I have news."

He smiled. He was used to Nahana's news and it was always delightful. A favorite fruit tree had ripened. A flower she particularly loved had come into season.

"Very important news," she added, her eyes wide and bright.

"All right. I'm ready."

She laid her smooth arms along his and looked up into his face. "We are going to have a child," she whispered.

Jameson had not expected this. Her words almost stunned him. "A child? Our child?"

Nahana laughed and nodded. Jameson lifted her off the sand in an enormous hug, whirling her around in pure ecstasy. "Oh, you wonderful, wonderful woman," he sighed.

From that hour he was changed. A child, a son, meant that Jameson must prepare for the future. Until now he had concerned himself only with a comfortable life for himself and Nahana, and with advising the king in his dreams of glory. Now Jameson began to have dreams of his own, dreams of the estate he would build for his son.

For years he had acted as the king's representative, forming casual friendships with men from many nations. He had regularly picked their brains for news of the world and conditions of trade. An idea began to form as the infant grew in Nahana's womb.

But the Spanish vessel for which he waited did not drop anchor until Nahana was close to term. Jameson's message brought ashore Carlos Mentez, flamboyant in a wide-brimmed hat and colorful sash. When an admiring crowd of Hawaiians had dispersed, Jameson led him along a jungle trail to a high promontory.

"Look," Jameson said, pointing to the valley beyond.

A herd of wild horses, dominated by a large stallion, grazed and nudged at one another. Even with their unkempt manes and rough hair, they were obviously well formed and lively. Beyond them, on the slope of the hills, sturdy cattle grazed lazily in the deep grass.

"What do you think?"

Carlos frowned. "The horses, they are very *fuerte*, very strong."

"No, I meant the cattle. I want to raise them and sell the hides."

Carlos studied the distant herd. "Possibly. They could take the place of the sandalwood. There's not much of that left, is there?"

"No." Jameson broke off a young stalk of sugar cane. He chewed on it a moment, then used it as a baton to point across the valley toward a hillside. Only ragged stumps remained of what had once been a small forest of trees. An occasional blackened tree, burned by lightning, thrust up among the saplings studding the bare area. "The sandalwood is almost gone. That's why I've been looking for something new to trade."

He nodded toward the swaying cane around them. "Sugar cane is a possibility. We'd need more fresh water to cultivate it. But I know more about the hide-and-tallow trade from Boston." He glanced over at Carlos. "Could I raise cattle on this land?"

The man gave an exaggerated shrug. "If the sugar cane grows wild, the land is fertile. Good for cows."

"But the cattle are wild now. Can they be bred? Domesticated?"

Carlos laughed. "Simple, my friend. First you catch a cow, then you catch a bull. God has planned the rest."

"Then there's one problem."

"I understand. The cattle do not belong to you. But that is nothing! In my country the cattle all belonged to the great *estancias*. But pretty soon many cattle belonged to me."

Jameson chuckled. "Maybe that's why you're on a ship instead of back in your country."

"You have a point of truth, señor, a valid point. But do not worry about these cattle. We will find a way to make them yours."

"That's not what I meant. They're forbidden. No one's allowed even to touch them. King Kamehameha put a *kapu* on them—the cattle and the horses, too."

"*Kapu!*" Carlos exclaimed, his eyes widening. "That is different. Then it is impossible."

"Maybe not. Kamehameha knows the sandalwood is running out, but he still wants *haole* goods from the trading ships. I may be able to persuade him to remove his *kapu*. But even if I can, I'll need help in running the business. I know something about the hide-and-tallow trade, and you know about raising cattle. What do you say, Carlos?"

A grin tugged at the corner of the Spaniard's mouth. "On the sea I get *mareda*, seasick. But there is not a horse I cannot ride. And I would have my compadres to work with me. So, I say yes."

Jameson shook his extended hand. "Then it's settled. That is, *if* I can convince Kamehameha."

With the passing of time, Kamehameha had transferred most of his passionate energy from the bedding of his wives to the pleasures of eating. Jameson chose a day when he and the king were sharing a noonday meal to discuss the subject of the cattle. Fine china dishes and silver utensils had been set out for Jameson's benefit, but since his host was eating his own meal in the old style, seated on a mat and dipping his meat from a bowl with his fingers, Jameson did the same.

Kamehameha listened absently to his opening remarks. "The cattle, yes. They were a gift from my brother king in Britain."

"I could catch the cattle and start raising them for their hides."

"There is a *kapu* on the cattle."

"I know. Which is a great pity. Because once the sandalwood is gone, we'll need some other commodity to trade with the ships that come to the islands. The cattle would provide hides, meat, tallow. It really is too bad there's a *kapu* on the cattle."

Kamehameha sat for a long moment holding a bite of meat before he popped it into his mouth and smiled. "It's *my kapu*."

"Yes, no one is allowed to touch the cattle."

"I put my *kapu* on the cattle so that one day five cattle would become ten and then a hundred and many more. Now that the sandalwood is almost gone, it is time to take away my *kapu*."

Jameson was delighted. "And on the horses, too? We'll need them to herd the cattle."

"Yes. On the horses, too."

"Wonderful! With hides and tallow and meat, there will be even more trade than before. And I've already found some men who know how to raise cattle—the sailors from the Spanish ship, the *Españolas*."

"*Paniolas*," the king repeated.

"I want to bring them to the island to . . ."

"No."

"But I have to have experienced help."

"No. You cannot bring foreigners to live on the island. Only you are allowed."

"You don't understand. I..."

The king shook his head firmly. "No, Jameson, I do not wish to listen to this anymore."

From her corner, Kaahumanu spoke softly. "I wish to hear him."

Kamehameha glanced at her, then sighed with resignation and signaled Jameson to continue.

"Just taking the *kapus* off the horses and cattle isn't enough. You can't raise cattle without labor. I need experienced men, men who know how to domesticate the cattle, breed them, and slaughter them. And we'll need other *haoles* to build a real dock and piers where the bay is, so more ships can come to load our goods."

Kamehameha rose and walked to where he could look across the broad, glittering bay. When he turned back, his expression was pensive. "You remember, Jameson?" he asked. "The cannon? The day we sailed off for Maui? You had doubts. But I knew we would conquer because the chants foretold that Kamehameha would be born under a fire in the sky and live to make all the islands one."

"And now that you've united the other islands, it is time to make them rich and powerful like other nations," Jameson pointed out.

Kaahumanu agreed. "Jameson is right. We are a nation. We must learn to be like the *haole* nations."

The old flash of irony shone in Kamehameha's smile. "Why? Let the *haole* nations be like us!"

"But they have things you need," Jameson said. "Medicines, machines, other things you want. And you can have all that in exchange for the cattle if you'll just let me bring in men to get it started."

"No. I will never give any of my land to those not of the land. Not even to you, Jameson."

"But you don't have to give them land. Just let them live and work on the island. There's sugar cane growing wild all over. We could grow that for trade, too, if we brought in those who know how to cultivate it properly. The people on the island don't know these things."

"My people know what they need to know, what they have needed to know for centuries. I have spoken. I will listen no more." Kamehameha stalked out of the palace into the compound.

Jameson banged his fist against the tapa mat on the floor. Then he sighed and said to Kaahumanu, "He always does that. He gives with the left hand and takes back with the right. The sandalwood's almost gone. There won't be anything to trade if he won't let me bring in *haoles* to raise cattle and sugar cane. Why can't he understand?"

"Because he is afraid."

He turned to stare at her. "Kamehameha? No, he's never been afraid of anything. I know. I fought beside him."

"It is not of warriors or guns that Kamehameha has fear. It is of the chant, of the prophecy that the gods will set the people against him. That they will tear away his cloak and he will die."

"But how could bringing in workers turn his people against him? There would be more for everyone. We can have the same things here as in the rest of the world."

Kaahumanu nodded. "That's what I want, Jameson."

"But not Kamehameha."

"Then we must make him want it. We will bring in the *paniolas* you need."

"How?" Jameson slumped down on the tapa mat. "Defy Kamehameha? No one can do that!"

"You can, Jameson." Her voice was soft and almost sad. "You are young. Kamehameha grows old. You are strong;

Kamehameha grows fearful." She gestured toward their sleeping mat. "I know. Defy him. Show him your strength and conviction, and *then* he will say yes."

But Jameson shook his head. "Not now. Not when Nahana is so close to having my child. I can't risk Kamehameha ordering me off the island and being sent away from Nahana."

Kaahumanu was clearly surprised. "I haven't seen you afraid before."

"In Boston they call it Yankee good sense. You don't try to open a locked door until you have the key."

As he left the palace, his eyes strayed to the blue bay beyond the trees. But it was a different sweep of sea that he remembered: Boston harbor under glowering clouds and the *Felicity Ann* swaying gracefully at anchor. How long ago that was! Jameson shook his head. There were more important things to consider now.

Kaahumanu's counsel was right, of course. How strong she was in contrast to her yielding beauty! And her surprise at his hesitation was understandable. He was being more cautious with the king than he usually was. But Nahana was due to deliver soon.

The future of his son who swelled beneath her garments depended on his skill at managing both the king and the island's resources.

Jameson had added a nursery room to their hut. He was proud of it, because its addition made the place seem more like a proper house. He especially liked seeing the crèche cradle there, waiting for his child.

Still graceful despite her bulk, Nahana walked toward him, her long, loose tapa robe swaying. "There is little sunshine in your face," she teased him.

Jameson filled his pewter bowl with warm water and honed his razor on the leather strop. "Your father," he explained, as he lathered his face. "He just won't understand. I want to build a future for us, and for our son—a cedar house sent out from Boston, more furniture."

"But we have a house, Jameson. If there is anything we need, others will give it to us. That is the way of our island."

"But it's not my way. I don't want people to give me things. I want to earn them myself, build them, own them. That's the way it's done where I come from. And I want you to have all the things I've shown you in pictures—dresses, pianos, carriages."

"I have you, Jameson. Would I have you more with all those things?"

He laid down his razor and tried to take her in his arms, but her great belly blocked his way. They settled for laying their hands on each other's shoulders and laughing at their ridiculous predicament.

"For such a small person, you certainly are carrying a giant inside you," he said as he leaned to kiss her.

Nahana reached for a tapa cloth to wipe away the lather he'd left on her face, but stopped abruptly, biting to keep herself from crying out.

"What is it?" Jameson asked. "It isn't your time yet, is it?"

Nahana nodded stiffly. "Yes. It started earlier."

"It could be something else. Are you sure?"

"I'm sure." Her face relaxed as the contraction ended. Very calmly she said, "I must go. It will be soon now."

"But there's an American ship coming from Kauai, with a doctor. If you could wait until he gets here..."

Nahana smiled at him and touched her stomach. "But *he* will not wait. Bring Pelika to take me now."

He paused nervously in the door, hating to leave her. But luck was with him. Pelika was only a few yards away. He gestured for her. When he turned back into the room, he saw Nahana pull something from a drawer in the maple dresser. It was a *kii* birth-charm necklace with a suspended fertility god.

At his sigh of annoyance, she moved guiltily as if to hide it in her clothing. Then, with a sharp lift of her head, a gesture Jameson had often seen in her father, she turned to face him with the necklace openly displayed.

"That's just a superstition, Nahana," Jameson insisted. "I thought you'd gotten rid of it."

"No, Jameson. This is a part of our tradition. I need to wear it." She slipped it over her head, adjusted the charm, and looked up into his eyes. "This I must decide for myself."

Pelika bustled importantly through the door and Jameson allowed the distraction to end their dispute. This was no time to teach Nahana the ways of his religion. He was disappointed that she still clung to the old ways, that she put her faith in such a primitive symbol instead of the things he had taught her, but it would be different with his child. From the start he would be able to bring the boy up with a proper understanding of God and civilized society.

He kissed Nahana, urged Godspeed on her, and allowed Pelika to guide her to the birth hut. When they disappeared inside, he paced restlessly back and forth in front of the ominous structure. It did not stand in an ordinary compound with other huts ranged around it; instead, it had been constructed in a flat, open field, all alone except for the carvings and figures that had been placed around the area.

The eight-sided building had no window openings and only a single entrance in front. Strips had been left open in the thatched roof to let in air and sunlight, and would let in rain, Jameson supposed, if one of the island's sudden, violent showers blew up.

He was not alone in his vigil. A small crowd had gathered around the hut: a few children, a couple of old men, and several women young and old. They were treating the birth of his child as an occasion for a picnic. They had brought food, which they shared as they talked quietly among themselves or stared curiously at him.

A tapa mat had been laid carefully before the door of the hut. Ranged on it, like surgical instruments on a tray, lay a row of highly polished birth rocks. Each rock had a different shape and, Jameson presumed, a different use. He would have considered surgical instruments more reassuring.

Aside from the muted conversation of the picnickers, the only sound was the low rhythmic humming of women's voices coming from inside the hut. Try as he might, Jameson could not distinguish Nahana's voice among them. Now and then he edged toward the entrance and peered in.

Except for shafts of sunlight crisscrossing the interior darkness, he could not make out any recognizable shapes. An ancient woman, most of her teeth gone, tugged at his trousers and smiled in reassurance. He could not understand the soft words she spoke, but he returned the smile nervously, knowing from her tone that she was offering comfort.

Encouraged by his smile, the woman pointed first at the hut and then at him, pantomiming the sexual act. One of the woman's companions giggled and the other women joined in, adding their suggestive gestures to the teasing. Embarrassed, Jameson turned away, then heard a sharp moan from inside the hut. By the time he reached the door, a second groan of pain came from inside. He lunged desperately for the door.

The midwife stopped him from entering. Although only of middle age, the woman was massive. Her light, sleeveless robe accented her immense size. In a no-nonsense fashion she barred his way with her huge, muscular arms. When Jameson persisted, she spoke to him in Hawaiian and pushed him aside. Then, kneeling by the tapa mat, she selected two birth rocks.

As she passed him to enter the hut, he pointed at the rocks and asked, "What are those for? *Kela? Kela?*"

Her rapid response and her unfamiliar words made it impossible for him to understand, nor could he figure out the accompanying pantomime. Now he was more apprehensive than ever. The gap-toothed woman was tugging at his clothes again. "*Eia a,*" she said, nodding and cackling. "*Eia aku!*"

A louder, sharper cry came from inside the hut. Jameson pushed past the old woman and rushed through the entrance. Momentarily blinded, Jameson stopped uncertainly, looking for Nahana. A cluster of young girls was gathered, enrapt, at one side of the hut, and the air throbbed with their low, monotonous chanting.

Jameson whirled at a cry from across the room, ready to rush to Nahana. But it was an old kahuna priest, draped with fertility charms, who let out the piercing wail of pain. The priest's stomach had been padded to simulate pregnancy. As he moaned, he pantomimed the pains of labor.

The midwife appeared in front of Jameson, her face distorted by fury. She gestured for him to leave.

"Where's Nahana?" he demanded.

She only shouted at him again, her voice rising with anger.

Nahana called softly from the darkness, "She says you must go out. Men are not allowed in the birth hut."

Jameson hurried to her side. Nahana knelt on a white tapa mat with her plump young servant-nurse Pelika at her side. Her face, looking up at him, was serene and composed. Not so much as a drop of perspiration shone on her smooth forehead. He stared at her in confusion, his own heart pounding wildly.

"But I thought you were in pain," he said. "I heard you cry out."

She shook her head and pointed to the old kahuna. "No, that is the kahuna Hannau. He feels the pain so I will not."

The midwife was still shouting for Jameson to leave.

"I'm staying right here with my wife," Jameson told her in careful Hawaiian. He pointed to the kahuna Hannau. "He's a man. If he can stay, so can I. I'm the father, and I'm not leaving."

Jameson was torn between fear of being in the way and his intense concern for Nahana. The midwife, grunting her annoyance, knelt before Nahana and set out the birth rocks she'd selected.

"What can I do for you?" Jameson asked Nahana.

"Hold me," she whispered, leaning against him. Although he closed his arms around her, he felt queasy watching the midwife pick up the stones and start toward Nahana. He looked away, feeling as if Nahana were supporting him. With Nahana's body tight against him, he felt the powerful contraction that wrenched through her body.

Across the room, the old kahuna gave an anguished cry. Jameson felt his own muscles contract painfully. Only Nahana was serene, stroking his face, comforting him. "It is all right, Jameson. It will be soon now. It is all right."

The midwife had settled in front of Nahana and indeed everything seemed to move very quickly. Within minutes Jameson caught his first sight of a blood-smeared infant. He fought wildly to keep from retching. Then the child cried, a hiccuping cry that grew to a lusty squall. The midwife lifted the child, turning it from side to side for all to see.

"Let me hold him," Jameson pleaded.

"Wahine," the midwife corrected him.

It took a moment for her words to register. Somehow, he had never expected to have a daughter. But he was quick to speak, for Nahana's sake. "Oh, a girl." Looking at the child, he struggled for words to cover his disappointment. "She's beautiful, perfect."

Nahana clearly didn't view the froglike, bloody child as he did. Her face radiated pride and delight. "Oh, Jameson," she cried. "She is so *haole*, so..." She reached out and touched his face tenderly. "So *melemele*, like you, Jameson. I am sorry it wasn't a boy, for you, but..."

Before she could finish, her eyes widened in shock and she clasped herself against a great contraction shuddering through her body.

"What is it?" Jameson asked. "What's wrong?"

The midwife was babbling in excited Hawaiian. Nahana, in the grip of her pain, did not reply. She didn't need to. His answer came in a fresh birth cry. Glancing down, he stared at the second baby in disbelief. "Twins! It's a boy! Look, Nahana, it's a boy!"

The midwife's face was no longer wreathed with joy as she lifted the child and held him up for all to see. Except for Jameson's exultant words, the room had fallen silent as the watchers stared at the baby. He was a bigger child than his sister, and darker in complexion. He squalled lustily, stretching long, shapely legs in protest at the cooler air. He looked truly Hawaiian, with a cap of black hair and high cheekbones like his grandfather, the king.

Only when the midwife, her eyes downcast, turned his son to face him did Jameson see the birthmark along one side of the baby's neck. It was a familiar shape and color, the outline of the deadly stingray fish that haunted the bay beyond the lagoon.

"*Lupe... ino, ino,*" the midwife said, her tone doleful.

CHAPTER FOURTEEN

SHRINES

Jameson spent his first night of fatherhood without sleep. After tossing restlessly on his tapa mat for a while, he walked the beach until he had shepherded the moon across the tropic sky. He had become the steward of those helpless, wailing children. Old sermons haunted him with their threat of the fate of souls who were not saved. His newborn son, as well as the child's sister, must be baptized properly, and at once.

Until he tried to set up the baptism, he didn't realize how poor his memory was. Too much time had passed, and he found himself unable to recall the details from his church back in Boston. All he could picture were the rows of stark wooden pews, the watery sunlight leaking through narrow windows, and the dark garments of the congregation. It troubled him that he couldn't make the church services come alive in his mind.

Setting up the baptismal altar outside his hut took the better part of the morning. Jameson moved the dining table outside and covered it with a tapa cloth that fell almost to the earth. He fashioned a cross by binding two straight sticks together with thongs. The altar might have looked drab and intimidating if not for the backdrop of a giant vine spilling scarlet blossoms.

Dressing suitably for a religious service strained Jameson's resources. Eventually he settled for the few *haole* garments that still hung together. Carlos Mentez and his men, attracted by this activity, joined Jameson as he filled his pewter bowl with water.

Kaahumanu had come to see the babies and stood watching Jameson's preparations. She was dressed in as unchurchly a style as one could imagine. Her blouse was cut low and tied in a sarong style that emphasized her voluptuous curves. With this she wore every possible kind of *haole* jewelry—necklaces, brooches, and elaborate bracelets and rings.

Curiosity overcame her as Jameson set down the bowl. "What is that, Jameson? To drink from?"

"No, it's . . . Just wait a minute and I'll show you."

As he turned back toward the hut she caught his arm. Her voice was low and conspiratorial when she nodded toward the men on the beach. "The *paniolas*. Are you talking to them about the cattle?"

"No, they're here because this is a christening. They're Christians like me. It makes it more proper."

She regarded him intently. "When their ship goes, they will go too, if you do not act."

"I'll try to talk to Kamehameha again before that happens. Maybe he'll change his mind."

"No. He will only change his mind if you force him. You must do that."

"Today is for my children. I don't want to think about anything else." Jameson pulled his arm away and moved to the door of the hut. "Come, Nahana," he called. "Bring the children out now."

They came at once, Nahana carrying one child and Pelika the other. Both infants were wrapped in soft tapa bunting. Jameson frowned. "They have to be wearing something white. Are they?"

Nahana spoke in a strangely flat voice. "Yes, white *kiapas*."

"I guess that will do." He pointed to a spot near the altar. "Hold them over there."

Nahana moved dazedly, as though she were numb. Jameson caught her hand and pressed it. "Don't be concerned. This won't hurt them," he said.

He moved to the homemade altar and waved the others forward for the ceremony. "First there's the part that's supposed to be said before the christening. There should be a proper minister, but I'll try to remember." Folding his hands and bowing his head slightly, he recalled a few opening words. "In the true sacrament of celebration before thee, and humbly..." He paused, forgetting what came next.

Carlos stepped forward tentatively. "Perhaps, señor, I could be of help. Just in the sacred invocation, if you will allow me."

Jameson nodded uncertainly and stepped aside. In front of the altar, Carlos crossed himself and then genuflected. *"Ego te baptismo in nomine patris et filii et spiritus sancti. Amen."*

"Was that Latin?" Jameson asked.

Carlos nodded. "When I was very young I studied to be a priest in the seminary. In truth, I believe I would have made an excellent cardinal, even Pope, perhaps."

"But what you did must be Catholic, and I'm a Protestant."

Carlos's tone was gentle, even a little amused. "I think God will look the other way this once."

"Of course." Jameson turned to the others. "It's time for the baptism and christening."

For a moment, Nahana looked as though she would speak. Jameson was relieved when she caught her lip between her teeth and silently handed him his infant son. With the baby in one arm, Jameson gestured to the sweep of land beyond. "My son, this is the land where we live now, our land. You will grow to be a man here, and share in everything I build for my family."

At the pewter basin he suddenly hesitated. "Wait," he said. "The girl was born first, and I think she's supposed to be baptized first." He handed the boy back to Nahana and took the girl from Pelika. At the basin he paused again and asked Nahana, "What was your mother's name?"

"Ahukai."

"Ahukai." The name did not sound the same on his tongue, but Nahana nodded without lifting her eyes. "And my mother's name was Elizabeth." He dropped the tapa bunting and held the howling baby directly over the basin of water. "I christen thee Ahukai Elizabeth Jameson in the name of the Father, the Son, and the Holy Ghost."

As he lowered the child into the makeshift baptismal font, Pelika cried out.

Kaahumanu frowned. "Are you going to drown her because she is female?"

"Of course not! It's just a little water. This is done so she can be a Christian and go to heaven to live forever. Otherwise, if she died, her soul would be cast forever into purgatory."

Nahana stared at him. "Like the place called hell you told me of?"

"No, no, nothing like that. There's no eternal fire in purgatory." He turned to Carlos. "Is there?"

Again the shadow of a smile played around Carlos's mouth. "No, señor. Some very excellent but unfortunate souls are now in purgatory, it is said."

Jameson wrapped the bunting around his daughter and

returned her to Pelika. When he reached for his son, Nahana held the child tightly to her breast.

Her eyes burned with an intense light. "Jameson, if this is done, this water, then he will live forever in the place of heaven?"

"That's right."

"Even if there is death and his breath is gone?"

"Yes."

Although she released the child into his hands, her expression remained uncertain. She watched solemnly as Jameson dipped the child into the water.

"I christen thee Robert Jameson, Junior," he said. "In the name of the Father, the Son, and the Holy Ghost."

Relieved that this important business had been taken care of, Jameson declared the ceremony over. The Spaniards came forward to congratulate him, laughing and slapping his back. Only Kaahumanu stood apart, watching thoughtfully.

Jameson stirred in his sleep, disturbed by footsteps in the room. Before he could tug himself awake, he felt a gentle touch on his head and his bare shoulder. Still struggling for consciousness, he grasped the arm, murmuring, "Nahana."

"No." The soft voice was very close.

Jameson opened his eyes to find Kaahumanu kneeling at his side, her face near his. He sat up, shrugging off sleep. "Kaahumanu! What is it? Do you want Nahana?"

She shook her head and gestured toward the other side of his bed. He stared in disbelief to find it empty.

"Nahana," he called softly, looking around the dark room. "Nahana!"

He grabbed his clothing from the floor and pulled it on as he climbed out of bed. Pushing aside the screen that separated the nursery from the rest of the house, he surveyed the dark room. Pelika was curled in sleep on a tapa mat between the two cradles. Ahukai Elizabeth slept quietly in one of them. The other crib was empty. There was no sign of Nahana in the room.

Jameson shook Pelika's shoulder until she awakened. "Where's Nahana? Where is my son?"

The frightened girl only whimpered in his grasp, either not understanding him or not knowing what to tell him. Kaahumanu waited silently beside his bed in the main room. He swung around to her. "Where are my wife and son?"

"Come. You will see."

The jungle paths looked unfamiliar by moonlight. Kaahumanu led him a long distance before she slowed her pace in a wooded area. When she stopped, he looked around in confusion.

"Where?" he asked. "Where are they?"

She made a gesture of silence and pointed down a side path. As soon as they started down the path he saw the flickering of torches ahead. Kaahumanu fell behind, barely keeping up as he ran toward the edge of a clearing.

Jameson saw a rounded shrine platform in the center of the open space. Nahana was on the shrine with King Kamehameha, Maakoa, the midwife, and several of Maakoa's priests. By the light of the torches Jameson saw the *kii* birth-charm necklace shining against Nahana's throat. She stood absolutely still with young Robert pressed against her breast.

The statues around the shrine were of the natives' benevolent gods—the gods of fertility, of love and peace, and plenty. A priest chanted softly. Kamehameha, in full royal regalia, stood rigidly beside Nahana. Puzzled, Jameson stepped back and whispered to Kaahumanu, "What is this, some kind of religious ceremony? A christening or something?"

"You will see."

Without leaving the cover of the woods, Jameson drew as close as he could to the shrine. When Maakoa approached her, Nahana cringed, holding her baby even closer. Maakoa spoke to her in a voice so gentle that Jameson barely recognized it. Nahana dropped her eyes and held the baby before her. The high priest made a sign over the tiny form and spoke words that Jameson could not hear.

When he fell silent, Nahana, walking as if in a deep trance, turned and carried the baby to the midwife. She stared down into her son's face for a long moment before handing the child over to the woman.

Jameson, suddenly struck by a sense of nameless urgency, raced toward the shrine. The infant began to howl as the midwife placed him on the flat-topped rock, lifted a small shale knife, and made ritualistic gestures over the small, heaving chest.

Fear doubled Jameson's speed. He reached the shrine in a matter of seconds. Acting instinctively, he grabbed the knife from the midwife's hand, not even noticing that he cut himself. He turned to Kamehameha and demanded in a loud voice, "What is this? What are you doing with my son?"

When the king didn't answer, Jameson wheeled on his wife. "Nahana, what is happening here?"

She pointed to the birthmark on the baby's neck. "That is *lupe*, the stingray, the black fish that kills our people. It is a sign of evil. I will be cursed, unable ever to bear another child if breath is not taken from him."

Jameson tried to absorb the enormity of her words. "Take away his breath? Kill him? They were going to *kill* my son?"

Furious, he strode across the shrine, shoved the midwife aside, and picked up the baby. "No one is going to touch my son. Not now. Not ever." With the infant clasped tightly against him, Jameson seized Nahana's arm with his free hand. Before he could move away, Maakoa and two priests stepped forward to bar his way.

Maakoa spoke of evil, but Jameson refused to listen.

Tugging Nahana behind him, he pushed his way past Maakoa and the priests, only to find King Kamehameha barring his path. For long minutes the two men stared at each other in tense silence.

Jameson finally spoke. His voice was soft, but his outrage gave the words a sense of menace. "The only way anyone is going to kill my son is to kill me first."

After another long moment, the king stepped aside and motioned Jameson past. Holding tight to both the baby and his wife, Jameson started back through the jungle. Kaahumanu was nowhere in sight.

Jameson didn't speak to Nahana through the long walk home. He didn't know what to say. The gulf of misunderstanding that yawned between them was too vast to be crossed by words.

The baby was sleeping soundly by the time they reached their hut. Jameson carried him into the nursery, placed him gently in the empty crib, and rocked it for a moment when the child stirred and stretched. Leaning down, he tenderly kissed the baby's dark forehead. Then he passed the other crib, pausing to straighten the tapa cover over his daughter before returning to the room where Nahana waited for him.

She stood very stiff and straight. "You are angry with me, Jameson."

"No," he lied. "Not angry, just..." The terror of the scene at the shrine recaptured his mind, and he shuddered. "You're my wife, Nahana. I have to be able to count on you to behave a certain way. Do you understand? That means you have to do things my way. No more *kapus*. No more believing in evil marks and curses. No more hanging on to things like that *kii* birth charm." He lifted the offending necklace that was suspended around her throat and clenched it in his fist. "From now on you can't believe in *any* of that!"

She nodded. "I will believe your way, too."

"No, not my way *too*. *Only* my way. I've had enough of curses and *kapus*. Human life is sacred! You don't kill people for stepping on shadows or eating something they're not supposed to, or sitting in the wrong place! My children are not going to grow up believing there are demons in volcanoes and evil spirits in rocks. They're going to be Christian, like us. Do you understand how it has to be from now on?"

Nahana's shoulders slumped. "If I must give up the ways of my people, the protection of my gods, I will be scorned by my family, shunned by my friends. You ask too much of me."

"Not too much," he insisted, drawing her against his chest. "If your gods had their way, our son would be dead now. For no reason except that he has a birthmark. No one thinks a thing of birthmarks in New England. They aren't the sign of curses or ill-fated omens. Nahana, this is all superstition."

"And what was that you did today?" she demanded, resentment overcoming her reticence. "What was that ceremony if not a kind of sacrifice to your God? You promised our children would obey him. And you placed great faith in the sticks you tied together, and the words you used. And you spoke of a Ghost. What is a Holy Ghost if not a spirit? You don't make any sense to me, Jameson."

He sighed and held her at arm's length. "In time I'll learn to explain it better, Nahana. You'll have to trust me. I'm your husband, and in my religion that means you must obey me. I want you to promise to obey me in this matter. It's very important."

Nahana straightened her shoulders and met his gaze, but there was a great sadness in her dark eyes. "I love you, and I will do as you ask, Jameson." She reached for the *kii* birth charm he still clenched in his hand. Reluctantly, he gave it to her. Nahana walked to the stove and dropped the charm into the dying embers.

Standing there in the faint glow, she said, "But you must not forbid me to teach our children that they are Hawaiians, too. It would kill me to deny the power of the land and the beauty of the flowers and the warmth of the sun and the greatness of their grandfather Kamehameha. They must never forget that this richness runs in their veins."

Jameson was watching the flames consume the *kii* charm. "Of course," he said, almost absently. "They will learn that they are part Hawaiian, and they will be proud of that heritage. You go to bed now. You must be exhausted." He crossed the room and kissed her tenderly. "I'm going to walk for a little while."

Outside, the landscape was shadowed by the moon. The beauty of the tropical night could not still his restlessness. When he had walked a short distance from the hut, Kaahumanu spoke to him from the darkness.

"I watched you, Jameson," she said, emerging from the darkness and falling in step beside him. "Kamehameha would have struck down a chief or an *alii*. But you are different. Kamehameha has deep respect for you and your *haole* strength."

She moved closer, her hand warm on his bare arm. "Do you still doubt what we can do, Jameson?"

"No. I know what has to be done, and I know that together we can do it." His gaze swept from the broad, moonlit beach to the hut where his wife and children lay. "Together we *will* do it."

Kaahumanu knew her king well. Jameson had established his strength, and Kamehameha listened and agreed to his plans. By following Kaahumanu's counsel over the next years, Jameson was able to fulfill many of his ambitions for the islands.

One of the first changes was the use of horses for on-land transportation. Carlos had always boasted that he could handle any horse. Now both his word and his skill were sorely tested in the unforgettable battle between the old stallion and the *haole* newcomer. The king of Kamehameha's wild herds was a giant in both size and spirit. And wily. And swift. Carlos finally tricked the fierce stallion into a rope. Into the corral he was thrown, snorting and spraying fury, but in time all the horses were broken, and with bridles slid over their heads they were led wherever Carlos wished. After nameless centuries of walking through the green, shaded paths of the jungle, men now crossed the island on horseback.

The wide-horned bull who had sired the island's wild cattle was the next to fall to the lasso of Carlos Mentez. The Hawaiians joined the *paniolas* to work as cowboys, adding Spanish kerchiefs and scarves to their *pii* and bark sandals.

After centuries of long, scarlet sunsets with sweet wafting winds, there was now the scent of death in the air. The valley that had swayed with thigh-deep grass and flowers was dotted with slaughter pens, and tanning sheds with huge vats of smoking acid, and lines of stretched hides.

And that was progress. Constant changes dragging the primitive society into the nineteenth century.

The years flew by. The Jameson twins grew to toddlers, then to curious children. And all the while their world changed around them. The masts of trading ships were frequently seen at the island. At the newly constructed dock, men from every nation were welcomed by *wahines* whose eager sensuality was a continual delight.

The trade items rowed in by side boats were different now. The docks still received shipments of maple furniture and barrels of fine china and *haole* linen for the houses of the king and the other *alii,* but most of the imports were more mundane. Saddles and bridles, tanning chemicals, tools, and machines lined the dock.

Jameson built a gaunt New England house from imported lumber. It stood on the site of their beach hut and echoed with the laughter and tears of the growing children.

Tom Haggers and his *haole* crew came, too. His job of bringing the sugar cane under control was every bit as difficult as that of taming the livestock. Left alone, the cane grew rampant in open fields and on the hillsides, yielding its sweet, uneven harvest. When men set the seedlings carefully in newly furrowed land, the plants yellowed and died. The fine dry soil eroded when it rained and blew away when the sun shone. No roots formed.

Not even an army of natives could carry enough water to the thirsty soil. Tom Haggers, gesturing and cursing, supervised the building of the scaffold and the setting of the drill. He harnessed Hawaiian workers four abreast, like steers. They circled endlessly, straining against leather to drive the drill bit deeper and deeper into the stubborn lava-born soil.

The natives had never heard anything like the rumble that rose from the heart of the island. When the sound grew to a deafening roar, Haggers warned his crewmen back. The island shuddered with a vast convulsion as the water broke free of the land. The geyser towered above the highest palm trees, a vast column of crystal artesian water filling the air with a multitude of rainbows.

The Jameson twins ran along the beach, under the watchful eyes of Nahana and Pelika, and shouted with delight at this spectacle.

And the artesian well was tamed into canals that carried sweet, clear water to the sugar cane fields, turning them lush and green behind *haole* fences.

Jameson welcomed the changes, applauded the signs of civilization, and continued to build an estate for his family.

CHAPTER FIFTEEN

ANCIENT PROPHECIES

At seven years of age, the Jameson twins were still as different in appearance as they had been at birth. Robert, his sweet nature apparent in his face, was a darkly handsome child with the black hair and glowing dark eyes of his mother. Elizabeth was as fair as her brother was dark. Her features were as fine as a china doll's, and she brimmed with liveliness and spirit. Though her movements were quick, her bright blue eyes were watchful.

A full moon hung over the island the night of the king's birthday party. Jameson, dressed in formal *haole* clothes for the event, walked proudly through the rooms of his proper house while he waited for the other members of his family. When he heard Pelika coming down the narrow stairway from the second floor, he called to her, "Where are the twins? Are they getting dressed?"

"Upstairs," she said tentatively, still a little insecure in the *haole* language.

"Try to hurry them up a bit, would you?"

Nahana appeared at the door of the back sitting parlor, slim and graceful as always. She was wearing a long draped tapa sarong, brightly patterned and knotted on one shoulder. When Jameson frowned, she turned to examine herself nervously in the mirror.

"What is it, Jameson?"

"Nothing. Just... Why aren't you wearing the dress I had sent from Boston? After all, it's your father's birthday."

"That's why I put this on, for him. But I will change if you don't like me in this."

"I like you in anything... or in nothing." He drew her close, inhaling the sweet scent of her hair. "How can I love you so much for so long?" he whispered.

The rare eloquence of the moment was shattered by the twins, who bounded down the stairs and danced around their parents. Jameson couldn't help laughing. "Look at you, Robert. What good is your cavalry uniform if you don't button it properly? What are you two doing down here anyway? Hurry up and finish dressing. I want to show you off. And remember what we have planned, Robert. Be sure your boots are polished!"

Robert clattered back up the stairs but Elizabeth didn't move. She was costumed as a Dresden shepherdess in a full-skirted dress with frilly pantaloons. Her glowing blond hair was trimmed with blue ribbons that matched her eyes. She gazed wistfully up at her father.

Jameson forced a smile, though he was becoming impatient. "You look very nice, too, Elizabeth, but we have to be leaving and you need to put on your shoes. Hurry now!" And he turned his attention back to Nahana.

* * *

Memories came unbidden as Jameson stepped into the clearing he had had decorated for Kamehameha's birthday celebration. Jameson remembered his first luau there, with Kekua at his side. How long ago that had been. How many changes. Nahana had been a girl then and he a lad of just twenty.

Instead of the steer that browned and sizzled in the huge fire pit, the meat that night years ago had been a whole pig and a carefully fattened dog. Jameson smiled to himself, remembering his shipmates' reactions. The only *haoles* in the clearing had been the wide-eyed crew members from the *Felicity Ann*. Now the *paniolas*, the other *haoles*, and the Hawaiians mingled everywhere around the clearing. Only the nobility sat apart.

Many of the Hawaiians had added *haole* touches to their clothing, but the chiefs who governed the other islands for Kamehameha were garbed in their native dress and the glorious feathers of their offices. As always, Jameson looked especially for Hanakea, the governor of Maui. He would never forget how close he had come to losing Nahana to this man. Hanakea stood apart with Maakoa. Neither man looked festive.

A line of *wahines* danced the hula to the leering delight of the *haoles* and the admiration of the Hawaiians. The crowd drew back, bowing, as the king approached. Kamehameha moved with the majesty of both size and station, with Kaahumanu on his arm and Keopuolani and Liholiho following.

The years had grayed Kamehameha, stooping his back and slowing his steps. They had been kinder to Kaahumanu. She had gained dignity and authority, but her beauty, unlike that of Keopuolani, was not buried under the massive burden of flesh that aging usually brought *wahines*. Liholiho, a young man now, was dressed elaborately in the most foppish *haole* attire.

Hanakea bowed respectfully before the king. "Many

things have changed since I last came here from Maui," he said.

"Yes," Kaahumanu agreed. "Jameson built all this."

Hanakea ignored her and gestured toward the women dancing. "Now women dance publicly before men."

The king shrugged. "That was not a sacred *kapu*." He pointed to the eating areas. "You see, women still do not eat meat and still sit apart."

"There are more *haoles* on our land now," Hanakea continued. "Some of the other island chiefs fear with me that still more will come."

Kamehameha straightened himself defensively. "The *haoles* do not have land. They will never own land."

The young chief studied his king for a long moment. "Does Kamehameha swear his word to that?"

Kamehameha stared at the younger man. Even in his great age he was taller than this chief, broader, and stronger. "You are Hanakea, chief of Maui," he reminded the young man. "I am Kamehameha, king of all the islands. Kamehameha swears his words only to the gods." He paused, glancing at the crowd in the clearing. "The people do not wish the *haole* to leave."

Hanakea bowed stiffly and moved away. Maakoa's soft voice just reached the king: "The gods see what people do not see. Remember the prophecy of the chants. He who makes the people one will be a god until the people tear away his false cloak and see he is not a god. Then he will be no more."

Carlos Mentez was resplendent in a Spanish costume with a brilliant sash. He led a well-groomed pony into the center of the clearing. Young Robert Jameson sat proudly on its back. The guests stepped back, smiling, as a *paniola* set a series of three barriers across the open space.

"Arriba vanquero!" Carlos shouted, giving the animal a sharp slap on the rump.

Robert, his handsome dark face shining with pride, jumped the pony over the barriers flawlessly and ended near his grandfather. King Kamehameha, laughing with delight, swept the boy from the saddle and held him high, then set him down by his sister, embracing them both.

"Everyone, listen!" he said. "Now my grandchildren will say the *mele inoa* for Kamehameha." For the sake of the *haoles*, he added, "The *mele inoa* is the name chant that unites our people for all time, through the names of all who came before, who are never to be forgotten."

To start the children off, he began chanting slowly, *"Kamehameha loaa inoa Kaloa..."*

The king's voice droned on and both children kept up with him for a short span. Then only Elizabeth was able to continue, going back and back and back. Jameson stared at his little Dresden doll, then at Nahana. He had not precisely forbidden that his children learn the name chant, but he certainly hadn't encouraged it.

Kamehameha smiled at Elizabeth and patted her head. "You look like the *haole*, and yet you are more Hawaiian than your brother," he said.

Jameson interrupted to promise, "Robert will learn the *mele inoa* for your next birthday. He's been busy practicing his jumps on the pony."

"Nothing is more important than learning the *mele inoa*," Kamehameha informed him coolly. His disapproval expanded to include Nahana, who stood with her head bowed. "You have forgotten where you came from, my daughter. Perhaps the big house and the *haole* clothes and the wood furniture have made you lose touch with your land and your ancestry."

Nahana shook her head fiercely but could find no words to defend herself. Jameson put an arm protectively around her shoulders. "No, they haven't. It was Nahana who taught Elizabeth the name chant. Nahana's heritage is very important to her." *Too important*, he thought to himself, but this was no time to speak such heresy. "It's late for the children. Pelika, take them back to the house."

The episode had soured the mood of the party. Jameson quickly assumed his role of host and took two glasses from a nearby table and handed one to the king. "I think it's time for a birthday toast. I'm not much of a hand at this, but I'll give it a try."

He filled both glasses with brandy and held up his own. "To the great and renowned Kamehameha, king of all the islands, on his birthday." He paused, smiling. "I'm not going to give his age away, though I could figure it out because he was born the year Halley's comet went around the earth."

"Comet?" The king sounded puzzled.

"Halley's comet. That's what made the light up in the sky the year you were born. It happened everywhere."

"No," the king corrected him. "Only here. Pele sent a fire into the sky to foretell that I would be born."

"All right, Pele," Jameson said, his tone soothing. He raised his glass higher. "To the great Kamehameha! May he live forever and always be young!"

There were cheers, and clapping, and raising of glasses in toasts, and more toasts. Jameson, having touched his glass against the king's, emptied it. Kamehameha sipped at his, made a face, and set down his glass.

Flushed with excitement and brandy, Jameson waved again for silence. "Wait! Wait! I've got something more to say. In Hawaiian, Kamehameha means 'the lonely one,' isn't that right, Nahana?" At her nod, he went on. "But to me, it should mean 'the farsighted one.' Everything that's here, all the new things, all the changes, none of it could have happened without King Kamehameha and Queen Kaahumanu."

He raised his glass and drank it down, as did the crowd. But although the king lifted his glass, he did not drink.

Carlos leaned down to whisper in Nahana's ear, "Señora Jameson does not look happy."

She withdrew her gaze from two young Hawaiian men she'd been watching. "My people aren't accustomed to strong drink."

"I wish the same could be said of my own."

Nahana smiled politely, but her eyes returned to the young Hawaiians whose flushed faces and angry expressions bothered her. And just as disagreeable were Maakoa and Hanakea standing apart from the crowd and glowering at Jameson and Kamehameha. Kaahumanu moved toward the king, blocking him from the approaching priest and Mauian chief. "Jameson is right," she said softly. "You *will* live forever. You will be forever young."

A little unsteady on his feet, Jameson signaled again for the attention of the crowd. "What's a birthday party without a present?" he cried. "Come, Carlos, over here."

Carlos, smiling broadly, left Nahana's side to join Jameson. He carried a bulky package concealed by tapa cloth.

"Do you remember the Portuguese ship and the captain's uniform you liked so much?" Jameson asked the king. "No, that's not what this is. It's better. Carlos, give it to him!"

Removing the tapa cloth, Carlos revealed an incredibly ornate royal cloak. The glowing velvet was richly decorated with swirling embroidery and patterns in metallic braiding.

"This," Jameson announced proudly, "is the royal cape of King Ferdinand of Spain. Isn't that true, Carlos?"

The Spaniard nodded soberly. "The sacred truth. It was sworn to me that this very garment was worn when he sent

Columbus to discover the world. And now it is yours. You must put it on."

Kamehameha held the cloak, hesitating. "This king of *paniolas*, he was a great king?"

"The greatest of all kings... except for King Kamehameha."

As he spoke Carlos lifted the cloak from the king's hands and draped it around his shoulders. Surprised, the king stirred beneath the cloak and stroked the unfamiliar fabric. Obviously delighted at the feel of it, the king took a couple of steps, watching the cape swirl around him. He beamed with pride and pleasure.

Liholiho watched his father with envy. Maakoa turned away in fury. The musicians—some American fiddlers and a number of *paniolas* with guitars—joined forces in a ragged attempt at a march of triumph as the king displayed his magnificent gift. What the music lacked in harmony, the audience made up in spirited clapping and shouting.

Carlos, holding a wine bottle aloft, leaped up on the pavilion beside the musicians and gestured toward Jameson and Nahana. "Compadres!" he called. "Now let us drink to our patron and his most beautiful wife. To Jameson and his Señora Nahana."

The younger members of the group, both Hawaiian and *haole*, seized this new opportunity to drink. Carlos called for music and commanded the company to dance. The musicians shifted from their mood of pomp and circumstance to a spirited flamenco tune.

Jameson led Nahana out onto the pavilion floor. Elated with wine and triumph, he held her close, savoring the sensual response that her nearness always brought him. The beat of the music seemed to be the beat of his own pulse against her. For some time he was carried away before remembering where they were. He held her apart and called to the guests, "Dance! Come, everyone dance!"

Paniola and *haole* men gradually took the floor with Hawaiian girls. It was some time before the first daring Hawaiian couples joined them. The tempo of the music quickened, and snatches of conversation and laughter rose all around.

One of the two young men Nahana had been watching earlier challenged the other to a wrestling contest. They chose a spot that was shielded from the king's view, and a crowd of supporters gathered behind each contestant, cheering their favorites.

Lomeoa, the older of the two men, bested his rival, Nakio, with a sudden burst of strength. Still wearing his *haole* stovepipe hat, Lomeoa triumphantly seized a bottle of whiskey from Nakio. Swaggering drunkenly past his opponent, he offered the prize to a sultry *wahine* who had been cheering Nakio on. The girl drew back, her gaze on Nakio.

Exploding with drunken fury, Nakio lunged at Lomeoa, knocked his hat off and stamped on it, and began punching with his fists.

Like wind-driven fire, the aimless drunken fight spread through the nearby young people. Pavilion posts fell in a tangle of decorations, and guests scattered before the random violence of the young men. Jameson realized the fight was not going to burn out on its own and motioned the musicians to silence. Leaving Nahana in the center of the dance floor, he made his way quickly to the spreading fight.

The king must have heard the commotion at the same time. Jameson saw him turn to observe the fray cresting only a few feet away. It surged toward him, a tidal wave of flailing arms and legs. Instead of fleeing the onslaught, the king stood immobile, frozen with disbelief.

Jameson plowed into the brawling crowd with Carlos and Haggers on either side. They shouted and pulled the fighters apart in an attempt to divert the drunken mob before it engulfed the king and his party. It was no use.

Kamehameha was a lion among jackals. He staggered from a random blow to his knees. As one drunken hand caught at his royal cape, another pulled it viciously in the opposite direction. The velvet ripped as the cloak was dragged from the king's shoulders and trampled in the dirt.

Kamehameha roared with rage. Silence fell at his voice. The Hawaiians cringed and backed away. The king stood alone, staring down at the destroyed cloak. Hanakea and the other chiefs watched with troubled eyes. Maakoa regarded the king sadly.

Only Kaahumanu dared approach the king. He held a torn scrap of the cape out to her, as if it were evidence. They spoke in voices too low for the others to hear. Then Kamehameha shook his head, dropped the torn cape, and turned away. The *alii* and the commoners alike stood back to let him pass. They kept their eyes lowered. No one spoke to him. Only when he had disappeared from sight did hushed conversations break out around the clearing.

Jameson and Nahana joined Kaahumanu, who stood staring after her husband. "It was all my fault," Jameson said. "I should have seen what was happening and stopped it before... Where is he going?"

"He chooses now to be alone."

"But was he hurt? What was he saying to you?"

Kaahumanu gestured toward the crumpled velvet on the earth. "He spoke of the prophecy of the old kahunas. When the people tear away a false cloak from the great king who has made them one, then his power will be no more, and he will die."

"But that doesn't make any sense. It's all just made-up words! He has to understand that. Someone has to tell him that it's wrong."

Jameson started to follow the king but Nahana caught his arm, holding him back. "He is Kamehameha. Only the gods can tell him that."

Impatiently he shook her hand away. "Prophecies! Curses! You know it's all nonsense."

"I know I have never given you more children. That was foretold," she said sadly.

A despairing sigh escaped him. Rather than argue with her, though, he turned to Kaahumanu. "This prophecy. You don't believe it, do you?"

Kaahumanu was silent for a long moment. "It doesn't matter what I believe, only what Kamehameha believes." Her wistful gaze strayed again to the path Kamehameha had taken through the jungle. "And Kamehameha believes that the prophecy is true."

CHAPTER SIXTEEN

THE KING'S BREATH

Kaahumanu only half-slept. On such a night, with the rain sweeping steadily out of a starless sky, the royal palace was too dark and confined for comfort. The thatched panels that were set into the entrance and windows to keep out the rain also blocked out all light and fresh air. They fluttered in the battering rain, an urgent whispering in the darkness.

Although the king slept beside her as usual, he was not enjoying his natural, sweet sleep. More than once she had been startled awake by his writhing. When she touched his face in a loving gesture, her finger came away moist with his sweat.

A heavy gust of rain swept against the roof. The king thrashed wildly. He moaned and screamed, then sat upright. Even in the dim light Kaahumanu saw his eyes open and staring. She rose on one elbow and touched his shoulder to bring him from this half-dream. He turned to her at once, but it took a moment for him to realize where he was.

"Did you have another bad dream?" she asked.

"This dream was different. Worse." His haunted eyes moved to her face. "Nothing can change the prophecy now."

She knelt beside him, caressing his bare shoulder. "It was only a dream. Come, lie next to me. I won't sleep. I won't let you dream again." She wound her arms around him, fitting her body against his. She stirred a little to warm him with the friction of their joined flesh. But as she trailed her finger across his chest, he turned away and stood up at the side of the bed. Her concern deepened.

"What are you doing?"

"I must go out." He disappeared into a dark corner and returned with his royal feathered cloak draped around his shoulders.

Kaahumanu caught him in her arms, using all her strength to hold him back until he listened to reason. "You can't go out now. There is rain and a strong wind."

He shrugged her off and moved to the entrance. When he pulled aside the thatched barrier, a fan of cold rain swept into the room. The wind was so strong that it rattled the canes in the umbrella stand. Kaahumanu ran to place herself between him and the storm outside. The icy rain stung her flesh.

"I beg you not to go," she pleaded. "You are a great king. The people need you to rule."

"It is too late."

Clinging fiercely to him, she moved her lips close to his, so close that his breath warmed her face. "Listen," she whispered. "We will rule together. You are my breath. I am your breath. We are one."

For a moment he held her shoulders and stared into her face. The tenderness of his expression and the softening of his grip on her arms gave her a moment of hope. But his indecision passed as swiftly as it had come. He pressed past her, thrusting the barrier out of his way. The sounds of the storm doubled as if in triumph.

"I will go with you," she cried, still clinging to him.

He set her firmly aside. "I must go alone."

Kamehameha disappeared almost at once into the darkness. Kaahumanu stood a long time in the doorway, clutching a tapa mat to ward off the rain. Finally she sighed and struggled to replace the thatched covering against the cruel force of the icy wind.

All his life Kamehameha had walked that hill with ease and vigor. Now the sloping incline had become a mountain. Kamehameha thrust his body against the wind's pressure. Rivulets of icy water coursed down his chest and back. The rain that stung his face pasted the feathers of his cloak against his skin.

At last he reached the platform where the rock he had lifted made a sacred monument. He braced his legs widely for balance against the gale and surveyed the circle of *kii* god figures. Kamehameha had to cling with both hands to keep the wind from ripping his sodden cloak from his shoulders. He stared, as if hypnotized, at the surface of the cracked, rain-polished marble slab.

His image was grossly, hideously distorted in it. He moved closer, trying to wipe away the rain streaks with his hand. Reflected beside him were the outstretched arms and talons of one of the god figures. They seemed to be clutching at him in the mirroring surface.

Kamehameha whirled to face this new terror. The god statue rocked on its base from the force of the wind, its talons clawing toward the king each time the figure swayed forward. With an effort of will, Kamehameha stood firm. He squared his shoulders and faced the swaying figure.

"I am Kamehameha," he shouted into the raging storm. "I am Kamehameha. I do not fear even the gods."

A blast of wind whipped the words from his lips. It swirled around him and ripped at the cloak on his back. The king sagged to the earth under the force of the gale, and the wind tore the ravaged feathers from his cape one by one until he lay naked and drenched. The rain still fell on the king and the shrine, and the *kii* god rocked ominously above him.

The storm had driven an American ship to drop anchor in the bay. Jameson had just heard the news of Kamehameha's illness and sent a message out to the ship's doctor, who came immediately. Dr. Hardcastle was a man in his forties. He looked capable enough with his half-glasses on his nose and a medical bag tight in his hand, but he protested volubly when Jameson hurried him on foot to the royal compound.

Two priests barred the way at the entrance to the royal palace. When Jameson tried to force his way past them, several *kapu* guards leaped forward. Jameson hesitated, then stepped back and shouted at the top of his lungs, *"It's Jameson and Nahana. We've brought a doctor for Kamehameha."*

Liholiho appeared at the doorway between two more priests. Jameson was astonished to see that the prince, who had appeared in *haole* peacock clothing for years, was dressed in traditional *alii* garb.

"There was a doctor on the American ship," Jameson explained. "I'm sure he can help your father."

Liholiho hesitated and glanced inside. "Maakoa prepares him now."

"Kamehameha needs a doctor, not a priest."

Kaahumanu appeared in the doorway. "Yes, Jameson," she agreed quietly. "You will come in with your doctor." At her gesture, the priests stepped aside so that Jameson could bring Nahana and the doctor into the room.

The four-poster bed had been taken away. The king lay on a plain tapa mat. Maakoa hovered over him, and Keopuolani, sad-eyed, watched from nearby. Although the king glanced at them as they entered, he showed none of his usual liveliness. His flesh was pale. Even his massive hands lay limp, as though his body had been drained of life.

Nahana knelt at his side and spoke softly to him. The king responded by pushing himself upward. But he said nothing when she told him she'd brought a doctor.

"I'd like to examine the patient privately," Dr. Hardcastle murmured.

Kamehameha said, "No."

Maakoa lowered the king to the tapa mat and crossed to speak quietly with Liholiho. "Maakoa says there is no need for *haole* medicine," the prince said. "The doctor cannot help the king."

"Is Maakoa afraid to let him try?" Jameson asked.

Liholiho chewed nervously on his lip. His mother, Keopuolani, was the first to speak. "My son, *haole* medicine saved your life once. Won't you see if it can save your father's?"

The young man was torn. His gaze shifted from his dying father to Maakoa and back to Kamehameha again. Keopuolani interceded with the priest, begging him to allow Jameson's doctor to look at Kamehameha. Maakoa reluctantly motioned the doctor forward.

As Dr. Hardcastle bent over his patient, Nahana shook her head unhappily, whispering, "I don't think it will do any good."

"But the doctor will be able to help him," Jameson insisted.

Kaahumanu spoke even more softly than Nahana. "I am

afraid he will die, if only because he believes it is the time for his death."

Jameson was used to arguing with such superstition. This time, the almost mystical acceptance of these two women silenced him. He frowned as he watched the doctor listen to the king's chest, thumping it slowly with his finger. After a moment or two the king stirred and waved the doctor away. Dr. Hardcastle shrugged, closed his bag, and rose. Jameson stepped forward to protest, but the doctor cut him off.

"Not here," the doctor said. "I prefer to talk outside."

As they left, Maakoa rose and returned to the king's side. Kaahumanu followed them out but Keopuolani and Liholiho stayed in the palace. Jameson waited, impatient with dread, for the doctor's words.

"He has edema of the pleural cavity. That's water in the chest. I'm afraid it's already affected his heart."

"But isn't there *something* you can do?" Jameson asked.

"I'm sorry. It's hopeless."

The doctor expressed his condolences to them, picked up his bag, and followed the child Jameson sent along to show him his way. No one spoke for several minutes, until Jameson turned to Nahana.

"I can't believe he's dying! I hoped, somehow..."

"But he is ready now for his death," Nahana explained.

"I'm not," Jameson protested. "Not yet. I promised Kamehameha many things that are still undone."

"And now they may never be, Jameson." Kaahumanu's gaze was faraway, as if she were trying to see into the future. "All the land, all the people, belong only to the king. When the breath of the king departs, all these things belong to the new king, and he may do with them what he wishes."

Jameson stared at her. "Liholiho! Surely he wouldn't try to change things."

"Liholiho fears Maakoa. And Maakoa and the other island chiefs would like to change everything back."

Nahana moved closer to Jameson. He put an arm firmly around her waist. "But the people like the *haole* ways."

"They also fear Maakoa and the gods."

"You're their queen. They'd listen to you. They did on Pele."

"Yes, I am a woman, and they won't listen to me unless they believe that Kamehameha had asked me to speak to them."

She turned and strode back into the palace. Nahana trembled in Jameson's arms.

A hush fell on the island. As Jameson hurried Nahana and the twins along the jungle trails toward the royal compound, only the rhythmic rolling of the surf broke the silence.

Jameson paused at the edge of the clearing, astonished at the number of people massed around the palace. It seemed that everyone on Hawaii had gathered there, as well as some chiefs from other islands.

The old order that had prevailed at other gatherings had been abandoned. Chiefs, warriors, and commoners stood side by side. Infants, still in tapa buntings, and ancient warriors, their faces contorted by grief, stood alongside doleful young Hawaiians. For this night, at least, these youths had abandoned their *haole* dress for traditional clothing. The silence was broken only by moans of grief.

As Jameson guided his family through the crowd, he caught sight of Carlos and Haggers with some of their men. The *paniolas* and *haoles* stood apart from the others, not wanting to intrude, but wishing to show their respect. Jameson nodded to them as he hurried on.

The two priests guarding the door of the palace allowed him to pass without question. Once inside the room, he felt

Nahana's body stiffen and heard her swift intake of breath. He squeezed her hand and fought the sudden anguish in his own chest. Maakoa's voice, oppressive and mournful, droned the sacred history of succession on the chant knots in a *mele kahuna* string.

King Kamehameha sat in a carved koa chair at the end of the long central room. He wore his elaborate feathered headdress and his limp feathered cloak, still damaged from the storm. Keopuolani stood at his right, looking almost as ill as the king himself. On his other side Liholiho stood with Kaahumanu. His aging wives were clustered silently at the end of the room with many of his children and his children's children.

Even from across the room it was plain that the king was near death. His flesh was pale and sallow, his face lined with pain. His eyes, half-closed, drooped wearily. The strain of sitting up interfered with his breathing, and each time his great chest swelled in its effort to draw air, he braced himself against the sides of the chair for support.

Yet his expression remained fearless.

Keopuolani, her great bulk half-supported by her son Liholiho, rose to embrace her king in a final farewell. As she moved away, Jameson approached the king's chair. Kamehameha gestured weakly for the others to move away so that he could be alone with Jameson. Although the effort cost him visible pain, the king held his arms out to Jameson.

"You came, my faithful adviser. As you see, I waited for you."

"I'll come every day, if you'll wait for me."

"No." The king smiled. "I have no cannon to trade for my breath, Jameson, as you once did. Suppose, instead, I had let you be killed?"

"There would have been no cannon."

The king waggled a playful finger at him. "And no

Jameson." A painful sigh racked his great body. "And there would have been none of the things that you have done!"

Jameson shook his head. "You would have found another *haole* adviser. Remember what you told me at the sacred rock before we went to fight on Maui? How you were chosen by the gods to raise that rock to unite all the islands, to build them into one kingdom, one nation?"

"And I have done it."

"Yes. Without you, it couldn't have been done."

Kamehameha's eyes rested on Jameson's face, but he seemed to see past him, searching for the truth. "Has too much of the old given way to the new? Have I given too much to the *haoles*?"

"I don't think so. You've never given them the land."

"Yes, yes." He fell silent a moment. "Do you know how a great war canoe is built? Koa wood for the hull, because it is heavy, strong, and even the greatest wave cannot break it. And lohu wood for the inside, because it is light, so that the canoe can go faster. But too much koa, too much lohu, and the canoe is without worth. It is better never to have built it than to have it sink halfway to a battle."

"What we have built will not sink."

The king's troubled eyes closed wearily. "Yes. I *want* to believe that."

After a moment's respite, he gestured for Nahana and the children. Nahana was pale, using all her strength to mask her sadness. With a tender smile, Kamehameha touched a finger to her cheek as if to wipe away the tears he knew she was holding back, never forgetting her role as the daughter of a king. His tone became crooning and playful, like that of a father amusing a small child. With his hand he pantomimed a tiny nesting bird growing, spreading its wings, then taking off in flight. This old game from her childhood brought a tremulous smile to her lips.

"You must remember always," he told the children,

"that your breath is the breath of kings, and of Hawaii." He reached out to touch their faces, but a sudden pain froze him. His eyes closed and he seemed not to breathe for a moment. When he opened his eyes he wasted no more strength. "Blessings," he said. "Blessings on your days!"

The king edged down into his chair and Jameson moved toward him, wanting desperately to postpone what he knew in his heart was happening. "Lie down for a while," Jameson pleaded. "Let me help you."

"No. I must finish now."

He gestured for the others to draw near his chair. Although his voice grew steadily weaker, his tone was still one of brisk command. "Liholiho!" he called.

The young prince stepped forward rather nervously. He bowed to his father and Kamehameha nodded, waiting for him to stand upright again before he spoke.

"Son of Kamehameha, are you ready to be the new Kamehameha? To serve as king to your people?" When Liholiho didn't answer, the king went on even more regally, "Will you be king after me, powerful and strong?"

Maakoa stepped forward to prod Liholiho. "Yes. You are ready," he told the prince. "The son of Kamehameha will be the new Kamehameha."

Liholiho managed to repeat the words.

"And I will guide him," Maakoa added firmly.

Kamehameha looked from the priest to his son, frowning. Keopuolani wore the same concerned expression at this demonstration of the priest's power over the prince. For the first time the king's expression turned uncertain. Abruptly he motioned Kaahumanu forward. He strained to reach out to her as she hurried toward him, his voice an inaudible whisper. Kaahumanu leaned closer, listening intently, holding him in her arms. Another spasm trembled through his body and he slumped in her grasp.

He was dying. Until that moment, Jameson had been

unable to accept Kamehameha's inevitable death. Sorrow and fear and a sense of panic raced through him. Nahana steadied him as he had steadied her earlier. With their hands linked tightly, they watched the last scene played out before them.

The king grimaced as he forced out his final words. They came so softly that only Kaahumanu, being so near, heard them. His head slumped against her breast and he lay still. Kaahumanu only held him tighter, as if her grasp could keep the breath from leaving his body.

Very gently she lifted his head and turned his face toward hers. Covering his mouth with her own, only a breath's distance apart, she gave him a last *honi*, the Hawaiian kiss that Jameson knew so well from Nahana's lips, the symbolic exchange of breaths and souls between lovers.

"Kamehameha one breath with Kaahumanu," she whispered. "Kamehameha, Kaahumanu."

And Kamehameha was dead.

The priests emptied the palace of visitors. Jameson, with Nahana trembling on his arm, led his family back through the silent, grieving throng. Memories of Kamehameha pierced through his mind like shafts of painful light in a sudden darkness. The grief that had begun to press in his breast at the sight of the weakened old king had become a barrier to every breath he drew.

Kamehameha was gone, and with him the special magic of knowing a living legend. Hawaii would never again be the same for Jameson. The friendship of many years had ended, and Jameson's position as adviser was finished. The promise of the future was blighted in too many ways to contemplate.

Through the long night, Jameson held Nahana close to him, warming his body against hers, sustaining his spirits with her courage.

*   *   *

A sunny morning dawned, golden on the water, brilliant on the sand outside the house. Jameson dropped the plate of fruit he was carrying when the quiet morning was suddenly blasted by a chorus of horrifying cries. Nahana sat immobile as the sound of screeching human voices and the cacophony of drums grew louder in the room.

Jameson ran outside to see what was happening. The smell of smoke came from everywhere, and the wailing voices rose and fell on the wind. A pillar of smoke began to trail skyward from a nearby bonfire. Through the woods, Jameson could see other fires, and torches being carried along the trails by wailing natives. The crying grew steadily louder and seemed to come mainly from the royal compound. He felt Nahana's touch on his arm.

"What is it? What's happening?"

"It is the time of *uhe*. The people must punish themselves for the death of a king, so they will be pure when Maakoa gives the *laau moi*, the royal scepter, to the new king."

"To Liholiho?"

The twins came racing from the house, with Pelika close behind them. Staring at the raging bonfires, Elizabeth shouted to be heard above the cries. "Why are they all wailing?" she asked.

"Can we go see?" Robert asked.

"No," Jameson told him, without even glancing at Nahana. "Pelika, take them back inside."

As the maid herded the protesting children away, he made another decision. "I have to find Kaahumanu. You stay here, inside with the children."

"No. I will go with you."

Jameson reluctantly agreed, for when Nahana had that expression on her face, she was more Kamehameha's daughter than Jameson's wife. Any words spent in arguing with her were useless. Smiling ruefully, he took her hand.

CHAPTER SEVENTEEN

THE HANDS OF THE GODS

The royal compound was a scene of mass hysteria. The light from the bonfires and the dancing torches distorted the appearance of the natives circling the area. Howling, screeching, crying, they milled about, some beating their heads on the hard earth and others scourging their flesh with thorns or sharp rocks. Liholiho and Maakoa stood together on the *heiau* shrine. People darted from the crowd to show them the flowing blood, the ravaged flesh of their self-mutilation.

Jameson and Nahana made their way slowly through the frantic mourners. To one side of the bedlam stood Carlos Mentez and Tom Haggers, watching the scene with disbelief.

"They are much loco, yes?" Carlos asked.

"If that means crazy, they sure are," Haggers agreed.

But Carlos had larger worries. "Some say now we will be *despechamos*, made to leave the island."

Jameson ignored the remark. "It would probably be better if you weren't here. Anything could happen."

The two men accepted the wisdom of this counsel and agreed to return to their homes. Jameson continued to lead Nahana through the melee toward Kaahumanu's separate hut. The crowd of flagellants seemed not even to notice their passing. Only the gazes of Liholiho and Maakoa followed their progress.

Kaahumanu stood quietly watching the scene in the compound from a side opening in her thatched hut. Nahana lingered near the door as Jameson entered and crossed to the queen.

"Why have you come, Jameson?" Kaahumanu asked.

"You've seen Liholiho and Maakoa together. Something must be done before it's too late."

"Yes."

He drew a deep breath of relief. "Then you *are* going to challenge them. Kamehameha *did* give you the power."

"He spoke it to me as his last breath fled."

Jameson stared at her. "You mean just as he was dying, when none of us heard?"

"Don't you believe me, Jameson?"

"Of course I believe you. But didn't he tell anyone else?"

"No, his strength had left him by then." She shrugged off Jameson's disappointment. "I will speak it. After the slave who has hidden Kamehameha's sacred bones is killed at the *iwi hoolewa,* I will say it to all the people."

Jameson and Nahana murmured words of good luck, but they looked doubtful.

Kaahumanu drew herself up sharply. "It was the wish of Kamehameha's last breath. I will rule with Liholiho."

Then she regally turned her back on them to stare at the scene in the compound, and Jameson and Nahana slipped quietly from the hut.

"Will they listen to her tomorrow?" Jameson asked his wife as they threaded their way home.

"She is a queen. The people love and trust her a great deal."

"Then they will listen."

"But she is still a woman," Nahana said with a sigh.

"I don't understand. What are you saying?"

"No woman has ever held power before. Just as we are forced to sit apart and not eat as men eat, we cannot rule as men rule."

"Then you really don't think they'll accept her."

"I do not know."

Jameson's temples pounded to the rhythm of the persistent drums.

The drums had diminished to one single, slow beat by the time the ceremony began. The solitary drum was as changed in mood as the crowd that gathered at the sacred monument. It beat slowly, in a dull, funereal cadence. The people stood hushed and reverent, staring at the altar on which lay the body of an impaled slave. With Liholiho at his side, Maakoa chanted over the young man's body. When he fell silent, four priests stepped forward to raise the body of the dead man and bear it away.

Jameson shuddered with revulsion. "Was that the slave who buried Kamehameha's bones?" he asked Nahana.

"Yes. Do not judge his death so harshly, Jameson. It is a great honor to bury the king's bones so that no one will ever find them. This man begged to perform this last service for his king."

The lesser priests began a low chant as Liholiho, in his father's restored feathered cloak, moved to the center of the altar with Maakoa. The young man stood stiffly, his eyes unmoving, his face gleaming with sweat. Maakoa's eyes were closed and he stood rigid as if in a trance.

Jameson could see Carlos and Haggers at the edge of the clearing. Haggers, a less subtle man than Carlos, looked openly apprehensive, his eyes darting from the dead body to the altar to the crowd of natives. On the other side of the clearing, Kaahumanu, Keopuolani, and several high *alii* chiefs watched as Maakoa stepped forward.

The funereal rhythm of the drums and chanters had been replaced by a different, brisker cadence. Maakoa picked up King Kamehameha's feathered scepter and held it for all the crowd to see. Instantly the drums and chanters fell silent.

"Liholiho will now become king over all!" Maakoa announced in his native tongue. "The gods have proclaimed that the spirit of Kamehameha will live in his son. With my counsel, he will rule. Liholiho our ruler."

The crowd swiftly picked up the chant. "Liholiho our ruler! Liholiho our ruler!"

Maakoa held the royal scepter out to Liholiho, who grasped it with nervous fingers. Kaahumanu rose and strode regally across the shrine to them. Reaching out, she placed her hand on the royal staff just above where Liholiho's hand clutched it.

Her voice rang out. "Mahele Kaahumanu! Kamehameha commanded me with his last breath that I, Kaahumanu, should rule equally beside Liholiho. It was his wish. It must be."

For one horrified moment, Maakoa was speechless. Then he began to swell with fury. "No woman can have power! It is the will of the gods."

Kaahumanu faced him serenely. "Kamehameha spoke for the gods and he commanded that I have power."

"No!" Maakoa roared. "It will never happen."

"Kaahumanu *will* rule," she insisted.

Before Maakoa could summon help from his priests or *kapu* guards, the crowd picked up the new chants, making them ring throughout the clearing. "Liholiho and Kaahumanu will rule!" and, "Kaahumanu will rule!"

Maakoa, his face set with hatred, raised his voice to be heard above the cries. "The final judgment must be placed before the gods. If Kaahumanu is lying, she will be punished." His gaze fell on Jameson as he spoke. "And the *haoles* will be banished."

The hut was hung with the trappings of the priests, knotted *mele* chant strings, kahuna masks. Kaahumanu sat motionless, facing her judges. The seven men were seated on tapa mats on the platform: Hanakea, governor of Maui, with his high kahuna, the governors of Oahu and Kauai, two high chiefs, one from her own island, and of course, in the center, Liholiho, staring down at his lap.

Kaahumanu knew these men like the clear water of the lagoon. She knew them as a woman knows the men whose eyes have followed her. And she knew Kamehameha's opinion of each of them, their strengths, their weaknesses, their ambitions. But her knowledge would do nothing to change the outcome of their decision, their determination of her fate.

Witnesses had been selected from the high *alii* of the islands. These nobles were grouped behind her so that she could not see their faces. They watched carefully as the judging started.

The bowl began to pass. Each judge held two closed fists over the bowl and secretly dropped in a stone. Each thud of pebble against pebble struck Kaahumanu like a blow. Though the bowl passed steadily, Kaahumanu felt the time stretch into an eternity of waiting. When the last stone had dropped, Maakoa took the bowl.

Turning to face her, and the witnesses behind her, he

began to lift the judging stones out, one by one. "Black," he intoned. "Black," he said a second time. His voice was rich with satisfaction as he drew out the third stone and said, "Black," again.

When the next two stones came out white, his voice tightened with annoyance. A whisper of nervous movement stirred the witnesses behind Kaahumanu. She allowed herself a flicker of hope. Maakoa lifted the next pebble and his eyes became cruelly triumphant. The last stone, too, was black.

"The gods have decided that Kaahumanu has lied. Does she forswear that lie?"

Drawing the memory of her king's love and trust around her like a cloak, she stood unflinching. "No."

Maakoa held up his hand with the black and white pebbles in it. "You have seen the decision of the gods," he said to the witnesses. "Now I will present Kaahumanu's betrayal before the people."

Jameson had writhed inwardly when Kaahumanu was led into the hut to face this test. Her judges were powerful, ambitious men. And Kaahumanu, for all her courage and strength, was still a woman.

The kahunas and *kapu* guards stepped away from the hut's entrance. Maakoa, fearless in his robes of office, emerged and stared sternly at the crowd. "The gods have spoken in judgment through those chosen," he declared. "Kaahumanu lied before the gods in order to bring false ways upon the people. She will be cast aside, and none shall ever bow to her again."

Before continuing, Maakoa sought out Jameson with eyes that blazed with hatred. Speaking directly to him, he said, "Liholiho will be proclaimed king of all the Hawaiians and every *haole* will be driven off the islands forever."

Satisfied with the impact this pronouncement had on his

stunned audience, Maakoa swung around and disappeared into the priests' hut again.

Nahana's eyes were filled with pain. "We will have to take the children and go far away."

"How? There's no ship. And even if we could go, we'd have to leave the house and everything else behind."

"I do not care about any of that."

"Well, *I* do. I'm not going to give up everything I've worked to build. Not without a fight. And I'm not going to let anyone take my family away from me. Certainly not Maakoa!"

"But what can you do?" she asked, fearful of his reckless words. "Maakoa has all the power."

"Not yet. Not quite yet."

The coronation luau was held at night in the open area in front of a *heiau* shrine. The regular trappings of a festive luau—feathers, flowers, bowls of fruit, platters of roasted pig—had been set out among the glowering *kii* gods. Even with the drums and the chanting, Jameson couldn't imagine anyone mistaking this event for a party. The warm night air crackled with tension. Coals blazed an angry scarlet in the cooking pits, though the fragrant meat had already been removed. The torches cast wavering shadows across Liholiho's face where he sat alone on a raised platform in the center of the luau. Maakoa stood pillarlike a few feet from the new king.

Jameson paused at the edge of the clearing, feeling Nahana's nervousness. "You don't have to come with me," he assured her, not for the first time.

"I must."

"But you don't completely agree with what's going to happen. It might be better if you went home."

She shook her head. "No, Jameson, I will stay." She walked swiftly to where the women were gathered.

When Maakoa raised his hand, the drums fell silent and the chanting stopped. Maakoa announced that Liholiho, now the king, the single ruler above all others, would eat first. Male servants, walking in deep crouches with their heads lowered, approached the raised platform, carrying bowls of meat to set before Liholiho.

Kaahumanu, too, was seated with the women. Jameson glanced over to find her eyes on him. As he watched, she rose slowly and gracefully to stand erect, magnificent in her dignity. The other women looked up at her in confusion. They hummed with puzzled questions as she walked majestically toward the platform where Liholiho sat with the bowls of meat. Maakoa placed himself in the queen's path.

Her voice was audible to everyone in the clearing. "I did not lie. Kamehameha spoke that I should rule equally. And I will!"

"You cannot rule," Maakoa said ominously. "You are a woman and the gods have already spoken."

"Then I will rule as a man," Kaahumanu said. "I will sit where men sit. I will eat what men eat." She turned to Liholiho. "I will eat meat with Liholiho."

Liholiho's face blanched, but he said nothing. Kaahumanu leaned down and took up one of the bowls of meat. A wave of alarm stirred through the clearing as she held the bowl out, at shoulder height, for all to see.

"Kaahumanu will eat this meat before all. Kaahumanu dares Maakoa's gods to strike her down."

In a tense and fearful silence, every eye followed the hand she plunged into the bowl. Slowly she raised the meat to her lips. A few women moaned, but most of the crowd were gripped by a frightened silence. They waited to see the gods strike Kaahumanu dead.

Not used to eating meat, she chewed the tidbit for a long time before forcing herself to swallow it. Then she scooped up another bite and ate it as well. At length she held the empty bowl aloft for all to see.

"Kaahumanu still lives. Maakoa's gods are not true gods." With the empty bowl still in her hand, she turned to the women, seated as always apart from the men. "There will be no more *kapu* for women. Come, join me. Do not be afraid."

The terrified women lowered their eyes. The men shifted uneasily on their mats. Maakoa addressed Liholiho, fury making his words hiss. "Kaahumanu has broken the sacred *kapu*. She must be killed. Order the guards to seize her!"

Liholiho was too inexperienced and too fainthearted to do anything of the sort. He had known this woman all of his twenty-two years, and she had been his father's favorite wife. Refusing to meet Maakoa's eyes, he sought his mother's for guidance. Keopuolani looked from her son to Kaahumanu.

"Come!" Kaahumanu urged, her voice as calm and confident as Maakoa's had been strident. "Eat! Nothing will happen to you. Do not be afraid!"

Jameson was shocked to see that it wasn't Keopuolani but Nahana who accepted this invitation. She was crossing the clearing, walking toward Kaahumanu, her spine rigid with determination. She didn't look over to where he stood, and she hesitated only a moment when her eyes met the blazing fury of Maakoa's glare.

At the platform she bowed to Liholiho before she lifted the second bowl of meat and held it up. "Now I, too, will eat," she said, dipping her fingers into the meat.

Jameson felt his body freeze with fear as she raised the meat to her lips. Tears gleamed in her eyes as she forced herself to break the *kapu*. Jameson bowed his head with humility. He knew too well how great a sacrifice she was making. More than that, he knew she made it only for him.

Her eyes met his as she displayed the empty bowl for all to see.

In the stunned silence that followed, Keopuolani braced her great bulk and rose to her feet. Her body swayed in the long, brightly flowered tapa dress she had chosen for her son's coronation. She walked to Liholiho and held out her hand for a bowl of meat. Without even glancing at Maakoa, he handed the bowl to his mother and watched her scoop the meat into her mouth and swallow it.

Kaahumanu gestured to the rest of the women. "Come! Eat!" she urged them, indicating the bowls of meat set before the men. "The *kapu* is no more."

The younger women rose first, then many others followed. They walked cautiously toward the men's side of the clearing. Encountering no resistance, they seated themselves and for the first time tasted the savory roasted pork.

Kaahumanu's eyes shone with gathering strength. She turned to the serving men who knelt with lowered heads. "Stand up!" she ordered. "Rise from your knees. There are no more *kapus*!"

They stared at one another, then slowly obeyed, smiling nervously around them at the gathering.

"The false gods of Maakoa are no more," Kaahumanu insisted. "I will show you they are without power. We *will* be free!" She crossed to the figure of a *kii* god and shoved it with her hand. It rocked for a moment in its place before falling to smash into pieces.

There was a shocked silence, followed by a frenzy of voices and motion. The most fearless among the crowd came forward and ranged themselves among the statues. One by one the *kii* gods were knocked from their perches to crash to bits on the ground. Two or three *kapu* guards leaped to stop this destruction, but they were quickly overpowered. Some of the guards fled, while others joined the demolition of the shrine.

Jameson made his way through the ecstatic, milling throng to Nahana's side. He took her trembling body into his arms. "You wonderful, brave woman," he murmured into her ear. "You've done more for our children today than I'll be able to do in a lifetime."

Maakoa's screams rose even over the shouts of the liberated and the pulse of the drums. "Stop!" he screamed, his rage out of control. "Stop!"

No one paid any attention to him. No one even yielded to him as he tried to force his way through the swirling mass of people. He was gasping and his ceremonial trappings were in disarray when he finally came face to face with Kaahumanu. Struggling for control, he said, "I ask to speak to the people."

After a second's hesitation, she nodded. "Silence!" she called.

"Why are you letting him talk to them?" Jameson asked in disbelief.

"So that everyone will know I have no fear of Maakoa."

The high priest stepped forward to face the silent mass. His voice came taut and subdued. "You have destroyed the sacred ways of the gods. You will be destroyed by the ways of the new gods. *None* will be spared, not even the children of our children's children. The land will no longer be ours. Our people will be no more."

The crowd parted to let him cross to the fire pit. Standing by the glowing coals, he raised his eyes to the heavens. "I choose never to see what will happen now to my people," he cried. Then he knelt and lifted a blazing coal in each hand. He held them without flinching as he raised and pressed them against his eyes.

Nahana shrank against Jameson's chest as Maakoa's shriek of agony filled the air.

"My God," Jameson breathed.

The crowd drew back from the blinded priest as he

staggered from the fire pit, his scorched hands helpless at his sides. Kaahumanu gestured to some lesser priests to help him. "Take him away," she told them. "Anywhere he wants to go."

Kaahumanu could tell that her people were shaken. Her manner skillfully combined control with reassurance. "What Maakoa has foretold will not be. He is an old man, disturbed by the death of the great Kamehameha. I will not allow anything bad to happen to my people. Liholiho and I, together with our people, will go forward to fulfill the destiny of our islands. May our islands endure forever!"

The chant of her words echoed through the clearing again and again, until no voice was silent. Kaahumanu joined hands with Liholiho, who stood stunned beside her on the dais. Then she turned to Keopuolani and Nahana.

"I will never forget what you did," she said. "Anything you wish, you have only to ask."

Keopuolani looked exhausted. A faint smile curved her lips. "I wish only that you and Liholiho will rule wisely." Slowly, she walked away, her feet padding heavily on the cool earth.

Kaahumanu touched Jameson's arm to get his attention. "Now all the things we planned for the island, we will do," she said, before she, too, walked away, this first Kahina-Nui with her regal stride and her new resolution.

Nahana stood very still. She stared, entranced, at the shattered remains of the *kii* gods. Jameson had to speak her name twice before she heard him. He pulled her into his arms gently, saying, "They're just pieces of wood. You know that, don't you?"

When she didn't reply, he lifted her chin with his finger and looked into her face. "Do you know that I love you, Nahana?"

"Yes, I know."

He pulled her hard against his chest, burying his face in

her fragrant hair. "No curse can change that. Nothing can change it, ever!"

As he led her from the clearing, she looked back over her shoulder at the smashed remnants of the broken gods.

PART FOUR

New Prophecies

CHAPTER EIGHTEEN

CHOICES

Jameson was half-dressed for the graduation when the significance of it struck him. By God, his children were grown up! At little more than Robert's age he had signed on the *Felicity Ann*. The fresh shirt crumpled in his hands as he dropped to the edge of the bed, lost in yesterdays.

Nahana appeared in the doorway. "Is something wrong?"

He shook his head. Certainly not with her, or between them, thank God. His devotion to Nahana had been the single constant in the hectic decades just past. Time had only ripened her beauty. Her skin glowed in the angled light streaming through the window and her eyes shone with curiosity.

"It's just that time has passed so quickly. I was struck dumb when I realized Robert is almost twenty."

"And Elizabeth."

"Of course. You can't imagine what a shock it gives me. At nineteen I was a green clerk shivering in a Boston warehouse with nothing to look forward to besides one day being senior clerk. I had none of Robert's expectations!"

"I'm just glad you came here."

Jameson rose and slipped on his shirt. All those years, and no two of them the same. Queen Kaahumanu had in many ways been no easier a ruler than Kamehameha. Liholiho, renamed Kamehameha II, had fulfilled his father's every grave doubt. Weak and vacillating to the end, he had succumbed to a *haole* children's disease, only to be followed by Kamehameha III, another immature and ineffectual descendant of the great Kamehameha, a young man not yet of age to rule.

Kaahumanu acted as his regent and her energy had never flagged. She had taken a new husband, almost half her age, to whom she was devoted. But she had supported Jameson in his projects. With her patronage he had been able to make the cattle and hide business prosper, and had put Hawaii on the sea charts as a primary sugar-cane producer.

The next step was a giant one, and a risky one. But Hawaii *had* to be freed from dependency on other men's ships, and Jameson was determined to make it happen.

Nahana stood in the doorway, fully dressed. "Are you still thinking about the past?"

"And the future." He smiled and took her arm.

More than the economy had prospered. The people now had a proper God to worship, brought to the islands by the missionaries the year after Kamehameha died, though Jameson secretly found the rector of the island church repelling. He had the eyes of a shark, and his wheezing diatribes on hell and damnation reminded Jameson more of poor old blinded Maakoa than they did of the sermons he remembered from Boston. But the church! It was a proper church, with hard pews, open rafters, and a plain cross behind the pulpit. The unadorned white spire pointing above the flowering jungle filled him with enormous pride.

The church was nearly filled when Jameson led his family to their pew. As usual, his *haole* business partners had gathered on one side of the aisle. These men, who had come to make their fortunes in his shadow, were as international as the ship flags at Honolulu harbor: Leon Bertelle from Belgium, the German Gustav Schmidt, Horace Tuttle from England, and Abner Holmes, the American.

Queen Kaahumanu and her handsome, petulant husband Kealiiahonui, and Kamehameha III, were already seated in a special pew set aside for the royal family. The rest of the Hawaiians in the church sat together across the aisle from the *haole* families.

The Reverend Matthew Brice, the rector's assistant, read the graduates' names. Brice was as little like his superior as a man could be. He had the solid, strong features of a twenty-five-year-old man who knew his own mind. Even in black ministerial garb he managed to look handsome.

He read the Hawaiian names of his students with the ease of familiarity. "Miss Elewila Hoomea, Mr. Kapono Kliener, Miss Milikeana Kakuna, Mr. Robert Jameson, Junior."

Jameson filled with pride. Young Robert bore a startling resemblance to Nahana in all ways except size. He was tall, with a powerful build and strong, deft hands. As he walked to the podium to receive his diploma, his step was as energetic as his grandfather's had been. His expression, though, was blank as the Reverend Proctor portentously gave his blessing: "Amen! God's will be upon thee."

Jameson seized his son's hand in congratulations as he returned to the pew. The young man remained solemn, and he refused to meet his father's eyes. Jameson assumed it was Robert's way of containing his emotions.

When the list of students was finally exhausted, the

Reverend Brice looked up and smiled. "And last, our honored valedictorian, Miss Elizabeth Jameson."

Every eye followed Elizabeth to the pulpit. No lovelier *haole* woman had ever graced the islands. Her fair skin and blue eyes gave no hint of her Hawaiian blood. A ray of sun touched her chestnut hair, finding hidden fire in its coiled abundance.

Elizabeth accepted her award from Matthew Brice with a subdued smile, though she could barely suppress her excitement. This was the moment she had waited for, when she would prove that she had become a part of her father's world, where reading and writing and skill with numbers were important. It was worth all the effort she'd expended to be rewarded in the presence of her father and his friends and business associates.

Naturally it was flattering when *haole* women praised her beauty and style. Women were expected to be beautiful. But she had excelled in scholarship as well. Her parents would be proud of her. She had proved herself her father's daughter, *haole* like him in looks and in her drive to succeed. She had earned his pride and respect.

Elizabeth had written her own valedictory address. Matthew Brice had offered to help her with the wording, but she knew exactly what she wanted to say and how she wanted to say it. Elizabeth had let him edit the opening thanks and the religious closing.

Her voice had the rich, firm cadence of her forebears. "I am humbled by the many blessings God has bestowed on me. The greatest among these is the dream of my grandfather, Kamehameha, to see Hawaii respected and honored among nations. My father has spent his life helping this dream come true. I wish to do the same. I can think of no worthier way to spend my life than to dedicate my energies and abilities to the continued fulfillment of that dream."

As she spoke she sought her father's eyes, but he was

leaning toward Robert in whispered conversation. Without a pause she continued her address, finishing on the proper note of humility. Applause pattered through the crowded church. Her father and mother and brother smiled at her as she descended from the pulpit.

The Reverend Proctor stilled the applause with a glare. With order restored, he thanked his assistant, mounted the pulpit, and began a variation of his usual harangue:

"We have seen in these young souls, the graduates of our higher school, the fruits of our labors in the fields of the Lord. Where once there was nakedness and lasciviousness, now there is Christian modesty. Where once there was ignorance, now there is Christian knowledge. The True Faith shall be proclaimed and spread until all Hawaiians accept it. Our late, beloved Liholiho accepted it, and our devout young king Kamehameha the Third does."

Proctor waited for the young king to acknowledge this statement with a nod before going on. "Nor shall I rest or set aside my burden while there are yet unsaved souls among us still living in Satan's awful darkness."

This was directed at Kaahumanu, seated comfortably in front of him. She was still remarkably attractive in a brilliant silk gown, her graceful hands and arms adorned with rings and bracelets set with precious stones. Proctor's words received only her regal disdain.

So he turned his stern attentions to the *haole* businessmen. "The True Faith cannot be bought or sold, for riches are but filth and ashes," he informed them with impassioned righteousness. "The rich can no more pass through the gates of heaven than a camel can pass through the eye of a needle.

"Work proclaims the glory of God," he continued. "It is sustenance to the soul. But work that panders to mere pleasure, unholy commerce that seeks only gain, these must cease. Only that which serves the one church of Christ is welcome on these shores. What is not of the spirit must be renounced. It must be stamped out root and branch, so that a New Jerusalem may rise upon these islands! Let us bow our heads and pray."

Queen Kaahumanu did not bow her head, which Kamehameha noted with a half-repressed smile. The Reverend Proctor was not amused. For a long moment the congregation sat silent, as the minister attempted to stare down the arrogant queen. Finally, he lowered his head and closed his eyes for the benediction.

The church emptied slowly. By the time Jameson and his family moved into the brilliant sunshine, Robert, Jr., had loosened his tie and collar and was carrying his constricting *haole* jacket over his arm. Elizabeth was at once surrounded by people offering her congratulations, which she accepted with poised charm. Robert, however, looked curiously ill at ease with the attention he too received.

Jameson excused himself to join his business associates, who were gathered nearby in heated conversation. He arrived in time to catch Holmes's irritated complaint, "Doesn't he realize what would happen to these islands now without trade?"

"I don't like it," Tuttle said. "He sounds as if he'd like to see this society we've dragged out of the Dark Ages drift back into them."

Jameson tried to divert their attention by changing the subject. "We're looking forward to seeing you at our party in honor of Mr. Ivers and his wife."

The German, Schmidt, frowned. "Will we discuss the financial arrangements with Ivers then?"

"No. I'll take care of it as usual."

Monsieur Bertelle objected. "And what if the Reverend Proctor interferes? He's not going to be happy with increased trade. Now that he's made a Christian convert of the young king, he has plenty of influence."

"Not with Kaahumanu." Jameson nodded to where the queen was being carried to her waiting carriage. Her chair still retained some of the ancient *alii* style, but it was inlaid with gold and ivory in the manner of King Louis XIV at Versailles.

The Hawaiians bowed and moved aside, offering homage as she passed with her young, handsome husband. They bowed also to the young king as he emerged from the church flanked by the two ministers. As the king climbed into his carriage, Proctor said, "I will see you at vespers."

"As always," the king agreed.

The Reverend Proctor approached Kaahumanu. "I had hoped when you and your husband came this morning that you were prepared to be saved, even as our former king Liholiho was."

Kaahumanu could not resist taunting him. "Liholiho was not saved. He died of the measles."

"His soul was saved," Proctor said. "He's now in heaven. Your soul can be saved, too, and you can help me lead others to salvation, and drive out the corruption of trade. Trade leads to drunkenness and lasciviousness."

"Perhaps, for the weak. But there will always be the weak. There is nothing I can do to change that."

"But *I* can," Proctor declared. "I can bring them the strength, the hope, and the comfort of belief."

Kaahumanu considered this seriously for a moment. "The people need gods. I understand that now."

"Good! Then you must convert so more will follow your example."

The queen stared at him. "There is nothing I *must* do. I am Kaahumanu." With a regal toss of her head she dismissed him as she turned to greet Jameson and Nahana.

Nahana reached up and caressed her chosen mother. "Thank you for coming. Elizabeth and Robert were so pleased."

"You are my *puna hele,* my sacred friends," Kaahumanu said. "The children of Nahana and Jameson are the children of Kaahumanu, too. I am very proud of them today. Robert so handsome. Elizabeth so . . . Well, Elizabeth reminds me of myself at that age."

As the carriage pulled away, Jameson was still thinking what a very strange remark that last had been. Elizabeth bore not the least resemblance to Kaahumanu in any way that he could see. But Nahana wore a secret, pleased smile that told him she agreed with the queen, and he could only shake his head with amused tolerance.

On the ride home, the Jamesons' carriage moved through lush countryside, with cattle grazing on one side of the road and rows of thriving sugar cane on the other. Shadows cast by the towering palm trees formed a changing pattern on the smooth, sandy beach. Beyond the bay, several buildings came into sight, but one structure stood above the rest, the one bearing the large lettering that read: JAMESON AND CO.

Jameson pointed to the open bay. "That's where it's all going to be," he said. "The docks, the moorings, the piers. A real port with our own shipping line."

He reached for Nahana's hand and gazed up at the hill where Kamehameha's sacred monument stood. "It won't be long before Kamehameha's dream comes true and we'll be a nation able to stand on our own. I promised him at the monument that I'd carry out what he started. And with Ivers coming in, it's finally going to happen."

"Has Mr. Ivers already agreed to join you?" Elizabeth asked, surprised.

"Not yet. But he will. He's too shrewd not to see the potential here. We'll have a shipping line of our own to carry on trade with the rest of the world, on our own terms. It's a shame Proctor and young Brice don't understand how important trade is for the islands and the people. Why, when I first came here there was nothing but raw, empty land."

"No, Jameson," Nahana corrected him. "When you came there were vines and flowers, there were wild fruits and many birds. Don't you remember?"

Jameson laughed. "Yes, I remember. Vines with thorns. I remember *that* from when I began to clear the land. I hardly knew how to go about it then."

"But you learned," Nahana said.

"The hard way." He turned to his children. "It won't be like that for you. And one day there may be a city like Boston right here."

"There's snow in Boston, though," Elizabeth remarked.

"And factories and smoke where Indian tribes used to hunt and fish," Robert added.

"Well, true. There's no snow or Indians here," Jameson assured them indulgently.

"There are Hawaiians," Robert insisted.

When Jameson did not respond, Robert continued. He leaned forward, eager to make a point. "Every book I've read says the same thing. When the *haoles* came to America, they took the land away from the native people, driving them from their hunting and fishing grounds."

Jameson sighed. "I can't defend what happened to the Indians. But look at the end result, Robert. A great new nation was built. When you visit America you will understand."

"I understand that once there were many Indians and they had plenty of land, and now there are few Indians and they have little land."

"Believe me, son, it's not that simple. Anyway, it's different here. The land belongs only to the Hawaiian people."

"Yes," Nahana said. "That's always been the way. That must never change."

Jameson nodded. "You see, Robert, it's not a matter of land here. These are islands and their lifeblood is trade, because we need things from other parts of the world and we have goods to trade in exchange."

"The Hawaiians managed without things from the rest of the world for centuries," the young man protested.

"Yes, and they killed people for eating the wrong foods," his father retorted impatiently. "You wouldn't have liked living in that primitive society. In fact..."

Nahana stepped sharply on his foot. It was a matter they never discussed with the boy, the fact that he wouldn't be living today if not for the challenging of that old society.

"Well, anyway," Jameson continued, "you will see. One day the bay will be teeming with merchant ships from all over the world. And I hope long before then the sign on my building will read 'Jameson and Son.'"

"But I've told you, Father, I'm not sure that's what I want."

Jameson began to launch his counterargument, but Nahana touched his hand. "Jameson, you promised."

"I know, I know." He sighed with exasperation. "I really do understand. I was restless at your age, too. But I didn't have a family, anything to be part of, the way you do. All of this, everything I've built, is for you and Elizabeth. It's here for you to carry on and expand."

Nahana pressed his hand, more firmly this time.

"Well, maybe this isn't the time or place to talk. At least promise me you'll think about it, Robert."

Robert glanced at his mother and nodded. "All right, Father."

"And I want you to make a good impression on Mr. Ivers at the party. All my plans depend on reaching an agreement with him."

Elizabeth's curiosity was aroused. "What kind of agreement are you proposing to him?"

"Oh, financial arrangements. It's complicated. I don't think you'd be interested."

"But I would! *I'd* like to work with you, Father, and be part of all the things you've talked about." When he merely smiled at her, she insisted, "Really I would!"

"You'll be getting married, having a family."

"Maybe Elizabeth doesn't want to get married this young," Nahana suggested.

"Why not? You did."

"Yes. But I was in love."

Jameson laughed. *"Was?"*

"Am. Now. Always!" Nahana allowed him to capture her hand, and the carriage rolled on in silence.

The house Jameson had built a few years back was an imposing structure. Both the blueprints and the gleaming white paint came from New England to make this building authentic. Every time he rode in his carriage up the long circular drive flanked with topiary bushes, he felt a rush of pride.

Usually he thought the house was as impressive as any of the finest homes in Boston. But now he frowned at it, trying to see it through the eyes of Mr. Ivers. Would this house impress his newest business associate? Well, in a few hours he would find out.

As the carriage drew up to the door, Pelika, who had graduated from nursemaid to cook and housekeeper, rushed to meet them, her wide face beaming with delight. She hugged Elizabeth and Robert, Jr., in turn, congratulating them profusely in English and in her native tongue. "With your new knowledge may you continue to flower like the great koa tree."

"The way you feed them, they'll soon be as big as koa trees," Jameson teased.

Pelika motioned the twins to follow her. "Come. Let me show you what I have made for you on this special day."

* * *

The spacious bedroom Jameson and Nahana shared open onto a wide veranda overlooking the front drive and a rolling hillside. To the right, the giant stone of Kamehameha cast its long shadow to the sea.

A sweet breeze swept into the room as Jameson and Nahana changed from their church clothes. Jameson was still struggling with the collar button of his damp shirt when Nahana, in a silk robe, came to loosen the button for him.

"Is my dress shirt all ironed for the party?" he asked.

"In your closet."

He slipped on a soft shirt, left unbuttoned in the heat, and walked out to the veranda, where the sea breeze cooled his bare chest. Leaning on the railing with both hands, he studied the garden and the land beyond. "You know, I think even Ivers is going to be impressed. A man like that, who's lived in London, New York, and China... He probably thought we'd live in a thatched hut." He swung around suddenly. "The lanterns! Have you told Kokino about stringing them along both sides of the drive?"

"Both sides. And I've taken care of the musicians and the silver and the chandeliers. Everything you said," she promised as she joined him.

He slid his arm around her waist. "I know you never miss a thing. It's just that this is so important. We have to get that financing from Ivers." He drew her close. "Then I'll be able to get you anything you want."

"I have everything I want. Don't you?"

"You know I do."

Tilting her head back, her lips barely brushing his, she put on a teasing pout.

"Do I have to prove it to you?" he asked.

She let her loose hair fall over his bare arm. Then, pulling him toward their bed, she whispered, "Yes."

He caught her in his arms, holding her back. "No."

At her puzzled look, he released the draw cord of the bamboo shade on the veranda. Pulling her close, he untied her kimono and let it slide to the floor. Nahana pressed her beautiful, naked body against his as she slid her hands inside his loose shirt, pushing it away from his body. Her ready lips soon found his.

Then they swayed together in urgent, joyous lovemaking.

CHAPTER NINETEEN

SOMEONE ELSE'S GARDEN

On her way downstairs to check the final arrangements for the party, Nahana heard a sound that drew her to Elizabeth's door. She listened a moment before tapping softly. At Elizabeth's muffled answer, she entered to find her daughter lying across her bed, sobbing helplessly.

"Oh, Mother, Mother," she wailed. "He didn't even hear me."

Nahana held her daughter until the storm of emotion passed. Elizabeth almost never gave way to tears. "Who didn't hear you, love?"

"Father. He doesn't even care that I won the top honors. He didn't hear my speech. And I wrote it for him, just for him."

"He's very proud of you," Nahana assured her. "Everyone heard your speech. It was wonderful."

Elizabeth wiped the tears from her face with a crumpled handkerchief. "No, he didn't hear. He was whispering something to Robert. He's always more interested in Robert. I'm the one who tries to learn his business and earn his respect, and he doesn't even care."

"Your father has you working in his office."

"Filing papers and serving tea!" Elizabeth said indignantly. "Mother, I want to work *with* him. I have more right than he does to help develop this country. I have Hawaiian blood in my veins."

"Your father loves Hawaii. He wants to see it become a powerful nation. It doesn't matter that he's *haole*. His blood joined with mine when we were married."

"It's not the same." Elizabeth pushed herself up against the headboard and crossed her arms over her chest. "I want to do something important with my life. I want to be part of Hawaii's future. Father thinks all I should do is get married and raise children."

"That's what most women do," Nahana reminded her gently.

"Well, I'm not most women. There's something... burning in me. Maybe that's not how to express it." Her bright blue eyes blazed with the fire of ardor. "I'm a descendant of Kamehameha, and of you, and of my father. Sometimes I think I could do anything I wanted! I could run a business, or make laws for my country, or design buildings!"

Nahana hardly knew what to say. She had understood when Kaahumanu said that Elizabeth reminded her of herself at that age. So much potential! So much intelligence! So much drive!

But Elizabeth seemed to be forgetting, or ignoring, the other element she had in common with Kaahumanu and Nahana—her sensuality. Elizabeth was more than beautiful; she was alluring. Her body was like ripe fruit hanging from the tree. Without doubt, a man would come along to pluck that tempting fruit.

And Elizabeth would not be prudish or shy. She was comfortable with her body the way *wahines* had always been. Because of her upbringing, she would not be indiscriminate. But all the moral lessons in the world could not divorce her from the sensuality that coursed through her veins.

Nahana stroked her daughter's head and sighed. "Things will be more difficult for you, I fear, with your burning desires. But don't despair. Give your father time to learn who you are and what you want. Teach yourself patience, and fill your waiting time with learning. I love you and I will do what I can to help you. But don't expect too much too soon."

"Oh, Mother!" Elizabeth was embarrassed by this shrewd evaluation of their positions. "You've given me more than anyone else in the world. Don't think I'm not grateful!"

"I know you are." Nahana patted her cheek. "Come. It's almost time for the party. Pelika has set out your new dress, and you're going to charm every visitor who sets foot in the house!"

Elizabeth's tears were gone now, and Nahana's encouragement, as always, revived her spirits. Elizabeth jumped up from the bed and held the pale blue satin evening dress against her exquisite figure. "Will he like it?"

Nahana knew very well that "he" meant Jameson. How important his approval was to Elizabeth! "You know very well he'll love it," she said lightly, rising to leave. "You'll look just like one of the finest young ladies from Boston!"

The lanterns flickered on either side of the drive and music filled the air as James Ivers's carriage approached the Jamesons' home. Ivers studied the handsome house and the preparations for the party. He watched the dexterity with which the servants leaped to the arriving carriages to help the formally clad alight.

His wife's delicate features glowed in the soft lantern light. He spoke to her in her native Chinese and she nodded in reply. The other occupant of the carriage, Ivers's assistant, also scrutinized the scene.

"You see, Jackson," Ivers said, "it's exactly what I expected. Jameson is trying to impress me."

"Yes, sir. Just as you predicted. Are you going to tell him your terms?"

Ivers considered a moment before shaking his head. "Not yet. I never like to make the first bid until I'm sure of winning."

An immense portrait of Kamehameha the Great dominated the main room. Music drifted in from the ballroom beyond. Handsomely dressed *haole* guests chatted and exchanged greetings. Hawaiian servants, colorful in native costume, circulated with hors d'oeuvres and trays of drinks. Uniformed naval officers and representatives of the consulates mingled with elegantly dressed women.

Elizabeth, radiantly feminine in her low-cut gown, smiled engagingly at her father's guests. When Jameson approached her, she asked eagerly, "Do you like my new dress, Father?"

"It's beautiful," he replied. "You look lovely. All the men are going to claim you for a dance." His eyes darted around the crowded room. "Have you seen Robert?"

"No, not for hours." She tugged at his sleeve. "Which one is Mr. Ivers? I keep trying to guess what such a powerful man looks like."

"Like that," he said, nodding toward a strong-featured man who was entering the room with his wife on his arm. His assistant, a drab young man in steel-rimmed spectacles, followed a careful step behind. Ivers, a man in his fifties, exuded the confidence of power. He also advertised his wealth in both the elegance of his clothes and his wife's impeccable jewels.

"Ivers, Mrs. Ivers," Jameson said. "I hope you'll enjoy your stay on our islands."

Mrs. Ivers, pencil slim in a clinging silk dress, responded. "Thank you. But I plan to take the packet boat on to Canton. Family business."

"You know my assistant, Mr. Jackson," Ivers said. "And this must be your daughter."

"Yes, Elizabeth." He then motioned to Nahana, who stood a few feet away, under her father's imposing portrait. "And this is my wife, Nahana."

"A pleasure, Mrs. Jameson." After introducing his companions, Ivers gestured to the portrait of Kamehameha. "I see the likeness."

"My father," Nahana said.

"Yes, I know. King Kamehameha. Magnificent. A man after my own heart—no fancy scholarship, just his native intelligence and determination. In Europe he'd have been a Napoleon or a Caesar."

Jameson caught sight of Robert, dressed in Hawaiian clothing, headed for the stairway.

"I would have given a great deal to have known him," Ivers said. "But of course you did, didn't you, Jameson?"

Distracted, Jameson switched his attention back. "I beg your pardon?"

"I said you actually knew King Kamehameha, didn't you? Quite well, I believe."

"Yes, I did. A remarkable man. Would you excuse me a moment?"

Elizabeth and Nahana were left to entertain a somewhat startled James Ivers.

In the hall Jameson managed to intercept Robert before he escaped up the stairs. "Where have you been?" he demanded. "We expected you an hour ago."

"Just walking by the ocean. I'm sorry, Father. I lost track of the time. I was thinking... about my future."

"And what did you decide?"

"It can wait until later."

"No, I want to know now," Jameson insisted.

"Well, you already know." Robert shrugged his huge shoulders. "I don't want to work in the company office, wearing a coat every day and being cooped up inside."

"But you can't just walk the beach for the rest of your life. What will you do?"

"You'll think it's stupid," he muttered, but continued nonetheless. "I want to try working in the fields, cutting cane. I want to do physical labor tied to the earth. Just to see what it's like for myself."

Jameson struggled to control his annoyance. There were people everywhere, the party was in full sway. "You'd better dress for company now. We'll discuss this later."

"I won't feel any differently later."

Jameson lost his control. "Do you know what it's like to cut cane? Do you have any idea? Stooping all day in the sun, hauling one bundle after another, working from sunup to sundown?"

"I've made up my mind, Father."

"All right, Robert, if that's what you want, try it. Maybe a little hard work is what you need to change your mind. But don't expect any favors. You'll be on your own."

"That's the way I want it."

Nahana appeared in the doorway. "Mr. Ivers is waiting for you, Jameson."

"Right away."

As Jameson returned to the drawing room, Nahana turned to her son as he started up the stairs. "Is everything all right?"

"It is now."

"Good. Hurry and get dressed."

"Like all of *them*, you mean."

"Yes, of course."

He shrugged. "All right, Mother, but I still won't look any more like them than you do."

With worry in her eyes Nahana watched her son trudge up the stairs and out of her sight.

It was two days before Jameson met with Ivers to conduct their business talks. In the meantime, Ivers had been given free rein to study the company's books and to explore the various operations. They did their talking not in Jameson's office but on the beach, with Jackson behind them testing the soil and studiously recording figures.

"Well, Ivers, what do you think?" Jameson asked. "There's a limitless future in these islands. There's almost nothing that can't be grown here, and ready markets for all of it."

Ivers nodded. "And with financing and a shipping line, you'd be able to choose your own markets."

"Exactly."

"This Reverend Proctor." Ivers frowned. "I understand he wants to restrict trade, turn the islands into some kind of psalm school. And I gather the young king listens to Proctor."

"But Queen Kaahumanu doesn't. She's on the side of progress, of increasing trade. And she has the power to get what she wants."

Ivers called to Jackson, "Can it be done?"

"I'd say so. We can dredge up to the mean line, and the footing's stable for piers."

Ivers turned back to Jameson.

"Well, it's settled, then," Jameson said.

"No."

"I don't understand. I'm offering you a half partnership, a chance at millions of dollars. If you're not interested, I'll go to a bank or a stock company."

"I happen to know you've already been turned down by Lloyd's of London, by the Rothschilds, by half a dozen financial houses west of Petersburg, because they wouldn't risk their money with an unstable native monarchy. Do you know the tale of the Thessalonians, Jameson?"

Jameson shook his head.

"The Thessalonians built palaces for the pharaohs until one of them died and the next pharaoh sent them packing off into the desert. I'm not a man to wander in the desert, Jameson. If I build docks, I want rights to the land I put them on."

"But that's impossible. Foreigners have never been allowed to own land. You don't understand the way the people feel about their land. It's sacred to them."

"I'll tell you what I do understand. If you want my financing, you'll have to secure it with land."

"But only Kaahumanu could authorize that."

"Then get her to do it."

"Anything else, but not the land. Like Kamehameha, she believes the people and the land are the same. One can't exist without the other."

"What I believe is not so fancy. Only a fool plants a tree in someone else's garden. Either I get a deed to the land, or there's no agreement."

Ivers turned abruptly and strode off to join Jackson, leaving Jameson looking after him, torn between annoyance and concern.

The rain began an hour after sunset. As always, the clouds formed swiftly, roiling into a clear sky within seconds. The downpour bent the tree branches, sent coconuts rolling along the beach, and pounded on the fields of lava rock with such force that the spray leaped upward.

Elizabeth Jameson pulled on her dark, hooded cape and let herself out of her father's house. On such a night she didn't need to be cautious, so she chose the shortest path to the church. Hawaiians, knowing how quickly the rain would stop, would wait it out in their thatched houses. *Haoles* seldom ventured out after dark, and never during storms.

The mission church glistened white in the rain. She barely glanced at it or at the dimly lit windows of the Reverend Proctor's rectory. She hurried along the path that led to Matthew Brice's one-room house. She could smell the smoke from Brice's oil lamp even before the opened the door. The flame fluttered at the draft she caused, but settled back to burn steadily once the door was closed. The room was deserted.

Elizabeth removed her drenched wrap and hung it on a hook. Her coiled hair was slightly disordered and she glanced in the mirror above Brice's commode. The looking glass was cloudy and dark but reflective enough that she could poke the wisps back into place. She adjusted the waist of her dress and seated herself on the straight-backed chair to wait.

Rain gusted against the high, narrow window, which was steamed over from the muggy heat inside. A skimpy bed, little more than a cot, stood beneath the window. The desk beside her held a number of books and scattered writing materials as well as the oil lamp. Compared to her room at home, this one was cramped, muggy, and primitive.

Brice burst in holding his frock coat tented over his head to ward off the rain. He closed the door carefully and crossed the room, eagerly taking her up into his arms. "I'm sorry I'm so late, Elizabeth. It's the Reverend Proctor. His pleurisy is worse. I had to pray with him and see he took his medicine."

"I'm sorry to hear he's worse," Elizabeth said politely. "I can't stay long this time. I pretended I was going out for a music lesson."

His shoulders slumped. "I shouldn't let you come here like this."

"But I wanted to! I always do." Elizabeth raised her eyes to his. He was very near. Her body felt as tightly wound as a spring when he stood so close to her. Her heart seemed to beat in her throat. And her eyes betrayed the intensity of her emotions.

Matthew groaned and hugged her tightly, raining kisses on her lips, her eyes, her nose. Caught in his arms, her body pressed against his, she felt a shiver of delight race through her. Suddenly he pulled back, his breath coming quickly.

"What is it, Matthew? What's wrong?"

"Everything, Elizabeth. You can't imagine the hours I've prayed about our being together. It's wrong. I'm your minister. You're my student." He ran his hand distractedly through his hair. "I've been a traitor to all I believe in by meeting you this way, but I can't seem to help myself. It makes me a sinner and a hypocrite. How can I stand in that pulpit preaching one thing and doing the opposite?"

"But I'm not your student anymore. Surely that makes a difference!"

"Very little. We're still deceiving everyone." He struggled for the words he had planned to say. "I want to marry you, Elizabeth. Right away!"

She frowned and drew back.

His voice turned fearful. "Don't you love me?"

"Of course I do. I love you very much, Matthew." It was the truth. She loved everything about him, even his rigid guilt, which continually held them apart. He was a *haole*, as *haole* as her father or any of the other foreigners who worked on the island. No hidden strain of dark Hawaiian blood flowed in his veins, as it did in hers.

Matthew's acute eyes searched her face. "Good. Then on Sunday I'll ask your father for his permission."

Elizabeth could imagine her father's reaction: he would be angry; he would refuse at once and be incensed by Matthew's asking. And yet she wasn't sure why. He was the one who wanted her to marry and have a family instead of working with him in the business. "I'm not sure he'd give his permission."

"Probably not," Brice admitted. "But it needn't matter. We can be married anyway, right here in the church, by the Reverend Proctor. Then your father will have to accept it."

He pulled her close again and she clung to him, but she felt no joy. After a moment she disengaged herself from him. "I can't, Matthew."

"I don't understand. If you love me and I love you..." His gaze moved slowly around his barren room. His voice hardened. "It's this, isn't it? You don't want to live like this. You don't want to be the wife of a missionary."

Elizabeth couldn't meet his eyes. What he had said was true. She didn't want to have to dress plainly, to live simply and be dependent on the charity of others for every pleasure. In her dreams of how joyous it would feel to be with Matthew, she had never thought of how poor and mean their daily lives would be.

Yet, she couldn't tell him that. Not Matthew, who preached that poverty was a blessed state. "I'm just not ready to be married yet. I'm sorry, Matthew. I wish..."

She looped her arms around his neck and kissed him tenderly. Before he could respond to her touch, she pulled away and reached for her cape. Matthew wordlessly adjusted the hood so that it would protect her face from the rain. She stood for a long moment in the doorway, oblivious to the rain pelting her back.

"I'm so sorry," she whispered, touching his cheek. Then she turned and ran off into the night.

* * *

The field Robert was assigned to was a living hell. Smoke from burning cane leaves hung over the valley like a shroud, spiked here and there by bursts of flame. The workers moved through the field bundled in heavy clothes, their heads swathed against smoke and ashes and their forearms wrapped in bulky rolls of tapa. After the leaves were torched and the fire was beaten down, they gathered and tied bundles of hot cane in an awkward, tortured rhythm.

From the first Robert found it grueling work. But as the sun rose higher, it became worse. Hot steam rose from the rain-saturated earth, scalding his ankles. His flesh crawled as rivulets of salty sweat coursed under his bulky clothing. He learned quickly not to wipe the soot and sweat from his face. Better to let it sting and itch than risk grinding the soot in deeper with his blackened hands.

He was humiliated by his own awkwardness. Around him Hawaiians of every age bent to the same task with a grim, joyless efficiency. An old man cut the cane with swift, deft strokes that Robert couldn't imitate. He was losing a clumsy battle with a bundle of cane when the Hawaiian overseer galloped through the field. Reining up his horse by Robert, he waved a long pole at him and shouted, "You! Faster."

A girl of about Robert's age who was working down the line cursed the overseer under her breath.

"Get to work!" he ordered. As he spoke, he jabbed his pole into the bundle Robert had been trying to tie up. The cane stalks flew apart at his prodding. "Look at that! No good. Do it over."

Robert glared at him. The overseer jabbed at him with his pole. Pushing the pole aside, Robert lunged toward the man. The girl stepped to his side and held him back.

"Now!" the overseer shouted. "You hear me? *Kanaka!*"

The girl shielded Robert from the pole and gestured toward the broken bundle. For her sake he bent to the task, though inwardly seething. When the overseer finally turned and rode away, the girl mocked a spitting gesture behind his back. Before Robert could speak to her she had returned to her work.

"Let me show you how to bind that," an old man offered. He looped the rope over one end of the bundle, then the other, and cinched it with a swift tug, speaking rapidly the whole time. "Do you see now?"

Robert smiled a little blankly. It was all done so quickly.

"Don't you know our language?" the old man asked with a frown. "Aren't you Hawaiian?"

"Yes, I'm Hawaiian," Robert said, his tone defensive. "But this is my first day and I'm not familiar with all the terms you use."

The girl stopped her work and said scoffingly, "Let me guess! They made you go to mission school and speak their *haole* language."

Robert nodded, a little uncomfortable with this half-truth.

The old man looked even more puzzled. "Then you can read and write. Why are you working in the fields?"

"Because he's still Hawaiian," the girl said. "Why do *you* have to work in the fields? Because you are only Hawaiian. Because the *haoles* feed their cattle where you used to grow taro, because they grow cane where you used to have your fish ponds. Even educated ones like him are still just Hawaiians to them."

"And you," she said, addressing Robert directly. "You won't even have this job long unless you learn to work faster. That *kumakaia* toad will tell the *haole* Jameson and you'll be fired."

"But they can't do that. I just started."

The old man was more conciliatory. "Lihoa and I will help you. It will be all right. Soon your hands will be like mine, and it won't hurt anymore." He pulled back the wrapping from his wrists and arms to show palms covered with crusted-over abrasions and calluses.

Robert was appalled by the old man's wounded, gnarled hands. Fortunately, a siren wailed just then and distracted everyone's attention. "Lunchtime," the old man said, straightening his shoulders with a sigh.

Lihoa pulled off her hood and shook her hair free. It tumbled gracefully around her face, as lustrous in the light as his mother's was. And then, to his surprise, she shrugged off her bulky clothing to stand, lithe and slender, in a thin muslin top and short pantaloons.

His response to her womanliness flustered him. He pulled off his shirt as he saw the men around him doing. As he wiped at the grimy sweat on his chest, he thought she was watching him. But when he looked up she had walked away and was dipping water from a bucket, pouring it over her head, washing the soot from her face.

"Can I use it, too?" he asked.

"It's for everyone."

He drenched himself with the water. She wiped her arms and shoulders with a wet cloth, making them glisten golden in the sun. Her eyes met his as he cleaned his face. Then the old man called to them that lunch was ready; he had set out poi for himself and the girl.

"Come," he said. "There's enough."

"In our village there is still the way of *alona*," the girl explained. "What is for one is for all."

Robert lowered himself painfully onto the earth beside Lihoa. "Thank you, and your father, too."

Lihoa laughed softly and glanced fondly at the old man. "He's my grandfather. My father died."

"Oh, I'm sorry. Was it from measles?"

She shook her head and pantomimed raising a bottle to her lips and drinking. "No, from *haole* liquor."

Robert fell silent. Lihoa dipped her fingers into the poi. It was the thick poi that Pelika made for herself in the kitchen, thick enough that one could lift a healthy bite by using three fingers at a time. The poi on his mother's table was thin and eaten with spoons in *haole* fashion.

"Eat," the old man urged.

They dipped the poi and ate hungrily, their fingers, mouths, and cheeks sticky with the food. Robert couldn't keep his eyes off the graceful girl.

"You're staring at me," she said, wiping poi from her lips with her hand.

"I've never known a girl like you before."

"Weren't there any *wahines* in your school, only *haole*?"

"I don't mean that. It's your strength, your determination."

"I'm all the son my grandfather has. And what about the queen? Kaahumanu was once only a *wahine* like me, except that she was beautiful."

Robert would have liked to tell her that she, too, was beautiful, but he didn't dare.

Her grandfather was gathering up their lunch supplies. "The poi is not good now. It's not fresh. But you will come to our village after work. There we will give you much to eat."

Robert sought Lihoa's eyes. "I'd like to do that. But only if Lihoa wants me to come."

She stared at him for a long time before nodding. "Yes," she said. "You will come."

CHAPTER TWENTY

OWNERSHIP

The new hotel had been completed before Ivers arrived. Jameson felt that it stood as tangible proof of the modernization of the island. Ivers had a second-floor suite with a french door that opened onto a balcony. All the furniture in the hotel was imported; the only Hawaiian touch in the room was a massive vase of pale orchids on a low table.

Ivers stood at the balcony door looking out over the bay and the ships anchored there. He listened to Jameson without turning around.

"You don't understand the islands, Ivers. The natives and their traditions."

"I understand business."

As Ivers spoke, the bedroom door opened. His wife, clad in a dark, heavy silk kimono, stepped into the room.

Through the open door Jameson saw a room cluttered with open trunks and stacks of folded garments.

Mrs. Ivers nodded to Jameson and joined her husband on the balcony, where she pointed toward the bay. After a brief exchange in Chinese, she returned to the bedroom.

"See that, Jameson?" Ivers asked. "They've raised the sailing pennant on the Canton packet boat. That means it will be leaving tomorrow."

Jameson groaned inwardly. "You're not a fool. Surely you're not going to back out now over nothing but a piece of paper!"

"No," Ivers said, "I'm not a fool. And neither are you, Jameson, or I wouldn't be here. I know what you want." He waved casually toward the vista beyond the balcony. "All of that. But you can't have it without me. And you know my price."

"You don't understand, Ivers. Foreigners can't have land."

"You do."

"No. My wife owns land."

Ivers smiled, his expression knowing. "Well, then..."

Jameson sighed. He had no answer.

Jameson found Kaahumanu on the upper floor of her spacious palace. Her rooms were in complete disorder, with clothing, jewelry, even a set of crested china scattered on such unlikely surfaces as the directoire desk and the spinet piano. Servants bustled around packing this collection of treasures while Kaahumanu turned in front of a full-length mirror. Kealiiahonui sat in a chair across the room, beside his own closed trunks. He wore an elaborate uniform and an expression of boredom.

Taking a beaded, brightly colored silk gown from a passing servant, Kaahumanu held it up to herself and remarked to Jameson, "This is from London. The same as for the great English queen, I am assured. Tell me why Kaahumanu should honor that rebellious governor of Lanai by wearing it when she goes there."

She tossed the dress aside and scowled. "Once I would have had him strangled, and then put his head up for all to see! There would have been no more talk of revolt. But now..." She sighed and shrugged. "What would Kamahameha have done? Would he have executed this governor and his followers?"

"Only if there was no other way. He probably would have charmed him, or tricked him into begging for forgiveness. Like he did with that Russian admiral who was going to annex Maui for the czar. Do you remember how Kamehameha confiscated all the man's vodka and only gave it back to him one bottle at a time until the admiral was drunk enough to apologize and promise to leave?"

Kaahumanu laughed delightedly. "Ah, yes. And made him sign a treaty of friendship, too. You are right, Jameson. Like Kamehameha, I will find a way to deal with the governor."

Kealiiahonui was restless. "You must hurry. The ship waits."

"Be patient, my love," she crooned. "I won't be long."

Jameson forced himself to speak now. "There's more I must tell you about Ivers."

"What can there be? Kaahumanu has given permission to Jameson to make an agreement with this Ivers."

"Ivers is a businessman. He wants collateral, something to back up his investment."

"What does he want?"

"Land." Before she could protest, he hurried on. "I've tried to explain to him, but he insists. He won't invest without owning the land."

"Own land? You know that cannot be!"

"I'm only asking just this once. Just with Ivers."

Her face was set. "No! Never! Kamehameha did not give land to the *haoles*, even to you, only to Nahana. The fathers of the fathers of Kamehameha did not give land. Kaahumanu will not give land."

"But things have changed. If the islands are going to continue to grow, we have to have more trade. If you want to keep putting up palaces, you have to let me get the financing and capital to build docks and bring in a shipping line to increase our profits."

"You will bring ships. You will build docks."

"How am I to do it if you won't let me offer Ivers land?"

Kaahumanu smiled tenderly at him. "Like Kamehameha, I will find a way to deal with the governor of Lanai. You will find a way with Ivers. It will be done."

Before Jameson's carriage was out of the drive, the servants were carrying down the trunks for the queen's visit to Lanai.

Unable to sleep, Jameson slipped quietly downstairs. The moonlight through the wide windows bathed the room in pale, cool light. He leaned against the fireplace mantel and stared at the complex pattern of the oriental rug. The colored lines of the design turned this way and that with a look of purposeful advance, though in the end each reached an impasse. How like his own frustrations!

From the very beginning there had been the immovable force of Kamehameha and his *kapus*. Later there had been Kaahumanu, who held the identical conviction that her will was the way things should be. Dealing with these rulers had required all his patience and ingenuity. But this time the only solution was much closer to home.

At the sound of Nahana's light step on the stair, he

looked up. She moved to him, her face concerned. "Can't you sleep?"

"No. I can't even think anymore. I feel like an animal in a trap."

"Ivers?"

"Nahana, I can't really fault him for what he's demanding. We're asking him to invest a great deal of money with nothing solid in return."

"But his money will earn money. I thought all *haoles* loved money."

He frowned at this but let it pass. "From a business perspective, it isn't wise for a man to invest all that money in land he could be forced off of."

"But Kaahumanu wants the dock. Why would she force him out?"

"Kaahumanu is only human and will not be here forever. Even today she's traveling to Lanai to quell a potential revolt. What if a revolt were successful and the victorious king took it into his head to banish all *haoles*?"

"That won't happen," she assured him. "The people want you. They want what you've brought."

"Yes, but there won't be more progress unless Ivers comes in, and he won't come without collateral. He won't invest unless he gets a right to own land, and Kaahumanu will never allow it." He hesitated, struggling with himself. Why did he shrink so painfully from what he needed to say? Nahana was the only possible solution.

"There is another way," he managed at last. "Kaahumanu wouldn't have to know. No one would know but us. There's our land . . . yours. Just a little part of it, I mean. Just the part where the dock would be, for collateral."

Her eyes were wide with surprise. "Kamehameha gave me the land, and I must give it to our children. It must be."

"But we would be doing it for them, don't you see? And

for their children's children. I want to help build Hawaii into a great nation, the way Kamehameha dreamed. If we can't complete this project, it will never be anything but a dream."

"But Ivers isn't one of us. He's not like you, Jameson. You understand how our people feel."

"Nothing would be that different, I promise you. There wouldn't be any problem with Ivers. I'd always be here. I'd still be in control of the land. The piece of paper would just be a promise that if the project failed, he'd have the land instead of the money he'd invested. He wouldn't have the right to anything else, ever. And the project can't fail."

Nahana was torn between her loyalties. Her hands jerked awkwardly and her face twisted with the strain of such a momentous decision. Jameson's words were strong, but her belief in the link between the land and the people was very powerful. It seemed wrong to her to jeopardize even a small piece of land. And yet, Jameson spoke of her father's dream. . . .

Jameson wanted to reach for her, to comfort her, but he held himself back. This was his last chance to see the project completed, but he would not add the insult of a caress to the force of his verbal logic. If he held her, he would be putting a demand on her love, and that would give her no real choice.

Her body tightened. To yield the land was to give up a part of herself. She was of the people, and the land and the people were the same. Yet, she was a part of Jameson, too, with the mingling of their blood. She leaned against him to brace herself against her painful decision.

"I am yours, Jameson. What is mine is also yours. I will do it."

For a moment he could only cling to her with relief. "You won't regret it, Nahana. I give you my word."

As he held her, Nahana's gaze rose to the looming portrait of her father. Then she quickly looked away.

Construction on the dock had stopped for the crew's lunch break but men were still working on the dirt road beyond. Even with the windows of Jameson's corporate offices closed, Ivers had to speak up to be heard over the road foreman's shouts and the clang of tools against the stubborn volcanic earth. Elizabeth served tea to the group discussing the progress of the work outside.

Ivers was frowning at a paper on his desk. "Mr. Jackson has tested for subsidence. According to his figures, those hinge pilings can't be sunk until the dray road is cut through."

"Then let's get the road finished," Mr. Schmidt said. "There's no point in having docks unless we can haul things on and off them."

"The problem," Ivers explained, "is that to finish the road, we may have to stop construction on the dock. There simply aren't enough workers to push both projects through at the same time. I should say there aren't enough *good* workers, ones who are ready to bend their backs to hard labor."

"But what about the contracts we've already arranged?" Tuttle asked. "Even when the docks are finished we aren't going to be able to meet the contract dates without the road."

"I think we can extend the contracts," Jameson said. He flipped through the files in a drawer and frowned. "Where are the lading contracts, Elizabeth? I can't find them."

"They're in the wall cabinet, Father. I rearranged them by sailing dates so we won't have drafts against them before delivery."

Jameson stared at her. What had gotten into the girl to

make a change in office management without consulting him?

"I thought it was a good idea," Ivers said. "When she suggested it, I told her to go ahead."

Before Ivers could take the contracts from Elizabeth, the door was shoved open unceremoniously and Jackson entered, his face flushed. "You'd better come, Mr. Ivers. It's those missionaries again."

Ivers leaped to his feet and hurried after Jackson, followed by Jameson and the other men. Elizabeth remained alone, holding the china pot. After a moment she restored it to the tray, blew out the spirit lamp, and went after the men.

The unfinished dock looked chaotic at first sight. Some of the pilings had been sunk, and the skeletal scaffolding for the piers was partly in place. Drying mud and sand were piled into untidy mountains where the bottom was being dredged for deeper anchorage. Beyond the dock, a dirt road had been hacked out of the base of the hill.

A cluster of *haole* foremen and skilled workers had seated themselves well away from the natives to eat their lunches. The majority of the workers were Hawaiian and they were grouped around a barrel of whiskey. As they ate, they passed the whiskey from man to man.

The Reverend Proctor and the Reverend Brice stood addressing the Hawaiians. Their message was received with a variety of responses ranging from men waving bottles, cheering them on, to solemn disapproval. The Reverend Proctor pointed to the whiskey barrel. "Mr. Brice, empty that vile potion into the cleansing waters of the sea."

Mr. Brice dutifully opened the spigot. The whiskey flowed golden onto the planking and down into the tide water below. With a grunt, a thick-muscled man seated among the *haoles* heaved himself to his feet. "'Ere, mate, what're you doin'? That's good rum, it is."

"I am carrying out the word of my pastor," Brice said, keeping his hand on the open spigot.

"Well, I'm foreman here. I say turn it off before I have to make you."

"Stand fast, Mr. Brice," the Reverend Proctor wheezed from behind him.

The foreman barely glanced at the older man. He wrenched Brice's hand from the spigot without the least bit of difficulty. But Brice surprised him by repositioning his hand on the spigot and twisting it right off the barrel. The thin stream of rum became a gushing current that splashed and steamed as it struck the hot wooden planks.

In the stunned silence that followed, Mr. Proctor, revived by this evidence of victory, spoke to the Hawaiians again. "Put aside the filthy whiskey. Cast down your implements and come now with me. In the House of the Lord there is room for all. Here you will reap only Satan's wages, but if you come to Jesus your reward will be eternal life. Come! Come!"

Several of the men moved forward, leaving their tools behind to join the two ministers. None of them was entirely sober.

Ivers watched the episode with disgust. "Jackson, tell the foreman to get the men back to work. I don't care how he does it, just see that it's done immediately."

"Wait, Ivers. I'll handle this," Jameson insisted. He approached the cluster of laborers who had joined the preachers. "It's time to go back to your work now," he told them in Hawaiian.

"These men have chosen to come with me and with Christ," Proctor said. "They will no longer toil for rum and false coin."

"Then their families will starve," Jameson informed him

curtly. To the other men, he said, "If any of the rest of you want to join the Reverend Proctor, you are free to leave. But if you go, don't come back. There will be no further work for you here."

None of them moved.

"Very well," he said. "If you're going to stay, get back to work."

Jameson watched as the men slowly returned to the work site. Some of the workers with the minister had changed their minds and picked up their tools. When only two men remained with the Reverend Proctor, Jameson made an effort to explain to him.

"Reverend Proctor, can't you understand that this port means many things for the island? It means jobs, and goods, and a market for the products of our labors."

"I understand that it means the undoing of all I've tried to accomplish." Proctor's voice strained painfully over his next words. "While I have breath I will never stop fighting against it."

"You're fighting against a livelihood for these Hawaiians, all in the name of religion. You can't turn back the clock; they don't want you to. The Hawaiians want to be as advanced as the nations that send merchandise here, not as backward as they were a few years ago."

"No one shall stand between me and my holy mission to save these innocent souls for Christ," the old man retorted.

Jameson shook his head sadly. "Then I'll ask you to leave now, and not come again. You're trespassing on my land."

"This is God's land," the Reverend Proctor informed him piously. But he gathered his small band together and marched off toward his church. The Reverend Brice brought up the rear and cast one last glance over his shoulder at

Elizabeth, who stood silent and watchful apart from the others.

Jameson was already remarking to Ivers that they'd have to find more men to hire.

"That won't do any good," Ivers scoffed. "They'll be just as bad as these. If they don't get their whiskey they run off, and if they do get it, they're not worth much as workers. Either way, the missionaries come and badger them."

"Do you have something better to suggest?"

Ivers pointed to the hill road. "Get those men down here to work."

"But without the road the port would be useless," Holmes said.

"There's a simpler way to get that done," Ivers insisted. "And faster, too. Every hour lost jeopardizes our contracts. We've got to blast through that hill to push the road forward."

"Blast!" Jameson cried. "There's a workers' village on the other side."

"There's no danger. It's just a matter of siting the charges properly."

"What about the monument on the hill?"

"You mean that pile of rocks up there?"

Jameson tried to keep his voice level under this provocation. Ivers knew that the "pile of rocks" had significance to the natives. "You don't understand, Ivers. It's a monument to Kamehameha for the unification of the islands. It has a sacred meaning to the people."

Ivers faced him squarely. "I understand that if we're going to let some rocks and grass huts stop us from paring costs and making a fair profit, we might as well give up now." He glanced at Schmidt, Tuttle, Bertelle, and Holmes. "The rest of you can see that, can't you?"

Jameson didn't give them time to respond. "We'll discuss this later, Ivers. Alone."

As he walked away he could feel Ivers's eyes on his back.

Lihoa carried the pail of oil the arduous distance from her village of Kamahameha's monument. Robert, walking beside her, was surprised that either of them had the energy to make this journey. He had never been so physically exhausted in his life as he was each day after working in the fields. His back ached, his hands and arms were raw, and his eyes still smarted from the smoke of the burning cane leaves. But Lihoa had asked him to come, and it seemed there was nothing she could ask of him that he wouldn't agree to.

The moon had laid a path of shimmering gold across the sea by the time they reached the monument rock. Robert had asked her what the oil was for and she had replied, "You will see. It is time for you to see." Now he watched as she tipped the pail, carefully feeding the oil into a rock basin where the faint flame was guttering.

Robert watched the flame leap higher as the fresh oil swirled into the depression. "Do you bring oil up here for the flame all the time?"

"Everyone does. The fire must never die. It is here to remind the people that they are one." She handed him the pail, still half-full of oil.

Slowly he poured a thin stream of oil as she had done. When the flames leaped high again, bright before his eyes, he felt a reverence that was new to him.

"Haven't you ever come here before?" Lihoa asked.

"Only on the commemoration day."

"My grandfather believes Kamehameha is here in the flames, his spirit. He sometimes comes to talk to him."

"Maybe Kamehameha's spirit *is* here. I can feel something special now."

"No!" Her voice was harsh. "If Kamehameha were here, even his spirit, he would drive them out."

"Them?"

"The *haoles*."

"But he liked them."

"If he were here now, he wouldn't like them. He would see what the *haoles* have done to you, to all of us. They teach us to read and write, but they have taken away our way of life. We were many when they came, and now we are few. Now we work in the cane fields to buy their clothes and their food and their whiskey. We even make love their way."

Robert was overwhelmed by his desire for Lihoa. In a low voice he asked, "Do you make love their way?"

Lihoa tossed her head and moved away. "That was just an example. It's not important."

He caught her arm. "Everything you think and do is important to me, Lihoa. I've never felt this way about anyone before. Every minute I'm away from you I wonder what you're doing and thinking." He stopped, embarrassed, and then smiled down at her. "Laugh if you wish, but I could watch you every minute of the day."

The militancy faded from her eyes. They became soft, dark mirrors of her emotions. "I wouldn't laugh at that. I watch you, too. I like it when we're together."

Robert enfolded her in his arms. "I've wanted to be close to you like this."

"For lovemaking?"

He shook his head. "I've imagined that, too, but it's more than that. I love you, Lihoa, and loving you makes me want you."

She put her lips close to his, warming him with her breath. "Our way," she whispered, pressing her body against his.

Her hands slid under his shirt and played over the hard

strength of his back. It thrilled her to touch his glorious body with its broad shoulders and slim waist. Her own body felt small and fragile next to his—until he touched her.

His callused hands lifted off her muslin shirt and cupped her breasts. His rough skin lightly chaffed her smooth skin, but it didn't matter. His touch sent bolts of excitement through her body. It was too late to reconsider. He picked her up in his arms and carried her to a secluded spot away from the monument.

She removed her pantaloons and stood before him, naked, trembling slightly as he stripped off his clothing. He was like a god standing there, magnificent, golden. His dark hair and black eyes gleamed in the moonlight. Some trick of the moonlight made it look as though he wore a feathered cloak. When Lihoa moved closer, she realized it was merely the fronds of ferns behind him, but the image stayed with her.

He was at once regal and primeval. Lihoa was as stunned by the force of his physical presence as she had been by his warmth and openness. Her body tingled under his gaze. A chaos of need swept through her as he held out his hand to draw her close. Her breasts rubbed against the coarse hair on his chest and her thighs softened against his throbbing manhood.

"You're like a queen," he murmured. "So proud. So strong. So beautiful." He bent to take her breast in his mouth. His hands pulled her buttocks toward him.

Linoa's body filled with passion until there seemed nothing else in the universe. His hands and mouth stoked her desire until the ache was almost unbearable. She couldn't touch enough of him. Her hands learned secrets from his skin, and revealed mysteries to his body. It felt as though a whole new language had sprung full-blown under her fingertips.

And when he filled her, when he strove to reach the ache in her, she could hardly believe the imprisoned power that he released. It burst upon her like a volcanic eruption. Flames and showers of sparks and a tumultuous rumbling shook through her, followed by an overflowing of love as hot and unheeding as lava.

"Now I understand what it means to be alive," Robert said with a sigh, holding her firmly against him. "Not just living. All those years before I met you are like a gray memory with no color or vibrancy. From today I count my real life."

If it was an exaggeration, it didn't matter to Lihoa. She understood what he meant. Suddenly there was a new significance to her life as well. And, somehow, a new hope for Hawaii.

CHAPTER TWENTY-ONE

THE FINAL STONE

Robert's skill in the sugar-cane fields improved daily, though he knew it would be a while before he became as deft at this grueling work as Lihoa and her grandfather. Yet, in spite of their skill, they greeted every sunset with a rush of impatient delight. They enjoyed the work no more than he did.

As the sun slid lower in the sky, he stopped to rest, wiping the grimy sweat from his eyes and looking wearily to the west. "It ought to be almost quitting time."

"Very soon, yes," Lihoa's grandfather said. "When the goddess Pele drinks fire from the sky."

Lihoa spoke indulgently. "He still believes in all the old kahuna ways."

"But you don't?"

"No! They didn't save our people." She bent quickly to

her work, hissing, "Quick! Back to work. The *haole hana* is coming."

Following her gaze, Robert recognized the smart buggy clipping along through a freshly cleared path in the field. His stomach lurched. Ducking his head, Robert turned his back and bent over his bundle of cane stalks.

The siren wailed. Lihoa and her grandfather stood up and stretched. Robert kept his head down, continuing to work. His father held the reins, while both he and Nahaha peered at the laborers along their way.

"Didn't you hear?" Lihoa asked. "You can stop work now."

"I just want to finish this bundle."

He heard his mother call his name. The horse snorted as the buggy came to a halt. "There you are!" his father cried. But Robert didn't look around, hoping his father would think he'd made a mistake.

Instead, Jameson quickly handed the reins to Nahana and jumped down. He strode to where Robert remained bent over his bundle and tapped his son's shoulder. "What's the matter with you?" he asked. "Surely you must have heard me."

Before Robert could respond, Lihoa had left her trembling grandfather and planted herself firmly at Robert's side. "He was working," she told Jameson. "He has done nothing wrong."

"It's all right, Lihoa," Robert tried to assure her.

"No, it's not all right! Just because he's the *haole hana* he thinks he can own you, the same as his cattle. Work is over. You don't have to do anything he says now."

Jameson frowned at her outburst. "This has nothing to do with you."

Lihoa stood on guard, her eyes flashing. When Jameson nudged Robert toward the buggy, Lihoa started after them.

Nahana said to her in Hawaiian, "He means no harm." Lihoa stopped, clearly confused.

Trapped and embarrassed, Robert challenged his father. "Why did you come out here?"

"We can talk in the buggy, on the way home."

"I have to wait until the overseer counts my bundles."

"I'll talk to him. I'll take care of it."

"No, I want to do this my own way."

Jameson grabbed Robert's arm as he turned back. "I'm proud of you, Robert. I mean it. I didn't think you'd last out the first day. But you don't belong here, working in the fields. Come with me now."

When Jameson tried to urge him toward the buggy, Robert balked. Lihoa, her lovely face flaming with color, instantly placed herself between them, grasping Jameson by the arm.

"He doesn't have to go with you. You don't own him."

"I've told you this has nothing to do with you. It's between my son and myself."

Lihoa's face registered shock. "Your father?"

At Robert's nod she turned and fled. Jameson still had a grip on his arm but Robert twisted free and ran after her. Jameson was about to start after them when Nahana called out, "Don't. What the *wahine* said was true. You don't own him. He's made a choice."

Jameson stared bleakly in the direction his son had run off, now out of his sight.

The table was set, as always, with fine china, proper silver, even the hand-dipped candles that Nahana preferred to oil lamps. Pelika entered the dining room carrying a tray laden with fish that had been steamed in ti leaves and squid cooked in a coconut milk.

It had been a long day and Jameson was hungry. Squid cooked this way tasted amazingly like the New England lobster he remembered from his youth. But he gestured Pelika away. "Not yet. Take it back."

Pelika glanced at Robert's empty chair. "I understand."

Jameson didn't understand. Hadn't he done everything possible for his son? He had saved his life and loved him with a father's passion and spent his life building an estate for him. And now Robert was changing, developing an arrogance that had to be curbed. If it had been Elizabeth, he wouldn't have been surprised. She had been willful from the first, with her watchful eyes and her devious attempts to get her own way. But Robert! Jameson's patience was exhausted. He rose and went to the foot of the stairway to call.

"Robert! We're waiting to say grace until you come."

Almost at once Robert's footsteps sounded on the stair. He stepped into the dining room dressed in baggy pants and sandals. His tapa shirt was hanging half-open. "I'm sorry. You shouldn't have waited for me. I'm going out."

Jameson waved aside his explanation. "I'd appreciate it if you'd join us. I have something particular to discuss with you."

"I'm sorry, Father, but I really can't tonight."

"There are going to be changes in the company that will involve you."

"If I don't leave now, I'll be late."

Jameson ignored him. "We're going to form a second company to handle all the trade through the new dock when it's completed. I hope you'll be interested in learning to manage it."

Elizabeth's face froze, but Jameson didn't notice. Robert did. "Why not let Elizabeth do it? She's the one who knows about business."

Jameson struggled to keep his tone level. The boy was mocking him by making such a ridiculous suggestion. "I'd like you to stay so we can talk about it seriously."

"I can't. This is something special, the Makahaiki."

"The what?" Elizabeth asked.

"Makahaiki," Nahana said. "It is an ancient festival to celebrate the land giving birth again with new fruits and flowers."

"The people must show the land they are grateful and swear never to foresake it," Robert added.

"But the Makahaiki was abandoned long ago, when the *kapus* and the *kii* gods were overthrown. We no longer celebrate it." Nahana's voice was wistful.

"Maybe not here," Robert said. "But in the villages they do a lot of things we don't do here."

"Robert, please," Jameson called as his son turned to leave. "I don't want you going to the village to see that girl."

"Her name is Lihoa. And I have every intention of seeing her."

"Why don't you bring her here?" Elizabeth suggested. "Maybe to dinner."

Robert glanced at the table with its ironed linen cloth and its rich place settings. "Because Father doesn't think she's good enough."

"That's not true," Jameson protested. "But she believes that all *haoles* are devils and that she has the right to destroy everything we've built for these people."

"All Lihoa wants is for the islands to be Hawaiian again, instead of *haole*. And it *is* their country, their land." His eyes moved to Nahana. "Can't you make Father understand? Don't *you* understand?"

Nahana could find no words to answer him. Jameson was watching the interaction with stern eyes; Robert was waiting for some sign that she sympathized with his cause. It was not the time to offer her son encouragement, and yet her heart had rejoiced to hear that the Makahaiki was still celebrated. Her gaze dropped to her plate, and Robert turned abruptly and left the room.

"He's young," Jameson said. "He doesn't know how far we've come."

Nahana said nothing.

The traditional Hawaiian dance was drawing to a close as Nahana reached the edge of the clearing. She had followed the sound of the drums to the festival in the workers' village. Beyond the darkness of the woods, the torches flared, bathing the dancers in light. Everything was as it had once been. The Hawaiians clustered around the luau fire pit were dressed in traditional native clothing and draped with leis. They were of all ages and their faces shone with reverence and joy.

Nahana closed her eyes. She could see the past, her own past. She could even imagine the stillness that would fall as her father, Kamahameha, strode into the clearing to begin the ceremony. But her father had been dead for many years. With a sigh she opened her eyes again to survey the scene.

Nahana saw Robert and Lihoa at once. Lihoa wore only a short tapa skirt and a lei, with her flowing hair loose around her shoulders. Robert, in pantaloons with a red lei across his chest, gazed at Lihoa with both love and desire. As the two young lovers began to dance, Nahana shuddered from the force of her own haunting memories.

A very old man began the chant of the ceremonial. Nahana drew nearer, behind a fringe of vines. She recognized the old man as the one who had been with Lihoa in the field. He stood before a mound of fruit and flowers, lifting his voice above the sound of the drums.

"When the gods looked down and saw our ancient fathers lost in the great ocean, they set these islands in the sea for them to find. The land gave its life to our fathers' fathers, and they promised forever to cherish it and never to turn from it. For without the land the people would be no more. Now again it has given us its life, and again we swear to cherish the land for always and never to turn from it. *Akua haawaii aina, aina haawaii.*"

The villagers repeated the chant and Nahana's lips moved in unconscious accompaniment. Across the clearing she saw her son, his eyes still on Lihoa's face, repeating the ancient words. "The land is for the people, the people are the land."

Jackson laid aside his surveying spirit-level and measuring rods. "I can clear for the road with just one explosion," he said. "Of course, I can't be absolutely certain of the effect on some of the substrata."

James Ivers frowned. "Then that native village *could* be endangered. Is that what you're saying?"

"No. The main fault line lies in the other direction. There's no way the village could be involved."

"You're sure of that?"

"Dead sure."

"And you can do the work at night?"

Jackson nodded.

Ivers thumped his fist into his palm. "Then get started preparing for it."

"But I thought you were going to discuss it with Mr. Jameson."

"I intend to. After I've done it."

Elizabeth had agreed to drive out with Matthew Brice, to give them a chance to talk. But they had exchanged barely a word on their long drive. She watched him covertly from under the rim of her bonnet, and he kept his eyes on the horse. She found a sensuous pleasure in just riding beside him on the buggy seat, feeling the warmth of his body, studying the line of his jaw, and remembering how his thick hair felt under her hands. Distracted by these delightful thoughts, she was startled when he reined the horse to a halt on a bluff overlooking the sea.

Without comment he got out of the buggy and tethered the horse to a giant koa tree. Elizabeth stared out over the water until he helped her down from the buggy. As they walked slowly along the rough path, Matthew tucked Elizabeth's hand inside his arm, pressing it firmly against his body.

"I needed to talk to you alone," he explained. "After we saw each other last, I wrote to my uncle in Philadephia and asked him if he could find me a place in the church there. He's an important man. I knew he could do something."

Elizabeth stared up at him. This was not what she'd expected.

"My uncle wrote that there's a possible opening. It's a wealthy congregation, and the rectory is spacious and very beautiful. All our needs would be taken care of. One day I could even become the bishop, with you there by my side. All I need is for you to believe in me."

"But what about your work here?"

"The Reverend Proctor has already done so much. And there will be others willing to help him. I can go back to Philadelphia with a clear conscience." He stopped and leaned closer to her. "Elizabeth, I need to have you with me."

A tremor ran through her. "But Philadelphia! It's so far away, Matthew."

"Ships sail here regularly now. You could always come back to visit your family. There's nothing else for you here."

Her eyes widened in amazement. "How can you say that? There will be everything here in the future when my father's plans mature. Hawaii will be a whole new nation, with cities and ports and people from all over the world. I want to be part of that. And I want to help my father build it."

"I need you, Elizabeth. I need you more than he does."

Elizabeth realized that this was true, and this truth hurt. Her father had never needed her the way she wanted him to.

Matthew needed her. And she loved him. She could have him as her mother and father had each other, forever, shutting out everyone else. She could take charge of her own destiny by marrying him. But Philadelphia? No, there had to be a better way.

"Let me think about it," she begged. "I do love you, Matthew, but this is where you're needed. And this is my world. I couldn't easily leave it."

"Pray," he urged, ducking his head to give her a quick, soft kiss. "That way you'll get the right answer."

Elizabeth smiled and said nothing.

Matthew followed his own advice. He prayed often for a resolution to their situation. A week passed, and then two, and he still could not concentrate on the open Bible on his desk, or even on the glorious sunset that set fire to the sky. It was images of Elizabeth that filled his mind, when a furious pounding on his door brought him to his feet in guilty distraction.

Two young Hawaiian converts seized his hands and tugged him toward the rectory, stammering in English, "Hurry, Mr. Reverend. He said bring quick!"

Brice ran along with the two boys. "Who said to come quick?"

"The doctor," they said, their eyes wide and frightened.

The door of the rectory was ajar. Matthew moved into the room as the boys drew back. His heart was hammering. The doctor was replacing equipment in his leather bag. He met Brice's questioning look and shook his head.

"I'm sorry. There was nothing I could do."

Brice walked numbly to the cot. The Reverend Proctor lay there unmoving, his eyes closed. His flesh, never colorful, was waxen in the light of the oil lamp. His lifeless fingers still clasped his Bible to his breast. Prayers for this solid, joyless soldier of Christ leaped unbidden to Brice's mind.

The doctor bent to pull the sheet over the body, but Brice stopped him with an upraised hand. As gently as he could, Brice disengaged Proctor's fingers clamped around his holy book. He was still standing with the rector's Bible in his hands when the doctor let himself out.

Ivers's assistant cautiously played out the coiled length of fuse line. The only light came from a vagrant moon that hid now and again behind banks of clouds. As Jackson reached the end of the fuse line, Ivers spoke from the darkness.

"Are you sure you've planted enough blasting powder to do the job? We aren't going to get a second chance."

"There's plenty," Jackson assured him. "It would be better if we could do this in daylight."

"I can't risk that." Ivers stared into the darkness. There was no sign of life on the hillside, only the jagged outline of the monument rock black against the sky. The moon swam free of the clouds. "Light it," Ivers said.

Jackson struck the flint and lit the end of the fuse. After a hesitant sputter the sparks raced along the line toward the blasting powder and the two men scrambled to take cover behind a boulder.

A thunderous explosion vibrated the earth under their feet. Pillars of flying dirt and smoke slowly cleared to show the saddle section of the hill blasted away. As Ivers and Jackson exchanged smiles of mutual congratulations, a rending crack trembled the earth once more, reverberating down the hill toward them.

The hill shuddered. In faint moonlight they witnessed the immense rock that Kamehameha had placed on the pinnacle of the monument break loose. It crashed, tumbling down the hill toward the sea, followed by the giant stones of the monument. In a matter of minutes the beach was littered with rubble.

Jameson reached the veranda while the land still trembled. He saw the pillar of dust rise to reveal the barren promontory. "No!" he cried. "It can't be!"

Nahana stared in the direction of the vanished monument, her eyes empty. Jameson touched her shoulder, but she didn't respond. He pulled on trousers and lunged out the door, and she made no attempt to follow.

Dazed, he stumbled through the rubble, recounting vivid memories of the great kings: Kamehameha striding up that hill with his golden cloak fluttering behind him, Kamehameha crouching and lifting the huge rock whose shadow reached to the sea. "You will be here when I raise that rock, Jameson. You will tell your children, and they will chant it into all time. Forever."

Jameson struggled with unanswerable questions all night. He needed to go back to Nahana, to comfort her, but he had no words to ease his pain, much less hers.

Within an hour, silent figures began to gather on the barren hill. By dawn, the crowd stretched as far as the eye could see. Wisps of morning mist wove through the silence shrouding the hill. The *haoles* sat in their carriages well away from the massed natives.

Jameson had pleaded with Nahana to spare herself the agony of joining the others. She had held her eyes on him until he finished speaking, then walked out of the house toward the hill. He stayed at her side, feeling helpless. Elizabeth threw a shawl around her shoulders and followed with Pelika. Robert, wearing loose trousers and sandals, knelt in the rubble to pick up a fragment of the shattered monument. He glared when he saw his father watching him, then turned on his heel to join Lihoa and her grandfather.

Nahana walked as if in a trance. She surveyed the ruins and knelt to pick up a shard from the marble slab Kamehameha had bought for his monument. The black surface was like a mirror of the past, captured in her hands. She gripped the ragged piece tightly and a trickle of blood ran down her wrist.

Jameson was instantly at her side, prying her fingers back, dabbing at the blood with his handkerchief. She glanced up at him, her face bleak with betrayal. When he tried to bandage her hand, she drew it away.

The crowd parted for the royal party's carriage. When Kaahumanu's husband helped her from her carriage, she looked different, almost frail. Kamahameha III was accompanied by the Reverend Brice. They all stood staring at the desolation, too stunned to speak. There was despair in Kaahumanu's eyes and she refused to meet Jameson's sympathetic gaze. When she stumbled on the path back to her carriage, her husband and the Reverend Brice supported her.

"Kamehameha's spirit cannot be destroyed," Brice told the young king. "His spirit did not live in the monument. It lives through you and Kaahumanu."

Kamehameha III nodded. "It is the same way the Reverend Proctor's spirit now lives on in the Reverend Brice."

As the minister passed Elizabeth, Jameson thought he was going to speak, but he merely nodded and passed on. The royal party returned to their carriage and slowly drove away, none of them glancing back at the empty shrine.

Lihoa left her companions to stand alone in the middle of the rubble. She raised her fist in a threatening gesture toward the carriages of Jameson's business associates. "You have defiled the spirit of Kamehameha," she cried in Hawaiian, pointing an accusing finger at Jameson.

Angry and embarrassed, he insisted, "I had nothing to do with this! I was here when Kamehameha set the rock in place. I'll do what I can to restore the monument."

Lihoa was scornful. "That's impossible. The breath of Kamehameha dwelled within it. You can't put *that* back."

He frantically tried to make Nahana understand. "I didn't know anything about this, Nahana. I swear to you. It was a mistake, a terrible, dreadful mistake."

She wouldn't meet his eyes. "I want to go home."

"But I must explain to them..."

"There is no way you can explain this to them."

CHAPTER TWENTY-TWO

INITIATIVES

Jameson waited by the window as Elizabeth let Ivers in, and wasted no words in greeting. "You went behind my back, Ivers! You had no right to do that. You promised me, and I gave my wife my word nothing would happen. Now you've destroyed the monument put up by her father!"

"I'm sorry," Ivers said. "I'm sorry about the monument. I didn't think there was any danger. At least nothing happened to the village. We made sure of that!"

Jameson fought to control his fury. "You don't seem to understand what this may mean. The people worshipped Kamehameha. Destroying his monument could turn them against us."

"You're making too much of this, Jameson. It'll all pass in time." He walked to the window and pointed to the street beyond the dock construction site. The people along the street were Hawaiians in *haole* clothing. "That's what they want, Jameson. They want English tea, American whiskey, French hats, Swiss clocks. Not some old rocks."

"Sacred rocks!"

"Sacred! In the Orient they believe insects are sacred. They sit around in trances, letting vermin crawl all over them. Well, I don't believe in sacred insects *or* sacred rocks. I believe in progress. In building new docks and roads like this."

"So does my father," Elizabeth said.

Jameson frowned at her. "Not at the price of destroying something sacred!"

Ivers was patient. "Listen, Jameson. You don't believe that I'm a man of faith, and by your terms I may not be. But I believe the Almighty put certain men here to build, to create, to prove their faith by their works."

"I agree with that," Jameson admitted through clenched teeth. "But I also know these islands. I know what can be done and what can't. And from now on, nothing's going to be done without my knowing about it!"

Jameson strode from the room, slamming the door behind him. Ivers sighed and looked at Elizabeth.

"Too bad. I wish your father saw things more the way you do."

"Oh?" Elizabeth smiled. "And exactly how do you think I see things?"

"Like me."

Facing Kaahumanu was one of the hardest things Jameson had ever done. As he rode to the palace, he was inundated with memories of Kamehameha. He remembered how they had shared lunch on the tapa mat in the old thatched palace. Jameson had dreaded that meeting, too, with its task of persuading the old king to lift his *kapu* on the horses and cattle and to permit the *paniolas* onto the island.

He reined in his horse before the palace, thinking now of Nahana. If only she would meet his eyes, would offer him the smallest assurance that she understood. Her distance made this meeting with Kaahumanu more difficult. The queen shared Nahana's strong feelings about the memorial to Kamehameha, about certain native customs that must never change. His stomach twisted with anxiety as he dismounted and entered the palace to face his oldest ally and newest critic.

The Reverend Brice barred his way at the entrance to Kaahumanu's rooms. "I don't think you should disturb her now."

"She's expecting me," Jameson said. "She wants to see me."

"The doctor said she should rest. She's in bed."

But Kaahumanu had heard his voice and called to him through the door. The Reverend Brice reluctantly stepped aside. Jameson found Kaahumanu propped against piles of pillows. She looked pale and spent. The ivory table beside her was crowded with pills, potions, and her bell gong.

"I know," he said, even before she could speak. "It was an accident, a terrible accident. I had nothing to do with it at all. But I've spoken with Ivers and I promise you nothing like this will ever happen again."

"He must go."

"Go? Leave the island? I know you're angry, but you don't understand. You can't just..."

"I am Kaahumanu. I rule. In the time of the *kapus*, I would have had him killed. Maybe I still will," she said wistfully.

"That time is gone. Ivers is English. You know England has many interests here now. If you even threaten Ivers, with his money and influence, they would send in ships and troops."

"Let them! Kaahumanu is not afraid." She tried to rise but fell back weakly. Jameson offered her a hand but she brushed it away and attempted to reach the bell gong on her table. "I will ring. I will order it now. He will be banished."

Jameson lightly blocked her hand from its goal. "Wait!" The right words wouldn't come. He struggled to find a way to tell her the bitter truth. "You can't exile Ivers. He owns the land."

Kaahumanu's eyes widened in disbelief. She stared at him and her words came slowly. "That cannot be. No *haole* can own land."

"I had to deed him the right to some of my . . . Nahana's land. It was the only way we could get financing."

He braced himself for her fury. He was not prepared for the hurt and betrayal in her voice. "Why, Jameson? I believed in you. I helped you. I pleaded with Kamehameha to save your life. We fought against Maakoa and the *kapus* together. Why? Why have you done this?"

"For the same reason we fought Maakoa and overthrew the *kapus*. So we could have progress, so we could build a whole new future for the islands. You believe in that!"

"Yes, but not in letting the *haoles* own the land. Never the land."

"I only did what had to be done. The *haoles* are here. And there will be more—powerful men like Ivers. No matter what you do or what you want, you can't change that. The days of Maakoa are over."

Kaahumanu seemed to age before his eyes. The muscles of her face slackened, and her eyes dulled with disappointment. But her voice remained strong, even harsh. "I can't trust you anymore, Jameson. I will have to turn to others. You have betrayed me, and you have betrayed Kamehameha."

She thrust away his hand and rang the bell gong. When

the servant appeared, she asked her to summon the Reverend Brice. The minister walked softly to stand beside her bed, awaiting her wishes.

"You will convert me now," she said.

Brice glanced at Jameson in confusion. "Convert you? But I don't understand."

"Don't you wish me to become a Christian?"

"Yes, of course I do."

"Good."

Jameson waited uneasily for her to acknowledge him again. Instead she glanced at her medicines, then back at Brice. "I will live forever in your Christian heaven when I accept your God. Isn't that true?"

Obviously she had not only dismissed Jameson as her counselor but had determined that he no longer existed for her. He forced himself to walk to the door. She didn't even glance in his direction.

"You will convert me now," she said again to the Reverend Brice as Jameson let himself out.

Jameson called for the next meeting of the Import-Export Association to be held in the conference room of his home. He felt this gave him a certain advantage over the others, as it took them out of the usual business surroundings and put them squarely in his domain. But the substance of the meeting remained the same, and tension mounted as steadily as the clouds of blue cigar smoke that tinted the air.

When Jameson attempted to take charge of the conference, Ivers leveled a furious finger at him. "Now see here, Jameson. You're falling down on your part of this bargain. You were supposed to have influence with the queen. You were supposed to keep her out of our business."

"And I *did* that! I could have continued to do it if you hadn't turned her and half the island against us with your dynamite blast. As for helping you, you would have been packed off the island or worse if I hadn't stopped her!"

"You certainly weren't able to keep her from being converted and handing over her power to Reverend Brice."

Tuttle leaned forward in his chair, tapping his fingers uneasily against the arm. "It's getting harder every day for us to find people to work for us. And Brice is at the root of that problem."

Schmidt nodded glumly. "Rumor has it that Queen Kaahumanu is really very sick."

"It's hard to bank on rumor, but no one's seen her for a long time," Bertelle agreed. "They say she's getting steadily weaker."

"Our problems will get even worse when she dies," Holmes said. "Brice has had the new king in his pocket for a long time."

Tuttle stirred in his chair. "Yes, Brice is the real problem. Now he's come up with this idea of banning all trade with countries that aren't Christian. Most of my business is with shippers from China, Ceylon, even Java."

Schmidt groaned. "Next it will be the Catholics. And that will rule out half of Europe right there."

Determined to keep the level of anxiety high, Ivers added another element to it. "Have you thought about what will happen if Brice succeeds in shutting down the grog shops and the bawdy houses? Sailors aren't choirboys, you know. Where do you think we'll get crews then for the shipping line?"

"He's right," Schmidt said. "What are we going to do about it, Jameson?"

"I don't know," Jameson admitted. "But I *do* know we wouldn't be in this mess if you'd listened to me in the first place."

Bertelle shrugged. "That's over. Our problem is what to do next."

"Our first business has to be deciding how to stop Brice," Ivers said.

"Do you have a specific plan, Ivers?" Jameson asked.

"Not yet."

"I thought not. We'll adjourn the meeting."

"Wait a minute, Jameson," Ivers protested. "It's a matter we need to pursue."

"Not until we've all had time to think about it. We can discuss our conclusions when I call another meeting."

Jameson rose and moved to the door, an obvious invitation for them to leave. Ivers hesitated. For a moment Jameson thought the argument was going to start all over again, but his opponent finally shrugged and stood up. When the last man had followed Ivers out, Jameson slumped into his chair with relief. He was gathering his papers together when Elizabeth appeared at the door.

"Father?"

"Hello, Elizabeth," he said absently. With his papers tucked under his arm, he walked past her into the hall, giving her a brief pat on the head the way he had when she was a child. She followed as he started up the stairs.

"Wait, Father. I wanted to talk with you about this matter Mr. Ivers has raised."

Jameson stared at her. "Were you listening out here?"

"Yes, and I have an idea about..."

"I can't believe my own daughter would eavesdrop on my business meetings! These affairs don't concern you."

"But they do!" Elizabeth insisted. "I'm a part of what you're doing, aren't I? I work with you!"

Jameson stomped up the stairs, his back rigid. Robert, Jr., wouldn't pay any attention to the business, and Elizabeth paid far too much. What difficult children he'd raised! As if it weren't enough that things were going sour between him and his business partners. All the years of hard work, all the risks he'd taken, and this was the result. He felt the burden of it like a crushing weight in his chest.

Elizabeth hurried behind him to catch up. "Father, please! I can help you with it. With Matthew...with Reverend Brice."

"How?"

Her expression softened and she ducked her head almost shyly. "I've been seeing him. I didn't tell you because I was afraid you wouldn't approve."

"So you went behind my back."

"I wouldn't have chosen to do that. But with the situation the way—"

"I don't want to discuss this any further."

"Well, I do!" Her eyes blazed with anger. "I know about the business, and I know a way to help with Reverend Brice. Why won't you just listen to me?"

"No!" Jameson made no effort to keep the fury from his voice. "I don't want to hear *anything* more from you. I won't have you involved in my company anymore, either. From now on you are to stay home where you belong. And you are not to see Brice or any other man without my permission."

Nahana came running out into the upstairs hall, wrapping a robe hastily around her. Her face was drawn with concern. Before she could say anything, Elizabeth shouted at her father, "I won't live like that!"

"You have no choice. You will live here exactly as I tell you."

"Just see if you can make me!" she cried as she ran back down the stairs.

Nahana called after her, but Elizabeth only glanced briefly at her mother before running off down the hall. Jameson, still looking furious, remained standing on the stairs. He reached out a hand to Nahana, but she didn't notice. Her eyes were locked on some distant place and her voice trembled with intensity.

"It is all my fault."

"Elizabeth?" Jameson asked.

"Yes. And Robert. And Kaahumanu. And the monument. All of it. Because I signed away the land. The gods punish those who turn from the land."

"That's just an old kahuna chant from a thousand years ago. You know that."

"Yes. I do know that."

She walked slowly down the stairs, passing him with glazed eyes. Jameson sighed and went to their room with his papers.

Jamee Ivers had spread the construction plans out on the desk of his hotel suite. He ignored the initial rap at his door, then frowned and slipped on his jacket when it sounded again, louder. When he opened the door, he found Elizabeth Jameson standing there. He looked nervously down the hall.

"Aren't you surprised to see me?" she asked.

He shook his head. "No. Not since I've heard you're no longer working at your father's office."

"Won't you invite me in?"

After a brief hesitation, he opened the door wider and gestured her in, leaving the door conspicuously ajar. "I wonder if this is wise, your coming here," he said. "It might be misunderstood."

"You're older than my father." Her smile was more mischievous than coquettish. "No one saw me. I waited until the clerk had gone."

He reached back and closed the door before taking her wrap. "I knew we had a great deal in common. Sit down."

Elizabeth took the chair he offered and arranged herself comfortably in it. Ivers could see no trace of native blood in her, unless it was the spirit of her grandfather. Determination gleamed in her eyes. He knew better than to underestimate this young woman. Her father wasn't aware of her keen business sense, but James Ivers didn't suffer from such blindness.

"You want something from me," he suggested.

"Of course. But I have something to offer you, too. We should be able to reach a fair bargain."

"I'm sure we can." Ivers leaned back in his chair, fascinated by her poise. "Tell me about it."

"How would you feel if I were able to make Reverend Brice our ally instead of our enemy?"

"I'd consider it something of a miracle," he admitted.

"Well, it wouldn't exactly be a miracle," she said with a laugh, "but I have some idea how important it could be to you. That's why I have something substantial in mind for your part of the bargain."

She proceeded to detail a very businesslike, very clever proposition to him. James Ivers, for one of the few times in his life, didn't even try to negotiate a lower price. Elizabeth knew precisely how valuable her offer was, and he had no intention of jeopardizing its success by trying to bargain with her.

Elizabeth was almost at the rectory door when she noticed a movement in the churchyard. Matthew Brice, his hands clasped behind his back, was walking between the graves, staring at the earth, lost in thought. Elizabeth saw no servants, so she took the path into the churchyard, softly calling his name. At the sound of her voice he swung around, his face glowing with pleasure. "Elizabeth!"

"I don't want to go on being away from you, Matthew," she said, laying a hand lightly on his arm.

"But your father's forbidden you to see me. And with Reverend Proctor dead, I have a great responsibility here."

"I know. And I know there's a way to work out each of

our problems and still reach the same conclusion. We will get married. I need to be with you, Matthew."

"I don't understand. Have you changed your mind?" He waved at the primitive rectory. "Could you be happy living here with me?"

"We wouldn't have to live in this house, Matthew."

He stiffened and moved back a pace. "I can't give up the ministry, Elizabeth, even for you."

"You won't have to." She knew that he was almost afraid to ask what she meant. "There *is* a way. If you love me. If you still want me."

"You know I do!"

She moved close to him, her raised lips only inches from his. "We'll be married, Matthew," she promised in a voice trembling with intensity. "And our love will be joined in body and soul. Together there's nothing we can't do!"

Lihoa stood a little apart from the workers massed in the clearing of the village. Under the light of the torches they pressed toward her, she saw how eager they were to hear what she would say next.

Her grandfather whispered close to her ear, "Maybe we should try to talk to them first."

"There's no use talking to *haoles*," she said. "They don't ever listen to us." She looked up at Robert. "Grandfather wants us to wait. Do you?"

He shook his head vigorously.

Lihoa gestured the massed workers to silence. "Now is the time to show the *haoles* that this is our island, not theirs!" Several of the younger workers cheered, but others frowned uneasily.

"How?" someone called from the crowd.

"They have destroyed what was ours. Now we will destroy what is theirs."

"But that means violence. People could get hurt!"

"Violence is all *haoles* understand. We must strike at them now to show them they can't crush us, to show them we must be taken into account."

In the silence that followed, several of the workers rose and began to walk away. Lihoa shouted after them, "Are you afraid? Then go! True Hawaiians have no fear for themselves. True Hawaiians are ready to fight for their land. Would Kamehameha have let the *haoles* rule over our people? Never!"

When only the hard core remained, she demanded, "How many of you are with me?" She nodded at their shouts of approval. "Good. We will show the *haoles* who the people are. *The land is ours!*"

The workers picked up the chant and sent it back to her. "The land is ours!" Their voices swelled, filling the clearing and spilling out into the quiet jungle. At her side, Robert raised his hand with hers as he joined the chant, "The land is ours!"

CHAPTER TWENTY-THREE

LAST EFFORTS

The afternoon sun had almost reached the top of Pele's mountain as Lihoa and Robert carried their hidden torches onto the construction site below the offices of Jameson and Company. They waited, crouched behind partially finished scaffolding. A few yards away, similarly concealed, Lihoa's grandfather knelt with another group of villagers.

When the sun balanced itself delicately on the tip of the mountain, Robert felt the seconds counting in his pounding pulse. That giant blaze of light would disappear in an instant. He must be ready. Even though he expected the blast of the siren signaling the end of work, it shocked him, tensing his muscles and shortening his breath. The sun was gone. He smiled at Lihoa.

The skilled *haole* workers left first, sauntering off in friendly groups. Behind them, the Hawaiian laborers, having laid aside their tools, stood to be searched before they could leave the construction site. The disappearing daylight cast shadows over the last of the workers, and the guards began to return to their huts.

Without moving, Robert whispered to Lihoa, "Now?"

She nodded. "But I must set the first fire at the farthest end. That will be the signal to the others."

"I'll do it," he said.

She shook her head, holding the torch fast. "Together, then."

Moving stealthily, darting from the shadow of one structure to the next, they worked their way toward the far end of the site. The joined planks of the newly constructed dock were freshly caulked with tar. Lihoa set the unlighted torches into the stripping.

As Robert knelt to set the planks ablaze, he felt footsteps vibrate along the dock. He darted behind a stack of lumber, watching a worker search for a forgotten tool, praying he wouldn't come close enough to notice the waiting torches. Robert was so intent on the approaching worker that he was unaware of a greater danger until he heard Lihoa's quick intake of breath. Farther down the dock, a guard was walking toward where her grandfather and the other villagers were hidden.

"We can't wait," Lihoa whispered. "If the others are found, it's all over. Light them!"

"But we were going to do it when there was no one around!"

"They'll be safe enough," she assured him. "It's the two of us who could be in trouble."

Only then did he realize how real the danger was. He struck the flint and touched the flame to their torches, handing one to her and keeping the other. Lihoa instantly thrust her torch at the tar strips, where the flame wavered only a moment before igniting spectacularly. The fire raced along the lines of tar, engulfing the end of the dock within seconds.

As the flames rose, crackling and hissing, the villagers at the other end of the dock lit their section. Most of them then fled according to plan, but Lihoa's grandfather stood motionless, waiting to make sure Lihoa was safe. Robert gestured furiously to the old man to leave, but he stayed rooted to his spot.

It was the cry of the Hawaiian guard from the dock below that caught Jackson's attention. He ran to the window overlooking the scene. "My God," he shouted. "The docks!"

Jameson and Ivers reached the window as the last of the villagers tossed their torches into the flaming structure below. Clouds of smoke billowed past them as Jameson raced down the stairs and onto the dock. He shoved a terrified *haole* foreman toward the equipment.

"Over there! Get the suction lines from the dredging pump. Spray wet sand on it." He shouted orders at the guards spilling from their hut. "Get the ones with torches. Use your clubs! Stop them!"

Lihoa saw the flames encircle her grandfather. Still he delayed, refusing to flee. He called her name, urging her to hurry. She shouted back as she ran, begging him to leave. But her voice was drowned by the growing tumult of the fire and the shouts of guards streaming onto the docks.

When the smoke cut Lihoa from his sight, her grandfather wept. She was lost, trapped with Robert beyond the consuming fire. The old man started toward them as Hawaiian guards broke through the smoke, wielding poles and swinging clubs. Blinded by smoke, and limping from a blow, he was suddenly thrown as the planking under his feet collapsed, hurtling him down onto the rocks below.

Flames and smoke cut Lihoa and Robert off from the main portion of the dock. She could no longer see her grandfather and she had to fight a rising panic. They had to find a way off the dock. Groping through the smoke, they moved along the edge of the dock. It crumbled under Robert's weight, and Lihoa kept him from falling by her strength alone.

Robert gripped her hand. "There! That way!"

Clinging to him, fighting for breath in the dense smoke, she followed his lead. They were gaining freedom when the whimsy of the wind swept the smoke aside. In that moment, Lihoa heard Jameson's cry.

"Robert!" he called, anguish filling his voice. "Robert!"

Jameson had been moving steadily among the workers, shouting directions, organizing the equipment to battle the blaze. Breathing the stinking vapors made his chest burn. When he caught sight of his son, Robert's name was wrenched straight from his heart. He saw Robert turn, his face blackened with smoke. He also saw a blazing timber breaking away above his son's head.

"Robert!" he screamed, this time in warning. "Look out!"

Lihoa heard the crack of the burning timber and reached for Robert, but she was too late. The huge, flaming scaffolding thundered down on him, pinning him helplessly.

The emergency hospital was set up in a tent not far from the site of the fire. In the shadows lay a line of shrouded corpses. Villagers huddled close by in grieving silence, waiting. Nahana stood with Lihoa at the edge of the clearing, with Elizabeth and Pelika nearby.

Jameson, closer to the tent, was pacing restlessly. A single kerosene lamp swayed inside the tent, casting grotesque images of the surgeon at his work. As Jameson recognized his son's cry of pain, he lunged for the tent. Two orderlies pressed him back, quickly, efficiently.

In his fury and frustration, Jameson wheeled on Lihoa. "This is your fault!"

She stared back without flinching. "No! It's yours, you and all the other *haoles* who have taken everything from us."

Jameson gestured to the corpses. "People getting hurt and killed, is that what you want? Do you think setting fire to some docks will change anything? They can be rebuilt."

"They will be destroyed again."

Dr. Sorrenson came through the flap of the tent, his surgeon's apron streaked with blood. For one brief moment they could see Robert on the cot beneath the kerosene lamp.

"He's not going to die, is he?" Jameson asked, his voice suddenly haunted.

"No, but I'm going to have to remove his leg to stop the gangrene."

Nahana looked as though she would collapse. "Please. There must be another way."

"I'm sorry," the doctor said gently. "He'll die if I don't amputate that leg."

Jameson grasped Nahana, cradling her head against his chest as the doctor went back into the tent. Elizabeth and Pelika clung to each other. When Robert's single, wrenching cry broke the stillness, Lihoa covered her face with her hands and stumbled off alone into the darkness.

Each day when Nahana arrived to visit Robert, Lihoa was there. His bed was always smooth, and fragrant fresh flowers battled against the acrid hospital stench. A bowl of fresh fruit was within his reach. Touched by these evidences of love, Nahana yearned to draw near to the girl. But Lihoa left the tent when Nahana came, and returned only when Nahana left.

Mostly Nahana sat at Robert's side, trying not to see the cumbersome, wrapped stump of his leg. It had been severed below the knee and was kept elevated, so he could not raise his eyes without facing the dreadful reminder.

Few words passed between them. Robert lay with his eyes closed most of the time. Her handsome, energetic son—crippled. She could hardly bear to think of it. When he was awake, he was groggy and stared at her numbly, unable to find words. Her heart overflowed with love and sympathy, but she, too, could not put this into words.

Pelika sent special foods, most of which went uneaten. Elizabeth sent books, which showed no sign of being opened. Jameson came, spoke heartily to his son, and waited.

On the morning of Robert's release, Lihoa did not leave. She stood expressionlessly in the corner. Jameson entered the tent with his usual brisk step, followed more hesitantly by Nahana.

"Dr. Sorrenson said we could take you home today, Robert," Jameson announced.

Lihoa stepped to Robert's side and took his hand. "No. He's not going back with you. Ever."

Jameson stared at her. "What are you talking about? This is my son. I'm taking him home."

When he leaned to assist his son, Robert shook his head. "I'm not going home with you. I don't belong there anymore." His eyes moved to Nahana. "I'm sorry, Mother."

Tears slid silently down her cheeks as she leaned to hug him farewell. It did not occur to Jameson until they were back in the carriage, on their way home, that he'd never seen his wife cry before.

* * *

Several weeks passed before Nahana decided to speak to Jameson. At sunset she rapped at his study door, interrupting his work. He was startled, for she had never done this before. But Nahana had changed since the day the rock fell into the sea. Even in his arms, she seemed distant.

"I'd like you to walk with me," she said.

He smiled and pushed aside his work. "Wonderful. Wouldn't you like to take the carriage?"

"No, I want to walk."

The path she chose led to the lagoon. The sunset colors that reflected on the face of the water stirred and changed like a shattered rainbow. "This is where we were first together," Nahana said. "Over there—that's where I hid you."

"I remember."

"And this was where Kaahumanu persuaded Kamehameha to spare your life." When he nodded, she gripped his arm, forcing him to look into her face. "*I want the land back.* You must take it back from Ivers and make him leave our islands forever."

"Do you know what that would take, Nahana?" he asked gently. "It would cost almost everything we've got."

"I want the land back," she repeated. "I don't care about anything else."

"This isn't a good time to convince my partners," he explained. "With the docks burned down, and having to start over again, Ivers's investment isn't protected. He'd probably want double his initial investment to pull out now. And that would take everything—the cane fields, the cattle and hide business, the trading company."

She listened without emotion to his arguments. When he said nothing, he continued, somewhat exasperated. "You see, I wouldn't be able to get cooperation from the others—Tuttle, Schmidt, Bertelle, and Holmes. They've started to side with Ivers, against me. They're talking about arming the guards, and bringing in Chinese coolies to work, and stirring up trouble among the natives against Kaahumanu, or getting Reverend Brice replaced with someone more to their liking. It's all crazy talk, but they aren't listening to me now."

Nahana regarded him with wide, sad eyes. "It is because of the land. Everything is going wrong because I gave away the land."

"That simply isn't true! These are business matters, political matters. They have nothing to do with who owns the land."

"When I owned the land, my children were safe. Now Robert has lost his leg, Elizabeth has become isolated and secretive. When I owned the land, my love for you was stronger even than my love for my heritage, or I would not have allowed you to persuade me to part with it."

Jameson suddenly looked horrified. "Surely your love for me hasn't changed! I still love you as deeply as I ever have, Nahana."

"Yes, but you love your things, your money, your businesses, almost as much. You've spent your life accumulating things, for me, for our children. But I don't want your things. I've never wanted your things, only your love."

"You have my love," he insisted. "You've always had my love."

As though she hadn't heard him, she went on in a tired, sad voice, "Your love has always been blind, Jameson. You gave me what *you* wanted to give me, not questioning what *I* want. You built an empire for Robert and never understood that his strongest ties were to the land and his people, not to money and business. You couldn't give Elizabeth the one thing she wanted more than anything else in the world."

"Oh, Elizabeth," he said dismissively.

"Yes, Elizabeth. Your beautiful, talented daughter. She just wants you to love her, to be proud of her. But you're too consumed by your adoration for your son to see how you have ignored her." Nahana stared out over the water. "And I saw it all, and I still loved you."

"Thank God!"

"But you used my love. You bargained it for a chance at another business deal. You said it was to make Hawaii great, but it is just one more way to make money. Perhaps you have convinced yourself that my father would have wanted this. But you are wrong!"

"Kamehameha wanted to build Hawaii into a great nation."

"Not at the expense of the Hawaiians. Never at the cost of dispossessing his people from the land."

Jameson felt a cold tremor in his heart. His shoulders began to ache with tension. It wasn't the argument about Kamehameha's wishes that most concerned him. "Don't you love me anymore, Nahana?"

"My love for you is inside me still. I can hear the whisper of it when all is silent. But a great darkness separates me from it. I should not have given away my land. It was wrong, and now I can't reach that love which drove me to betray my people, my land. I must have the land back, Jameson."

He sighed. "It's inevitable that foreigners are going to own land here one day, Nahana."

"But not my land. Not the land my father gave me."

"I'll see what I can do to get it back," he promised, reaching for her hand. He couldn't bear the thought of living without her love. But the land! Ivers would never part with the land for less than everything Jameson was worth. And perhaps not even that.

He held tightly to Nahana's hand as they made their way back to the house. He was afraid she was slipping away.

Elizabeth was waiting for them at the house. Her chin was set at its most determined angle and she refused to let her father put her off with the excuse of the lateness of the hour. "I have a number of things to tell you, and if you don't let me do it tonight, you're going to be embarrassed by finding them out for yourself tomorrow," she informed him.

Jameson grew impatient, as he often did with Elizabeth. It had been a difficult day and he wasn't looking forward to a confrontation with his demanding daughter. Nahana was watching him closely, though, so he tried to treat Elizabeth fairly. "Let's at least sit down in the saloon," he suggested, unaware that his voice made it perfectly clear he was humoring her.

With a shrug, Elizabeth followed him, the set of her chin and her shoulders just a little more rigid now. His attitude simply made it easier for her to justify what she had done, all the manipulations and negotiations behind his back. But it hurt to present her mother with this evidence of her disloyalty. Nahana wouldn't understand. She would support her husband, as always.

While her parents seated themselves, Elizabeth remained standing. There was so much to say, it was hard to know where to start. Perhaps with the most important matter.

"I'm twenty now, and old enough to make my own decisions, just as Robert is. He's chosen to live away from you because he feels he doesn't belong here, because he sees life differently than Father does. I've always had a great deal in common with Father, as far as my interest in building Hawaii and taking part in business, but that hasn't made living here any easier."

"You have all the luxury the islands have to offer right here," Jameson interjected.

"Father has decreed that I give up the two most important things in my life—Matthew Brice, and working in the family business." Sudden tears pricked at her eyes, but she forced them back. "And I know I have to have both of those things to give my life any meaning, to have even the smallest measure of happiness."

"Oh, Elizabeth," Nahana whispered. "My poor child."

"And I know how important it is to have Matthew on our side. Father wouldn't listen to me, but Mr. Ivers did."

"You went to Ivers?" Jameson bellowed. "What have you done?"

Elizabeth drew a deep breath. "I've made it possible for all of us to work together. Mr. Ivers and Reverend Brice have come to an agreement. They have decided that their purposes are not, after all, opposed. The Hawaiians need employment, the company needs employees. The church needs revenue for expanding its programs."

"And where would the revenue come from?" Jameson asked through tight lips.

"The mission will become a member of the association, by every other member signing over a share to it. That's already been agreed."

"They had a meeting behind my back? How dare they do such a thing? I won't sign over a share to the mission," Jameson warned.

"They're prepared to buy you out if you don't. It's a unanimous decision, except for you."

As his fury grew, a pain inside his chest tightened. "And you did this to me, my own daughter. Go! I never want to see you here again."

"You haven't ever accepted me as I am, anyhow," she cried. "And I have solved a problem for you, not made one. These associates of yours would have done far worse if I hadn't managed to turn things around."

Nahana's soft voice pressed through the tension that filled the room. "But how did you do it, Elizabeth?"

"I used my influence with Matthew." She met her mother's eyes for a brief moment before looking away. "I love Matthew. I've loved him for a long time. And he loves me.

There was no sense in letting this conflict between the mission and the company continue. I brought Matthew and Mr. Ivers together and helped to sort out their differences."

Her father eyed her coldly. "And what do you get for it?"

"Just what I wanted," she replied coolly. "I get to marry Matthew. And I'll handle business matters for the mission, sitting in with the association. I'm your daughter, after all. I decided what I wanted, and I went after it."

"You're selfish, and willful, and ungrateful. I can't imagine how you turned out this way, with such a fine example in your mother. The sooner you move out of this house, the better I'll like it."

Jameson rose to his feet, feeling almost breathless with the small exertion. When he was still suffering from his son's horrifying injury and even more distressing departure from the family, Jameson felt he couldn't bear this second betrayal. And all this on top of Nahana's confessing that she no longer loved him as she once had.

His whole life seemed to be crumbling around him. Nothing he had hoped and planned for had worked out as he'd expected. His children hated him, and the close bond he'd always treasured with Nahana seemed to be fading away.

The burden grew in his chest, swelling painfully. Sharp stabs of light flared behind his eyes, flashing scenes of an earlier Hawaii, an idyll of simple pleasures that no longer existed. "But the *kapus* are gone," he muttered. "The *kii* gods are gone. There have been the good things, too."

But suddenly he couldn't remember the good things he had brought to the islands. He was back at the waterfall many years ago, watching Nahana wash her hair, her beautiful wet body shining in the sunlight. How rich their life had been, and how uncomplicated! Swimming and fishing and making love. Sleeping and eating, talking and laughing. Could his life now compare with that?

A ragged shock of pain struck his body. His flesh burned with perspiration. Had he been struck by lightning? His chest throbbed, his breath came in frantic, useless gasps. Hard and fast after the pain came the fear. Something was happening, something awful. Then suddenly his legs gave out. When he regained consciousness, he found himself lying on the floor, dazed, with soft hands holding his head.

"Nahana?"

"I'm here." Her voice was choked with tears. "Get a doctor, Elizabeth. Quickly! Quickly!"

"Oh, God! I'll be back as fast as I can." Elizabeth bent over Jameson and whispered fiercely in his ear, "Don't die! I'll get help. I love you, Father! Please don't die."

Jameson could hear her running feet as she left the room, but he felt paralyzed and weak, unable to move. Nahana cradled his head in her lap, stroking his temples. Her touch soothed, as did her words, Hawaiian words of love, of courage, of mystical pleadings to the gods. His mind carried him back to the first night in her arms. The remembered ecstasy helped to block out the pain that was closing over him.

With the last of his consciousness he forced his eyes to take in Nahana's stunned, beautiful face. "I've never regretted staying. Not once. Your love made my life special." He moistened his dry lips, trying to finish what he had to say. "Remember that I loved you. If I did things wrong... I didn't mean to. I wanted to make your life as rich as mine was. Tell Robert..."

A last, fatal tremor raced through him. Nahana knew his breath left his body. She continued to sit with his head in her lap, chanting the old songs for the dead in a trance, a trance that protected her briefly from thought, and feeling, from realizing her loss.

* * *

Elizabeth was shaking with fatigue by the time she and Matthew reached the house. The doctor was on his way and a message had been sent to Robert to come home. She had done all she could. And yet she knew in her heart that it was too late. There had been a moment, not long after she left the house, when she felt an almost unbearable weight on her heart. When it lifted, she was sure her father had died, but she continued, desperately refusing to accept that he was gone.

Everything looked exactly as Elizabeth had left it. The one lamp still burned, and Nahana sat on the floor with Jameson's head in her lap. But Jameson was still, and a steady stream of silent tears washed down Nahana's face. She could no longer avoid the truth. Elizabeth reeled under pain that struck her like a blow. Matthew held her shoulders tightly.

"Mother," she said softly.

Nahana looked up with wounded eyes. "His breath is gone, Elizabeth," she said carefully.

At first, Elizabeth could not speak. She swallowed hard, her eyes moist with unshed tears, her throat aching. Finally, her voice returned, shaking. "Do you blame me?"

Matthew looked astonished at this question, but Nahana seemed not at all surprised. "Of course not," she said firmly. "No one is to blame. He heard difficult words today, but he knew we loved him. He knew he made a mistake, a grave mistake, but he understands now. His spirit will understand."

Matthew cleared his throat. "Would you . . . like me to say some prayers for him, Mrs. Jameson?"

For a moment Nahana looked confused. Then she nodded. "Of course. Please. He would have wanted that very much."

Elizabeth moved to her mother's side and held her while

Matthew prayed aloud, filling the room with his fervent, masculine voice. It seemed almost sacrilegious for Matthew to be the one who prayed over her father, after what had happened earlier. But in death Jameson was a Christian soul and Matthew was a man of the cloth. Elizabeth would simply have to accept the irony, along with her grief.

Robert arrived at the door of the saloon with Lihoa's help. He was learning to manage by himself, but he was too distraught now to remember what he'd been taught. All he could think of was that he hadn't yet thanked his father for the horse Jameson had sent to the village for him. In fact, he hadn't spoken to his father since leaving the hospital.

And now he would never speak with him again. By the time he arrived, Pelika had already laid Jameson out according to custom and he lay stiff and white and unreal. Robert turned helplessly to Lihoa, but she had already drawn back as his mother and sister moved toward him.

"What was it?" he asked. "What happened?"

"His heart, the doctor thinks. It all happened so quickly." Nahana hugged him tightly against her. "He loved you. And he knew you loved him, too, despite your differences."

Though Robert accepted her comforting, he was racked with guilt. He had been such a disappointment to his father. Jameson's expectations had always been a burden to him, and Jameson's love had been suffocating. They had driven him to find his own way of life, a life so different from his father's that not even their close relationship could overcome it. He reached out for Lihoa's hand, drawing her with him into the room.

In silence, Jameson's family surrounded him for the last time. Robert, with Lihoa's supporting arm around him, balanced on his one good leg. Elizabeth stood defiant, with Matthew's hand on her shoulder.

And Nahana, dazed with grief, remembering all the years spent together, kept coming back again and again to their first months in the beach hut. Life had been perfect then, and life was seldom perfect. And love . . . well, her love had not been perfect at the end, but Jameson would understand. Now he would understand everything.

PART FIVE

*Hawaii Ponoi!
(Our Own Hawaii)*

CHAPTER TWENTY-FOUR

THE WILL

Jameson's funeral drew a large crowd of Hawaiians and *haoles*. Inspired by his personal feelings of guilt, Matthew Brice conducted the service with a dignity enhanced by his usual religious enthusiasm. Kaahumanu was too ill to come, but out of respect for Nahana and her former allegiance to Jameson himself, she sent a representative, an *alii* chief, to speak of all the accomplishments this *haole* had brought to Hawaii. Several of Jameson's business associates also paid glowing tribute to him, secretly grateful, no doubt, that he had died so conveniently.

Elizabeth found the service an agony. Everything about it seemed hypocritical to her. Especially her own position. No matter what her mother said, she felt her betrayal had contributed to her father's death. Elizabeth was angry with her father for dying, and she grieved for his loss. Now she would never have a chance to win his love or earn his respect.

Through the service she sat rigidly, unemotional, clasping her mother's hand. Nahana stared straight ahead, her expression dazed, with tears slipping unnoticed down her cheeks. Robert sat on Elizabeth's other side. He looked pale and strained, as if this tragedy had set back his recovery. Lihoa wasn't with him.

"Robert Jameson was the American pioneer who worked with the great Kamehameha to start Hawaii on its road from primitive isolation to modernization and progress. Jameson's vision of Hawaii's future held firm through his entire life, and led him to bring commerce to this island. No other man is more responsible for the advancement of civilization here."

It was all true, but it disturbed Elizabeth that it was Ivers speaking, and not Kaahumanu's representative. These words should be spoken by the Hawaiians, not the *haoles*. Even though Robert's Lihoa didn't believe this to be the truth, there were plenty of Hawaiians who did. Kaahumanu's representative was far too mild in his praise, as far as Elizabeth was concerned.

As she walked back down the aisle with her mother and brother, the realization of Jameson's death struck her again. Her knees suddenly felt weak, and Nahana, ever a source of strength in times of need, supported her out into the blazing sunlight. Elizabeth blinked back the tears, surprised at the intensity of her emotions.

For an hour Elizabeth stood there with Nahana and Robert, accepting condolences from the other mourners. "A wonderful man," they said of her father. "A truly generous man." "A man of vision." "A man of principle." The phrases fell from every tongue. They were all true, but they weren't Elizabeth's idea of her father.

Her father had been like a god to her. Greater than

Kamehameha. His unqualified love and approval, constantly withheld, had been the most important things in the world. And now she could never have them.

"Come, Elizabeth," her mother was saying. "We're going back to the house now."

Thank heaven for the numbness that helped one through these occasions, Elizabeth thought as she climbed into the carriage beside her mother. It was painful to watch Robert struggle in after them, using his hands and his cane and his one functioning leg. How different from their graduation day!

"Jameson's attorney is going to be at the house," Nahana said carefully. "Your father wrote a will some time ago, just in case of... well, in the event of his death."

Elizabeth felt a sinking in her stomach. Why hadn't she thought of that? Of course her father would provide for this contingency. And it would be one more trial to bear, his last chance to repudiate her.

"I don't want anything," Robert said.

"You aren't going to be able to work in the fields ever again," Nahana reminded him. "You're going to have to find something different to do with your life."

"I'm not going to be forced into running his business. I wouldn't do it when he was alive, and I won't do it now that he's dead."

Elizabeth saw that his bitterness distressed her mother. But Nahana simply shrugged. "I think you should wait to hear what the attorney has to say."

"Don't you know what's in the will?" Elizabeth asked.

"No. He didn't discuss it. Your father took care of financial matters." She gazed off toward the bay where sunlight danced on the water. Her hands had tightened into fists at her sides. "But whatever he's arranged, I want the land back that I signed over to Mr. Ivers. I should never have agreed. Only awful things have happened since. I can't bear if anything else should go wrong."

Robert immediately assured her that the problem would be taken care of. Elizabeth was silent, thinking through the possibilities. There seemed one highly risky move that could be taken. Every other solution would prove either useless or economically disastrous. But she said nothing. First she would have to see how her father had disposed of his property.

The attorney Jameson and his business associates had used for years lived in Honolulu but journeyed frequently to the big island to do their work. Because of the negotiations that had been going forward, Mr. Waggoner was on Hawaii at the time of Jameson's death. He offered to come to the house to explain the terms of the will to Jameson's widow and children.

Mr. Waggoner was one of the many *haoles* who had gotten a second chance in the islands. In America he had disgraced himself in some fashion that was rumored but not actually known in Honolulu. His work had proved excellent, and his fees were reasonable, so no one dug too closely into his past.

He was a cheerful fellow, probably not a day over thirty, with a shock of red hair and a bouncing step. He wore spectacles that slid down his narrow, freckled nose until he carelessly pushed them back up again. Looking at him, Elizabeth had always wondered if anyone could take him seriously.

But when he settled down to discuss matters he was efficient and businesslike. Nahana led him to Jameson's study, where he found a copy of the will with no difficulty. He sat at Jameson's desk, nodding as he flipped through the document. "Yes, exactly as I remember it," he said. "Shall we go over it here?"

They brought in chairs and settled quietly to listen. It

wasn't a long document. Jameson had made provisions for Pelika and several of the other servants, but the main thrust of the document was twofold: Robert was to have half of the estate; Nahana was to have the other half in trust for Elizabeth for the duration of Nahana's life.

It was even worse than Elizabeth had imagined, an insult to her maturity and her intelligence. She bit down hard on her lip, refusing to display the anguish she felt. Robert was the one who broke the stunned silence.

"What a rotten thing to do to her!" he blurted. "Well, she can have my share. I don't want it. I wouldn't know how to handle it."

Mr. Waggoner frowned. "Mr. Jameson's estate is worth a great deal of money. It would be rash of you to make a decision on the spur of the moment. I'm sure we can resolve the matter in a better way."

Nahana pressed a hand against her chest, a gesture she had adopted since Jameson's death. "Mr. Waggoner, it's important to me to recover the land which I've signed over to Mr. Ivers. Robert would be willing to see some of his inheritance used for that purpose."

"Buy the deed back?" Waggoner asked, startled. "I can't imagine he'd be willing to sell it, Mrs. Jameson, for any price."

"But I must have it back!"

"It's a relatively small piece of land," he said soothingly. "You own quite a bit of other land, and perhaps you could purchase more with money from the estate."

"You don't understand." But Nahana shook her head. It was useless trying to explain to these *haoles*. "Never mind."

The attorney's head cocked at an inquisitive angle. "Surely you're not suggesting that you'd take everything Mr. Jameson left to reclaim that particular parcel of land. That would be most unwise."

Nahana didn't answer. Elizabeth agreed that they shouldn't tell this man, who after all represented the association as well, anything concerning their plans about the parcel of land. She wasn't sure that she could trust his discretion, no matter how friendly he appeared.

"I'm sure we'll be able to manage under the terms of my father's will," she said. "Mother does have plenty of land, as you say. And I'll be marrying shortly, so..."

"Marrying?" Robert looked genuinely confused. "Who are you going to marry, Elizabeth?"

"Matthew Brice."

Her brother stared at her. "A missionary? I can't believe it!"

Disconcerted, Elizabeth rose and walked to the window. Her brother was immediately contrite. "It's not that he isn't a good man, Elizabeth. I'm sure he is. He was certainly a fine teacher. It was just that you surprised me, I guess."

For the first time, Elizabeth realized that her mother and brother had thought she would marry a Hawaiian. Even though she looked so *haole* herself, they had thought that the blood of Kamehameha that flowed in her veins would lead her to some *alii* chief who was her Hawaiian match. It was a disappointment to them that she had chsen a *haole*, who was not only a foreigner but a minister.

They were determined to respect her choice. Where Jameson had decreed that she shouldn't see Matthew again, her mother and brother were trying to adapt to her decision. This consensus that he wasn't right for her didn't change her mind, but rather made her want to see him, to hold him, all the more.

"Are we finished here?" she asked brightly. "I have some things I really should do. If you don't need me."

Mr. Waggoner seemed reluctant to see her go before matters were fully discussed, but Nahana smiled and waved her away. Relieved, Elizabeth escaped from the house.

* * *

Nahana knew that Elizabeth needed to get away from them for a while. Too many disappointments, too much grief. Let her go. There was plenty of time to sort things out later. For all of them.

Jameson was dead.

In the nights, the knowledge haunted her. Her dreams were often painful. She rose in the mornings burdened with her grief, but in the light of day she could call forth the memories she chose, the good memories, the best of her times with Jameson.

She was left with two grown children, both of whom she loved dearly. They each had something of Jameson in them, though it wasn't necessarily what they thought. But they were both hurt in some ways and she didn't know how to heal them. That would require time... and luck.

Elizabeth found Matthew at the rectory writing his monthly report to the missionary society. He kept meticulous notes on conversions, marriages, and deaths, and especially on the progress of his students. The society was supposed to send him an assistant but had not found someone ready to accept the post. In the meantime, Matthew managed both his old duties and those of the departed Reverend Proctor.

"How are you holding up?" he asked as he seated her in a chair across from his desk. The rectory was marginally larger than the hut he'd first been in. It had three rooms, but none of them large enough to be called a sitting room. Elizabeth was in his "study."

She raised one helpless shoulder. "We've just been informed of the contents of his will. Robert gets half of the estate and Mother the other half, in trust for me until she dies."

Matthew shook his head. "I know it must be a grave disappointment to you, but perhaps it's for the best."

"How could it be for the best?" she wailed.

"It will keep us in moderate circumstances. Wealth is always corrupting." He raised a hand to forestall her objections. "That's how I see it as a minister, of course. I would want more for you, especially since you're accustomed to so luxurious a life. Still, Elizabeth, it will mean you can make your own way. You won't owe anything to your father."

She smiled at such a blatant attempt to win her over. "Who would have thought a minister would have such powers of persuasion, and such a devious mind? In some ways it's true, though. If he didn't have enough faith in me to give me a share outright, I'd rather earn my own."

"When was the will made?"

"I don't know, exactly. A couple of years ago, I guess."

"That might explain it. Long before you and Robert graduated and set out on your separate courses."

Elizabeth gestured impatiently. "He could have changed it at any time. It doesn't matter. I knew he didn't believe in me the way he did in Robert. If he'd lived to be a hundred I'd never have been able to make him love me that way or respect me for my abilities. It doesn't matter," she said again.

Of course it did. Matthew knew it mattered to her a great deal, but he was ready to drop the subject for her sake. "How's your mother doing?"

"Not too badly. But she's convinced all these terrible things that have happened recently are caused by her signing over her piece of land to Mr. Ivers. She and Robert are willing to use Father's whole estate to buy it back."

"And you don't agree?"

"I know Ivers better than that. He's not going to give up the deed. But there may be a way. If you'll help me."

Matthew looked dubious. He had already stretched his moral values to the tearing point in his negotiations with Ivers. It was hard for him to refuse Elizabeth, especially when what she said made so much sense. But there was his duty to think of. His calling. His responsibilities.

And his love. With a sigh, he said, "Tell me what you have in mind."

Kaahumanu was dying. Elizabeth remembered the time when she was taken as a child to say good-bye to Kamehameha. In dying he had shown the same acceptance, the same staunch inevitability as his queen now exhibited. Ever since the explosion had destroyed Kamahameha's monument, Kaahumanu had been drifting toward death. It was as though she had no wish to live after Kamehameha's presence was gone from the island.

In his role as the queen's minister, Matthew visited her regularly and provided what Christian comfort he could. He even turned a blind eye to her backsliding into Hawaiian ways on occasion. He was sympathetic to the force of the old habits in the aging population; his hope was for the younger generation.

Matthew wasn't at all sure how Kaahumanu would receive Elizabeth under the circumstances. There were times when the queen was still gracious and hospitable, but often she was withdrawn and uncommunicative. When he had expressed his reservations to Elizabeth, she had said she would take her chances. "After all," she'd said, "there's really nothing to lose."

The queen was surprised to see her with the Reverend Brice. Recently Elizabeth had come to visit only with Nahana. "How beautiful you are!" she exclaimed, before remembering the sad event that had occurred so recently. "My condolences on the loss of your father. Jameson did many important things for our island, and he was my personal friend for many, many years."

Elizabeth appreciated this ambiguous way of stating the case. She kissed Kaahumanu on the cheek and said simply, "Thank you. We miss him."

"Sit down." The queen waved them to two chairs close to her bed. The room was, as always, littered with knickknacks from all over the world, as well as an assortment of medicines from both Dr. Sorrenson and the native healers. She eyed Elizabeth more closely. "You have something important to say to me."

Surprised at this astute observation, Elizabeth nodded. "I'm hoping we can solve a problem." An impertinent smile played around her lips, and her eyes sparkled. "And perhaps settle a score at the same time."

"You intrigue me. Go on."

"My mother is frantic about the piece of land she signed over to Mr. Ivers."

Kaahumanu's face froze. "It was a terrible thing to do. Not that I blame her. She did it for Jameson. He should never have asked it of her. He knew that the land and the people are one." In case this was somehow inappropriate to say in front of the Reverend Brice, she added, "This is a Hawaiian belief which your God would approve of."

"No doubt," he said.

"Mr. Ivers was responsible for the explosion that caused the great catastrophe," Elizabeth informed her unnecessarily. "You sent him word of your displeasure, but it hardly seems punishment enough for his vile deed."

"They burned down his docks," Kaahumanu said with great satisfaction.

"Yes, but he will build them again. And if they should be destroyed again, perhaps he would not try a third time. Which would mean that he might do something worse with the land. Sell it to another *haole*, perhaps."

Kaahumanu was at her most imperious. "Never! I would not allow it."

"No, of course not. But in order to stop him, you would have to exercise your royal prerogative, you and Kamehameha the Third." Elizabeth realized Kaahumanu was not following her. "Kamehameha gave the land to my mother. The king owns all the land and gives it to whomever he wishes. This has always been the way, from king to *alii* chief, to the common people who live on the land. And what one king gives, another can take back."

Kaahumanu was shaking her head. "But it is seldom done, and we have new laws. The foreigners would refuse to come here at all if the king or queen behaved in such a fashion. We cannot take back land we have given."

Elizabeth was prepared for this argument, since she quite agreed with it. "Yes, but you can put restrictions on the land. You can take back the land and give it to the people, with the stipulation that it is to be used for docks by the association. That if at any time it does not serve the people in this way, it will revert to their use."

The queen looked from Elizabeth to Brice and back again. "Is this true? Could I do this?"

"You have the power, yes," Matthew admitted. "They won't like it, but it won't harm their project, either. It would be a good lesson to Ivers for his carelessness in blasting through the mountain. And if it's explained to the people, they shouldn't try to burn the docks down again. It's an ingenious solution."

A slow smile spread across Kaahumanu's pale face. "I told your parents once that you reminded me of myself when I was young," she said to Elizabeth. "I see I was right."

"She can't do it!" Ivers bellowed. "I have a deed to the land."

"Unfortunately," Mr. Waggoner said, running a hand through his already disarrayed red hair, "she *can* do it, with the young king's cooperation. And he has undoubtedly agreed. It won't make much difference to your project, only to you personally, since your deed is worthless."

Ivers glared at him. "A lot of help you are. I've a good mind to find myself another attorney."

"Do as you please," Waggoner retorted. "No one else could have done anything more about it than I did. And you may find, in the end, that it's a boon to you. That crazy bunch of natives isn't going to find much support for burning down docks that are built on *their* land, for *their* future progress."

This was small consolation to Ivers, who prided himself on his careful handling of his business affairs. "And you'll never convince me that it was Kaahumanu's idea. She may have been furious with me about the explosion, but she would more likely have had my head chopped off than come up with this ploy. So who got to her?"

Waggoner shrugged. "I haven't the slightest idea. Jameson wanted the deed back for his wife, but I doubt if his ghost whispered in the queen's ear. Brice may have been involved, but he's not worldly enough or clever enough to have come up with this scheme."

"There's only one person it could have been," Ivers growled. "The rest of them are sheep."

His attorney didn't even wish to hear his theory. "Put it behind you," he advised.

"For now."

Nahana listened to Kaahumanu with stunned attention. The queen was explaining exactly what she had done about the parcel of land. "I won't give you anything to replace it," she said. "You were wrong to part with the land. But I understand. Your Jameson was very convincing, and you loved him very much."

"I didn't want the land back for myself. So long as it

belongs to the people, I am more than content. I can never thank you enough."

"Thank your daughter. She did me a service as well."

Nahana's brows rose. "This was Elizabeth's idea?"

"Yes. She's going to be a powerful woman one day, your Elizabeth."

Nahana nodded absently. She was wondering if Elizabeth would remember her Hawaiian heritage at times when it wasn't simply useful to her. But Nahana was immensely grateful to her daughter for easing this weighty burden from her shoulders. The land once again belonged to the people. Her family would be safe.

CHAPTER TWENTY-FIVE

JOINED TOGETHER

Elizabeth was stunned by her mother's decision to live in the beach hut. "But there's nothing there! Things have changed since the days you lived that way, Mother," she protested. "Don't you like the way you live here? The big beds, the stove, the carpets, comfortable furniture? There wouldn't be room for anything like that in the beach hut."

"I know. It doesn't matter. For a while I want to live that way again."

"Oh, then this is only temporary." Elizabeth smiled with relief. "You'll come back to the house in a little while."

"No, I won't come back here. Perhaps to something larger than the hut in time, but not here." She drew a deep breath. "I want you and Matthew to live here when you're married."

"Is that why you're doing this?" Elizabeth demanded. "So Matthew and I won't have to live in the rectory?"

"No, of course not."

"Because I *can* live in the rectory. I know it's not what I'm accustomed to, and I'd make a lot of additions and improvements, but I can certainly live there. I don't even know if Matthew would be willing to live here," she added. "He's very disapproving of too luxurious a way of life."

"There's a certain austerity about him, yes. I hope that he'll agree for your sake. Talk with him about i "

After a moment's hesitation Elizabeth agreed.

Elizabeth was considering what it would be like for the two of them to live here when the buggy drew up to the front of the house. Nahana had insisted that Robert take the buggy, that he had a great deal more need of it than she did. She had also insisted that he bring Lihoa with him when he returned.

Because it was painful to watch Robert climb the front stairs, his mother and sister waited in the main room. Robert entered with Lihoa at his side, her face stern. No more than half a dozen words had ever passed between Elizabeth and Lihoa, who remained hostile and ill-at-ease when confronted with Robert's beautiful, light-skinned sister. Lihoa was slightly more comfortable with Nahana, though it wasn't obvious. She held her head at a stiff, proud angle that firmly denied any possibility of the Jameson women getting close to her.

The large portrait of Kamehameha dominated the room. Lihoa managed to frown at it in a meaningful way, somehow suggesting that this family did not deserve to be related to the great ruler. She refused the chair facing the looming portrait and instead seated herself on the floor a few feet from Robert. He seemed not to find this behavior awkward. Elizabeth assumed he was used to her doing such things.

For a while no one said anything. Robert cleared his

throat and adjusted his damaged leg to a more comfortabl position. Finally he said, "I understand Elizabeth has take care of the land pledged to Ivers."

"The people don't want docks," Lihoa informed th room at large. "They want their birthright, their fishin ponds and taro patches. What good will a dock do them?"

No one responded to her. Robert had obviously covere this ground with her before, for he said carefully, "Consid ering the situation, it's perhaps the best solution that coul be reached. I don't think anyone will try to burn the dock down again. Too many people suffered last time, an Kaahumanu has at least given the land to the people."

Lihoa's grandfather was dead, and Robert was seriousl handicapped. Certainly it was unlikely that the people woul attempt such a project again. Lihoa refused to allow anyon to see the pain these misfortunes had caused her, but bot Elizabeth and Nahana were aware of it. Her goal of destroyin the docks had been accomplished, but her losses had bee much higher than anyone could have anticipated. Liho turned away from the others now, her back stiff an uncompromising.

Robert laid a hand gently on the nape of her neck, surprisingly tender gesture under which Lihoa seemed t relax slightly. It was as though she needed the consta reassurance of Robert's forgiveness and love. Despite wh she had said to Jameson the night of Robert's amputation she obviously did consider herself responsible for the catas trophe. Elizabeth realized this, and felt sorry for the youn woman.

Nahana said to Elizabeth, "I've already spoken wit Robert about my plan to live in the old beach hut, as soon a it's been repaired. He's agreed to oversee the work, and h knows that I want you and Brice to live here."

"In fact," Robert added, "we want to set it up so yo have your rightful share of Father's estate right now. Mothe doesn't feel she'll need much to live on, but I think we should set aside a third of the estate for her and each take a remaining third. Do you think that would be fair?"

"It would leave you with less than Father intended."

"It will leave me with a great deal more than I need or want," he insisted. His gaze shifted briefly to Lihoa and back to Elizabeth. "You know I'd be hopeless at running Father's business. But I thought we could sell my share to you, or one of the partners. I'd use the money to buy a ranch on the northern part of the island."

Lihoa finally spoke again. "We'd pay our workers a living wage, and we'd hire only Hawaiians. And we'd set up villages where the people could have taro patches and fishing ponds. They could live the old ways."

Elizabeth had been thinking that she would have to guide Robert in the sale of his association stock so that it wouldn't give Ivers an advantage, but she was caught off guard by the latter part of their plans. "You'll need to hire *paniolas* at least at first to teach enough Hawaiians how to do the work," she suggested. "But it sounds like a good idea for you, so long as you don't expect to make money at it."

"We're not interested in making money," Lihoa assured her. "We're interested in seeing that Hawaiians can live the way they used to, without *haole* things, and without *haoles* telling them what to do."

"You're not forgetting that Robert is half-*haole*, are you?" Elizabeth asked, her voice under careful control.

But Robert only laughed. "Lihoa tries very hard to forget I'm half-*haole*. She only remembers the half that's descended from Kamehameha."

"Your father was a wonderful man," Nahana told him. "I don't want you ever to forget that you are descended from him as well, and be proud of your *haole* heritage, too."

"I won't forget." He touched Lihoa's cheek. "We'll tell our child."

Elizabeth was surprised to see Lihoa blush. "You're going to have a baby?" She hadn't realized until that moment how jealous she would feel to hear such news.

"Yes," Robert admitted with a grin, "we're going to have a baby. In a month we'll be married, the Hawaiian way, in our village. I want you both to come and give us your blessing."

"That's wonderful news. My blessings to both of you." Nahana remembered the night she and Jameson were married. She had thought at the time that he would leave her, that he would return to Boston, to the woman in the locket. And he would have, except that he had fallen in love with her and couldn't let her die of cholera. He might have caught it himself, might have died as so many Hawaiians had. But he had stayed and saved all those lives. Nahana wondered if Lihoa knew this about Jameson, but she wouldn't ask. "We'll be there," she said.

Elizabeth had intended to postpone her wedding. It was all right that Robert and Lihoa were to be married so soon after Jameson's death, because Lihoa was pregnant. And there was something so moving in the Hawaiian ceremony, something that glorified fertility and the renewal of life. With Lihoa's grandfather and Jameson dead, it was a hopeful sign to see the young couple exchange their promises. Their blood was joined through the tiny marriage cuts at their wrists before they went off to the marriage hut draped with colorful leis and feathers. The chants and the flaming torches contributed to the exotic atmosphere. Nahana had stood as still and watchful as a bird, obviously remembering the past, and pleased with their marriage.

For just one moment Elizabeth wished she could be married in such a colorful ceremony, steeped in native tradition. But she brought herself up short, remembering that she would be married in a Christian church, by one of Matthew's colleagues who would come from another island for the marriage.

In her heart she vowed to make their physical joining something more full-blooded than she pictured the usual missionary-and-wife joinings were. How austere and pious the missionaries seemed! She had had hints of Matthew's passionate nature, and she refused to let it remain buried under the moral stance once they were married.

When she'd made this decision, she was somehow unable to hold to the idea that she and Matthew should wait an appropriate length of time before being wed. Her body felt continually on fire with desire for him. Since Nahana had never seen any necessity for Elizabeth to wait, and in fact seemed eager to have her settled, Elizabeth began to plan in earnest.

The *haole* community and the Hawaiians closest to the family were invited to the ceremony. Elizabeth had thought there would be no special attention paid to the event ahead of time and was surprised to come home one evening to find that Nahana had gathered together several of the Hawaiian women Elizabeth knew best, both of her mother's generation and her own.

They ate a traditional meal and gathered casually in the small back room that had always been reserved for Nahana's use. There wasn't much there in the way of furnishings—tapa mats and lengths of tapa cloth used for decoration on the walls. Nahana gestured for the women to sit and explained to Elizabeth that these women knew things that would have been passed on to her throughout her life if she had been raised a few years previously.

It seemed to Elizabeth that this would be the most embarrassing thing that had ever happened to her, but she found she was mistaken. The women talked among themselves, passing along the sexual wisdom they'd learned, which had been passed on to them. Their voices were like chants, their pantomimes like dancing. They started and finished the sayings for one another, as though this knowledge were so ingrained in them that they thought the same thoughts.

"Don't be satisfied..."

"...with just pleasing a man."

"You have to know how he can please you..."

"...and teach him the way if he doesn't understand."

"With the *honi* you can combine..."

"...the joy of spiritual love with the delight of physical love."

No one needed to explain the *honi* to Elizabeth. It was something she had always known. Whether it was from having been told about it by her mother, or by Pelika or some other Hawaiian, she couldn't say. Perhaps it was something her native blood instinctively comprehended, this merging of body and soul.

The myths of Kaahumanu's sexual prowess had reached even Elizabeth, as they had been whispered from one person to another for as long as she could remember. And Kaahumanu had passed on her secrets, which were now passed on to Elizabeth. She welcomed the information, though it made her almost dizzy with thoughts of passion.

Elizabeth lay in bed that night filled with her new knowledge. Somehow, though, she felt these were things she had already known, somewhere deep inside her. The sensuousness that was born in her had ripened into a need so strong she could barely suppress it.

But what of Matthew? His church taught that pleasures of the flesh were to be severely restricted. Would he hold himself to that goal? He was a passionate man; Elizabeth felt sure of it. He must allow that element of himself to find expression once they were married. It would be a sin, surely, not to lay claim to this God-given delight.

Elizabeth wore a flowing white gown that had come by ship from New York. Her long chestnut hair was twined with island flowers. Matthew wore his clerical garb, as was to be expected, though it added a somber note to the ceremony. These Christians, she found herself thinking, were never going to convince the Hawaiians that there was anything joyful about their religion if they continued to look so funereal.

The officiating minister was an older man, somewhat reminiscent of the Reverend Proctor, with his steely eyes and uncompromising tone of voice. It was obvious that he had assumed Elizabeth would look more Hawaiian and that he didn't exactly approve of Matthew's marrying someone who was even part native. Elizabeth was demure in his presence, saying little and doing nothing to indicate that she was anything but an appropriate wife for a missionary.

During the wedding Elizabeth was aware of no one but Matthew, his intense eyes, his unsmiling mouth, his voice that resonated within her. This commitment meant a great deal to him, and in a different way from her. He took on responsibilities, made sacred promises before his God, vowed his devotion to her. Almost as though it were a burden.

Elizabeth felt otherwise. She experienced joyous release from her celebate status, her restricted girlhood, her family. What the commitment meant to her was that two people in love had a chance to live together always, to entwine their bodies and produce a family, to do as they chose.

When they had made their separate promises and he had placed a ring on her finger, Matthew and Elizabeth were declared husband and wife. Elizabeth felt a tiny shudder pass through her body. She tucked her hand through his arm, just so she could touch him, and wished that they were already at the house. Their very first night they would spend at her house because Nahana had already moved out. Robert's old suite of rooms had been readied for them, and she could hardly wait until they were alone.

Because of the recent death in her family, Elizabeth had forgone the usual festivities, but she found now that the *haoles* had planned a surprise gathering. On the beach they had set up tables with food and drink, though nothing with spirits, in deference to the missionaries.

Suddenly, any somberness that might have been attached to the ceremony disappeared in the glorious Hawaiian sunshine. Laughter and good wishes filled the air, from Pelika to James Ivers, from Robert and Lihoa to Carlos Mentez and his Hawaiian wife. Matthew relaxed a little, trying to convince these people that Elizabeth had not, after all, made a bad choice. Elizabeth had never seen him so charming, and her heart ached with love for him, as her body ached with desire.

There were hours of feasting and talking and dancing. Finally Nahana pressed Elizabeth's hand tightly as she wished them well, and Robert hugged her with more enthusiasm than she had expected. As the carriage pulled away from the gathering she waved happily, feeling almost regal in her good fortune. When they had rounded a bend and were out of sight of the others, she looked up for Matthew's kiss.

"My beautiful bride!" he whispered, and enclosed her in his arms. His lips touched hers with only minimal restraint. "All this time. I can hardly believe you're finally my wife."

His mouth covered hers with all the fervor stored up from months of waiting, hoping, planning. Elizabeth felt engulfed by his kiss, drawn into the intensity. When she returned the pressure with her own excitement, he shuddered against her. Their eyes met in an acknowledgment of physical need. Elizabeth ran her fingers over his face, touching the slight moisture above his lips and the roughness of his chin. How wonderful that she had a perfect right to touch him now!

There was no one at the house. Elizabeth was almost trembling by the time she stood in the hallway. She caught their reflection in the mirror—Matthew tall and handsome in his black suit, she glowing with inner fires, her eyes sparkling, her cheeks flushed.

Once, years ago, she had seen her parents reflected in this glass on their return from a party, when they had been so totally caught up in each other that they hadn't noticed her standing nearby. She had desperately longed then for the kind of love they knew, an engrossing love, a physical love, that excluded others and yet had an overflow, a different kind of love that spilled forth for their children.

She could see that kind of love in their eyes in the mirror now. She and Matthew had that wondrous kind of love. It was almost too good to believe, that this could have happened to her. And yet it had. They turned to each other, their eyes locked, their hands joined, and pledged another silent vow, that this would last forever. Through the hard times, and through the monotonous times. Through the good years and the bad. Their love would triumph.

And then Matthew led her up the stairs to the prepared suite. Sun still filled the room, and the breeze was sweet drifting past the flowering vines. Elizabeth stood patiently while Matthew unfastened the dozens of buttons down the back of her wedding gown. She could feel his fingers trembling as they touched the bare skin of her back. Then she stepped out of the dress and watched as he laid it carefully over the back of a chair.

The weather was always too warm to necessitate any undergarments. She stood entirely naked, unembarrassed but filled with a burning need. Her breasts rose firm and soft above her narrow waist and long legs. The thatch of hair at the top of her legs was the same chestnut color as the shining hair on her head. The sun blazed on her with a gleaming light that made her skin glow. Matthew was so moved he couldn't speak for several minutes.

"My God, how beautiful you are," he finally said. With awkward movements, so foreign to his usual calm competence, he began to remove his garments one at a time until he, too, was naked. Except for his hands and face, he was startlingly white. Only in contrast to her warm skin was it apparent that she did, indeed, have Hawaiian blood.

But there was a marblelike strength to his body. Every curve and angle seemed perfectly sculpted from the broad shoulders to the firm feet. He was already hard with desire, and the sight of him made Elizabeth quiver with need. She glided toward him, pressing her entire body against his. The impact of their contact made her draw a sharp breath.

"I want to teach you a Hawaiian custom that is called *honi*," she said. "It's another way to pledge our love, and I'm sure it wouldn't offend any Christian. It's like a kiss, except that our lips don't touch. We exchange breath, which Hawaiians think is where the soul is."

"So we're exchanging souls?" he asked, dubious.

"We're joining our souls." She smiled then and held her lips close to his, breathing softly into his mouth. His eyes widened with astonishment, and he merged his breath with hers. "Now we are one in almost every way," she said, taking his hand and leading him to the bed.

Matthew had little knowledge of female anatomy and his lust made him nervous. He wasn't comfortable with this passion that had gripped him. He was tempted to do the only thing he felt sure about, simply to consummate their marriage, and to release himself from the throes of this painful need.

Elizabeth sat on the edge of the bed and kissed him with such tenderness and excitement he could scarcely keep his senses from deserting him. And he knew, without thinking, that he should follow her lead. It was not that he thought her experienced; he was sure she was no more experienced than he. But there was a sexual confidence in Hawaiian women that could not be denied. As a minister, he had tried to discourage this awareness because it led to an appalling promiscuity when unchecked. In a married couple it couldn't possibly be wrong. Could it?

As though she could read his thoughts she said, "If you listen, you will hear your body speak to you, as it speaks to me. It will tell you about pleasure, and about what excites. This is what we're meant to feel."

He trusted her completely. She ran her hands across his chest and he understood that she was showing him what to do. Hesitantly he lifted a hand to cup the soft swell of her breast. Her satin skin excited him, and he knew from her slight shiver that she too was aroused.

Elizabeth felt her whole body come alive at his tentative touch on her breast. As his finger slid along her skin, following the curve of her flesh, a deep urgency developed in her. His finger found the tip of her breast, the sensitive spot that sent waves of pleasure through her body, joining other sensations deep within. Her very being seemed to resonate with the arousal.

Where his hands were timid, hers were bold. She touched and stroked and pressed, eager to discover what pleased him. In her tropical environment she had seen naked men, but she had never touched one, had never known the excitement of feeling a man's reaction to her touch. Her love gave her a daring that took Matthew's breath away and coaxed his body to heights of excitement that were almost too much to bear.

And her assurance gave him courage. Looking at her, touching her, he knew he wished to taste her. She sighed with delight as he kissed her breasts and rubbed his lips over her hardened nipples. With his tongue he licked the little buds and finally, greedily, took one into his mouth and sucked on it. Elizabeth shuddered with ecstasy.

In imitating her touch, his hands moved down her body, coming to the thicket of hair and the hidden treasures beneath. His exploring touch was gentle and yet amazingly potent. Elizabeth gasped at the intensity of the pleasure his touch ignited. "Oh, Matthew, how wonderful," she sighed. "I'm filled to bursting with need for you."

He came to her then, filling her so she did in fact feel as if she had burst, as if pleasure had exploded through her whole body, engulfing her and sweeping her away. Matthew cried out his release. And then, holding her tightly against him, he spoke of his profound wonder. "I had no idea it would be so glorious. And now we're joined in body as well as in spirit. I'll always love you, Elizabeth."

"And I will always love you."

CHAPTER TWENTY-SIX

THE QUEEN IS DEAD

Kaahumanu died two days after Elizabeth and Matthew were married. Nahana grieved for the passing of her favorite mother and for the passing of another way of life. There was no chance of returning to those carefree days now that Jameson was gone, and Kaahumanu, and the children were grown and married.

Nahana lived in her beach hut and remembered how things had been. Too much had happened too quickly. She needed time to mourn her dead properly and to find a new way of life for herself. She cultivated a taro patch and restored the fish pond. She gathered breadfruit and coconuts. But it wasn't the same, even for her, who had known this way of life in the past.

When it was almost Lihoa's time, Robert urged Nahana to come and be with Lihoa. "It would be better if you brought her here," she had written. "Here there is a doctor who can care for her."

"Here there is a Hawaiian midwife who can care for me," Lihoa wrote back indignantly. "I don't need a *haole* doctor. But we would like you to come."

Nahana came—and mourned with them the loss of their infant daughter.

"Everything I do to preserve the old ways turns against me," Lihoa said bitterly when she and Nahana were alone one morning in the ranch house. She lay on her bed, still weak from the disastrous childbirth. "It's wrong, I know it's wrong for the *haole* ways to swamp our old traditions. And yet when I try to do something the way it used to be done, it only brings disaster."

Nahana held her while Lihoa sobbed, racking, heartbroken sobs that she wouldn't allow her husband to see or hear. To Robert, Lihoa was a rock, the source of his strength, and it imposed an awful burden on her. Nahana understood this, and called forth all her own strength, all the strength she drew from the land, as she had so many times in the past, to give to those in need.

With a trained doctor's attendance, the child would probably have lived. Both Lihoa and Nahana realized this, though it was never said. If Robert suspected, he said nothing. But he suffered, as they did, from the loss of the tiny baby. He had made a cradle with his own hands, as his father had before him, and now it was hidden away so as not to remind them.

When Lihoa's tears were spent, she leaned back on her bed and closed her eyes. Nahana thought she was falling asleep, but her daughter-in-law was simply drawing the courage to tell Nahana more about her many plans gone awry.

"We set up the village so they could live as Hawaiians. And what do they do but complain that they don't have any of the *haole* things they want—the lamps and tools and finery. We pay them a good wage and they spend it on drink and fancy furniture." Exhausted, her face swollen from crying, Lihoa opened her eyes to meet Nahana's. "What are we going to do?"

"I don't know," Nahana admitted. "Jameson thought it was progress, and said it couldn't be stopped, that it shouldn't be stopped. And there are the good things."

"You can't keep out the bad and only have the good. They come together, and there are always more of the bad."

"It seems so," Nahana said. She stroked the younger woman's forehead, trying to give comfort. "We'll find a way."

Lihoa, discouraged, shook her head. "I don't think there is a way. For years I've tried different things, and always with the same result. The *haoles* are here to stay, and they intend to be in charge. They are more interested in money than in people, and they infect the Hawaiians with their disease."

"The missionaries are concerned with people."

"Only with saving their souls for their civilized God. We had gods of our own, gods who suited us."

"Gods who caused too many deaths," Nahana reminded her sadly. "If the old gods had always been obeyed, Robert would have died as an infant."

Lihoa stared at her, and then gradually understanding dawned on her. "The stingray. He would have been sacrificed so that you could have other children."

"Jameson saved him." She dropped her eyes. "I would have let them kill him. It was our way."

In an agony of frustration, Lihoa cried, "How can we know what's right? How can we bear to live with all the terrible *haole* things when they are destroying the best of our Hawaiian ways, as well as the worst? What are we to do?"

"I don't know. Perhaps, given time, we'll learn," Nahana said.

Lihoa pounded her fists against her legs in impotent rage.

Elizabeth gave no thought to preserving Hawaiian ways. The entire time she was pregnant with her first child she worked to build up the church's and her own share of the association. Her youth and her sex would have made her the object of a great deal of hostility had she not been Jameson's daughter.

It was easy for her business associates to say, "She's inherited her father's business sense." They were more than willing to forget any disagreements they'd had with Jameson. He had had a way of assuming a superiority, a knowledge of Hawaiian matters, that infuriated them. Just because he had been the first *haole* on the island and the one to initiate commerce did not, in their opinion, give him any special dispensation to be in charge. Elizabeth was much easier to deal with.

And Elizabeth was much more subtle in her manipulation of the association. She didn't try to tell them what they could and couldn't do, as her father had. Because she was a Hawaiian, they accepted certain things she said as true. If she wanted to be especially effective in a discussion, she wore the ring Kaahumanu had bequeathed to her, and toyed with it as she spoke. It reminded them both of the old queen's power and of the monument of Kamehameha that *haole* carelessness and overconfidence had destroyed.

As a missionary's wife, Elizabeth wasn't quite as successful as she was in business. The Hawaiians recognized her as one of their own, unaware that on the other islands the wives of ministers spent their time working for the Cause right along with their husbands. It was the other missionaries, and sometimes even Matthew, who found her a disappointment, though he would never have admitted it.

He loved her as much as ever. Perhaps more so, as they became more familiar with each other. If she didn't live up to his expectations as a missionary's wife, she more than lived up to them in their intimate relations. When he worried that his physical pleasures were too great, Elizabeth teased him out of his condemnatory mood. He would have been more comfortable if she'd involved herself more in the good works of the church and less in making money.

Yet, his church grew moderately wealthy under her handling of the shares of association stock. There was money to send to the other missionary groups and enough to purchase teaching materials and Bibles and all the things Matthew had longed for when he first came to the islands.

It just seemed wrong somehow for a church to have such a close association with a business.

Elizabeth was at home alone when she felt her first labor pains. Because of Lihoa's tragic experience, Elizabeth had arranged to be near help at all times, with the doctor only minutes away. Pelika had only stepped out to get fruit for her lunch, though, and Elizabeth was not particularly concerned.

She sat down to write a note to the doctor, ready for Pelika to take when she returned. And then, when the pain became debilitating, she lay down on her bed to rest. Nahana and other women had told her a great deal about childbirth in the last few months and she tried to remember all of it.

"There's always plenty of time with the first baby," one of the women had said with a laugh. "The first one takes its time."

Well, that was a relief, Elizabeth thought, because the pain seemed to be almost constant, and Pelika hadn't yet returned. Elizabeth rubbed her enlarged belly. She could feel it contract under her hands. When the pain had passed, she walked unsteadily to the window and scanned the vicinity for Pelika's familiar figure.

Nothing.

Before she could get back to bed another pain racked her. A little frightened now, Elizabeth held on to the bedpost for a moment, then reached for the bell beside her bed. She gripped the handle tightly and walked to the window. Holding it outside the house, she rang it over and over again with all her strength, right through the next contraction.

And then, having done what she could, she crept back to her bed and waited.

Pelika arrived, puffing and breathless, just as Elizabeth delivered her own son. He squalled furiously as Elizabeth tried to lift his slippery body from between her legs. The stunned Pelika hurried across the room and pushed Elizabeth back against her pillows.

"I'll take care of things from here on," she said firmly. "Imagine your not waiting for me."

"I waited as long as I could," Elizabeth said, tears of relief and laughter in her eyes. "He looks so tiny, Pelika. Will you hand him to me?"

"Let me wipe him off, poor little fellow."

They had already decided to name a boy Samuel, after Matthew's father. Elizabeth accepted the small bundle from Pelika, breathing his name. He had dark eyes and a heavy mop of black hair for such a small creature. Though his skin was no darker than her own, he looked more Hawaiian with his dark hair and eyes.

"He looks a little like my mother, doesn't he?" Elizabeth asked Pelika.

"Why, yes. Or like the reverend. It's hard to say when they're first born."

Elizabeth studied the small face for a long time, wondering what he would be like, this child only a few minutes old. Like her mother, or her husband, or her brother, or her father, or Lihoa, or Pelika, or even herself? So many influences. And in a world of such changes. By the time he became a man, life might be quite different on this island.

She looked up into Pelika's smiling face. "Send for Reverend Brice, Pelika. And for my mother. They'll want to see our baby."

Nahana found new meaning in her life with the arrival of her grandson. Samuel was a bright, happy child, always in a hurry, as his arrival might have indicated. He was followed in rapid succession by a sister, Ruth, and a brother, Adam, as well as a cousin.

Robert and Lihoa's son, Nahilo, was born three years after the miscarriage. As more years went by it became obvious that he was going to be their only child, and they devoted themselves to teaching him the old Hawaiian ways as well as the newer methods they'd adopted for the ranch.

With each new arrival Nahana sang the songs she'd heard as a child and sung as a mother. She insisted that her grandchildren learn the Hawaiian language as well as English, so they could speak with any Hawaiian and understand the old chants and songs. So they could recite the *mele inoa*, as Elizabeth had done for Kamehameha at his last birthday party.

As a mother Elizabeth was tolerant, if casual, about her children's learning the old language. She couldn't see any harm in it, nor could she see much advantage. Matthew didn't wholly approve, believing that the old language was used for spreading un-Christian myths among the people.

"They're Hawaiians," Elizabeth insisted whenever he voiced an objection. "They should know their own language. English is an import."

"English is the language in which we teach the Gospel."

"Here, perhaps. But in France they teach it in French,

and in Spain they teach it in Spanish. It was taught here originally in Hawaiian."

Matthew sighed with exasperation. "But your mother teaches them about the old gods and the kahunas and the charms."

"Not for them to believe in." Elizabeth put her arms around his neck and kissed him softly on the lips. "She doesn't want them to lose their Hawaiian heritage."

"I've never heard her talk to them about God," he muttered.

"Well, she wouldn't, would she, with their father a minister. I'm sure she knows you'll teach them what they need to know about religion."

"And you'll teach them what they need to know about business."

He couldn't resist taunting her with her business interests from time to time. Elizabeth understood that it was a great trial for him to have a wife who was so different from all the other missionary wives. He would have liked her to stay at home with the children or take up parish work, like Alice Farmer, his assistant's wife.

"Yes, I teach them about my business. Man may not live by bread alone, but he'd be hard pressed to live without it," she retorted.

"But you're more interested in the association and its plans than you are in the children!"

Elizabeth raised stricken eyes to his. "How can you say that? I love the children. I spend every bit as much time with them as Alice Farmer does with hers."

"The rest of her time she spends doing God's work."

"And the rest of my time I spend making God's money."

Her sharp, irreverent tongue frequently unsettled him. He had yet to win this argument, but he knew he was right. What Alice Farmer did was far more traditional, and far more useful to the church, than the tainted activities Elizabeth involved herself with.

Elizabeth could tell that he was truly upset now and she burned with frustration at his lack of perception. "Alice Farmer is a sweet, unimaginative cipher. She thinks what she's told, she does what she's told, and she would bore the pants off any man with the least intelligence. Fortunately, Tom doesn't have much."

Now she had shocked him, but she didn't care. This harping on doing her duty was more than irritating, it was galling. She stalked away with a haughty step reminiscent of Kaahumanu's. In the doorway she turned to add, "Perhaps it's because I'm Hawaiian. If you'd married a *haole* you might have just the sort of woman you want. But I promise you you wouldn't have a woman with my kind of fire in her veins, and you wouldn't spend your nights the way we do. They're as thin-blooded as cattle, these *haole* women!" And she stomped from the room.

Their quarrels never lasted long. Matthew was too polite, and Elizabeth too forgiving, to hold grudges. The love they shared, both spiritual and physical, bridged the frequent chasms that separated them.

For despite Nahana's efforts, Elizabeth's children seemed very *haole*. They were light-skinned and surrounded by other *haoles*. English was the language they spoke easily, with Hawaiian a distant runner-up. Even their cousin Nahilo, with Robert and Lihoa as parents, was attracted to the foreign goods and foreign ways.

Elizabeth was unconcerned about this attraction her children had for things un-Hawaiian. She herself had been raised on toys imported from Germany and England, music boxes and egg puzzles, miniature globes and landscapes operated with sand. Matthew frowned on such luxuries, but many of the toys were brought down from the attic, and not bought new at all.

When Samuel was five years old he discovered the ladder to the attic. It was in the closet of Nahana and Jameson's old room, which was off limits to the child since Nahana stayed there when she visited. But he was a curious boy and he clambered up the wooden rungs with his monkeylike agility, and managed to push aside the trap door that covered the rectangular hole in the ceiling. It was some time before anyone realized he was missing.

Elizabeth was sitting on the floor with Ruth and Adam when Pelika brought in a plate of fruit for their morning snack. "Isn't Samuel with you?" she asked casually.

"He was in here the last time I saw him."

"Well, see if you can find him. He'll be hungry."

Pelika discovered that he was nowhere to be found. She searched through each room and stood outside on the porch calling his name. Soon Elizabeth joined her in the search, but she was no more successful. The two women looked at each other with alarm. Samuel was such a quick child, he might well have wandered off and gotten into some kind of danger.

An icy fear formed in Elizabeth's chest. So many things could have happened. There was the ocean, and the cliffs, and blind bends in the road. She hurried back to where Ruth and Adam played contentedly in the back parlor that had once been Nahana's special room.

Not wishing to frighten them, she sat down on the floor again to ask, "Did you see Samuel leave the room?"

Ruth, her bright eyes and chestnut hair a miniature duplicate of Elizabeth's, looked up and frowned. "He went out to get a pencil, I think, when we were playing with the puzzle."

"Why do you think he went to get a pencil?"

"Because he had a piece of paper," Ruth explained patiently. "And he didn't have anything to draw with."

The child's logic was always impeccable. Ruth was a complete contrast to Samuel—deliberate where he was impulsive, calm where he was energetic. She was a sturdy, thoughtful girl, content in a quiet way. Elizabeth hugged her and got to her feet.

"Me too. Me too!" Adam insisted, holding out his arms to be hugged.

Here was the happiest of all of them. From morning to night his infectious giggle rippled through the house. A roly-poly boy with chubby legs and plump cheeks, every day was a delightful adventure for him. Nothing pleased Elizabeth more than to see this merry child climb into his father's lap and change Matthew's face from somber to joyous.

Elizabeth hugged the cuddly body against her, murmuring at the same time, "If I could be sure he didn't go outside..."

"Well, of course he didn't," Ruth assured her. "We'd have heard the door slam if he'd gone out."

Pelika met Elizabeth's eyes with a shrug and a nod. It was true. Samuel couldn't go through a door without banging it shut behind him, a habit that accompanied his perpetual hurry. But if he was in the house, what could have happened to him? Why hadn't he come when they called? He wasn't a disobedient child.

Turning to Ruth, Elizabeth asked, "Where would he go to get a pencil?"

"To Grandma's room, of course."

"Why there?"

"Because she always has pencils for us and we know where she keeps them in her drawer."

Elizabeth shook her head. "You shouldn't take them without asking."

"Oh, Samuel would tell her, next time she came."

So the four of them trooped up the stairs to Nahana's old room, the finest room in the house. Matthew insisted that it be kept in readiness for her at all times, and resisted Nahana's urgings that he and Elizabeth make it their own suite. He still had twinges of unease at living in her house instead of the comfortless rectory, and he seemed to think Jameson would not have approved of the use they made of his former bedroom.

In any case, Nahana visited regularly, during which time the children loved to play in her room. Though they weren't supposed to go there when she was absent, Elizabeth was aware that they did occasionally, especially Samuel, slipping in to sit at her extravagant dresser or stand on the balcony looking out over the sea. But they had searched this room already, and Samuel was nowhere in sight.

Adam tumbled into the room after them, rolling on the soft carpet that glowed in the late morning sun. Pelika looked under the bed and Elizabeth lifted the fabric on the dressing table. Both hiding places were empty. The door to the balcony was closed.

"I bet he's in there," Ruth said, pointing to the closet in the far corner of the room. "Grandma keeps a box of pencils in there behind her shoes."

"I looked there earlier," Elizabeth remarked, but she opened the door again, to please her daughter. The closet was empty, except for some old shoes of Nahana's. And the box of pencils behind them. And the ladder to the attic.

A whisper of sound drew her eye upward, to the gaping hole where the trap door should have been. "Good heaven," she murmured. There were areas of the attic that had no floor. What if Samuel had fallen through one of them?

She moved quickly up the ladder to discover a profound blackness above. But the whisper of sound continued. "Samuel? Are you here?"

From far down at the other end, a husky little voice, filled with guilt, answered. "Yes, Mama."

"Are you all right?"

"Yes, Mama."

"What are you doing?"

"Well... I've found some toys."

The heavy fear that lingered in Elizabeth's breast finally lifted. "Come along. You're not allowed up here. Be careful."

"Can I bring one toy with me?"

"Just come, Samuel. We'll discuss that later."

When her son was safely in the room below, and Elizabeth had refused to let Adam climb up the ladder, Ruth said, "Are there many toys there, Mama?"

"I don't remember," Elizabeth answered honestly. "But it's not safe up there for children and I'm going to have the ladder taken away so this won't happen again."

"Won't you look at the toys?" Samuel asked. "Can't we have them?"

"I'll look at them," Elizabeth promised, brushing a cobweb from his hair. "Run along now and have your snack. You frightened us."

"I didn't mean to, Mama."

"I know."

She sighed as she watched them leave the room. How precious they were to her! And how frightened she had been that one might have been harmed. She thanked Matthew's God for keeping Samuel safe. Then she closed the bedroom door behind her and followed her family down the stairs.

CHAPTER TWENTY-SEVEN

MAI PAKE

By the time Elizabeth and Matthew celebrated their fourteenth wedding anniversary, there was an English-language newspaper for the islands, and the first legislature had been convened. So many things were influenced by the *haoles* now, and especially the Americans.

For a brief time, three years before, the frigate *Carysfort* had forced the Hawaiian islands to cede to the British government, but the incident had passed over, with Kamehameha III and the islands restored to their former sovereignty.

Now it wasn't the overt force of foreign ships so much as the more subtle pressure of *haole* business that shaped much of Hawaiian policy. Like her father before her, Elizabeth thought this was only realistic, since it was the businessmen who had brought civilization to Hawaii.

Matthew was less certain of his feelings on the subject. In

some ways it had been easier to bring Christianity to a primitive people than to this restless, changing society that confronted him now. There had been an abundance of conversions, and many of the Hawaiian people belonged to his church, but most belonged in a casual, almost unthinking way. As many of the congregations in New England belonged, Elizabeth had shrewdly guessed.

It had been easier to believe he was serving God's purpose when he was poor and lived in the one-room hut and prayed ceaselessly for guidance. Now he lived in a huge house, with every comfort attached, and he was personally worth a small fortune. Elizabeth had invested his meager salary from the Missionary Society and built it until he was embarrassed to think of his wealth, let alone of hers. He refused even to contemplate sharing the money, despite their marriage.

Wealth necessarily led to corruption, in Matthew's view. Through the years he had resisted compromises for himself, but he was unable to deny his family. Elizabeth could always convince him it was needlessly ascetic to refuse the children what would make their lives fuller.

If he was an unlikely companion for this talented, ambitious woman, he knew he had been a good influence on her, the very person to temper her excesses. Her influence on him was something he was seldom able to consider at any length.

Pelika had come to Elizabeth early one morning to say she must leave.

"Leave? I don't understand. We love you," Elizabeth said, holding out her hands to this old friend. "Are you not well?"

Pelika's fingers fluttered like birds as she nervously withdrew them from Elizabeth's grasp. "I'm old. Fifty-five. Too old to care for such active youngsters."

Samuel was thirteen now, and Ruth twelve. Adam would celebrate his tenth birthday in a week. They didn't require the kind of care Pelika had given them as children. And there were several other servants to cook and care for the house.

Elizabeth was puzzled. "You don't need to do a thing, but we'd like you to stay with us. You're our family. The children wouldn't know what to do if you weren't here."

"No, I have to go." Pelika had never been stubborn, but her voice was firm. "Today."

"Today! Surely not! Why, Reverend Brice won't even be home until late this evening."

"You will say good-bye to him for me."

Elizabeth shook her head. "There's something wrong. Something you aren't telling me."

Her companion stood mute before her, eyes downcast.

"Where will you go? Would you go to my mother?"

Pelika shook her head vigorously. "No. Far away. Alone."

"But you can't do that! How awful. Why, Pelika? Please tell me."

Slowly, the older woman extended her hand. Elizabeth could see a darkened path of skin. She frowned, vaguely disturbed, but she didn't say anything. Then Pelika removed a scarf from around her neck to expose a running sore.

"What is it?" Elizabeth asked, leaning closer. "Have you seen a doctor?"

"I didn't have to. It is *mai pake*—leprosy. My sister has it."

"Leprosy?" There had been a few cases verified, but Elizabeth had never had any contact with them. Her immediate reaction, though, was fear. People with leprosy couldn't be cured. Their flesh rotted away, deforming and eventually killing them. "Oh, Pelika, are you sure?"

"My sister came last night to tell me. She saw a doctor. I'm sorry."

"Oh, God, no. I'm the one who's sorry. Our poor Pelika. But you mustn't just go off alone. How will you survive?"

Pelika raised her shoulders in a hopeless shrug. "It doesn't matter. I would almost rather die now than later."

"Please don't say that! We'll think of something. We'll find a doctor who can help you."

But Elizabeth remembered with certainty that leprosy could not be cured. And what if... She couldn't bear to think of it. "Come. We'll talk with my husband. He'll know what best we can do for you."

When Matthew had sent Pelika off to collect her things, he turned to Elizabeth. "You know what this means? Any one of us could have it. They think it's contagious. Certainly Pelika must have gotten it from her sister. Have you...?" He couldn't force himself to finish the question.

"No, but I haven't looked. Not on the children. On myself I'd probably have noticed." Her hands tightened into helpless fists. "We'll have to check the children first thing. I haven't seen any blotches on you, and I know your body better than my own."

They were in the tiny room at the back of the church where the vestments were hung. Matthew was too alarmed by the possibilities of disaster to register this reference to their lovemaking. He put his arms around Elizabeth and hugged her close. "I'll pray for us, and for Pelika and her sister," he said. "And you'd better let your mother know right away."

The children were inspected thoroughly for any sign of the dread disease. Elizabeth felt as though a lump had stuck permanently in her windpipe. When each child had been declared free of blemish, the lump gradually disappeared.

But she felt shaken, and was relieved when her mother came to visit.

Nahana was still a lovely woman at almost sixty years of age. Her eyes had regained the brilliance dimmed by Jameson's death. There was a strength about her, in the way she carried herself, in her lively step, that was a comfort to Elizabeth and a delight to her children. She still lived simply in the beach hut, but visited Robert and Lihoa frequently, and she came to stay at her old home for long periods of time.

"I wish I could have seen Pelika before she left," Nahana said sadly. "She's been so close to all of us for so long."

"She wouldn't stay, even for an hour. Even to say good-bye to the children." Elizabeth bit her lip to restrain the tears that threatened. "She was so afraid she might infect one of us."

"Poor dear. Where will she go?"

"Matthew's arranged for her and her sister to live in a hut on the mountain. He'll have food and anything else they need taken to them. But it's an awful fate."

"Yes." Nahana seemed almost not to be listening. Her eyes drifted past her daughter to the window that looked toward the volcanic mountain. "Once I was at the crater, dying of cholera, ready to be sacrificed to Pele. Your father saved me. But so many died. So many died. This *mai pake* must not spread. It must not kill off more Hawaiians. We have lost too many already."

"Matthew's talking with the doctor, trying to find out what he can."

Abruptly Nahana brought her eyes back to Elizabeth. "Yes, he's a good man, your Matthew. Jameson would have grown to like him, you know."

Elizabeth sighed. "Perhaps. But I wonder if he would ever have come to like me, to understand what I am."

"One day he would have seen Kaahumanu's spirit in you, and he would have respected you. He never realized how much he loved you because you were too much like him, and too little like me."

"Am I so unlike you?" Elizabeth asked, surprised.

"Not really. But he couldn't see it." Nahana smiled reminiscently. "When he first came here, he had a locket. In it was a miniature of a girl from Boston. He thought every girl should be like that. And though he loved me more than he ever loved her, he thought he wanted his daughter to be a Boston lady. Thank heaven you're not!"

Elizabeth laughed. "It wouldn't do me much good. Even now, this is hardly Boston."

"If we're lucky, it never will be."

Tom Farmer taught the children at the mission school. Matthew had done the teaching for years, but shortly after his assistant arrived, he reluctantly handed over most of this duty. It was easier not to teach his own children, though Tom's own were in the classes. And, as Elizabeth had once charged in the heat of argument, Tom was not particularly intelligent. Matthew still worked with some of the oldest children.

He stood now looking out the door of the church across the fields to where Tom was giving the boys a break from their studies. The youngsters were running races, two at a time. Matthew smiled as Samuel galloped far ahead of his opponent. The boy was one of the fleetest he had ever seen.

Adam had lost his baby chubbiness, but he still wasn't much competition for the boy who ran against him. As always, Adam was clowning as he ran, skipping and dancing, with no concern about winning the race. Matthew saw him take a tumble, and shook his head with mock exasperation. No one could help laughing at Adam's antics, for they were always good-natured and harmless.

In the distance, Matthew saw his son holding his wrist, and thought he might have sprained it. Tom Farmer came over to check the damage and a very strange thing happened. Tom dropped Adam's hand as though it were a live coal. The boy stood staring at the Reverend Farmer as he backed away, shaking his head.

Though he felt frozen, Matthew ran. *Please, God, no*, he prayed, begged, as he lunged across the field. It was two months since Pelika had gone into the mountains with her sister. They had checked the children for weeks afterward. Only recently had they begun to feel secure.

Matthew arrived breathless before his son, this happy, shining boy, and reached for his wrist. Behind him he could hear Tom saying over and over, "I'm sorry. I'm so sorry." Matthew bent to look at the wrist, blinking his eyes to clear them. How could he bear to see? There was a darkened spot on Adam's wrist, raised and slightly crusted. One of Pelika's sores had looked exactly like it.

He crouched beside his son. "When did you get this?"

The boy shrugged. "I don't know. A couple days ago, maybe. It's a scratch from when I fell, I think."

Matthew looked into his son's eyes, so trusting and uncomprehending. How could you tell a ten-year-old boy that he had leprosy? Matthew swallowed hard against the pain in his chest. Nothing was going to make that pain go away, now.

Samuel, frightened, had moved to stand beside his father. "What is it?" he whispered. But Matthew could tell he had guessed.

"Let's go home now," Matthew said.

"But it's only a sprain," Adam insisted.

"Let's go home."

All the way to the house Matthew debated what to tell the boy, and whether he should break the news before they got there. He walked in silence with one arm around each boy's shoulder, too stunned to think clearly. With every step he had to force himself not to hold God responsible, not to blame anyone at all, not even himself.

As they neared the house he tried to think how to tell Elizabeth, but his heart shrank from the task. They started up the curving driveway, walking slower now by unspoken consent. She was sitting on the porch, her head bent over a book in her lap. Matthew recognized it as the ledger for the sugar cane plantation.

Though she could not have heard them yet, her head suddenly jerked up and she stared at the three of them. Her hands clenched the arms of her chair. It was much too early for them to be coming home. She sat without moving, watching them walk closer and closer. A wisp of hair blew across her eyes but she didn't try to push it away.

At the foot of the steps Matthew and Samuel hesitated, but Adam climbed the stairs and held his wrist out to Elizabeth. "My baby?" she said hoarsely. The ledger fell from her lap as she leaned forward to take him in her arms. Tears streamed down her cheeks and her eyes met Matthew's with such agony that he could barely meet her gaze.

"What is it, Mama?" Adam finally asked. "What's so awful?"

Matthew hurried up the stairs, leaving Samuel where he sat on the bottom step. "Do you remember why Pelika went away?" he asked Adam gently.

The boy nodded. "She had *mai pake*. You said so."

Elizabeth tried to speak, but she could only hold him more tightly.

"Leprosy is a disease that . . . eats away at the skin. We don't know how to treat it." Matthew's voice cracked under the strain of trying to explain.

Elizabeth felt the child's body tremble in her arms. His voice was hollow with despair. "Do you mean that I have *mai pake*? That my skin will rot away? They've talked about it at school. They say your hands fall off and your eyes fall out."

"Adam, we'll take care of you," Elizabeth insisted. "Children always exaggerate. People are afraid of this disease because they don't know where it came from or how to cure it. We'll find someone who can help you."

"But you couldn't find anyone for Pelika. She had to go away."

Elizabeth met his wide, frightened eyes. "We'll try harder. There must be something..."

"And God will give us all courage," Matthew said. "Will you try to trust Him?"

But Adam wasn't thinking about God. He was remembering Pelika. "Will I have to go away?" he asked in a small, terrified voice.

Matthew and Elizabeth looked at each other. "We'll have to talk about that," Matthew finally said.

"You'll never be alone," Elizabeth promised.

The nightmare wouldn't end. At first Elizabeth had thought a miracle would happen and the patch on Adam's arm would somehow turn out not to be leprosy. The doctor came and verified their fears. Then she hoped that this would be one of the rare cases that did not enlarge or spread. But even by the next morning the pustule had grown.

Samuel and Ruth were almost as distraught as the afflicted Adam. Terrified that they too would contract the disease, they refused to come near him, though they talked to him awkwardly through his closed door. Elizabeth had to put aside her own pain to comfort each of them in turn, to find some words of solace that would help lighten the unremitting darkness.

When the exhausted children had finally fallen asleep for the night, Matthew and Elizabeth clung to each other in their bed, trying to clear their minds enough to discuss the matter rationally. The enormity of their tragedy made it almost impossible to consider.

"Everyone at the mission school probably knows about this by now, and has spread the news," Matthew said. "People are frightened of leprosy, almost superstitious about it. We won't be able to keep Adam here long, even in isolation. There'll be a hue and cry."

"I know." Elizabeth shivered. "How could this happen to a child? It's so unfair. Why wasn't it me?"

"Sh. Don't say that! There's never any explanation for disease. It's something we have to learn to accept."

"I don't think I'll ever be able to do that." She was trying hard not to say any of the things that raged through her mind, because all of them would offend him. And he needed her love and support as much as the children did. His own efforts at comforting her, all of which relied on trusting in God, were of little help to her right now, but she couldn't say so.

"I'll go with him," she said finally, softly. "He'll need me. We'll join Pelika and her sister in the mountains."

"No. Please listen to me, Elizabeth, because this is important. I know you'd do that for Adam, and he will know it, too, but the other children need you, too."

"They would have you, and your faith."

He winced at her valiant effort to make this sound a positive virtue. Turning her face up to his with a tender finger, he said, "I have to do it, Elizabeth. It's not generosity on my part, or even penance, it's just what I know I *have* to do. There's a piece of land I saw once when I first came to the island. It's accessible only from the sea, and I'm sure we could make an arrangement to buy it. I'll start a colony there, for people with leprosy. And I'll bring them the Gospel, and comfort them, and care for them."

Elizabeth fought against the knowledge that this was

exactly what would happen. If Matthew felt a call to do this, he would do it, because even the sacrifice would be part of the bargain. He would leave her and the other two children, and he would watch their third child gradually rot away.

But because of his faith, he would be able to help the wretched outcasts who suffered from their grotesque disease.

The pain had become too great for her to bear in silence. She sobbed desperately against his chest, pounding impotent fists against the bed. Until that moment she had not realized how much she depended on Matthew's being there, loving her, lending his strength to her aspirations, his stability to her passions. What would she do without him?

When her storm of emotion had calmed in his arms, she forced herself to meet his anguished eyes. "I'll manage, Matthew," she promised. "Somewhere I'll find the strength to accept what I have to."

"God will give you the strength."

"I can't bear to think of what will happen to Adam. It tears at me inside. And I know it tears at you. We won't be together to comfort each other. Will I be able to bear not being with you? I love you so, Matthew."

They hadn't intended to make love. All the fear and pain made it the farthest thing from their minds. But their bodies craved the intimate contact, and the cathartic release of their joining. In the face of desolation, their union was somehow life-renewing.

Afterward Elizabeth clung to him in the darkness, hearing the gentle sound of the ocean, the whispering of the vines against the house. Her mind was filled with terrible pictures of her poor Adam, distorted by his disease, playing against a backdrop of flaming hibiscus and waving ferns. How could such a contamination flourish in this paradise?

It was hours before she fell asleep. Matthew too was awake for some time, both of them trying to come to terms with this disaster, and their own obligations, in their own way. By morning Elizabeth felt exhausted. The bitterness had abated, though, and been replaced by a temporary courage that would see her through one day.

For tomorrow she would have to search again. Each day she would have to search again.

CHAPTER TWENTY-EIGHT

ALOHA!

Where the coral-and-lava beach met the restless ocean, there were ancient canoe-mooring holes chipped in the rock. This was the location chosen for Matthew's leper colony, because the fishing was good and the constant strong winds seemed to clear the air of the awful disease. The old stone walls of a *heiau* shrine lay a few yards away from the new "church" that had been built. This simple hut would serve the Reverend Matthew Brice very well.

It had taken three months to make all the arrangements. Only when the land was still untainted by the sick was Elizabeth able to bring in workers to build the huts, to clear areas beyond the beach for taro patches. In these three months, while Matthew sought permission from the missionary society to set up a church at his own expense,

Elizabeth learned from Robert and Lihoa how a simple society could support itself.

Not that the colony wouldn't receive continuous supplies, but Robert and Lihoa had pointed out that they would take pride in being basically self-sufficient. This was not to be a place of hopelessness, where the afflicted waited to die. There would be tapa making and mat plaiting and taro growing and ocean fishing as well as schooling and religious training. They would nurse one another.

Elizabeth lived in fear during those months that one of her other children would develop the disease. Or that Matthew, living in the mountains with Adam and Pelika and her sister, would. But the preparations were ready for the colony, and Samuel, Ruth, and Matthew remained uninfected.

Nahana stayed with the older children when Elizabeth made the final arrangements at the still-uninhabited leper village. Robert, Lihoa, and Nahilo had spent the last week there, too, and were ready to depart. Elizabeth stood with them beside the outriggers and fishing nets, her eyes focused farther up the coast. It wouldn't be long before her husband and son arrived.

At the sound of movement beside her, Elizabeth turned. It was hard for her to see Nahilo, who was just Adam's age, so strong and healthy. He seemed to understand this, and reached silently to squeeze her hand in farewell. Lihoa was deeply disturbed by what had happened and more sympathetic toward Elizabeth now. She hugged her sister-in-law and handed her a necklace she had made from shells in the area.

"It might help you feel a part of this place when you're not here," Lihoa said.

Elizabeth slipped it over her head and touched the ridged shells that brushed against her skin. "Thank you. I know it will."

Not since the years when they were children had Elizabeth

felt so close to Robert. They had gone in such different directions, and yet here they were, working together again, sharing the same emotions. For it was obvious that Robert ached for her, that he shared the burden of her hurt, as she had perhaps never quite shared his after the amputation.

Tall, strong, and handsome, he looked like Kamehameha must have in the prime of his life. Except for the missing leg. "We'll go before they come," he said. "There will be enough confusion. But I'll come when they're settled. Of course I'll be careful," he hurried to add at her fearful expression. "And your Matthew will be careful. He knows he's needed too much to take chances with his health."

No one else had been able to say it to her. It helped to hear it from her brother, her twin. If it was only the echo of her own self-assurances, it hardly mattered. "Yes, he'll be careful."

"And he'll help Adam adapt. Adam's such a happy child, he'll learn to love living the old Hawaiian way, Elizabeth. He'll love fishing and swimming and running on the beach."

But he can't love what will happen to his body, she thought. *He can't love having no friends to play with, and no brother or sister or mother.* "He'll have his father, and Pelika," she said bravely.

"Oh, Elizabeth." He swept her into his arms and hugged her tightly. "I don't know what else to say. I know how much you love him and how much this hurts."

"I know you do. Thank you."

Robert released her and shoved the outrigger into the water. Lihoa and Nahilo climbed in and waved good-bye. Elizabeth watched them out of sight and sat down on the rough beach to wait.

The double canoe rounded a finger of land almost two hours later. Elizabeth was still sitting in the sun but she hardly noticed its heat. She'd been thinking about something Robert had said, that Adam would like living the old Hawaiian way. Adam's upbringing had been very *haole*, and she wasn't sure he would be comfortable with the more primitive ways, as most of the other, older lepers would.

In the hut Adam would share with Matthew, Elizabeth left the last of the toys from the attic. He was a little old to play with them, but without the companionship of children his own age, he might welcome the diversion. She looked back over the cleared area, thinking what a limited horizon it must present to a child of Adam's boundless enthusiasm. And there was nothing she could do about it.

When the canoe was close enough to her to see its occupants, she waved to the familiar faces. Adam, Matthew, Pelika. And yet Pelika's face was not entirely familiar, that face that had hovered over her own childhood. Already the neck and jaw were dissolving on one side.

Elizabeth forced back the tears that threatened. Her son was not yet disfigured in any horrifying way. But seeing Pelika, how could she doubt that he would be? She rose to her feet and hurried to the edge of the ocean. Adam held his arms out to her.

Before Elizabeth could grasp him, Matthew gently caught hold of Adam's arms. "You mustn't touch your mother," he said. "We have to be very careful not to spread the disease to people outside our colony."

"I don't care!" Elizabeth cried. "I want to hold him."

"Please think of Samuel and Ruth," Matthew urged. "If you don't care for yourself, think of them. Adam will understand."

The boy's eyes were huge on her, dark and wistful. After a long moment, he nodded his head. Pelika put a comforting arm around him and smiled at Elizabeth. "He's a good boy," she said. "Sometimes he forgets and he's happy as a bird."

And Adam laughed, to show it was true. Elizabeth bit hard on her lip, and laughed with him. "Come and see what's here," she urged.

He dashed off, eyes bright with curiosity. Pelika and her sister followed, leaving her with Matthew. "Can I hold you?" she asked.

"You probably shouldn't," he admitted, bending to kiss her.

The kiss, meant to be swift and simple, became a conduit for all the tenderness, passion, hope, and fear they both felt. Elizabeth couldn't allow herself to express this any other way. She had missed his touch with a stony desolation, and her warm lips spoke of how much his absence diminished her.

"Samuel and Ruth miss you," she said. "And I do. So much."

"I've written a long letter for the children. Not full of lectures and lessons," he promised. "Just telling them what we're doing here. And how much I miss them. And you."

Slowly they followed the others to the little village of huts, exchanging news, explaining the details of their lives. Never quite able to express the profound loneliness that being apart caused them. But trying, always trying, to make clear how strong their love was. Words came with difficulty; they were too used to affirming their feelings with their bodies, as lovers.

For the first time the knowledge impressed itself on Elizabeth's heart that probably they would never make love again. All the passion she felt for him must stay contained in her body, locked up against the living hell of his exile. He would not be free to come and go from the colony because of his close contact with the lepers.

She would be able to visit from time to time, to see for herself how they were getting on. They would be painful visits, heartbreaking for what they revealed and for how helpless she would feel. Yet she knew she wouldn't be able to stop herself from seeing her husband and son.

When Adam had seen what would be his new home, and Elizabeth had talked with him for a long time, Matthew called him over. "Your mother mustn't stay any longer," he said. "We don't want to take any chances with her."

"I'll come again," Elizabeth said. "I won't be able to stay long, ever, but I'll see you and I'll bring you letters from your brother and sister and I'll bring you anything you need. Oh, Adam, my son. I love you so much. If only... But you'll be with people who care about you here, too. God bless you, my love."

Her throat was too choked for her to go on. She backed away from him, stumbling. There were tears in his eyes, and then on his cheeks. She drew a deep breath. "I know you'll be brave because you're a wonderful boy," she said, before turning and fleeing toward the shore.

"I'll be brave," he called after her, in a gruff little voice.

Matthew caught up with her before she reached the canoe where one of Pelika's relatives waited patiently to take her away. "How can I leave him?" she demanded. "How can I leave you?"

"It's out of our hands. We're all doing what we have to do, Elizabeth. I think it's hardest for you, but you'll find the strength." Matthew's hand automatically came out to touch her, then hesitated and dropped to his side. "You and Robert and Lihoa have accomplished wonders here in so short a time. We've heard of others with leprosy who will come soon. We'll have plenty to keep us busy."

He lifted her net bag into the canoe. When he straightened, his eyes locked on her face. "I love you, Elizabeth. Please remember that. Always. I'll take good care of Adam."

There was nothing more he could say right now. Elizabeth lifted her lips for his lingering kiss. Without a need for words they then exchanged breaths and joined souls in the magical Hawaiian *honi*. Slowly they drew apart, as though it were an effort to put more than a few inches between their bodies.

Elizabeth climbed into the canoe, and it immediately plunged out into the sparkling waters. She looked back at Matthew, and Adam beyond him near the hut. "Aloha!" she called. "Aloha!" And she waved for a long time, until her arm ached, until her canoe rounded the point that took her out of sight.

Then, regardless of Pelika's nephew, she curled up in the bottom of the canoe and wept.

Nahana stood in the doorway of her old room looking out toward the ocean. She had already decided that she would accept Elizabeth's invitation to live here permanently. This tragedy had drawn them all together, forcing them to lean on one another.

Robert and Lihoa had stayed for several days before returning to the ranch with their son. Nahilo spoke better Hawaiian than English, and he'd been raised with a knowledge of the past that surpassed anything Nahana had been able to impart to her other grandchildren.

Strange, how the years had shaped all their lives since Jameson's death. The American influence grew stronger and stronger on the islands, and yet Nahana could still hear the old kahuna legends whispered among the people. Of course, there were also whispers that the kingdom of Hawaii would be annexed to the United States. Surely Kamehameha III and the government on Oahu would not allow that!

"Mother?"

Nahana turned at Elizabeth's voice. Her daughter had suddenly developed an uncertainty in her speech, the questioning note that made her seem so terribly vulnerable.

"Yes, dear. Come in. I was just watching the light change."

Elizabeth moved to stand beside her. "It's beautiful.

Father planned the house so well. There is a window to catch every aspect of life here."

"Do you remember when you could see the giant stone Kamehameha raised, from the main room?" Nahana asked.

Elizabeth nodded. "And its shadow stretching down to the sea. I used to like to play in the shadow. Somehow I felt safe there."

Nahana smiled at her. "Yes, his spirit seemed closer then. But it's still here. I know it's in the land. Especially this land, where he lived and died. There's strength in this land."

A fragrant breeze swept through the open door and played through Elizabeth's chestnut hair. She thought of the wild winds on the point where she'd left Matthew and Adam. A shiver ran through her. "I've lost touch with the land."

"Only temporarily." Nahana put an arm around her waist, holding Elizabeth tight against the fears that shook her. "The land and the people have always been one. But things are changing and I fear the Hawaiians will lose their heritage, their strength, engulfed by *haloe* ways. I want to use some of the money Jameson left me to preserve the old traditions."

For the first time in months, Elizabeth felt a spark of interest ignited in her. "How would you do it?"

Her mother shrugged. "I thought perhaps you'd know."

Elizabeth did know. A plan sprung full-blown into her mind, as though she'd been considering the project for months. "We'd have scholars write down the old kahuna chants. And we'd set aside a piece of land for a museum, where we'd collect all the old wood *kii* statues we could find." Her brow clouded. "You don't think Matthew would object, do you?"

"I'm sure he'd respect the need to save our heritage. His children are descendants of the great Kamehameha. If

Kamehameha is forgotten by his people, the strength of Hawaii will bleed away."

"Matthew believes that all strength comes from God."

"The *haoles* do not understand Hawaii," Nahana said. "In Hawaii the strength is in the land. When the missionaries brought their God, He was in the land." She stroked Elizabeth's hair, much as she might have done when her daughter was a child. "In the land you will find your strength again, Elizabeth. In the land and in your Hawaiian heritage."

Later Elizabeth stood on the porch looking up to where Kamehameha's monument once stood. Her fiercely Hawaiian passion, so easily indulged until now, would have to find a different course. As a stream wanders through the land, skirting rocks and hills in its path, she would have to seek a new direction around her private disasters.

This time she would give more than she took, would preserve the important ways of her people instead of thoughtlessly discarding them.

Behind her she could hear Nahana teaching Samuel and Ruth the *mele inoa,* the name chant that united the Hawaiian people for all time through the names that came before. Elizabeth still remembered it, and silently mouthed the chant, along with her mother and her children, pausing when they stumbled, moving forward when Nahana continued alone.

Strength flowed into her, filling her with a new hope. She would find the courage to survive this awful fate. The blood of Kamehameha still flowed in her veins.

The Best Of
Warner Romances

___BOLD BREATHLESS LOVE (D30-849, $3.95, U.S.A.)
by Valerie Sherwood (D30-838, $4.95, Canada)
The surging saga of Imogene, a goddess of grace with riotous golden curls—and Verholst Van Rappard, her elegant idolator. They marry and he carries her off to America—not knowing that Imogene pines for a copper-haired Englishman who made her his on a distant isle and promised to return to her on the wings of love.

___LOVE, CHERISH ME (D30-039, $3.95, U.S.A.)
by Rebecca Brandewyne (D32-135, $4.95, Canada)
"Set in Texas, it may well have been the only locale big enough to hold this story that one does, not so much read, as revel in. From the first chapter, the reader is enthralled with a story so powerful it defies description and a love so absolute it can never be forgotten. LOVE, CHERISH ME is a blend of character development, sensuous love and historic panorama that makes a work of art a masterpiece." —*Affaire De Coeur*

___FORGET-ME-NOT (D30-715, $3.50, U.S.A.)
by Janet Louise Roberts (D30-716, $4.50, Canada)
Unhappy in the civilized cities, Laurel Winfield was born to bloom in the Alaskan wilds of the wide tundras, along the free-flowing rivers. She was as beautiful as the land when she met the Koenig brothers and lost her heart to the strong-willed, green-eyed Thor. But in Alaska violence and greed underlie the awesome beauty, and Laurel would find danger here as well as love.

WARNER BOOKS
P.O. Box 690
New York, N.Y. 10019

Please send me the books I have checked. I enclose a check or money order (not cash), plus 50¢ per order and 50¢ per copy to cover postage and handling.*
(Allow 4 weeks for delivery.)

_____ Please send me your free mail order catalog. (If ordering only the catalog, include a large self-addressed, stamped envelope.)

Name _____

Address _____

City _____

State _____ Zip _____

*N.Y. State and California residents add applicable sales tax.

By the year 2000, 2 out of 3 Americans could be illiterate.

It's true.

Today, 75 million adults... about one American in three, can't read adequately. And by the year 2000, U.S. News & World Report envisions an America with a literacy rate of only 30%.

Before that America comes to be, you can stop it. . by joining the fight against illiteracy today.

Call the Coalition for Literacy at toll-free **1-800-228-8813** and volunteer.

Volunteer Against Illiteracy. The only degree you need is a degree of caring.

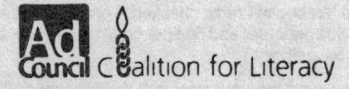

Ad Council Coalition for Literacy

Warner Books is proud to be an active supporter of the Coalition for Literacy.